12/6/02

DATE DUE

RESURGENCE

Baen Books by Charles Sheffield

The Heritage Universe series:
Convergent Series
Transvergence
Resurgence

The Amazing Dr. Darwin
My Brother's Keeper
The Compleat McAndrew
The Mind Pool
The Spheres of Heaven
Proteus in the Underworld
Borderlands of Science
The Web Between the Worlds
Between the Strokes of Night

RESURGENCE

A NOVEL OF THE HERITAGE UNIVERSE

CHARLES SHEFFIELD

RESURGENCE

A Baen Books Original

Baen Publishing Enterprises
P.O. Box 1403
Riverdale, NY 10471
www.baen.com

ISBN: 0-7434-3567-2

Cover art by Bob Eggleton

First printing, November 2002

Library of Congress Cataloging-in-Publication Data

Sheffield, Charles.
    Resurgence: a novel of the heritage universe / Charles Sheffield.
        p. cm.
    "A Baen Books original"—T.p. verso.
    ISBN 0-7434-3567-2
    1. Life on other planets—Fiction. I. Title.

PS3569.H39253   R47   2002
813'.54—dc21   2002028046

Distributed by Simon & Schuster
1230 Avenue of the Americas
New York, NY 10020

Production by Windhaven Press: Auburn, NH
Printed in the United States of America

10   9   8   7   6   5   4   3   2   1

DEDICATION

To Ann, Kit, Rose and Toria; to Maureen, who proposed the title; and to the fans who kept asking, when will there be another Heritage Universe book?

PROLOG

Before we begin a systematic exposition of Theories of the Nature of the Builders (of which theories there appear to be at least one hundred and seventy-seven) it seems appropriate to provide what may be termed the Facts of the Builders. This is far easier than any enumeration of theories, since the facts are few in number:

Fact 1: No living being, and no dead being whose word carries any semblance of validity, has ever seen or met a Builder.

Fact 2: Various inorganic constructs possessing some form of intelligence have been found on, in, or in conjunction with objects created and left by the Builders. These constructs all claim to be of great antiquity. They also claim a full understanding of the Builder purposes in creating them. There are reasons to doubt the validity of all such testimonies, not least the fact that no two testimonies agree.

Fact 3: The Builders made and left behind in the Orion Arm of the galaxy, and possibly in other galactic arms, a variety of constructions which are generally referred to as Builder Artifacts. More than a thousand of these are scattered around the Orion Arm alone. The purpose of many or most of them remains obscure. They range in size from a few meters, to lightyears across. The technology that went into their creation is beyond that achieved by any other species, living or dead, inhabiting these regions of our galaxy.

Fact 4: There is no evidence that any Builder Artifact was constructed to be specifically inimical to organic life forms. Large numbers of deaths have been reported associated with different Builder Artifacts; however, in every case these deaths resulted from the unwise curiosity of beings seeking to explore, understand, or exploit the Artifacts.

Fact 5: With one notable exception, every Builder Artifact was completed and set in position at least three million years ago. Any changes in Artifacts more recent than three million years appear to have been planned as part of their original design.

Fact 6: Four years ago, there was unmistakable evidence of new, rapid, and unprecedented change in many if not all of the Builder Artifacts.

Fact 7: At the same time, a completely new Artifact, named as Labyrinth by its discoverer Quintus Bloom, appeared near the star known as Jerome's World.

Fact 8: Soon after the appearance of Labyrinth, every other Artifact in the Orion Arm quickly vanished. Labyrinth itself was the last to disappear.

Fact 9: Since the disappearance of Labyrinth, no evidence of any kind of Builder Artifact or Builder activity has been found in the Orion Arm.

These, and these alone, are the facts concerning the Builders and the Builder Artifacts. We now proceed to the Theories themselves, which are legion.

—from the introduction to the volume,
A SURFEIT OF NOTIONS: Theories of Builder
origins, activities, nature, and artifacts.
Author: Professor Darya Lang, Artifact
Research Institute, Sentinel Gate.
This is an advance publication copy,
and may be subject to additions
and amendments.

CHAPTER ONE

On Candela, in the Phemus Circle.

As a last meal it left a lot to be desired.

Hans Rebka stared down at the mess on his plate, then up at the guard.

"Kolker, what's this supposed to be?"

Rebka was naked. He was shackled at the ankles and his hands could move only far enough from the iron chair's arms to allow him to eat. Even so, the guard took a step back at the prisoner's scowl.

"Isn't it what you asked for, Captain?"

"I requested as my last meal the best that the planet could provide. Take a look at that plate. I've seen more inviting pig shit. Smell it for yourself, and tell me what happened."

"Wait a minute. I'll try to find out." Kolker did not take up the offer to smell the plate of food. That would have brought him within reach of Rebka's hands. He took another step back, close to the room's bare stone wall, and his lips moved. Through his implant he was in contact with more senior officials. After a few seconds he nodded.

"Captain, that meal was provided on instructions from Minister Schramm. Apparently it *is* the best that the planet can provide. But not this planet. It is the best that can be had on your home world, Teufel." The guard hesitated. He

3

knew that every word and gesture was being recorded. "The minister thought that you would appreciate a little joke."

"Did he?" Hans Rebka picked up the spoon. It was, like the plate and little tray that it sat on, made of a thin and flexible plastic that no amount of treatment or hardening could turn into a weapon. "I must be losing my sense of humor. But the terrible thing, Kolker, is that he's right. I've been away from Teufel so long, I'm spoiled. Do you know what they say about Teufel?"

"Yes. I have heard it many times."

"Then I won't bother to repeat it." Rebka dipped the tip of the spoon tentatively into the black goo on his plate. He tasted it, grimaced, and laid down the spoon. "Once I'd have gobbled this up and gone back for seconds. The minister knows what's what in the worlds of the Phemus Circle. This *is* as good as it gets on Teufel."

"Are you going to eat it?" In the weeks that Rebka had been in captivity, a peculiar relationship had developed between guard and captive. Rebka had done his best to become friendly, and he was good at that. But Guardsman Kolker, who suspected—rightly—that given half a chance Hans Rebka would kill him and try to escape, had remained respectful but aloof.

"I told you," Rebka went on. "I've become picky these past few years. I'd rather die hungry than eat that." Hands chained together, he waved the plate away. "It's all yours. Do what you like with it."

The guard approached warily and snatched the tray out of Rebka's reach. "I can't bring you anything else, you know."

"I understand. And you can't share your food with me, either, right? Don't feel bad. I've been hungry before. And people waiting to be executed are not expected to enjoy their final night."

Kolker nodded and retreated to the metal door. He pushed the tray through a narrow horizontal opening at waist height, then stood motionless. He seemed to be listening. At last he nodded, turned to Hans Rebka, and said, "Minister Schramm asks if you have any last request."

"Certainly. Tell the minister that I would like to be allowed to write my memoirs."

The guard frowned. Finally he said, "You are joking, are you not? Excuse me, Captain Rebka, but I do not think it would be a good idea for me to transmit that message."

"Very wise of you. It's my impression that Minister Schramm only like little jokes that come from him." Rebka glanced around the bare, dimly lit and windowless cell. "So. What now, Kolker my friend? Dinner is over and death is twelve hours away. We have the whole night ahead."

"I am to remain here with you. If you would like to talk, or if—"

The rest of Kolker's words were cut off by a metallic rattling at the door of the cell. The guard spun around, pulling his weapon from its holster. He stood poised to fire as the door swung open.

The four men who entered were equally wary. They wore guards' uniforms, and all held drawn guns.

"Stay right where you are, all of you." Kolker, part of his attention still on Hans Rebka, backed up against the stone wall. "I have absolute orders to admit no one. If you do not leave this room at once, I must shoot."

"You got orders? Well, so do we." The biggest of the newcomers held an envelope out to Kolker. "I'm Colonel Toll. Check with Guard Central if you don't believe me." Toll stared at Rebka. "He's the one who caused all the trouble? He sure don't look up to it. Anyway, we've come for him."

"For Captain Rebka? I cannot allow that. I have orders from Staff Advisor Lanski to remain here with the captain until morning, when he will be taken away for execution."

"And we have orders from Minister Schramm to take Rebka away with us. Do I need to tell you who's higher in the line of authority?"

"I was warned that there might be some kind of rescue attempt. If I do not obey my orders—"

Kolker was interrupted by a laugh of disbelief from Rebka and by an impatient, "Read the bleeding papers, mister. We don't have all night," from Colonel Toll.

"They seem to contain the right authorization." Kolker was trying at the same time to scan the document he was holding, keep one eye on Hans Rebka, and train his weapon on the quartet of guards standing in the doorway. "But this makes no sense at all. The prisoner is scheduled for execution at dawn, on the basement level of the building where we are now. This instructs you to take him to 132-B. That's above surface."

"More than just above surface. 132-B is Minister Schramm's suite, up at rooftop level." Colonel Toll waved his gun at Rebka. "Can you walk?"

"Try me."

"Right. Get him out of those shackles, Guardsman Kolker. We'll take over from here. Anything that happens to him after he leaves this cell will be my problem, not yours."

Down in the basement cell there was no day-night change of lighting. Hans Rebka had been chained in near-darkness for more than three weeks. The elevators were almost as dimly lit as his cell, and sudden emergence into the brilliance of evening sunlight of Candela made him flinch and throw up his forearm to protect his eyes.

A familiar and outraged voice said, "He is naked! How dare you bring a prisoner naked into my quarters?"

Rebka lowered his arm and blinked away tears. His eyes could see only fuzzy outlines in the large, windowed room, but the voice told him that the figure a few paces away was Minister Schramm.

"I'm sorry, Minister." That was Colonel Toll. "I was ordered to bring him here at once. No one mentioned clothing."

"Did no one also tell you to use your common sense? Find clothes for him at once—or give him your own."

"Don't worry on my account, Minister." Hans was beginning to see more clearly. "Once I'm executed I doubt if I'll care what I'm wearing."

"You will not be executed." Another figure standing behind Schramm swam into focus. "Is that not correct, Minister?"

"It is correct."

Schramm was a tall, fleshy man in a style of dress that for the impoverished worlds of the Phemus Circle represented extreme opulence. He spoke without enthusiasm, but Rebka paid him little attention. The man at Schramm's side held his eye. He wore the shimmering white suit with gold epaulets and light-blue trim of an inter-clade Ethical Councilor. If any such councilor had ever before made a visit to Candela, or any other world of the Phemus Circle other than Dobelle, that was news to Hans.

"Though I should point out," went on Schramm, "that the execution of this prisoner is more than justified. He attempted to bring down the authorized government of the Phemus Circle—"

"I am aware of the charges against him." The councilor stepped forward, placing himself squarely between Rebka and the minister. "Don't push your luck, Minister Schramm. There are those of the Council who believe that such a change to the Phemus Circle is long overdue. However, that is not my business today. Captain Hans Rebka?"

"Speaking."

"I am Inter-clade Councilor Jeremiah Frole. I am here to inform you that you are needed on Miranda, and that you will leave with me."

"As simple as that?" Rebka waved a hand toward Schramm. "With no objection from your friend the minister?"

"I provided the necessary . . . explanation." Jeremiah Frole nodded toward a wall screen. Hans Rebka glanced across at it for the first time and realized that it showed a view of Candela as seen from space. The whole planet wore a circlet of bright points of light.

"Armed ships," the councilor went on. "Two hundred of them. We had a previous unfortunate experience with the Phemus Circle. We sent for one of their political prisoners, rather than coming to collect her in person. She suffered, we were told, a fatal accident before she could leave the surface of Candela. We did not want that to happen again. We brought forces designed to discourage such a possibility."

Schramm said, "Councilor, the previous case was no more than a regrettable—"

"Just so, Minister. I feel sure that nothing similar will happen this time." Jeremiah Frole turned to Rebka. "Captain, how soon can you be ready to leave after you have clothing?"

"Forget the clothes. I'm ready to go right now."

"Don't you have possessions that you want to take with you?"

"Not one thing. Since we're leaving, I guess I can do without this, too." Rebka had been standing with his fists clenched. Now he opened his right hand palm upward, turned it over, and allowed a gram or so of blackish powder to fall to the floor. While the others stared, he said, "Pepper. The best I could manage. Took me nearly three weeks, saving it from my food."

"What did you plan to do with it?"

"Whatever I could. At the very least, I'd give somebody a faceful. I wouldn't go down without a fight." Rebka turned to face Schramm. "I can't say I'm sorry to be leaving—but don't worry, I'll be back."

"If you have any thoughts of starting up another rebellion against the Phemus Circle government—"

"Of course I don't. At least, not as my top priority. I'll want to settle a few personal scores first with the people who sentenced me to death and locked me away. From now on you'd better watch your back, Minister. Every minute of every day."

Rebka turned away without waiting for Schramm's reaction, but Jeremiah Frole saw the instinctive movement of hand toward belt.

He shook his head. "Not this time, Minister, or you may not care for the result. We'll be clear of Candela orbit and make our first Bose transition in half a day. After that you can do as you like—but it won't be to this prisoner."

He followed Hans Rebka out of the room. As they moved along the corridor he noticed for the first time the condition of the naked man's legs and bony back.

"You were tortured!"

"I was?" Rebka turned his head and saw what the councilor was staring at. "Oh, you mean the sores. That wasn't torture."

"Then what was it?"

"Just what you expect when you have no clothes on, and they chain you to sit in an iron chair for a few weeks."

"They did that to you? That *is* torture."

"Not by Phemus Circle standards it isn't. I've slept in worse beds. But don't get the wrong idea, Councilor, I'm really happy that you came along when you did. I was beginning to wonder just how I was going to make it out of there. Gratitude doesn't begin to express it."

They had reached ground level and begun walking to a waiting car. They passed half a dozen men and women, but only Jeremiah Frole seemed concerned about Hans Rebka's nakedness.

"We will provide you with clothing as soon as we are on board the ship," he said. At the car he hesitated. "Your file describes you as a problem solver and troubleshooter. I hope that remains true."

"Why? Seems to me you just got me *out* of trouble."

"Perhaps. I notice that you have not asked why I came here to take you to Miranda. That is just as well. For if you were to ask, I am not at liberty to tell you."

The councilor held open the car door for Rebka. "However, when you do learn the reason why you are being removed from Candela, I hope that your feeling toward me and the Council will still be one of gratitude."

CHAPTER TWO

On Xerarchos, at the far end of the Zardalu Communion.

For the full three weeks while Hans Rebka sat naked in a rusty iron chair, Louis Nenda had lived the good life. Thirteen hundred lightyears away from Candela, he sat now in lordly ease and surveyed the arid surface of Xerarchos.

True, the planet beyond his ship's ports was not most people's idea of a garden world. The dust storms came every season and raged worldwide for months on end. The air was thin and dry and tasted like powdered iron. If you went outside without a suit, fine grit worked its way into your teeth and eyes and every body cavity. Water was so scarce on the scoured surface that no gemstone or precious metal could match it in value, ounce for ounce. The natives were warlike and bloodthirsty. An honest man was defined as one who stayed bought for more than a day or two.

But now you had to look on the good side. Louis Nenda had come here voluntarily, knowing that his ship was well-armed and if it came to a fight he could kick the ass of any native group. He did not have to breathe Xerarchos air, or eat food grown on Xerarchos. Best of all, the water generators on board the *Have-It-All* made him the richest being on the planet. The locals would die to learn their secret. And if that's what it took to keep control, Nenda was quite willing to let them do it.

He placed his boots on the lip of the rounded observation port, leaned back, and scratched his hairy rib cage. He yawned. A few more weeks, to squeeze out the limited best that Xerarchos had to offer, then the *Have-It-All* would lift off and seek another source of commercial advantage. The local arm of the galaxy was full of them. There was a new sucker-world born every century.

Pleasant thoughts were interrupted by a faint sound from behind. He jerked around, and confronted a nightmare. The creature stood on one pair of its six dark-brown legs, rearing twice the height of a man. The segmented underside was dark-red, rising to a short neck banded by scarlet-and-white ruffles. Above that sat a white, eyeless head, twice the size of Nenda's own. A thin proboscis grew out from the middle of the sightless face and curled down to tuck into a pouch on the bottom of the pleated chin. Yellow horns in the middle of the broad head constantly scanned whatever stood before them. A pair of light-brown antennas, long even in comparison with that great head, were unfurled to form two meter-long fans that quivered delicately in the ship's warm, moist air.

"For God's sake, At, I wish you wouldn't come crawling in quiet like that." Nenda swung his boots to the deck, stood, and turned. "You give a man the creeps. It shouldn't be too hard to let me know you're on the way."

"I did exactly that." Atvar H'sial's message wafted across to Nenda as a complex interplay of pheromonal molecules. They carried more subtle information than any human language ever could—mild irritation, admonition, amusement, and a hint of something else. "You were too busy daydreaming and gloating to take notice."

What was that other message? A touch of alarm, maybe? Nenda concentrated. The Karelian augment on his chest was a dark array of pits and nodules, sufficient to permit him to understand and to speak the Cecropian language natural to Atvar H'sial. However, no augment could ever provide the fine distinctions of meaning available to Cecropians, or to their Lo'tfian slaves and interpreters.

"What's up, At? We got trouble?" He spoke both phero-monally and using human speech.

"Not on Xerarchos. Everything here is quiet, and payments to us were made this morning. But this came to the ship's message center a few minutes ago."

Atvar H'sial held a brown flimsy in one bristled paw. The fine pattern on it was designed for ultrasonic scan by a Cecropian reader.

"You know I can't read that stuff, At. What's it say?"

"It is the highest level of command from the Cecropia Federation's Central Council, an order I cannot disobey. I am told to report to Miranda, in the Fourth Alliance, with all possible speed."

Nenda took the output and stared at it. "You sure you're reading this right? I thought all charges against us were dropped after the Builder artifacts disappeared, and we helped everybody get out of Labyrinth."

"They were dropped. This is not an accusation of crimi-nal actions. It appears to involve some entirely new matter."

"And you feel you have to go?"

"I must, for reasons I will not specify. More than that, Louis Nenda, I suspect that there may be similar orders waiting for you. When this directive arrived, a separate message came to the ship's communications center in human output format. At the time, Glenna Omar was giving me another lesson in human speech, which she interrupted in order to take the message. She read it, gasped, and hur-ried off aft. She carried the message with her, and I sus-pect that she was seeking you."

"Heading in the wrong direction. Why didn't you tell her?"

"I did. I told her exactly where you could be found. However, I continued to employ human speech, which may have been a mistake. I spoke this." The Cecropian folded its proboscis into the pleated region on its chin and inflated the thin tube. After a wheezing like a leaky bellows, sounds emerged: " 'lusnnda 'sn 'sfrd k-kbn.' "

" 'Louis Nenda is in the forward cabin'? Yeah, that's very good, At. But with all due respect, those sounds could just as well have come out of either end of you. I better go see what's happening."

Nenda marched off along the corridor. Somehow he felt more resigned than surprised. Things had been going far too well for far too long. Just when you thought you had the universe by the tail, it turned round and bit you on the ass.

He came on Glenna drifting back in his direction. If he hadn't known that Atvar H'sial was female, and that the Cecropian found all humans repulsive in appearance, he might have wondered what kind of lessons Glenna had been providing. It was not yet midday, but her makeup was perfect. Her pale blue negligee showed off her long, graceful neck and upswept blond hair. As usual, the very sight of her made him gulp.

They were by the entrance to one of the *Have-It-All*'s comfortable observation lounges. Glenna moved into it and sank onto a long, soft bench. She gave Nenda a worried smile and waved the paper that she was holding. "This came for you, sweetheart, from somebody called Julian Graves. He says he's a Council member for the Fourth Alliance."

"I know him. He's part of the Ethical Council."

"But just look at this." She pointed to the sheet. "He says he's *ordering* you to travel as quickly as possible to Miranda. He can't make you do that, can he?"

"I don't think so. Let me take a look."

Nenda ran his eye down the sheet. A group of words close to the bottom of the page sprang out at him. . . . *to reach Miranda in at most twelve days. Otherwise, I will re-open the old investigation into the plundering of a medical-supply capsule en route to Lascia Four.* . . .

"Julian Graves can. Order me, I mean. The son of a bitch. I'll have to go."

"But what does he want you for?"

"I've no idea. Nothing pleasant, you can bet on that. Something dangerous and dirty and desperate. We'd better get on our way as soon as we can."

"We?"

"Yeah. Atvar H'sial got the same sort of message, though she didn't give details. And of course, J'merlia and Kallik wouldn't let us go without them, even if we wanted to."

"But J'merlia and Kallik are your *slaves*. They're supposed to do whatever you tell them to."

"I know. It never seems to work out that way. So I guess we'll all be going to Miranda."

Glenna motioned to Nenda and patted the bench at her side. Her negligee had opened at the bottom, to reveal an inordinate length of smooth white leg.

"Louis, you don't mean *all*, do you? You know I'm no good at dangerous things. I'd just get in the way."

"You mean you'd rather stay on Xerarchos?"

She patted his arm. "Silly man. Of course I won't stay *here*. This is an awful place."

"I've seen worse."

"Not with me you haven't. Now, you say you must go to Miranda. And Miranda is just one Bose transition away from Sentinel Gate. You can drop me off on the way."

"But what will you do on Sentinel Gate?"

"I'll take my old job. I was a Senior Information Specialist."

"You told me you hated it."

"Oh, it wasn't all that bad, just a bit boring. It will only be until you come back, you know. And there was the occasional diversion."

Occasional diversion. A male visitor to Sentinel Gate, where Glenna's challenge was to hustle the stranger into bed before he left the planet. Apparently it didn't matter what he looked like, or how badly he behaved, provided that he was an off-worlder.

Nenda knew all this. Glenna had once explained it to him, and anyway, he could be thought of as a beneficiary of her policy.

He nodded. He didn't resent the proposal that she should not go with him to Miranda. A woman with real nerve was something to be admired.

He thought of asking, "We'll wait for each other, won't we?" then changed his mind. There were some things so stupid, you ought not even to think them. Instead he said, "That's it, then. Sentinel Gate for you, and the two of us will have a good time on the way. An' after that, At and me will see what Miranda has to offer."

"Maybe fame and fortune, Louis. When I was growing up, my house-uncle always told me that every trouble could be thought of as an opportunity."

An opportunity, in Nenda's experience, to find even more trouble. But negative thinking never got you far.

He slipped his arm through Glenna's and they stood up together. Miranda was well-known as one of the richest worlds in the spiral arm. Maybe he and Atvar H'sial would find a chance to skim a little off the top.

CHAPTER THREE
Miranda and Miranda Port.

As always, travel through the Bose Network induced a faint sense of hallucination. There was something unnatural about an instantaneous jump of a hundred or a thousand lightyears, and even the best human brain apparently needed a few seconds to orient itself to its body's new circumstances.

Darya Lang stood with her eyes closed. Five seconds ago she had stood at the Bose transition point closest to Sentinel Gate, near the outer limit of Fourth Alliance territory. When she opened her eyes, the sight that met them would be of Miranda and Miranda Port, six hundred and twenty lightyears away.

All right. You've had enough time to adjust. Now—do it!

A blink. And there it was, although the sight failed to do justice to the reality. The Shroud hanging by the disk of the planet was too far away for Darya to make out details, but the countless flyspecks within the gauzy web must be spacecraft: starships of all sizes and types, more than a million of them netted and warehoused in the Shroud: the biggest collection in the spiral arm, everything from Primavera body form-fits to the monstrous Tantalus orbital forts.

She was to be allowed little time for sightseeing. Already a hand clutched at her arm.

"Professor Darya Lang?"

She turned. "That's me."

"Finally, you are here. I am an assistant to Councilor Graves." The man was polite and nondescript, but he did not release his hold on Darya's arm. "If you would come with me. Today's meeting is already in progress and may be close to its conclusion."

A meeting *here*, out by the Bose transition point and at Upside Miranda Port, rather than down on the surface of the planet? But as Darya allowed herself to be led away from the glittering splendor of the Shroud, she said nothing. There were bigger questions to be asked and answered.

The puzzles had started in Darya's study at the Artifact Research Institute on Sentinel Gate. Twilight was approaching, and the first nightsingers could be heard through the open window when Professor Merada ambled in.

His visit was not expected, but it was also not surprising. Merada was a stickler for accuracy and formality in every element of analysis and reporting, but he felt that research work done under his auspices thrived best in an informal atmosphere. Putting it another way, he felt free to butt in wherever and whenever he liked.

Darya lifted her head from her notes. She had been collating reports of the final days of the Builder artifact known as Maelstrom, but now she was down to the hearsay and rumors, and this was a logical stopping-point to ease off for the day.

One glance at Merada's face was enough to ruin her relaxation. She thought, "Uh-oh. What have I done now?"

She knew he had always disapproved of her galloping off to inspect Builder artifacts at first hand, but the last of those journeys was years in the past. Since then she had settled down in her office at the Institute to write the definitive history of the Builders, including every scrap of information on the more than twelve hundred Builder artifacts that had once been scattered around the spiral arm.

The only sin she could think of was a possible excessive use of Institute communication privileges. She had sent dozens of messages to a planet of the Phemus Circle in the past two months, although not one of them had been answered.

Was that it? Merada was waving a sheet at her and scowling.

"This is inexplicable," he said, in his thin, penetrating tenor. "It is also, to be honest, somewhat insulting. If there is to be an important meeting concerning the Builders, anywhere in the spiral arm, it would seem like common courtesy to address such an invitation to me, as Director of the Institute. But this document requests—more than requests, *insists*—upon the presence of *you*, of all people." He peered down at Darya, vaguely aware that he might have said something less than tactful. "Not that I am in any way criticizing your credentials, my dear. You are, after all, the editor of the past two editions of the *Universal Artifact Catalog.*"

The *Lang Universal Artifact Catalog*. But Darya said that only under her breath.

"May I see?"

More than a certain irritation, she felt puzzled. Why would anyone choose to hold any meeting at all about the Builders, except here at the Artifact Research Institute where Builder history was a major interest? Odder yet, how could a meeting be described as an *important* meeting concerning the Builders, when the Builders had vanished three million years ago, and every last trace of Builder artifacts had disappeared more than two years ago?

The sheet was not very informative. In fact, it added to the mystery. First, it insisted, with the full force of the interclade council, that Professor Darya Lang be present "in person." No virtual presence through the Bose communications network would be accepted. Second, the meeting would take place on Miranda, a planet which formed the major power center of the Fourth Alliance. Third—Darya stared at the date. Somebody in the Institute had been sitting on this message for a long time. She would barely get to the meeting in time even if she left at once.

Which she had done. And here she was, still dizzy from the Bose transition, walking unsteadily alongside the man who had greeted her.

She had traveled six hundred and twenty lightyears in a handful of days. She was late, late, late. And she had not the slightest idea why she had been summoned.

The chamber that Darya entered was almost totally dark, but she had an impression of an echoing, cavernous vastness. The man who had led her there slipped unobtrusively away, leaving Darya to fumble her way forward to a seat. As her eyes began to adjust she realized that the great room was lavishly equipped, even by the high standards of a rich world like Sentinel Gate. Directly in front of her was a personal privacy shield and Bose link connection. Did each seat have one? If so, any bewildered participant could call home, and (with luck) receive a reply soon enough for it to be useful.

A sudden flash of light right in front of her eyes ended any opportunity to see more of the room. Her seat was also provided with a large 3-D display, which had just filled with an image. The principal clade territories of the spiral arm were delineated in their characteristic colors. Within them, scattered like sown handfuls of fiery sparks, Builder artifacts stood out as brighter points of light.

There was the dull orange of the Zardalu Communion, a region that thinned out as the distance from the galactic center increased. At its outermost edge, Darya recognized the outpost of the Needle. That was an artifact she had longed to visit, but now never would. The eye of the Needle had provided an acceleration-free boost in speed to any ship that traversed it. Now it, like all the rest, was gone.

To the right of the fifteen-hundred-lightyear sprawl of the Zardalu Communion sat the dark void of the Empty Quarter, a region where stars were plentiful but artifacts were almost unknown. Darya's catalog showed just two of them, Lens and Flambeau. Neither she nor anyone else had ever offered an explanation for the Empty Quarter.

Below the Empty Quarter showed the pale green of Darya's own clade territory, the Fourth Alliance, where the sentient species were largely humans. Her home world of Sentinel Gate sat far off to the right, close to the artifact of Sentinel.

Below and to the left of Fourth Alliance territory, stretching off toward the galactic center, the clade worlds of the Cecropia Federation showed in electric blue—a color which the Cecropians, who "saw" using sound waves and echolocation, could never experience.

Darya looked for the Phemus Circle, and found that little cluster of twenty-three suns and sixty-two habitable planets limned in muddy brown, at the point where the overlapping boundaries of the three dominant clades converged. The color seemed appropriate. The worlds of the Phemus Circle were desperately poor and primitive. "Dingy, dirty, dismal and dangerous." "Remote, impoverished, brutish, backward, and barbaric." It was no coincidence that the three major clades had never fought for possession of the Phemus Circle.

The stylized map was infinitely familiar to someone who had spent a lifetime studying Builder artifacts. Darya could have drawn the whole thing herself. But then the display began to shift and shrink, revealing a larger region of the galaxy. The bottom of the display no longer ended in the usual place, at the lower boundary of the Cecropia Federation. As the volume shown increased in size, more of the galaxy became visible. First the Gulf came into view, a void many hundreds of lightyears across that sat at the inner edge of the local spiral arm. Only the thinnest sprinkling of stars and solitary planets drifted there. Beyond the Gulf, the Sagittarius Arm gradually appeared. The Sag Arm was another branch of the whole spiral, the next one in from the local arm and closer to the galactic center.

Darya had never studied the Sagittarius Arm in detail and knew no one who had, although it was a region as big and star-filled as the local arm. The Gulf provided a formidable barrier. Only the most long-lived of species would invest the centuries needed for a crossing. Humans did not belong in that select company.

So why was someone bothering to show a large part of the Sag Arm? And who was that someone?

Darya realized that staring at the bright display actually hindered her eyes from adjusting to the dim light. She was aware of a crouched figure in the seat next to her, of inhumanly odd proportions, but she could see no details. A perfume—not unpleasant, an odd mixture of cinnamon and peppermint—diffused toward her. She heard a scuffling sound, like a struggle going on to her left. Then a hand patted her thigh, and she squeaked in surprise.

A hoarse voice said, "Professor Lang! It is you. I thought At was giving me the runaround."

"Where are—who are—" Darya saw the dark figure by her feet at the same time as she pushed the hand away from her leg.

"It's me—Louis Nenda. I had no idea you would be here."

Darya's rush of warm feeling surprised her. "Nor did I, until four days ago. Louis, why are we—"

That was as far as she got when Nenda was hoisted suddenly into the air and whipped away to the left. The other figure next to Darya silently unfolded, to rear high above her. From its proportions it had to be a Cecropian. She heard a hissing sound and felt something else, thin and angular and with a hard and unyielding exoskeleton, push against her knees.

"With respect," said a voice from close to the floor, "We do not think that this is the best time for the renewal of old acquaintance."

"J'merlia?"

"This is J'merlia's person, but I am of course speaking on behalf of my dominatrix, Atvar H'sial, who is seated next to you."

More scuffling sounds from Darya's left. A hiss, a series of clicks, a thump, and a guttural curse from Louis Nenda. The display in front of Darya vanished and bright lights filled the whole chamber.

"I had intended," said a deep, hollow voice, "that we would end today's meeting in silent study of the Orion and Sagittarius Arms, since that knowledge will prove essential to all of us. I did not anticipate that some of us would choose to indulge in private discussion and personal squabbling."

Darya could see the speaker now. He stood at the front of the great chamber, a lanky man with a bald and bulging cranium. She should have expected him. Julian Graves was a native of Miranda, the only one on that world whom she in fact knew personally. The Ethical Councilor's deep-set blue eyes were staring right at her and she nodded a greeting.

"Ah." Graves nodded. "Professor Darya Lang. Of course. I should have anticipated this difficulty. A vortex of emotional disturbance surrounds you still, as ever. Welcome to this assembly. Better late than never, though in truth you are not the last. I am expecting one more participant, who will, I am informed, be arriving within the next half-day. Given that, and the present state of disruption, I feel it will be to everyone's advantage if I postpone further discussion and explanation until then." Julian Graves glanced—glared?—around the chamber. "Study the displays. I will leave you now. For the remainder of the day you are free to resume old acquaintances in any way that you choose."

Julian Graves spoke as though Darya was somehow *responsible* for ruining his meeting. All she had done was come in and quietly sit down, at a point when the meeting was in any case almost over.

Darya stared around her. She had come here expecting to know almost no one, but to be surrounded mostly by humans. In fact, she thought she recognized every one of the half dozen beings in the room—and most of them were aliens.

Still crouched at her feet in an eight-legged sprawl of limbs was the stick-figure form of J'merlia, the Lo'tfian who interpreted the pheromonal speech of his Cecropian mistress, Atvar H'sial. J'merlia stared up at Darya, and in greeting rolled his lemon-colored compound eyes on their short eyestalks. Darya liked J'merlia, although she objected strongly to his insistence on voluntary servitude to Atvar H'sial. And she had grave suspicions about the honesty and intentions of the latter.

Which made her fondness for Louis Nenda even harder to explain. Nenda was Atvar H'sial's business partner. He had told Darya, in so many words, that he was a man with an awful and criminal past. He was a native of Karelia, in the far-off reaches of the Zardalu Communion, and others had hinted to Darya of monstrous acts which meant he could never return there. He even possessed his own Hymenopt slave, Kallik, and unlike Atvar H'sial he could not offer the excuse that he needed an interpreter.

Kallik sat at Louis Nenda's feet, on the other side of Atvar H'sial. The Hymenopt was short and barrel-shaped, her meter-long body covered with short black fur. With her small round head, set with a ring of bright black eye pairs, she looked mild and defenseless.

Darya knew better. Invisible was the yellow sting, retracted into the end of the rounded abdomen. That hollow needle could deliver squirts of neurotoxin with no known antidote. At will, Kallik could vary the composition from mild anesthetic to instant kill. Also invisible was the Hymenopt nervous system. It provided Kallik with a reaction speed ten times as fast as a human's. The eight thin legs would carry her a hundred meters in two seconds, or let her leap fifteen meters into the air under a standard gravity.

The miracle was that Kallik regarded Louis Nenda as her absolute master and allowed herself to be led around with a collar and leash. Nenda bullied and blustered. Sometimes he even carried a whip. However, Darya had direct proof that the master/slave relationship was more complex than it seemed. She had been on board Nenda's ship, the *Have-It-All*. Nenda's private quarters were opulent, even by the standards of a rich world like Sentinel Gate. But Kallik's were just as large, and just as well-furnished. The little Hymenopt even had her own additional private area, equipped with powerful computers and scientific instruments.

Kallik squeezed past Atvar H'sial, whose great body was blocking Louis Nenda, and came scuttling over to Darya. The Hymenopt and J'merlia exchanged a brief burst of clicks and whistles, then Kallik said, "Greetings. With your arrival we will perhaps begin to receive some explanation for our presence."

It was an embarrassment to Darya that J'merlia and Kallik, whom she had thought mindless pets when she first met them, could pick up languages with such ease. In the time that it had taken Darya to comprehend a few basic Hymenopt clicks, Kallik had achieved fluency in half a dozen human languages.

Darya shook her head. "You won't get explanations from me. I have no idea why I was summoned."

"Master Nenda says that it is a meeting which involves the Builders, and Builder artifacts."

"So I was told. But the Builders vanished from the spiral arm more than three million years ago, and now all their artifacts are gone, too."

"You sure of that?" Louis Nenda must have done an end run on Atvar H'sial, moving round the back of the row of seats. He had appeared now on Darya's right-hand side.

"Sure as anyone can be." Darya quietly pushed his hand away from her shoulder. "The Artifact Research Institute is the clearinghouse for all activities or information concerning the Builders or Builder artifacts. I examine the data bases every day, personally. Absolutely nothing new has come in for the past few months—not for years, in fact."

"But they put the heat on you to come here?"

"I suppose they did. I felt that I was given no choice."

"Same for me, same for At. Makes no sense at all. I mean, she's an expert on the Builders, and so is Kallik. So are you. But me, if you bet on what I know about the Builders, you'd lose your ass and hat."

"You were involved in the disappearance of the artifacts, starting with Summertide on Dobelle and ending at Labyrinth, out by Jerome's World."

"Sure I was, but that's all history. I don't remember more than half of what happened, even though I was right in the middle of it. I'm tellin' you, something big has to be brewing."

"Based on a gut feeling, or do you have evidence?"

"Mostly gut. But when your guts have rumbled with danger as often as mine have, you get to trust 'em. And yeah, I do have one bit of evidence. When the word came to us, me an' At an' Kallik an' J'merlia an' . . . another person, we were on Xerarchos, in what you might call the Lesser Armpit of Zardalu Communion territory. It's a long way from there to here, so I called Miranda and said we'd need financial help to pay for the cost of the Bose transitions."

As usual, Louis Nenda's clothes were crumpled and his eyes were bloodshot and his battered face needed a shave.

And as usual, there was an intensity in the way he looked at Darya that both pleased and disturbed her.

She glanced away from him and said, "It was reasonable to ask for help if you were short of funds. I assume that they gave some to you?"

"Yeah. But that's not the point. As it happens, me an' Atvar have had a good year or two an' we're rolling in money. We sort of try to disguise that, of course, but you can't hide everything. A simple credit check would have shown we didn't need no help. And when I made my request, I deliberately sky-highed what I said we'd need. I do mean sky-highed, too, because I wanted to see if I could learn anything from their reply."

Darya found she was looking back at him in spite of herself. "And?"

"Not a murmur. Instant approval of everything I asked for."

"What do you think it all means?"

"Haven't a clue. Except that somebody thinks this meeting is real super-important. But since we're supposed to find out tomorrow from Julian Graves, I'm not goin' to worry about it 'til then." Nenda leaned closer to Darya, ignoring the angry hiss that came from the giant Cecropian on her other side. "Nothin' else on the agenda for today. So how about you an' me havin' dinner an' catchin' up on things?"

CHAPTER FOUR
Sleepless in Miranda Port.

When you have something to do, do it. When you have nothing to do, sleep.

Hans Rebka had learned that rule on Teufel before he was six years old. It had served him well through two decades as a troubleshooter in the Phemus Circle, and even better during the nerve-racking two years while he tried to overthrow the Phemus Circle's corrupt central government.

That effort had not been a success—he had come within twelve hours of his own execution—but once he was on the ship leaving Candela he put all such thoughts out of his mind. The trip to Miranda would require careful piloting through a number of Bose transitions points, but that was not his responsibility.

Hans ate until his skinny belly bulged, went to his cabin, and fell asleep within thirty seconds. The weeks in prison had pushed his body to its limits of endurance. For the next five days he intended to do nothing but gorge, snooze, and wonder occasionally why the inter-clade council might think it worthwhile to drag him out of gaol and all the way to Miranda.

A dozen close calls had given him a lot of respect for his own abilities. He had survived the fearsome *Remouleur* dawn wind on Teufel, saved a whole colony on Pelican's Wake, and flown an expedition on Quake to safety at the height of Summertide. But every one of those had been a marginal world, a place on the threshold for human existence. Miranda was rich, safe, and self-satisfied. It had been settled for millennia.

Hans yawned, turned over, and snuggled deeper under his blanket. So why Miranda? Well, when somebody told him why they wanted him there, he would know. Until then . . .

The final Bose transition and transfer to the Upside Miranda Port entry point took place in the middle of the local sleep period. He was told by the bleary-eyed woman who came to his quarters that since he was a late arrival, he might as well spend the rest of the night on board the ship. Meetings would continue the next morning, and nothing would happen until then. Hans nodded. As soon as the woman left he rose and dressed in his borrowed uniform. It was something learned through experience: in an unknown situation, any bit of extra knowledge might be the edge you would need. Examine your environment.

He left the ship and stared around him. Unlike Darya Lang, he wasted no time marvelling at the vast magnificence of the Shroud with its myriad netted ships. He had been to Upside Miranda Port before, and when he left the last time he had felt in no great hurry to return. On that occasion he and Julian Graves had been mocked when they tried to persuade the Council that the Zardalu, believed extinct for eleven thousand years, were once again at large in the spiral arm. Could this call involve the Zardalu again? If so, this time it would be the Council's job to convince him that he should take them seriously.

His previous visit had provided him with a vague layout of the docking center and station administrative quarters. He moved silently along corridors deserted except for cleaning and maintenance crew, low-level intelligences that froze in position until their motion sensors showed that he had passed. The meeting rooms were all empty. One of them contained a giant holographic display big enough to fill the whole chamber. He walked through the middle of it. The first part was the familiar territory of the local arm. He came to the nimbus of muddy brown that marked the Phemus Circle, and placed his index finger on the tiny bright spark of Candela. It winked out of existence. If only it were so easy to blot out the government there . . .

The spark reappeared as soon as he removed his finger. Government corruption would be the same, returning to full strength throughout the Phemus Circle now that he was no longer there to wage war against it. Next time— if there could ever be a next time—he would seek allies from other clades before he took on an entrenched power structure.

He continued through the chamber, wandering past Dobelle and into the beginnings of the galactic region dominated by the Cecropia Federation. The display here showed unfamiliar stars and the scattered sites of old artifacts, Zirkelloch and Tantalus and Cusp. At Cusp he halted. He had been heading in the display toward the galactic center, and he was at the edge of Cecropian influence. This marked the end of the local arm, the place where the Gulf began. Nothing lay beyond but thousands of lightyears of empty space, until finally a determined traveler who went on and on would reach the other side of the Gulf and find the stars and dust clouds of the Sag Arm.

But something *was* here. In the display, the darkness of the Gulf was broken by a line of pinpoints of light. Stars? Rogue planets? Monstrous artificial free-space structures? The Builders could conjure such things from nothing. They had placed Serenity thirty-thousand lightyears out of the galactic plane. Hans had been carried to that great enigma— involuntarily—and after his return he still he had no idea of its purposes. Now, without some key, he could not guess what he might be seeing in the chain of lights that spanned the Gulf.

He left the chamber and prowled another dark corridor. Everyone should be in sleeping quarters, but by instinct he moved silently. That same caution made him pause at the entrance to another room. The sliding door was open a fraction.

Hans froze, all his senses alert. He peered through the

one-centimeter crack, but saw and heard nothing. The room beyond was totally dark. He told himself that his imagination was working overtime. Still he did not move. Something—what?—convinced him that the room beyond was occupied.

The argument was no less fierce because it was conducted wholly through pheromonal communication. The chemical messengers passing between Louis Nenda and Atvar H'sial reeked with overtones of suspicion, anger, and denial beyond anything that mere words could offer.

"I am betrayed." The pair of fernlike antennas on top of the Cecropian's head were tightly furled in indignation. "You insisted that the Council's call for our presence indicated their desperate need."

"Hey, I think it does."

"Also, you spoke on the journey here of the possible commercial advantages that accrue to us on such a rich world. And I, in my innocence, agreed."

"Innocence! You lost your innocence before you left the egg."

"I was innocent of particular knowledge. I had no idea that the human female, Darya Lang, would be here. *You knew.*"

"I sure as hell didn't. I was as surprised to see her as you were."

"Say what you will, the warmth of her pheromonal greeting to you was unmistakable. And you sought her company later."

"I suggested *dinner*. What's wrong with dinner, for Croesus' sake? Hell, I gotta eat. *And* she said no."

"To your obvious disappointment. It is clear now why you insisted that your faithful companion and my valuable human-language teacher, Glenna Omar, be abandoned and left to her fate on Sentinel Gate."

"Nuts. I've told you a dozen times, Sentinel Gate was Glenna's idea, not mine. She thought we might be heading for something dangerous. Danger isn't Glenna's style."

"But treachery is your style."

"Sure. Why else would you accept me as a business partner?"

"Do not play word games, Louis Nenda. Treachery toward *me* is a different matter. I am now convinced that you know exactly why we are here. In fact, I strongly suspect that you engineered this from the beginning. You *arranged* to have messages—"

The flow of pheromones abruptly halted. Nenda said, "At, I'm telling you for the last time—"

He was interrupted by a paw across his mouth and another on the nodules of the augment on his chest. A powerful burst of pheromones said, "SILENCE. We are not alone. If you must speak, do so softly and only through the augment."

Nenda glanced around the darkened room and saw nothing. "What? Where?"

"Beyond the door. A human male."

"You sure?"

"Of course I am sure. The odor cannot be mistaken." Atvar H'sial's proboscis quivered. The yellow horns turned, and the antennas above them unfurled to their fullest extent. "I can also provide an identity. It is Captain Hans Rebka— your old rival for the sexual favors of the female, Darya Lang."

Nenda gritted his teeth, but he said only, "I didn't know Rebka was here at Upside Miranda Port!"

"He was not, earlier in the day. To be more specific, if at Upside Miranda Port he was nowhere near us. Had he been present, even half a kilometer away, J'merlia or I would have smelled him. Wait a moment."

Again the antennas quivered. Atvar H'sial said at last, "He does not know that we are here, yet somehow he is suspicious. His odor betrays uneasiness. Now—he is moving away along the corridor. I wonder how he knows?"

"Rebka's a snooty bastard, but I'd never say he's a fool. He can smell danger nearly as good as I can, and he knows how to look after himself. But At, you wanted proof that I'm not keeping information from you. Now you have it. Will you admit that I hate Rebka's guts?"

"You have never been able to disguise that fact, at least from me. You and he, in your incessant bickering over the human female—"

"Forget the goddamned human female. Or better still, *don't* forget her. Ask yourself this: If I had the hots for her the way that you claim, would I have brought Hans Rebka to Miranda Port?"

"It seems unlikely." The pheromones held an overtone of grudging admission.

"Unlikely? It's preposterous."

"So you *are* admitting your interest in the female."

"No such thing. I don't know why the Inter-clade Ethical Council called this meeting—I wish I did. And I had nothing to do with Hans Rebka being here, either. I wish he weren't, but that has nothing to do with Darya Lang. He's a troubleshooter. A good one, too, who's dug himself out of some desperate fixes. But his being here means we're lookin' at trouble, with us likely to be in the middle of it."

Louis Nenda had been crouching in the shadow of Atvar H'sial's broad carapace, the location where he found pheromonal communication most easy. Now he stepped clear and went to slide the door wide open. He peered along the corridor.

"No sign of Rebka. But I can tell you one thing for certain. If he's part of the meeting, we're not being called in for a garden party. Better be ready, At. I don't know what's coming up tomorrow, but you can bet it'll be a real doozy."

Standing at the narrow opening in the doorway, Hans Rebka had sensed—or imagined—the faintest odor from within the chamber. It was sulfur-grass, with an overtone of something less familiar. *Alien.* Which alien, he neither knew nor cared. Without a sound, he retreated as fast as possible along the corridor.

Originally, his wanderings within the Upside Miranda Port administrative station had been more or less random. Now he had a destination. He sought the nearest of the external chambers, where an observer could settle in to stare at the stars.

Before he got there he experienced one more distraction. He passed one of the numerous chambers that housed the station's distributed computer facilities. A row of windows permitted Hans to see everything inside the brightly lit room, including a solitary male human seated cross-legged before a gray instrument panel. The man had his back to the windows, so Hans had a view only of neatly trimmed black hair square-cut at the nape of the neck. Some kind of thin tube or cable led from the instrument panel toward the man's hands or hidden chest. Hans guessed at a neural bundle, though what the man could possibly want with such a thing was anyone's guess.

And none of Hans Rebka's business. He watched for a few more seconds, then moved on.

The observation chamber sat at the end of a short tunnel that projected from the outer shell of the station. Hans could sit in a swivel chair, orient himself in any direction that he chose, and study every part of the heavens not obscured by the body of Upside Miranda Port station itself. Of course, in keeping with the natural cussedness of things, what most interested Hans was at the moment shielded from view.

That could never be more than a temporary problem, because the whole structure of the Upside Miranda Port station slowly rotated. Hans faced maybe a five-minute wait.

He occupied the inevitable delay doing what he had earlier declined to do, and examined the contents of the Shroud. The nets held ships of all sizes, shapes, origins, and ages, in dizzying variety and numbers for as far as the eye could follow. One nearby vessel caught his eye, from its strange yet familiar outline. He had seen that design, like a hammer with a head at both ends, only once before. On that occasion he had been far out in Zardalu Communion territory, where the outpost world of Bridle Gap orbited its neutron star primary, Cavesson. And Hans had at the time confirmed that the alien ship had been manufactured nowhere in the local arm: it was something built in a far-off time and place, by the species known as the Chism Polyphemes.

What was such a ship doing here? Was it intended to provide proof of the boast made by the Miranda Port sales staff, that you could find in the Upside Shroud examples of every ship ever made?

The slow rotation of the station was bringing what he

wanted to look at into view, and that pushed consideration of the alien ship to the back of his mind. Visual inspection of the glowing band of light that was now appearing would tell him nothing, and he stared at it for only a few moments. The Milky Way shone brighter without the diffusing effects of a planetary atmosphere, but the spiral arms beyond the local arm were still shrouded by interstellar dust and gas clouds. He had known that in advance, and already selected the observation wavelengths that he wanted. He switched to them. The chamber had been designed so that a viewer need not be aware that the "windows" now displayed the readings of radiation and particle monitors in spectral and energy regions far beyond what human senses could experience directly. Suddenly, Hans could "see" through the obscuring veils of dust and gas.

See to the edge of the local arm. See across the Gulf. See the Sag Arm, looking no different now from the way it had appeared at other times when he had done deep galactic viewing. And see, beyond the Sag Arm, the galactic center itself, with the million-star-mass black hole lurking at its hidden heart.

Hans brought his attention back to the Gulf. It appeared empty, as it had always been empty. It offered no sign of the pinpoints of light provided by the giant display he had walked through inside the station. So those bright points did not represent stars. They were a creation of the display itself, not something visible in nature.

But what were they? Hans had no idea. He lay back in the swivel chair and selected visible wavelengths, so that he was once more seeing by the natural light that came in through the chamber's transparent walls.

The view was familiar and relaxing. The chair was comfortable, more comfortable than most beds that he had slept in.

As the heavens turned slowly about him, Hans decided that although he had learned little, it was all that he was likely to get tonight.

There was always tomorrow. Which would take care of itself.

When you have nothing to do, sleep.

Within seconds he was drifting off. In his final moments of consciousness, he imagined he was walking out along the staggered line of lights that lay like stepping-stones across the Gulf.

CHAPTER FIVE
A cry from the grave.

It had been Darya's intention to be early to the meeting and take a place as close to Julian Graves as possible. That way there could be no accusation that any new disruptions had anything to do with her.

Her plan changed abruptly when she came to the corridor leading to the chamber where they were due to meet. Someone—something—was ahead of her. She smelled an ammoniac odor, and saw a huge midnight-blue form wide and tall enough to block the corridor.

A shiver passed through her body, at the same time as her mind told her to turn and run. Thirty meters ahead of her, standing more than four meters tall on its thick, splayed tentacles, was an adult Zardalu. The bulbous head was twice the width of a human body. The creature was—thank Heaven—facing away from Darya, but she knew that the front of the head bore two great lidded eyes of cerulean blue, each as big across as her stretched hand. Beneath the eyes was a cruel hooked beak, more than big enough to grasp within it a human body.

The Zardalu had been the bogeymen of a dozen different species and a thousand worlds, monstrous land-cephalopods believed extinct for eleven thousand years but still the living nightmare of myths and legends. Darya knew that the Zardalu were again a presence in the local arm—she had been on their homeworld of Genizee, and considered herself lucky to escape—but she had never expected to encounter an adult Zardalu *here*. No Zardalu should be free to move without watchful guards ready to annihilate it at the first sign of trouble.

Darya took a couple of steps backward—and was grasped firmly from behind.

Her heart froze in her chest, until she realized that those were human arms encircling her. Louis Nenda, pawing her again! She felt a little guilty at refusing to go to dinner with him, but didn't the man ever learn? Terror changed to anger, and she spun around ready to give him the hardest slap he had ever felt.

Her hand was already raised and moving when she saw who was behind her.

"Hans!"

"Who else has hugging rights on you?" He was smiling.

"Hans, I had no idea that you were coming to Miranda Port. Where have you been? I've sent message after message for two months, and never had one word of answer."

"None of them got to me. I wasn't where I could be reached." He was holding her at arm's length. "Darya, you're looking really good."

"I wish I could say the same for you. Hans, what have you been doing to yourself? You look like hell."

"If you think this is bad, you should have seen me a week ago. Darya, I didn't get your messages because I couldn't. I was in jail on Candela."

"Why?"

"I'll tell you about it later. Just now, I want to know why I'm at Upside Miranda Port. Being called here probably saved my life. Let's get to the meeting room."

"Hans, there's a Zardalu in this corridor." Darya stared ahead. "Or there was. Where did it go?"

"The only place it could possibly have gone—into the meeting chamber." He was moving forward.

"Hans, slow down. I'm telling you, it's a *Zardalu*."

"All right, so it's a Zardalu. I feel sure it's sedated, or

brain-dead, or some form of simulacrum. Otherwise nobody would let it loose."

He had reached the entrance to the chamber, where he paused. Darya followed and moved cautiously to where she could see what was happening inside.

Her idea of getting to the meeting early had occurred to plenty of others. A fresh-faced, dark-haired human male whom she did not recognize was already seated where she wanted to be, right at the front. Behind him was the Cecropian, Atvar H'sial, flanked by the little Hymenopt, Kallik, and the Lo'tfian, J'merlia. And behind *them*, in the chamber's biggest open space, stood Louis Nenda.

She owed him an apology, but this wasn't the time for it. Because in front of Nenda, sprawling its great length along the floor, was the Zardalu. It was making a series of clicking and snorting sounds.

Nenda snorted right back at it. He said, "Yeah, yeah. Don't gimme that," and made his own set of clicks. After a few seconds of hesitation, a thick meter-long tongue of royal purple emerged from the Zardalu's head.

Louis Nenda said, "I should think so. That's a damn sight better." He stepped forward and placed his right boot on the outstretched tongue.

Darya gasped in horror, expecting to see Nenda picked up in thigh-thick tentacles and dismembered. He heard the gasp, glanced her way, and nodded a greeting. "Morning. Archie here has been gettin' above himself while he was down on Miranda. I had to use Zardalu slave lingo to remind him who's boss an' who brought him here in the first place."

He lifted his foot from the Zardalu's tongue. "Now, Archie, you get over to the back of the room. You're too big and ugly to sit in front with the rest of us." He produced another set of clicks, and the Zardalu rose, bowed its great head, and slithered away to the rear of the chamber.

Nenda turned back toward Darya and seemed to notice Hans Rebka for the first time. "I'd say that *little* and ugly ought to sit in the back, too."

"Don't let me stop you, then. Go there if you feel you ought to." Rebka calmly made his way toward the front row of seats.

Louis Nenda growled and was heading for Rebka when Atvar H'sial placed her great body between them. She raised her forelimbs, one over Nenda's head and another above Rebka, and hissed menacingly.

"All right, all right." Nenda stepped around the Cecropian so that he could see Hans Rebka. "Just so you don't get the wrong idea about why I'm layin' off now, it's because Atvar H'sial says that the meeting's ready to start—she can smell Julian Graves in the corridor. If we try to fight she says she'll hold us upside down an' shake sense into us. She can do it, too. You don't understand pheromone talk, but J'merlia will confirm her words if you have any doubts."

"I'll believe Atvar H'sial." Rebka continued to the front row of seats, followed by Darya Lang. "As for you, we can take this up some other time."

"The pleasure will be mine." Nenda squeezed into the last place up front, next to Darya, just as Julian Graves entered the room.

If the councilor felt surprise at finding an audience already in place—it was well before the official start time of the meeting—he did not choose to reveal it. He nodded his bald, domed head at Hans Rebka, said, "I heard of your arrival. Good," and turned to face the whole group.

"Since everyone is here, and since you all know each other, I'll get down at once to business."

Darya glanced past Hans Rebka at the dark-haired man on her left. The Zardalu at the back of the room—Archie, an incongruous name for such a giant beast—must be the one that Louis Nenda had dragged along, trussed and wriggling, when they all escaped from Labyrinth. But who was the strange human?

She decided not to ask. Julian Graves already blamed her for interrupting yesterday's meeting.

The councilor went on, "Perhaps the composition of this group has allowed some of you to guess why we are assembled here today. But let me be specific.

"We, like everyone else, grew up with the knowledge that there were Builder artifacts scattered around the local arm. The artifacts had been present for millions of years, and we assumed that they would always be there. Some of us devoted a large part of our lives to studying the Builder artifacts and seeking to understand them."

Darya felt it was safe to nod. She certainly fell into that category.

"However," Julian Graves continued, "two years ago, an astonishing thing happened. Following the event known as Summertide, in the Dobelle system, the artifacts started to change. I have heard half a dozen proposed explanations as to the cause of those changes, but one fact cannot be denied: one by one, the artifacts vanished. We saw the appearance of a single new artifact, Labyrinth. And shortly after that, Labyrinth disappeared along with every other artifact. All of you were present during that climactic event. Since then, we have seen no signs of an artifact anywhere in our local arm of the galaxy. For the past two years, all has been quiet."

Perfectly true, and well-known to any five-year-old. So why are we having this meeting? But Darya remained silent.

Graves said, "At least, we assumed that all was quiet. Then, two months ago, a ship carrying a Chism Polypheme arrived at Upside Miranda Port. The Polyphemes are a species rarely seen in our local arm, since their home world is somewhere in the Sag Arm. The Polyphemes are famously reluctant to give accurate information on its whereabouts."

Louis Nenda, next to Darya, sniffed loudly. "Why don't you tell it like it is, Councilor? Any Polypheme would rather lie than tell the truth. They're the most crooked, unreliable, deceitful species in the galaxy. If you believe anything that the one who came here said, you're a fool."

"You may be right, although the Chism Polyphemes accord the doubtful honor of maximum duplicity to humans. However, in this case it was not necessary to take the Chism Polypheme's word for anything, since it could speak not a word. The ship finished the journey on automatic pilot. The Polypheme was dead on arrival."

Darya felt a spasm of movement on either side of her. Hans Rebka and Louis Nenda were hard to shock, but they were shocked now. So was she. The Sag Arm was thousands of lightyears away. Only a vastly long-lived species, like the Polyphemes, would face the prospect of a Gulf crossing from one spiral arm to the next. As for one *dying*, she had never heard of such a thing. By human standards, a Chism Polypheme was immortal.

Julian Graves went on, "Normally, the interior of a ship arriving at Miranda Port is considered private property and off-limits. However, in this case there were exceptional circumstances. The port authority felt a need to know what event, be it natural or unnatural, had killed the Polypheme. To ensure that suitable procedures and propriety were observed, they called in a member of the Ethical Council to be present when the ship was entered. Upon an initial investigation she was unable to determine the cause of death. The body appeared quite intact, although a closer examination revealed that almost every cell within it had been ruptured and burst by some unknown agent. Soon afterwards, the councilor called for my assistance. She had, as a move to determine if there might be some danger of contamination, examined the ship's log. And what she found was almost beyond belief. The Chism Polyphemes, astonishing as it may seem, have perhaps been *lying* to the species of our spiral arm—and for thousands of years."

Louis Nenda said, "It's like I told you—"

"There is therefore no need to tell me again. The ship's log contained a complete listing of Bose transition points visited. The coordinates of the most recent transition nodes were *in the Gulf.*"

Darya felt the tingle all the way up her spine. No one in the Fourth Alliance, or in the Cecropia Federation whose boundary lay much closer to the Gulf, knew that those Bose nodes were there. Did it mean . . . ?

It did. Julian Graves was continuing, "A chain of Bose nodes exists, forming a link between this spiral arm and the Sag Arm. The Chism Polyphemes certainly did not create such a chain, but obviously they have been making use of it for millennia. The notion that the Polyphemes endured enormously long crossings of the Gulf is a myth of their own devising. The Polypheme's ship log showed that it had crossed the Gulf using exactly eleven Bose nodes. The total travel time to Miranda was a matter of weeks."

Julian Graves made a gesture with his right hand, and

the display of the principal clades and neighboring Gulf that Darya had seen the day before appeared. "As you see, the Bose nodes begin at a location easily reached from here, and they continue to points deep within the Sag Arm. A new and easy path exists from this arm to the neighboring one.

"That, however, was not the main reason why the councilor called me, nor the reason why I called this meeting. The ship contained other information within its data banks. The councilor concluded—and I agree with her conclusion— that there is evidence of Builder artifacts in the Sagittarius Arm."

It was Darya's turn to jerk upright in her seat. A suggestion of existing Builder artifacts—even from such a known unreliable source as the Chism Polyphemes . . .

Graves went on, "Furthermore—"

He was interrupted by a quiet voice from Darya's left. "May I speak?"

With those words came instant recognition. Darya said to the dark-haired man sitting next to Hans Rebka, "Why, you're Tally! But you are in a different body."

"Yes, indeed. I am E. Crimson Tally." The embodied computer grinned horribly at Darya. "I perceive that you did not know me until I spoke. That is because, one month ago, it was necessary to place me within a new setting. For some reason, the bodies into which I have been placed suffer an abnormally high failure rate."

Darya could imagine—the embodied computer had a disregard for danger that only a being with a totally replaceable body could match. And the installers still hadn't managed to get that ghastly smile right.

E.C. Tally said again to Julian Graves, "Councilor, may I speak?"

"I have in the past found no way to prevent you. Go ahead."

"I merely wish to point out that the evidence of Builder artifacts in the Sag Arm is not new. Extra capabilities were added to my newly embodied brain, plus improved data access channels to my body. Last night I downloaded everything in the general data banks. Information there about the Sagittarius Arm indicates the presence of Builder artifacts."

"That is true. Do you know where that information came from?"

"No sources were quoted. The information has perhaps been in the data banks for thousands of years. I do not know its derivation."

"But we do." J'merlia raised a stick-thin limb. "Atvar H'sial offers apologies for this interruption, but the matter is important. She says, long ago, members of the Cecropia Federation interested in Builder artifacts did a complete survey of all knowledge of the Sag Arm relating to possible Builder activity there. The conclusion was that everything originated in statements made by Chism Polyphemes."

"Which means it's all a load of crappo." Louis Nenda swiveled in his seat and looked along the row to Tally. "E.C., didn't you spend time with Dulcimer?"

"Indeed I did."

"Well, Dulcimer was a Chism Polypheme, an' didn't he give you all that garbage about Polytope, an' how it was a world built by the free-space Manticore?"

"Garbage? I thought it was all true."

Julian Graves said firmly, "E.C. Tally, what a Chism Polypheme tells you is almost certainly *not* true. More important, I will not have this meeting turned into an irrelevant series of digressions."

"May I speak?"

"You may speak as much as you like—after I have finished. The facts are these: we have no absolute proof that there are Builder artifacts in the Sagittarius Arm. However, a strong possibility exists that there are. This alone would be enough to encourage some investigators to make a trip to the inward arm. However, there are other and more compelling reasons for an interest in the Sag Arm. When the ship of the Chism Polypheme was thoroughly explored, a group of other alien beings was discovered within their own sealed living quarters. There were eighteen of them. They were of a species unknown to us—and every one was dead. Like the Chism Polypheme, their bodies were outwardly undamaged. But like the Polypheme, all their body cells had been burst open by some unknown force."

Graves waited for the murmur to die down before he continued, "With considerable difficulty, we have been able to decipher their records. They came here to seek our advice and our assistance, although there is no suggestion that they ever thought the trip would prove fatal to them. They call themselves by a name which our translation machines offer as *Marglotta*. Their home world is in the Sag Arm, and it translates as Marglot. It is somewhere in here."

Graves again gestured, and the Gulf with its pattern of Bose nodes vanished. It was replaced in the 3-D display by a long, twisting volume of space, dotted with the beacons of supergiant stars and great obscuring clouds of dust and gas.

"The Sag Arm, in detail. Here"—a blinking point of blue appeared—"is our best estimate for the location of the Marglot system. Either we are misunderstanding their records, or the Marglotta come from a strange world indeed. There seem to be four poles, defined as North, South, Hot, and Cold. No explanation is offered for this. The Marglotta apparently did not feel it necessary to keep in their files descriptive details of their own home world. However, you will have plenty of time to puzzle out the significance of the four planetary poles later."

Later? But if no one else asked the question, Darya was not about to interrupt. The councilor's big, domed head, with its powerful mnemonic twin memory and misty blue eyes, still had the power to intimidate her.

Graves went on, "Now for a question which you may already have asked yourselves. Why was I, a member of the inter-clade *Ethical* Council, called in? I have perhaps had more contact than other councilors with Builder artifacts, but I am by no means an expert on the subject. How are ethics involved? I can give you a simple answer. We may be dealing with attempted genocide. The Marglotta say that their world is changing. Some great destructive force is at work in the Sag Arm. It has spread steadily for many millennia, possibly for millions of years. The Marglotta suspect the influence of the Builders. I cannot speak as to the truth of that conjecture, but we have made our own observations of the Sag Arm. We find a region utterly lacking in light and life. Observe."

The chamber dimmed. The new 3-D display seemed to grin back at Darya. It was as though something had taken a bite out of the spiral arm and left a small sphere of black nothing where stars should be.

"Scary picture." Louis Nenda spoke softly, as much to himself as to Darya. "And hard luck on Marglotta and friends."

She whispered back, "Scary, and strange. Anything on that scale has to be Builder activity. But no Builder artifact in our arm ever destroyed whole stellar systems."

Julian Graves was staring at them. Louis Nenda said, more loudly, "Somethin's doing a number on the Sag Arm. But Councilor, it's a zillion lightyears away. We're safe enough."

"I do not share your confidence on the latter point." Julian Graves's deep voice filled the hall. "Our own clades—*all* our own clades—could be in danger. We went back to observations of the Sag Arm made millennia ago. The dark sphere is growing, and as it spreads, its outer boundary will come closer to an edge of the Sag Arm—to the place, in fact, where nodes of the Bose network stretch across the Gulf toward our own spiral arm."

Darya could sense Hans Rebka moving restlessly at her side. He said, "I see what you're getting at. But what are we talking about here? We sure don't need to worry about next week, or next year. How long do we have?"

"Precisely?" The lights came on, and Graves was frowning. "I do not know. E. Crimson Tally? An estimate?"

"From the data available, the affected area could reach the far edge of the Gulf somewhere between twenty-nine and thirty-two thousand years from now."

Graves nodded. "There's your answer, Captain Rebka. But I wonder why you ask."

Rebka stood up restlessly, although squeezed between Darya and E.C. Tally he had no place to go. "Because of who I am, and what I've done all my life. I can see why Darya might get excited when there are signs that the Builders are busy in the next arm over. I can see why you are involved, because the immediate danger to the Marglotta is an ethical question. But me, I'm strictly short-term. Get in a fix today, maybe I can get you out of it by tomorrow. At least I'll try. But when you talk thousands and tens of thousands of years, I'm as much use as feathers on a fish."

"Which goes doubled for At an' me." Louis Nenda stood up, too, leaving Darya sitting sandwiched tightly between him and Rebka. "An' our slaves, J'merlia an' Kallik—"

"They are not your slaves, Mr. Nenda. I object strongly to the use of that word. They are free beings."

"Try tellin' that to *them*, Councilor—maybe you'll have more luck than I've had. But don't get me off the point. Me an' At don't specialize in ethics."

"I am not unaware of that point. In fact, I am relying upon it."

"Eh? What kind of crack is that? Anyway, not only ethics. I've been mixed up with Builder stuff ever since Summertide, but nobody in their right mind would call me an *expert* on them."

"This also is a fact well-known to me."

"So why am I here? Why is At here? Why is that"—Nenda seemed ready to use something insulting, but finally he just jerked a thumb toward Hans Rebka—"why is *he* here? Hell, why is any one of us here? We were forced to come, you know—we didn't want to."

Graves nodded. "That also is no surprise. Mr. Nenda, and Captain Rebka also, I am afraid that one element of this whole affair has apparently escaped you. I should have been clearer at the outset. You were not brought to Miranda Port simply to be provided with information concerning the new Bose nodes that lead to the Sag Arm. You were not brought here to learn about the Marglotta, or the destructive force at work in the Sagittarius Arm. Nor were you brought here to offer your advice, valuable as that may be. You were brought here because you, and I, and everyone present in this chamber, have a more active role to perform."

"Like what?"

"Like, Mr. Nenda, to discover what threatens to destroy Marglot, and what one day may destroy us." Graves bowed his head, so that light gleamed on his bald dome with its pattern of radiation scars that for some reason he had never bothered to have removed. "Miranda Port represents no more than a point of embarkation. As soon as possible, we will all be on our way to the Sagittarius Arm."

CHAPTER SIX
Through the Gulf.

Darya, even though she was from one of the richest worlds in the Fourth Alliance, had never dreamed that ships like the *Pride of Orion* existed. It was a miracle of compact structure. Although it was not especially large, and although it looked like and operated as one perfectly integrated body, the ship could divide into six self-contained vessels. Each had its own drive and its own Bose transfer capability. The ship had been renamed before they set out from Upside Miranda Port. Darya suspected that was a Council act. The *Pride of Orion* and everyone within it would be the first representatives of the local arm to visit its inward neighbor.

Or not quite the first. The *Pride of Orion* was about to pass through yet another Bose transition. Just ahead, a mere pulsating speck on the screen, flew a much smaller ship. Even as Darya watched and wondered, the *Have-It-All* entered the node and the signal beacon vanished.

Its presence on the expedition was the result of a terrific argument with Julian Graves on the eve of their departure; an argument, moreover, in which the unheard-of took place: Hans Rebka and Louis Nenda had agreed with each other completely.

"The *Pride of Orion* is effectively indestructible." That was Julian Graves.

"I don't care if the *Pride of Orion* is made of solid neutronium and could fly up the wazoo of a Bolingbroke giant and come out in one piece." Nenda stood arms akimbo, glaring at the councilor. "Smart people don't do things that way, an' I can't believe you don't know it."

"Nenda's right." Hans Rebka poked an accusing finger at Graves. "You saw it for yourself during Summertide *and* on Genizee. No matter how secure you feel, you don't travel without a backup. Especially when you're heading beyond known space."

"We have a back-up ship, for Heaven's sake. We have *six* back-up ships, right on the *Pride of Orion*. If you want to inspect them, you have my permission to visit every one."

"Yeah, an' that's real easy to do." Nenda looked around as though seeking a good place to spit. "You know why? Because they *are* right there on board the *Pride of Orion*. It gets zapped, they get zapped."

"What could possibly, as you put it, 'zap' the *Pride of Orion*?"

"If we knew the answer to that, we'd be a lot less worried." This time Rebka's outstretched finger actually touched the councilor's chest. "I don't understand your logic here. Taking an extra ship along will cost the Council a negligible amount."

"Cost *nothin'*, you mean." Nenda jerked a thumb toward the silent Cecropian. "At an' me, we'll fly the *Have-It-All* in scout position *for free*."

"Even better. Councilor, are you listening? You have somebody willing to fly on ahead of the *Pride of Orion*, to make sure that there are no problems waiting. "Hans Rebka gave Nenda a quick sideways glance at that point—the offer to lead the way into possible danger sounded a little too good to be true—but he went on, "A lead scout is in everyone's best interests."

"It would not be right to ask Mr. Nenda and Atvar H'sial to expose themselves to risks not borne by the rest of us. In any case, we will have a special group of humans on board the *Pride of Orion*, with unique training in survival techniques. The inter-clade council insists on it."

"Oh yeah? Training acquired where? Sitting on their asses on one of the cushy worlds of the Fourth Alliance? If you took 'em to Karelia—"

"—or to Teufel."

Nenda glared at Hans Rebka. "Hey, Captain, we're not competin' on this one." He turned back to Graves. "Take 'em to Karelia or Teufel, an' the locals'd eat 'em for supper an' spit 'em out with the pits."

"I have no reason to question the survival team's competence. They were trained under the direct supervision of Arabella Lund, whom I happen to know personally. And I do not want you to take unnecessary risks."

"Fine. You're not askin' me an At to do that. *We're* askin' *you*. An' we're not offering miracles. If there's trouble on the way, all we'll give you will be a few minutes of warning."

The argument went on and on. But Hans and Louis had finally won. The proof of that was the presence on the expedition of the *Have-It-All*, which had already made its next Bose transition. Darya stared hard at the screen, seeing nothing but knowing that the node entry point for the *Pride of Orion* could be no more than a few minutes away. One advantage of this ship's curious structure was the existence within its hull of scores of private chambers where a person could retire with her thoughts and hide away from others. Each room had access to the *Pride of Orion*'s external viewing sensors, and what Darya wanted to see on the display was the reassuring beacon of the *Have-It-All* as soon as their own ship completed its transition.

Crossing the Gulf was nothing like normal interstellar travel, where you were always comforted by the sight of nearby stars that might send help if your superluminal travel modes failed. Around the *Pride of Orion* lay only a vast sea of emptiness. The spiral arm from which they had come lay far behind. Ahead the Great Unknown of the Sag Arm sprawled across half the sky.

And within that unknown, perhaps, lay completely new Builder artifacts. Darya had not been able to focus on anything else since Julian Graves mentioned the possibility. She had rejected from Louis Nenda a suggestion that they compare notes on what they knew about the Sag Arm—"I'll show you mine an' you show me yours." She had also been unable to return to her previous intimacy with Hans Rebka, and it had little to do with the fact that they had been apart for two years.

Even the delivery of what Councilor Graves clearly thought of as a warning seemed to lack reality.

That had come in answer to Hans's protest, at the end of the first meeting. "You're crazy if you think a handful of us can run off and in a few weeks sort out the problems of a region as big as all our territories put together."

Graves's forehead added a few more worry lines. "Captain Rebka, I have never suggested any such thing. Our goal is the exploration of what is happening on Marglot, and possibly an attempt to help the Marglotta. We do not expect to understand the mystery of dying worlds, or to determine the fate and future of the whole Sag Arm. However, I would be remiss if I failed to inform you of another important point concerning our journey. As you remark, we are small in numbers, even if large in experience of the Builders and their artifacts. But our expedition is as small as it is because this is viewed by the Council as a high-risk endeavor."

In other words they don't want to send too many of us, just in case we don't come back. But even that thought hadn't had as much effect on Darya as it should. Artifacts! What wouldn't she give to see new Builder artifacts? She realized now how boring it had been for the past couple of years, sitting in her office at the Institute on Sentinel Gate and methodically recording every element of the disappearance of Builder presence. It had been like making notes on your own death.

With that thought, Darya felt within her the near-imperceptible quiver that told of impending passage into and through a Bose node. She peered at the screen, seeking that other dot of light.

And there it was, a signal beacon blinking its message. The *Have-It-All* was safely through, with the *Pride of Orion* following close behind. But the thing that made Darya catch her breath lay beyond the two ships. They had attained the far side of the Gulf. A final and short Bose transition should take them to the Marglot system. However, even before that there might be evidence of Builder artifacts.

Darya eagerly scanned the glittering starscape that filled the sky ahead. Many years of experience told her that she was probably wasting her time. Builder artifacts were infinitely varied in appearance. They ranged from apparently normal structures, like the Umbilical that ran between Opal and Quake, to the near-unfathomable space-time convolutions of the Torvil Anfract. An artifact could look like anything or nothing.

She looked anyway, swinging a high-resolution scanner across the sky. Stars and to spare—they seemed more thickly clustered than in the home Orion Arm—but nothing to hint at Builder presence.

She jumped as a voice behind her said, "Too soon, I fear."

She turned to see E.C. Tally standing there.

"How did you know what I was looking for? And how did you know where I was?"

"The latter question is easily answered. The *Pride of Orion*'s central data bank contains a complete occupation directory for every chamber at all times."

"So you know where the survival team is housed?" For whatever reason, Julian Graves had kept his team of survival specialists in seclusion.

"Of course."

"Do you know how many of them there are?"

"There are five, all of human form. None, alas, appears to be an embodied computer. As to what you were seeking as you scanned the sky, I assume that it is what all others seem to be seeking: a first look at the Marglot system."

"Are we close enough for that?"

"No. Nor will we be, until the final Bose transition is accomplished. However, logic is not at work here. Every being on board, in spite of known facts, stares impatiently at the screens. It is curious, but even I, who according to my designers lack circuits for the emotion known as excitement, feel a sense of impending fulfillment."

"But you're not staring at screens."

"No. Logic still plays a significant part in my actions. Our final Bose transition to the vicinity of what we hope will be the Marglot system lies an hour in the future, and I have calculated that the whole system subtends less than a second of arc from our present distance. It is therefore invisible to the naked eye. I sought you out in order to ask for your assistance on something else, something for which the data banks provide no guidance."

"Then it's not likely that I can help."

"Councilor Graves suggests otherwise. The subject calls for opinion, rather than fact. May I speak?"

Had Julian Graves sent Tally to her just to get rid of the embodied computer, with his endless what-why-how? Darya gave up on screen-watching. The chances of finding evidence of Builder presence in the first five minutes in the Sag Arm was as low as that of seeing the Marglot system itself. She resigned herself to an E.C. Tally lecture. "What's your problem?"

"The nature of the Builders."

"You're out of luck. Nobody knows that."

"My question is specific, and concerns the generality of their distribution. Were you present during the dissection of the Marglotta corpses?"

"No, I was not." And *Ugh!* as well. From what Darya had heard and the pictures she had seen, the bodies had been shrunken mummies by the time they were discovered in their sealed chamber on the Polypheme's ship. She wondered just when they had died.

"Nor, regrettably, was I present. However, I understand that the Marglotta are very different in external body structure and internal organs from any creatures in our local arm."

"That's not surprising, E.C. The Sag Arm is so far away, you'd expect the development of life to have occurred there independently. Their beings should look and act utterly differently."

"So Councilor Graves suggested. Yet tests of the Marglotta living quarters on the Polypheme ship suggest that they were not segregated because they breathed different air from the Polypheme. In fact, they could have breathed the same air with no difficulty. And the Chism Polyphemes—who also developed in the Sag Arm—can breathe the same air as humans and Cecropians. Analysis of material in the Marglotta digestive tracts shows that they were also able to eat the same kinds of food as humans. Now, you are of course familiar with the ancient theory of panspermia?"

Darya groaned mentally. One problem in dealing with E. Crimson Tally was the embodied computer's built-in urge to acquire as much information as possible—no matter how old, no matter how useless. She shook her head.

"Really? Then I will explain." E.C. Tally casually fitted a neural cable from the room's terminal to the socket on his chest, and went on without missing a beat. "Panspermia posits that life on many worlds was seeded there from outside. This leads at once to a question: Could such seeding take place not merely among the neighboring stars of a galactic arm, but clear across the Gulf?"

"I have no idea."

"But I do. I performed the necessary calculation of Gulf crossing-time for spores of living matter when propelled by light pressure. I made plausible assumptions as to the mass/area ratio of such spores. And the result I obtained was a survival probability so close to zero that it can for all practical purposes be ignored."

"And?"

"I decided that interstellar seeding can indeed take place, but not across so great a span as the Gulf. From which one would conclude that any living beings who inhabit the Sagittarius Arm must have arisen as and be descended from independent life. And yet we can breathe the same kind of air as the Marglotta and Polyphemes."

"That's because of the Principle of Convergence." It was rare for Darya to find simple facts of which Tally remained ignorant. "We have good theoretical grounds for expecting all worlds within the habitable zone of a star eventually to tend to develop one of just two kinds of atmosphere. Either they remain hydrogen-rich, or photosynthetic forms develop and they become oxygen-nitrogen rich. Taskar Lucindar proved that principle using very general arguments, more than three thousand years ago."

"Indeed she did. She also pointed out that the Principle of Convergence applied to biospheres as a whole, but not to the living forms that might inhabit them. To explain observed similarities in edible materials, Taskar Lucindar invoked the principle of panspermia; which, as I have proved to my own satisfaction, cannot operate across any empty space as wide as the Gulf."

Go away, Tally. You make my head ache. What was the old comment about the ancient who knew everything? "He not only overflowed with learning, but stood in the slop."

Darya said mildly, "So what's your question, E.C.?"

"Why, it is as I said: the Builders. They occupied our spiral arm long ago, and they filled it with their artifacts. Did they also occupy the Sag Arm, and perhaps the whole galaxy? Were they, rather than panspermia, the instrument by which life forms with similar metabolic requirements were able to appear on both sides of the Gulf?"

E.C. Tally now had Darya's full attention. For years it had been her conviction that the Builders would not have confined their presence to a single galactic arm. Her unplanned and uncontrolled trip to Serenity, the huge Builder artifact thirty thousand lightyears out of the plane of the galaxy, had supported her belief, although Professor Merada and others at the Artifact Research Institute on Sentinel Gate still regarded the story of that journey as a pure flight of fancy. *Proving* that the Builders had been active in the Sag Arm (and beyond) required access to that arm—which had until now been impossible. True, there were the wild tales told by the Chism Polyphemes. But Darya, like Hans Rebka, lacked faith in Polypheme pronouncements on that or any other subject.

She said, "If the Builders were active all over the galaxy, that explains a lot of things." She added, "Kallik and Atvar H'sial can tell you—" Then she paused.

She had been going to say that the Hymenopt and the Cecropian probably knew as much about the Builders as she did. Unfortunately, Kallik and Atvar H'sial were aboard the *Have-It-All*, along with Nenda, J'merlia, and the hulking Zardalu, Archimedes.

She glanced up to the display. The flashing beacon of the other ship was pulsing at a higher rate.

"E.C., that's a Bose entry signal. They're about to make another transition."

"That is correct. Another, and the final one."

"So soon?"

"As I said, this last stage of the journey is short and simple. Unless they return a warning drone after Bose node entry, our own transition is only a few minutes away. However, as to my earlier question, and our discussion of it—"

"Not now, Tally. If you don't mind, I'd rather not talk."

Unlike E.C., Darya definitely did have circuits for emotion. At the moment they were close to shorting out with overload. So many elements were converging. Louis Nenda was about to take a leap into unknown dangers—she found it hard to forgive herself for refusing his simple request for a meal together; mixed with worry for Louis came the excitement of encountering a new stellar system that sounded like nothing anyone had ever seen; and finally, most powerful of all, there was the promise of renewed Builder interaction. That hit her like strong wine after a two-year drought.

Darya watched and waited until the beacon of the *Have-It-All* vanished, then watched and waited again through the long minutes preceding their own Bose transition.

The moment came at last. The universe blinked. Darya sighed, leaned forward, and opened her eyes wide.

And saw nothing. She felt bewildered. The records left by the Chism Polypheme and the dead Marglotta should have brought the *Pride of Orion* to a system where the central primary was a greenish-yellow star alive with hydrogen prominences. Before her eyes lay nothing but darkness, lit by the wan gleam of far-off stars and galaxies.

At her side, E.C. Tally was not limited to wavelengths visible to humans. The embodied computer was in direct contact with all the sensors of the *Pride of Orion*, which had completed a first full-sky survey within milliseconds of transition. Darya heard Tally's exclamation of surprise.

"What is it, E.C.?"

"One star, but many planets—more than forty of them."

"Where? I can't see a single one."

"Nor can I, even with the superior eyes of my body. But the *Pride of Orion* reports the presence of a central star less than two hundred million kilometers away from us, orbited by a large train of planets."

"Then why don't we see them?"

"Because they are all, even the central star, at low temperatures. The *Pride of Orion* employs bolometers, able to detect and measure the radiation from objects only a few degrees above absolute zero. This is ridiculous!"

"What is?" Darya had heard—or imagined—excitement in Tally's voice.

"Why, the readings. The star and most of the planets are cold, no more than a couple of hundred degrees absolute. But one of those planets—a big one, in a close-in orbit—is at only 1.2 kelvins. That is *lower* than the temperature of the universe's microwave background radiation."

"Isn't that physically impossible?"

"According to the accepted theories of human and Cecropian scientists, it is. But perhaps the scientists of the Sag Arm employ different theories."

Darya hardly heard E.C. Tally's reply. A more disturbing thought had come into her head. Where was the beacon? Where was the flashing sign assuring them of the safe arrival of the others? Where was Louis Nenda?

Darya called for a new full-sky survey, centered on the frequencies of the signal beacon. She concentrated totally on the monitors as the results came in, ignoring E.C. Tally who was still babbling on at her side.

Nothing, nothing, nothing. The *Have-It-All*, along with all its crew, had vanished without a trace.

CHAPTER SEVEN
The wrong place.

Louis Nenda wished to travel separately from the *Pride of Orion* for a very specific reason. Julian Graves, as you might expect of a numb-nuts Ethical Council member, was a hopeless pacifist who did not believe in the use of weapons. Maybe it hadn't been Graves's idea to add a "survival team" to the party, but it was unlikely that he had fought against it. Arabella Lund—whoever she might be—had trained them, and she was one of Graves's buddies. So he trusted her and them. Nenda, on the other hand, trusted nobody but himself, and he had made too many blind and desperate leaps through Bose nodes to leave to chance whatever might lie on the other side.

Long before the *Have-It-All* made the final Bose transition, the ship had every weapons port open and every weapon primed. All warning sensors were on full alert. The ship was ready to fire on command, to make another Bose jump, or to run a high-speed route for whatever cover might exist. Nenda had also silenced any device that might signal their presence to an unfriendly listener. If anyone's signal beacon served as a homing signal for enemy fire, it would not be Louis Nenda's. What those morons on the *Pride of Orion* chose to do was up to them.

The *Have-It-All* emerged from the node and floated free in space, its drives turned off. Nenda took one look at the warning displays and released a long-held breath.

"Nothing. Not one blessed thing."

He meant that he saw no signs of anything dangerous, but Atvar H'sial, at his side, was receiving the input of other sensors tuned to her own echolocation vision. Her pheromonal output murmured, "Less than nothing." When Nenda turned to stare, she became more specific. "We are supposed to find here the home world of the Marglotta, are we not? It is the presumed source of much strangeness and who-knows-what wonders of alien technology, priceless when returned to the Orion Arm. Tell me, then. Where are these treasures?"

Nenda turned on the raft of displays not dedicated to warnings. The *Have-It-All* should have emerged close to the Marglotta home star, somewhere within a complex stellar system. All that showed on his screen was a central disk of darkness against a faint background of distant stars.

He scanned the other monitors. "Nothing at any wavelength. What gives? Has the Marglotta star been turned into a black hole? And where are the planets?"

The pheromonal reply from Atvar H'sial was tinged with uneasiness. "There are planets, in abundance. But all are cold. Too cold for liquid water, too cold for a breathable atmosphere."

"No air, no water. So there's no life. Unless the Marglotta don't need any of that?"

"But they do, Louis. Remember, they were air breathers just as we are air breathers. They could not survive on any of the worlds we see."

"Master Nenda, if I may with respect add to this discussion." Kallik, crouched at Nenda's side, had access to the same displays and was following Nenda's spoken version of the conversation with Atvar H'sial. "The main body that you see on the screen cannot be a black hole. Our mass detectors indicate that it contains as much matter as a large star, and this is confirmed by the periods of revolution of the planets. However, a black hole of such a mass would have a diameter of only a few kilometers. What we observe is a dense object several tens of thousands of kilometers in diameter, at just a couple of hundred degrees above absolute zero."

"The size of a large planet, but as heavy as a star. A white dwarf?"

"Except that it gives off no energy. I wonder." The Hymenopt hesitated.

"Spit it out, Kallik. No time to get coy with me."

"The body that we see does not lie at the end of any natural stellar evolutionary sequence known in our own spiral arm. It appears to be solid matter in a cold, crystallized form. Could it be that the laws of physics are different in the Sag Arm?"

"That is at best a remote possibility." Atvar H'sial had been receiving pheromonal translation through Nenda, and her response revealed her chemical scorn at such an idea. "The laws of physics are the same throughout the universe."

"Maybe. But either way we got us a mystery."

"I think not. Louis, there is one other possible answer. Ask Kallik if she believes that the star arrived in its present state through natural processes."

As soon as she received the question, Kallik shook her round head. "I can see no way for natural processes to achieve such a result."

"Very good." Atvar H'sial nodded as Nenda gave her that reply, and went on, "Tell Kallik, then it must have reached its present state through *unnatural* processes. The star has been *drained* of its energy, by some external agent."

"I concur. And the same is true for the big planet." Kallik gestured to the bank of monitors. "Observe. It is supernaturally cold. Nothing in this whole system is warm enough to radiate significant amounts of energy."

"Not quite nothing. Not any more." Nenda pointed to one of the monitors, where the signal beacon of another ship suddenly flashed bright against the dark span of the Gulf. "Look at those dummies. They're certainly radiating energy. They come through the Bose node into possible danger, an' they're all lit up for the holidays. I'll bet you Hans Rebka is foaming at the mouth, but he don't have final say on the *Pride of Orion*. Lucky for them there's nothing sittin' here waitin' to wipe 'em out."

"Nothing *now*." The chill in Atvar H'sial's words was that of the frozen stellar system to which they had come. "But at some time, Louis, the fusion processes of that star were halted and it was depleted of its energy. Something has been at work here on a scale that I find hard to imagine."

"The Builders?"

"They are certainly capable of it. Yet this does not fit with my perceptions of Builder activities."

"Kallik? Do you think the Builders might have done this? Atvar H'sial says no."

"With respect, Master Nenda, I must agree with Atvar H'sial. This does not have the feel of a Builder artifact."

"So where do we go from here? At, do you think we're safe in this system?"

"I believe that we are safe *for the moment*. The continued existence of the *Pride of Orion* supports that idea. Its crew must be as puzzled as we are, since this is clearly not the system of the Marglotta."

"We should have known that all along. We told 'em that no Polypheme ever tells the truth unless it has to."

"Congratulations to us on our own perspicacity. However, self-praise does us little good. This is not the place where we thought to arrive. I repeat, it is not the system of the Marglotta."

"Damn right. It's colder than a witch's cul-de-sac."

"And I am at a loss to suggest what we should do next."

"Ten heads might be better than five. Let's go an' see if Graves and his bunch have any bright ideas."

"In order to do that, Louis, we must either travel or send signals to them."

"Then that's what I guess we gotta do."

"Either signals or motion will reveal our existence and our position."

"But according to you, At, for the moment we don't need to worry too much about that." Nenda turned on the *Have-It-All*'s signal beacon. "There. Now everybody knows we're here." He activated the intercom to the pilot's cabin. "Hit them buttons, J'merlia, an' take us to rendezvous. It's time to compare notes. Let's give the others a chance to show off how smart they are."

The *Have-It-All* was Louis Nenda's pride and joy and his most treasured possession. Allowing J'merlia to serve as its pilot represented a triumph of reason over emotion.

Nenda's homeworld, Karelia, wasn't the sort of place that went in for formal education. Survival was the limit of most people's ambition. Maybe because of that, Louis despised anything that might be labeled as philosophical thought. But he had learned a thing or two in the school of hard knocks, and one of them was that if somebody or something did a job better than you ever would or could, it made sense to let them. J'merlia had instincts and eyesight and reflexes that Nenda could not match. So, J'merlia would fly the ship.

In the same way, Kallik had superior analytical ability, while Atvar H'sial possessed a great knowledge of Builder history. Nenda suspected that Darya Lang knew even more, but he wasn't about to head into that territory. Atvar H'sial's satisfaction when Darya was left behind on the other ship had sent a pheromonal message you could read at a hundred meters.

And amid all this talent, what did Louis Nenda himself do? He knew the answer to that. He did anything left over that had to be done, and he examined anything that made his guts rumble uneasily for no defined reason. While the *Have-It-All* and the *Pride of Orion* closed in on each other, he took a closer look at the planets orbiting their frozen primary.

Ignoring the usual space rubble of minor planetoids and comets, the count was unusually high. The tracking equipment on the *Have-It-All* reported forty-seven sizeable bodies, eighteen of them massive enough to maintain some kind of atmosphere. Few of them did—most were simply too cold—but one oddity would have caught the eye of a space traveller far less seasoned than Louis Nenda. Of the five worlds orbiting within the life-zone region of a normal star of equivalent mass, one planet was a monster larger than all the others combined. It was also the coldest one, almost as big as the star around which it orbited. Based on diameter alone that should make it a gas-giant with a gravitational field strong enough to sweep clear a broad swath of space. That had not happened. The deep ranging system on the *Have-It-All* revealed the existence of celestial debris, including objects no bigger than orbiting mountains, criss-crossing the orbit of the monster world.

You could not expect to see much from eighty million kilometers, but Nenda focused the *Have-It-All*'s best scope on the planet.

The instrument's smart sensor complained at once. *This target provides no emitted radiation at any wavelength useful for imaging. The body is close to absolute zero.*

"I know. Do the best you can."

That may still prove unsatisfactory. There is nothing to work with but a meager supply of photons provided by the reflected light of distant stars. Image dwell time may be unacceptably long.

"I'll be the judge of that. Show us what you're gettin' as you go, and stop moanin'."

The image built slowly. At first it was no more than the faintest speckling of points of light, providing the ghostly outline of a disk that might well be no more than a man's wishful thinking. Louis Nenda waited. He had the patience of a man who had once spent two days and nights immersed in the oozy swamps of Doradus Nine, ears and nostrils stopped while he breathed through a narrow straw and troops of Doradan Colubrids sought to exact revenge for the death of their ancestral leader. No chance. If necessary, he would have waited a week.

Photon by unpredictable photon, the picture on the screen strengthened and solidified. Nenda was not seeing the banded cloud patterns of a typical gas-giant. He did not expect it. At such low temperatures, all gases must change state to become liquids or solids. Rather, he thought to see the typical fractal cracking of a methane or nitrogen iceworld surface. But that too was incorrect.

Just what *was* the pattern, slowly building on the display? He saw linear features, straight as though ruled on the distant ball. Or did he imagine them? He was well aware of the tendency of human eyes to "connect the dots," making from random patterns of light and dark a structured mental picture.

He said to the sensor, "Hey, I need an independent check. Am I really seein' straight lines on the image you're producin', or am I making 'em all up?"

They are real. Would you like an enhancement of linear features?

"Not yet. Wait another ten minutes, then you can—"

The blast of a siren through the interior of the *Have-It-All* cut off his instructions. It was followed at once by J'merlia's soft voice. "We are about to make our rendezvous with the *Pride of Orion*. Be prepared for possible anomalous accelerations."

With J'merlia at the controls, the chances of a rough ride were close to zero. But either you did what your pilot told you, or you looked for a different pilot. Nenda said to the imager, "Any problem with building the picture while we rendezvous?"

Yes and no. The ship's movements experienced during rendezvous can readily be corrected using image motion compensation algorithms. However, the planet is turning on its axis. Even if we continue imaging, our final result will be of variable definition, since the dwell time for the whole surface will not be uniform.

"Times are hard all over. Do the best you can, an' keep addin' photons to give us a good picture." Nenda took a final look at the image on the display. Numerous dark dots were coupled by narrow lines to form a fine web over the whole planetary surface. It was exactly the kind of pattern that the mind liked to conjure up—except that in this case, the sensor assured him that what he saw was not just the result of human imagination.

There was one more thing that had to be done before rendezvous. Nenda turned to Atvar H'sial, who had been listening intently to some mysterious two-dimensional data stream of sound.

"At, can I borrow J'merlia for a while? I have a job for him."

"If it will extend into the time of our meeting on the *Pride of Orion*, you will deprive me of my interpreter."

"I'm not as good with the pheromones as J'merlia, but I can run you a pretty good simultaneous translation."

"Then I agree. You will, of course, owe me a favor. I will go now to J'merlia and command him to follow your instructions."

The Cecropian glided out. Nenda turned to Kallik. "I have a tough one for you."

"Master Nenda, I will operate to the best of my abilities."

"This will need them. While Atvar H'sial and I are gone, I want you and J'merlia to plot out the locations of Bose transition points in the Sag Arm. Mark as many of them as you can, along with associated closest stars and distances."

"Master Nenda, we lack data about the Sag Arm. How are we to locate Bose nodes?"

"If I knew that, would I be askin' for help? You can make a start with the data base from the Polypheme ship. It was all loaded into the banks on the *Pride of Orion*. You should be able to access that from here."

"Data provided from Chism Polypheme sources are notoriously unreliable."

"Sure they are. But that doesn't mean everything in them is wrong."

He heard the faint sigh of equalizing air pressures. J'merlia had already docked them with the *Pride of Orion*, and so gently that Nenda had not even felt the contact. Which meant that Louis had to get a move on—the last thing he wanted was somebody on board the other ship deciding to take a look at the interior of the *Have-It-All*. He had closed the weapons ports as soon as he gave the command to seek the *Pride of Orion*, but there were plenty of other things he did not want exposed to prying eyes.

He gave a few final instructions to Kallik and hurried out. Behind him, the instrument sensor was turning for sympathy to Kallik, the only organic being remaining in the chamber.

This task cannot be performed well unless the ship moves closer to the target. A simple accumulation of photons will not suffice to provide a first-rate image. There is also the question of resolution. Even with diffraction-limited optics—

Nenda was barely in time. But for the actions of Atvar H'sial he would not have been. The umbilical between the two ships was already in position when he reached the hatch, and Atvar H'sial was standing in front of it. The Cecropian had towered up to her full height, with her black wing cases stretched as wide as they would go to block the whole umbilical. The pheromones wafting from her were wordless, but they betrayed a smoldering anger.

"What's up, At? Give us a bit more room there." Nenda squeezed his way through on her right-hand side. He pushed the wing cases and delicate vestigial wings out of the way, and found himself face to face with a human female. "I see. And who the hell might you be?"

But he could already guess the answer. The only strangers on the *Pride of Orion* were the "survival experts." This had to be one of that team of five, kept in strict seclusion by Julian Graves.

Nenda could see now why Graves had hidden them. The woman in front of him was fresh-faced and slim. With her big blue eyes and curls of golden hair, she looked about sixteen years old. She ignored his question and stared at Atvar H'sial with obvious curiosity.

"So this is a Cecropian," she said. "Funny, I thought he would be bigger."

"*She*, not he. The only Cecropians you'll ever meet away from their home world are females. You were standing in Atvar H'sial's way."

"No. She was in mine."

"Same thing. You're lucky she didn't pick you up and squash you flat. Cecropians are strong, an' they don't have much patience with humans. Weren't you briefed on this sort of thing before they let you out of the creche?"

The woman again ignored his words, but she did stop staring at Atvar H'sial. She turned those innocent blue eyes on Louis, and said, "I suppose you must be Nenda. Graves warned us about you."

He knew it was a deliberate come-on, but he couldn't resist. "Warned you of *what* about me?"

"Oh, that you are a thief, and a villain, and probably a murderer. Is it true?"

"Go to hell."

"Graves said that you would cuss and flame and generally act like an uncultured barbarian."

"What do you mean, *act*? You got the real thing here."

As they spoke, Nenda was reevaluating the woman in front of him and providing an edited pheromonal version of their conversation to Atvar H'sial. The impression of youth came partly from the pale and flawless skin, but beneath it he could see strong tendons in her bare arms. Her eyes might seem innocent, but they were everywhere, scanning him and Atvar H'sial. Her movements were unnaturally rapid and precise, and he guessed at hidden enhancements.

He said, "Do you have a name?" and as the woman in front of him answered he passed a pheromonal message to Atvar H'sial: *"Keep crowding us forward along the umbilical. We definitely don't want her near the* Have-It-All.*"*

"I am Sinara Bellstock. Born on Miranda, trained on Persephone."

"Louis, I do not like this human female. Her pheromones suggest a desire for continued badinage and intimate discourse with you."

"That's crazy. At, if I listened to you I'd never speak to a human woman."

He said to Sinara Bellstock, "Trained to do what?" At the same time he moved past her, forcing her either to follow him or come into contact with Atvar H'sial. The Cecropian was gliding steadily forward and blocking the whole corridor.

"Trained in martial arts, trained in weapons, trained in diplomacy. Trained to endure pain, trained to be patient, trained to evaluate a situation quickly and then act. Trained to *survive*."

But not trained to lie, and cheat, or disbelieve half the things that you are told? Then good luck, lady. Because you're going to need it. Without all those other things you wouldn't last ten minutes on half the worlds in the local arm.

Louis did not speak those words to Sinara Bellstock. Nor did he convey them pheromonally to Atvar H'sial, who continued to transmit bursts of suspicion and displeasure. They were at the end of the umbilical, and as they entered the docking chamber of the *Pride of Orion* he could see four people waiting for them. There was Julian Graves, and E.C. Tally, and behind those two were Darya Lang and Hans Rebka.

Louis Nenda experienced multiple feelings of relief. The effort of speaking to a human and simultaneously holding a pheromonal conversation on a different subject with Atvar H'sial made his head feel like it would split in two. It would be a luxury to sit for a while and just *listen* to what others had to say.

And then there was the behavior of Atvar H'sial herself. Preoccupied with Sinara Bellstock, for the first time in years the Cecropian was not reacting with suspicion and annoyance to the sight of Darya Lang.

Louis moved forward. He had never thought it could happen, but the sight of Hans Rebka's scowl of greeting and of E.C. Tally eagerly poised to speak brought a smile to his face.

CHAPTER EIGHT
Theories, theories, theories.

With every passing hour, Hans Rebka became more convinced that his presence on the expedition to the Sag Arm was a mistake. Sure, it was nice to have been saved at the eleventh hour from what, even being optimistic, still looked like certain death by execution on Candela. But saved to do what? No one on the *Pride of Orion* seemed willing to let him do anything.

He had tried to make Julian Graves see reason. The Ethical Councilor simply shook his bald head and muttered to himself for a few moments.

"I hear you, Captain Rebka," he said at last. "And yes, I admit that so far you have been given little or nothing to do. That does not change my opinion. I possess a deep inner conviction that at some point you will prove to be essential to the success—even the survival—of this group."

"Doing what? How can I be needed for survival, when you brought along your own specialist survival team to ensure that?"

Hans Rebka's tone was sarcastic. He had met the "survival specialists" just before the ship made the final Bose transition to the great, frigid stellar system within which the *Pride of Orion* now floated. He had been appalled—appalled at their youth, at their lack of experience in dangerous situations, and most of all by their utter self-confidence. If you wanted to get yourself killed, there was no better way than to think you knew all the tricks. It took experience to make you realize that the universe could always pull another one out of the bag and throw it at you.

The irony of his words was lost on Julian Graves. The councilor frowned, pondered, and replied, "It is difficult for a logical mind to accept the idea that a redundancy of talents for survival might be a bad thing. In any case, my belief does not stem from logic alone. It draws also from personal experience. You saved my life in the past, not once but at least three times. I rely upon you to do it again."

So far as Graves was concerned, that ended the conversation. It was left to Hans Rebka to grit his teeth and sit on the edge of his seat when the *Pride of Orion*, signal beacon turned on and a dozen transmission devices blaring to betray its presence, made its Bose transition to a new stellar system which Hans had every reason to suspect might be dangerous.

That upon their arrival it seemed more dead than dangerous was nothing for which Hans or anyone else on board could take credit. He was wary as the survival team children—his term for them—oohed and aahed over observations of the cold, dark star and its frozen retinue of planets. The return of the signal beacon from the *Have-It-All* was less reassuring to him than to anyone else on board. He knew, even if they did not, that Louis Nenda had silenced the beacon and all other emanations from his ship until the crude but shrewd Karelian human felt there was no immediate danger. The *Pride of Orion* must have helped, a sacrificial goat that had bleated its beacon message non-stop from the moment of its arrival in the new stellar system.

Now Nenda was here, on board the *Pride of Orion*, and Hans didn't think for a moment that he had come to help. Nenda was here to improve his own chances of survival—and who could blame him?

Hans nodded a wary greeting as Nenda arrived. He placed himself at a point in the meeting room where the two men could keep an eye on each other. Behind Nenda, towering over everyone, was the Cecropian, Atvar H'sial. The twin yellow horns on the eyeless white head moved constantly from side to side. Hans knew that those horns received return signals from high-frequency sonic pulses emitted by the pleated resonator on Atvar H'sial's chin. They provided the Cecropian with vision through echolocation. What else they received, and whether or not human speech could be collected and interpreted, was anyone's guess. Atvar H'sial's slave and interpreter, the Lo'tfian J'merlia, was not present. He must have remained behind on Nenda's ship. How much could Nenda, with his pheromonal augment, tell the Cecropian of what was going on?

Louis Nenda was not about to say. He remained as silent as his Cecropian partner while Julian Graves introduced to them the five members of the survival specialist team.

"Ben Blesh, Torran Veck, Lara Quistner, and Teri Dahl." Graves waved a hand at the five, two men and three women sitting in a tight group. "And Sinara Bellstock, whom you have already met."

Nenda nodded. From his inscrutable smile, Rebka decided that the man was as underwhelmed as Rebka himself by the youthful "survival specialists." Nenda was squat and grubby and uncouth, but as the man at your back in a crisis you'd choose him over all five.

"We are here," Graves went on, "but clearly we are not where any of us expected to be. This is not the Marglotta system. Therefore we must decide what to do next. To aid in that, we should pool any new knowledge. Mr. Nenda, perhaps you would begin by telling us what you and your associates have learned. I assume that you will be happy to speak for all."

Nenda's smile vanished. Starting the ball rolling was obviously not his first choice, and from the way that the Cecropian behind him reared up and back, the information had been passed by Nenda to her and was not welcomed.

"Mr. Nenda?"

"Right." Nenda paused for a moment—for more communication, Rebka suspected, with Atvar H'sial. "One dark star, small enough and dense enough to be a white dwarf, but drained of all its internal energy by some process we do not understand. Forty-seven planets, just as cold. Nothing living or able to live on them, at least in any form known to us. And one other oddity. The biggest of the planets in the region where you might expect to find life in a normal system is a monster, bigger than the star it's goin' around, but it doesn't have the strong gravitational field to go with it. We detected all kinds of smaller bodies in nearby orbits, where the region ought to have been swept clean. The big planet is also the coldest of the lot, impossibly cold. We are tryin' to build up a detailed picture of the surface, but from this distance that will be a long job. As for explanations, we don't have any. This is all on a scale to suggest the work of the Builders, but we don't believe the Builders have been active in this system."

Almost from Nenda's first sentence, Hans Rebka noticed Darya Lang stirring in her seat. At first she was nodding agreement, but at Nenda's final words and his mention of the Builders, she burst out, "No! Wrong, wrong, *wrong*."

While Louis Nenda stared at her, apparently more in surprise than annoyance, she went on, "Oh, I don't mean most of what you said—I came to many of the same conclusions. This system isn't our final destination, it's a halfway-station used by a lying Polypheme, probably one Bose jump from where we really want to go. But Louis, when you say the Builders haven't been at work here, you are wrong."

Nenda opened his mouth, said, "Well—" and paused. Atvar H'sial had reached out to place one black paw on his shoulder, and was leaning over him so closely that the Cecropian's pleated pouch touched the top of his dark hair.

After a few seconds Nenda nodded. "Yeah, yeah, yeah." He turned back to Darya Lang. "Atvar H'sial says she knows the *Lang Universal Artifact Catalog*—all editions—forward, backward and sideways. And in none of those, dealing with more than twelve hundred artifacts in the Orion Arm, do you anywhere suggest that the Builders destroyed a whole stellar system. Why are you changing your tune now? Is it just because we're in the Sag Arm?"

"No. I'd say the same if we were back in our local arm. Louis, you had all the evidence staring you in the face, you just ignored it. The planet you mentioned is amazingly cold. In fact, according to the physics that we know, it is as you said impossibly cold. Colder than the microwave background radiation of the universe, which means there must be some mechanism at work on that planet to *get rid* of incident radiation falling onto it all the time from space. Otherwise it must increase in temperature to match its surroundings. Mentally, I tagged the place as *Iceworld* as soon as I made the first measurements. It's huge, just as you say, but it has hardly any gravitational field. You realized that, because it hadn't swept a region clear around its orbit. But you didn't take the next step. If you had measured the orbital periods of Iceworld's satellites—it has seven of them, all small—you could have calculated the planet's mass. I did that. The result is tiny, something you would expect from something one hundredth the diameter. What does that tell you?"

Nenda shook his head. He seemed to be waiting for Atvar H'sial to provide an answer, but a survival team member—one of the women, Lara Quistner—got in first. "Big diameter, small mass. Are you suggesting that your Iceworld is *hollow*?"

"I am. And that has other implications, ones that you don't know because you weren't with us on our earlier explorations. First, a hollow object that size can't be created by any natural processes that we understand. Second, we were led once before to a system and a giant planet, Gargantua, that seemed totally dead. But one of its moons, Glister, was hollow, and the evidence of Builder activity was *inside* it—including a transport vortex that could take you to other places. I bet that's happening here. If we want to reach our true destination, we have to go down to the big planet and explore below the surface."

Julian Graves said gently, "Professor Lang, even if you are right you didn't answer Atvar H'sial's question. Did the Builders destroy this whole stellar system, in order to make a single artifact on Iceworld?"

"I don't know. But Atvar H'sial is correct, in no other case have we found evidence that the Builders did such a thing."

"Not the Builders, Professor Lang. Then who?"

"*Others*. Destroyers, Voiders, Dead-Zoners, call them what you like. Whoever or whatever it is that the Marglotta believe is at work destroying the Sag Arm. Councilor, I have spent my life studying the Builders and their actions. What we find here does not match my instincts."

"But you may be wrong."

"Of course I may be wrong. It's only a *theory*. So let me go to the planet—and find out if I'm right! Something inside Iceworld should lead to our real destination, Marglot."

It was not Hans Rebka's job to tell Darya to stay away from inexplicable and probably dangerous worlds. He would have interrupted anyway, but Julian Graves saved him the trouble.

The councilor shaded his misty blue eyes with his hand and said, "Destroyers, Voiders, Zoners. Professor Lang, you desire to resolve a mystery by the somewhat risky procedure of introducing a greater one. Rather than one kind of super-being, the Builders, you now propose that we consider two. The avoidance of unnecessary complications has been a known working principle since the dawn of human history. Also, as you point out, what you have is no more than a theory. Others may have different ideas and suggestions."

As though on cue, E.C. Tally jumped in. "May I speak?"

The embodied computer was sitting well away from the others. A gleaming fiber-optic cable connected the socket on his chest with the computer system of the *Pride of Orion*.

Julian Graves glared at him. Tally was apparently not on the list of candidates likely to offer useful theories. "Is this relevant?"

"It is indeed most relevant. When we made the final Bose transition, I happened to be in the observation chamber with Professor Lang. However, after the transition she appeared uninterested in further conversation with me."

Hans Rebka saw Darya looking in his direction, and raised an eyebrow. *You threw him out?*

She smiled and shrugged, as E.C. Tally went on, "I then decided that I could perhaps employ my own extensive data bases to good effect. I made observations of my own. First I examined not the dark star system to which we have recently come, but our general stellar environment. I found an unexpected asymmetry in incident radiation. More starlight is coming to us from one region of the celestial globe than from its antipodes. It did not take long to discover why. The distance of the nearest visible stars varies from less than a lightyear in one direction, to more than twenty lightyears in the opposite direction. I asked myself, why should there be such a difference? But I found no obvious explanation. I therefore set out to make more observations, looking not at our local environment, but back toward the Orion Arm. Even across the distance of the Gulf, it is possible to identify certain of the supergiant marker stars employed in celestial navigation within the Orion Arm. And from their apparent locations, I could by triangulation compute an accurate position for us in the Sag Arm."

The embodied computer paused. E.C. Tally sensed that for the first time ever, others might be hanging on his words. "Before we started on this journey," the computer went on at last, "I had made my own estimates of the place in the Sag Arm where the Marglot system might be located. I was, unfortunately, wrong."

Graves said, "You trusted the Chism Polypheme's navigation files?"

"Regrettably, I did. However, my earlier error is not the point I wish to make. I believe from my observations and calculations that I know where we are *now*. If I might employ the displays?"

"You're hooked in? Then go ahead."

The lights dimmed. E.C. Tally said into the darkness, "This is a presentation of the Sag Arm as we observed it before we left Upside Miranda Port. Do you see the spherical region which, as Councilor Graves remarked at the time, is utterly lacking in light and life? Good. Now I am going to shift the origin of coordinates of the display, to one centered on a particular position at the extreme edge of that dark region."

The display seemed to zoom through space at an impossible speed, crossing the Gulf in seconds and plunging into the depths of the Sag Arm. When it slowed, a new and strange starscape revealed itself.

"You will probably not recognize this," Tally went on.

"Nor might you expect to, since you could presume that no one from our spiral arm has ever been at such a location in the Sag Arm. This is, in fact, merely a portion of the Sag Arm as seen from the place that I computed by triangulation as our location. You would, however, be wrong in your assumption. I will now display the sky as it *actually appears* to sensors on the *Pride of Orion* at this very moment."

The image flickered. Tally continued, "If you fail to observe any difference, that is because there is no difference. We are where my computations suggested that we would be: at the very edge of the zone of darkness."

The lights in the chamber brightened. E.C. Tally, who had been standing, sat down to a baffled silence. It was finally broken by Julian Graves.

"Very good. So we know where we are. I do not see how that is of much help to our present situation."

"May I speak?"

"I rather wish you would."

"We are at the extreme edge of the region where the stars have ceased to shine. The Marglotta, who came to us and sought our assistance, may be presumed to be just beyond that edge since their home system is currently in danger. And since we were *directed* here, it is logical to assume that the Marglotta home world is at no great distance from us. I therefore propose that we travel to and explore the nearest stellar system. It will be, with high probability, the Marglot system."

Hans Rebka had listened carefully to every word. He decided that he understood the problem: although E.C. Tally was totally logical, the embodied robot was also totally crazy. Unless you got lucky, and found either another Bose node or a Builder transport vortex, a subluminal trip to the nearest stellar system was a multi-year proposition.

But maybe you didn't have to be crazy—just have an indefinitely long life-span, like an embodied computer.

Julian Graves said, "You leave one important point unspecified. Who would undertake such a journey?"

"Why, I would. Who else?"

"Who else, indeed? I need time to consider your

suggestion, and also Professor Lang's. Does anyone have other ideas to offer?"

Graves was already on his feet, ready to end the meeting, when Louis Nenda coughed and said, "Yeah. Well, maybe. Though the last thing I offered got shot to hell. Thing is, At and me figure the rest of you are missing a big piece of all this. What about the Polypheme?"

"Mr. Nenda, you are the one who pointed out that Chism Polyphemes are the most crooked, unreliable, deceitful species in the galaxy."

"Absolutely. Did I mention they're also totally self-serving? If I didn't, I should have. But you had a Polypheme piloting the ship with the Marglotta on board. More than that, by the time it reached Miranda it was a *dead* Polypheme, something nobody I know ever saw or heard of. Polyphemes may not live forever, but they do their best to. So At an' me, we asked ourselves, why would a Polypheme get mixed up in tryin' to help the Marglotta? We can come up with only one answer: the Polyphemes are involved because they're scared light green. An' why? 'Cause their home world is next on the list, or maybe next but one. Otherwise, they wouldn't give a damn what happened to the Marglot system. So if anyone can tell us what's goin' on, the Polyphemes can."

"Mr. Nenda, what you say may well be true. There is, however, a fatal flaw in your argument: we have no idea where the Polypheme home world might be, and we know they will do everything they can to conceal that knowledge from us."

"The hell with their home world. We don't need it. Polyphemes gossip and gabble like nobody's business. You can bet your ass and hat that if the whole species is in trouble, any Polypheme you run into is likely to know about it. I don't want *all* the Chism Polyphemes. I just want one, and a chance to pull information out of it."

"How would you do that?"

"Don't you worry your head. I got my methods."

"I would be concerned by that statement, but for one thing: you have no Polypheme."

"Not yet. But I think I know a way to snag me one. Only

thing is, it's going to take a few more hours of work before we know what we got."

"Indeed? Then a few more hours is what you will have. Not, I should add, for your benefit but for my own." Julian Graves surveyed the group. "I am sure it is hardly necessary to point out that we have gone from a paucity of ideas as to where we are or what we should do next, to a superabundance of theories. It is perhaps also unnecessary to remark that when three suggestions appear equally plausible, there is a better than fifty-fifty chance that any given one of them is wrong. I will inform you tomorrow of the result of my deliberations."

Julian Graves stood up and left the chamber. It was obvious that he was in no mood for further discussion, but Hans Rebka hurried out after him.

"Councilor, I know you have not yet made a decision but I want to point something out to you. It would be absolutely criminal to permit Darya Lang to head down to the surface of Iceworld unless someone who knows what he is doing goes with her."

"It certainly would, Captain Rebka." Graves turned in the doorway. "Your concerns are noted. They are, however, premature. I request that you, like everyone else, wait until tomorrow before you jump to conclusions. Please do not pursue me further."

A wave of his arm, and the door closed.

Hans Rebka was left alone in the corridor with another mystery to ponder: How could somebody with so little idea of danger be placed in charge of an expedition so far beyond the boundaries of known space?

CHAPTER NINE
The parting of the ways.

Louis Nenda was out of the meeting chamber almost as quickly as Hans Rebka. He, however, had no thought of pursuing Julian Graves. His interest was in returning to the *Have-It-All* as fast as possible.

He left Atvar H'sial to make her way back at her own speed, and as soon as he was in the corridor leading to the ship's computer center, he was calling, "Hey, how are you doing?"

His question was intended for Kallik and J'merlia. The doorway, however, was blocked by the massive body of Archimedes. Rebka was presented with a view of the Zardalu's midnight-blue hind end.

He kicked at one of the thick tentacles and tried to squeeze past. "Kallik? J'merlia? What the hell's going on here? I didn't tell you to let Archie push his way in."

"With respect, Master Nenda, Archimedes did not enter unsanctioned." J'merlia's voice came from beyond the mass of leathery flesh. "Kallik and I invited his presence."

"Why'd you do a thing like that?" Louis pushed, and the Zardalu wriggled a little to one side. "Archie doesn't know a damn thing about Bose nodes."

"That is true." J'merlia, in the absence of his dominatrix

Atvar H'sial, tended to speak too much rather than too little. "Archimedes knows nothing of such things, nor does he need to. Kallik and I completed that phase of the analysis more than an hour ago. As you instructed, we began with the data bank from the ship of the dead Polypheme. It contained many thousands of Bose point references within the Sag Arm, many of which doubtless follow the Polypheme custom of providing spurious data to confuse other would-be users. We sought to eliminate those from consideration by correlating them with star positions. We argued that although Bose transition points in empty space certainly exist—such points led us across the Gulf—the ones in a navigation catalog are likely to lie at reasonable sub-lightspeed travel distance from habitable worlds. This reduced the number of nodes to be considered, to nine hundred and twenty-seven. This, however, is still far too many to be of practical value—"

"Hold on. I didn't ask for a lecture. I asked what this lump of fat and gristle is doing in here."

"With respect, Master Nenda." Kallik pushed around the other side of the Zardalu. "The presence of Archimedes was not relevant to the Bose node analysis. He was, however, essential to the task that evolved from it. My eyesight is excellent, and so is that of J'merlia. But neither can compare with that." The Hymenopt pointed to Archimedes's head. The eye-pupils of the Zardalu were each the size of Louis's fist. "The spatial resolution that Archimedes can achieve is so good that we have trouble believing the results."

"I still don't get it. What did you have Archie looking *at*, that anybody cares about?"

The Zardalu must have understood the sense of the question, if not the full meaning. Archimedes produced an urgent series of clicks and held out toward Louis a big sheet of hardboard.

"Our apologies if we have exceeded your orders." The little Hymenopt bowed her round black head. "If I may continue with what J'merlia was saying, we reduced the number of stars with associated Bose nodes to nine hundred and twenty-seven. However, you had suggested as you left that you were most interested in Bose nodes close to neutron stars. You did not say why, but I made an inference as to your intentions. A Chism Polypheme, as we learned from our earlier experiences with them, enjoys hard radiation. Hence, a natural question: Do any neutron stars close to Bose nodes possess planets? Unfortunately, this was not a question that either J'merlia and I could answer using our instruments and our observations. Archimedes, however, was able to do so. He has been transcribing his results."

"Is that what you've been trying to show off? Gimme a look at that." Louis grabbed the sheet of hardboard, slightly slippery to the touch from the Zardalu's waxy skin. "Archie, next time I tell you you're a useless sack of gas and blubber you can talk right back to me. I brought you along thinkin' we'd need your strength. It never occurred to me you might have other uses."

A veil of pheromones drifted from beyond the long body of the Zardalu. "Louis, what game is being played here? Why is this *object* blocking my way?"

"It's all right, At. Give Archie's rear end a poke and he'll move. I think we're going to see action—at last! We get the go-ahead from Graves tomorrow. Then, we make a jump and we're out of here."

"You presented your plan to me yesterday as a certainty." Atvar H'sial was again sitting behind Louis Nenda in the main chamber of the *Pride of Orion*. "Do you still adhere to that view?"

"Hell, I don't know." Louis stared around the room, about half of which seemed to be taken up by the great body of Archimedes. "Julian Graves is crazy, so you never can tell what he's goin' to decide. But I don't like this setup at all."

"Too many are present?"

"You got it. *All* are present, except Graves himself. Me, you, Archie, Kallik, J'merlia, Rebka, E.C. Tally. Why involve everybody? Why even hold a meeting? What we need from him is a simple yes or no."

"And if Graves says no?"

"We reevaluate. We got a ship, we have a set of Bose nodes and stars and planets to go with 'em. We could take off and explore the Sag Arm."

"What of our return to the Orion Arm?"

"Why would we go back? We're no better off there than we are here—maybe safer here. Nobody's chasing our tail in the Sag Arm."

"Louis, for you that may be an option. For me it is not. Ultimately I must return to the Cecropia Federation and mate. If I do not, I die."

"The end of your travels?"

"By no means. After mating is complete I will again be free to wander as I choose."

"An' we'll be back to work. None of my business, but I was told that Cecropians mate for life."

"It would perhaps be more accurate to say that Cecropians mate for death." Atvar H'sial's forelimbs made a reflexive motion, pulling something toward her and crushing it hard against her chest. "Louis, the process is a rapid one, quickly accomplished. I suggest that you do not require details."

"Damn right I don't."

Although J'merlia was present, the silent interaction was wholly pheromonal and did not involve the Lo'tfian interpreter. J'merlia was following what was said, but the idea that he might interrupt a conversation with his dominatrix, or pass any of what he heard to a third party, was to a Lo'tfian literally unthinkable.

Half a dozen other conversations, by no means silent, had been going on around the chamber. They ended with the sudden arrival of Julian Graves.

The councilor glanced around. "I see that everyone is present. Good. I will not keep you long. Here is my decision. We have pursued the path to the Sag Arm as far as the end point of this dead stellar system. The path leads no farther. It would be logical to say, no more, and use the Bose network to return to the Orion Arm by the same route that brought us. The node sits there, it is available and waiting. You might argue for that course of action, since any other option seems to expose all of us to danger.

"Against that, we must set the fate of a whole species, the Marglotta. And, still more important, in the longer term we must consider a possible threat to everything in our own

Orion Arm. My conclusion is that the larger danger outweighs any personal one."

Louis Nenda muttered, "Get on with it!" But he spoke silently and pheromonally.

Graves went on, "That conclusion does not dictate a best course of action, which I come to now. Three alternatives were suggested. Rather than taking the risk of choosing the wrong one, we will pursue all three. The *Pride of Orion* will be divided. Professor Lang, you will take one of the sub-ships to Iceworld and explore that planet. To assist you in that effort and alert you to possible dangers, survival team specialists Ben Blesh and Lara Quistner will accompany you. Captain Hans Rebka will serve as your pilot. Does any one of you have questions?"

"Yes." Hans Rebka spoke up. "You can't have four different people in charge. Who makes the decisions?"

"Until your ship touches down on the planet, you do. After that, you will follow the instructions of survival team member Ben Blesh. Professor Lang will of course be in charge of scientific investigations."

Louis normally had little sympathy for Hans Rebka, but he knew what he would do if somebody told him to take orders from some freshly weaned child. He saw Rebka turn red. However, the other man said nothing more.

"E.C. Tally," Graves continued, "you proposed to take another of the sub-ships and travel toward the edge of the dark zone within which we are presently located. That effort is approved. You will seek the Marglot system, but you will of course explore anything on the way that you find interesting."

"Councilor, may I speak?"

"What is it now?"

"I find everything interesting."

"Dear me, I suppose you do. Very well. Let me be more specific. You are to explore only those matters which seem relevant to the goal of this expedition. I hope that such things will be found at no great distance. However, there is a possibility that your journey will extend indefinitely. You will therefore travel alone."

"Naturally. When may I depart?"

"I will defer that decision. I may need your help." Graves turned to face Louis Nenda and Atvar H'sial. "This brings us to our third course of action. You wish to seek a Chism Polypheme. Very well. You will be free to do so, in your own ship. *However.*" Misty blue eyes stared into Louis's. "Based on previous experience, it would be less than honest of me to say that I trust you to follow the agenda of the expedition rather than one that represents your own private interests. Therefore, I insist that a survival team member go with you, and use your equipment to report back to me regularly as to your movements and actions. You are, I know, already acquainted with Sinara Bellstock."

"Now just a minute." Louis knew exactly why Hans Rebka's face had turned red. He stood up. "The *Have-It-All* belongs to me, not you and not the Ethical Council. I won't have some snotty-nosed infant tellin' me when and how I use my own communications system."

"Louis, desist." Atvar H'sial placed a hairy paw on his shoulder. *"Once we are on the way, we can deal with the problem of Sinara Bellstock in our own fashion. She need not trouble us for long."*

"Mr. Nenda, I am in command of this expedition. Are you saying that you refuse to follow my direction?"

"No, no, nothin' like that." Louis sat down again. "You know how it is, we get used to runnin' our own ship in our own way. I overreacted. I'll be happy to have Sinara Bellstock come with us, an' send you messages from the *Have-It-All* any time she feels like it."

"That is much better." Graves actually smiled at Louis, before he turned again to face the whole group. "Which brings me to my own role, and the role of our other survival team members, Torran Veck and Teri Dahl. One thing that we must keep in mind is that, no matter how far in space we are separated, we remain a team unified in our objectives. We need both a nexus of communications, and a reserve capacity available to act in an emergency in support of any team component. I, Torran Veck, and Teri Dahl will serve in that capacity."

"And Heaven help any poor bugger who has to rely on that lot to get them out of trouble."

Louis's remark went only to Atvar H'sial, and he had time for no more. Julian Graves, apparently well pleased with himself, was saying, "Now, I urge you to go ahead and make all necessary preparations for your assignment." At the same time, Darya Lang and Sinara Bellstock were both on their feet and heading in his direction.

Darya pushed in front of the younger woman. "Louis, I want to wish you good luck and success. I'm sure we'll be seeing each other again before long." As she turned away, she added, "Last time you asked me, I refused to have dinner with you. Next time we meet, please ask me again."

She gave him an enigmatic smile and slipped away. Before Louis had time to react, Sinara Bellstock was standing in front of him and throwing a mock salute. "Captain Nenda, survival team specialist Sinara Bellstock reporting for duty and at your service. I will be aboard the *Have-It-All* in less than half an hour. Whatever you want me to do, just let me know."

She turned and headed across the chamber, leaving Louis with his mouth open and Atvar H'sial behind him, saying, *"Louis Nenda, it is beyond logic why I continue a relationship with you as a business partner. The mating rituals of humans never cease to shock and amaze me. In ten thousand years of supposed civilization, they have made no progress whatsoever. Have you no shame? In the course of a lifetime, not only do you permit multiple mates, but you seek to enjoy more than one mate at the same time. Come, J'merlia."*

The Cecropian's pheromones seethed with disapproval, as she in turn headed away and out of the chamber.

As the room emptied, Louis was left with Kallik and Archimedes and his own thoughts.

It makes no sense, no sense at all. The only woman I've had sex with since I met Atvar H'sial has been Glenna Omar, and At totally approves of her and thinks she's wonderful. But women I've never even considered having sex with, like Darya Lang and Sinara Bellstock, make At crazy. She's right, it is beyond logic why we keep going as business partners.

Below those thoughts, running at a far deeper level than the conscious, was an admission that Louis was not willing to make: Atvar H'sial had the power to read in detail the pheromonal products from Darya Lang, Sinara Bellstock, and Louis himself. And the other reluctant admission: pheromones don't lie.

CHAPTER TEN
A useless diversion?

Hans Rebka deliberately steered clear of Darya Lang during the day before departure. If she thought that he was angry because he would not be in charge of the expedition on Iceworld, that couldn't be helped. Two years ago she and Hans had been so close that she could sweet talk him into revealing almost anything. In some ways he'd like to think that was still true, but he didn't want her knowing his current intentions. He wasn't sure he understood them himself.

To avoid Darya, he sought out and spent as much time as possible with the two survival team members assigned to his group. Ben Blesh and Lara Quistner might not know the value of understanding your team members *before* you got into trouble, but Hans had learned it in a score of dangerous situations.

At Hans's suggestion, the three of them took a ride outside the *Pride of Orion* in one of the ship's pinnaces. There he watched with amazement as the main vessel reconfigured itself to permit two smaller vessels to be spun off from the main body. The process resembled the reproduction of some great animal, as a new ship grew out of and finally separated from the mass of the old. It occurred to Rebka that

89

the analogy might be more than that. Could it be that the *Pride of Orion* was a mixture of biological and inorganic components? If so, the technology of Fourth Alliance worlds had advanced far beyond what that group was willing to admit to the poorer clades. It also offered the promise of flexible structure for the sub-ship they would be using.

The casual attitude of Ben Blesh and Lara Quistner convinced Hans that what they were seeing was nothing new to them. They treated Rebka himself as though he were the odd and interesting phenomenon.

"Didn't you have medical treatments and curative drugs available when you were a child?" Lara Quistner asked. "If we'd had anything as bad as your condition, we would have been treated before we were old enough to remember."

Until he encountered the fortunate inhabitants of the rich planets of the spiral arm, Hans Rebka had not realized that he had a *condition.* A large head and a small frame, on his birth world of Teufel where a shortage of food and essential trace elements was taken for granted, had been the rule rather than the exception. He considered explaining this to Lara Quistner and Ben Blesh, then decided it would be a waste of time. He could quote what residents of the Phemus Circle said about his home world—"What sins must a man commit, in how many past lives, to be born on Teufel?"— but he suspected that the other two would still have no idea what he was talking about.

He contented himself with a shrug, and ended the conversation with, "Where I grew up, I was considered normal— and pretty lucky."

The new ship was full-sized now, and taking final shape before his eyes. Hans inspected it from bow to stern. Fully equipped for interstellar or interplanetary travel it might be, but no one would call it large. Four people would be a tight fit—even if they all got on with each other, which Hans knew would not be the case once they were on the way.

It was time for a change, to a subject that might reveal more of his companions' personalities. He said, "We're going to be flying in a vessel that never flew before. We ought to have some kind of naming ceremony. Any thoughts as to what we should call it?"

Lara Quistner glanced at her companion but said nothing. Fair enough. Ben was the senior member. Regardless of her individual competence, she was someone who would respect authority and a chain of command.

After a few moments, Ben Blesh said, "I agree that the ship should have a name. But don't you think that Professor Lang ought to have a voice in what we call it? I certainly do."

Blesh was pointing out, fairly directly, that he would not go along with any suggestion made by Hans. Maybe he was looking for an argument, and given what Hans had in mind once they were on the way, argument with Ben Blesh was almost certain. Until that time, however, it was best to avoid confrontation.

Hans said mildly, "Oh, I wasn't by any means trying to exclude Professor Lang. We certainly wouldn't decide anything until she gave her opinion. I was just asking your preliminary thoughts."

"In that case, what about *Savior* as a good name?"

Ben Blesh's suggestion came without any pause for thought, and the proposed name told Hans a lot about the speaker. Blesh must have a greatly inflated idea of what a small exploration team to Iceworld might accomplish. They were seeking *facts*, and only facts. Savior? Saving anything more than themselves and whatever they might discover was too grandiose an ambition. If Lara Quistner deferred to Blesh on the basis of his seniority, and if he was consistently unrealistic, difficulties for the group were guaranteed. Julian Graves had not helped. He had put Hans in a position where after they reached Iceworld he could offer advice until he ran out of breath, but there seemed little chance that Blesh would take any notice.

Well, it would not be the first time that Hans had been forced to lead from behind. He said, "*Savior?* Yes, that has a lot to recommend it. We'll see what Darya Lang thinks."

He had a good idea of her response, even if they did not. She would remain neutral. Unless it involved the Builders, Darya went along with most things. Unfortunately, that might not include what Hans had in mind as soon as they were on their way.

He stared at the new ship, fully formed and gleaming. He wanted to make sure it contained a few extra features. Apart from that, he would smile and lie low. There would be plenty of time for feuding after they left. And plenty of reason to expect that feuding would occur.

"Councilor Graves was quite specific. Call him if you wish, and confirm his intentions. But I know he said that until this ship touches down on Iceworld, I make the decisions."

"And I know he never had anything like this in mind." Ben Blesh was standing behind Hans, who sat at the ship's controls.

Rebka did not look around. He could hear the anger in the other man's voice. "Ben, I'm not sure that I understand your objection. We will still arrive at Iceworld in a few days. I'm simply trying to add to the store of information that we will have when we get there."

"By a pointless diversion to examine a dead planet? I don't see how that tells us a thing. If I'm wrong, explain to me what I'm missing."

"I can't guarantee that you are missing anything. All I know is that the world we are heading for sits smack in the middle of the life zone for a normal main sequence star with mass equal to the one at the center of this system. There's no life on the surface of the planet at the moment, it's far too cold. My question is, was life there once? Might there even have been intelligence, before the sun dimmed and every living being was condemned to freeze to death?"

The members of the survival team were emerging as distinct personalities. Lara Quistner might be good at her job, but she was certainly not a controlling type. She would go along with what her boss, and maybe anyone else, suggested. Ben Blesh was not only interested in being that boss, he made snap judgments and didn't like anyone to disagree with him. Hans Rebka's announcement that they would visit a different planet first, made when after a full day of powered flight Iceworld was clearly no closer, had provoked loud and instant disagreement from Blesh. Darya Lang had come down on Hans Rebka's side. Her support was unexpected, but it was no more than reasonable—

Hans's actions had saved her skin often enough to earn her respect.

Behind Rebka, Ben Blesh said, "I'm not going to let this stand. I intend to find out what Julian Graves has to say. He'll put an end to the nonsense."

Hans, his attention on the planet growing in size on the display, was inclined to agree. Graves *would* put an end to it—when he erred, it was on the side of caution. Given any small chance that a visit to another planet would increase the odds of survival on Iceworld, the Ethical Council member would be all for it.

As for Ben Blesh, his disappearance to use the ship's communications equipment at the very time when a new world was coming into view was, in Hans Rebka's opinion, one more piece of evidence that he was dealing with a fool. What else could you call a man who was more interested in having his authority confirmed than in increasing his chances of living? And what did that say about the general selection of survival team members? It was a pity that Lara Quistner and the others could not have been dropped off on Teufel for a few weeks during training. One encounter with the *Remouleur*, Teufel's terrible dawn wind, would be worth a year of lectures from their "famous"—according to Graves—trainer, Arabella Lund.

The time for philosophical speculations on the training of survival teams was past. Hans concentrated on the planet ahead. It was about fourteen thousand kilometers in diameter, which together with the readings of the mass detectors suggested a world possessing a metallic core beneath rocky outer layers. The substantial magnetic field confirmed that idea. Surface gravity was about fifteen percent more than standard, a bit high but well within the tolerable range. Surface temperature was another matter. There was an atmosphere, and it contained oxygen as well as nitrogen and argon. But the spectra revealed no hint of water vapor or carbon dioxide.

Detailed maps of what lay below that frigid atmosphere would have to wait until they were in a parking orbit. However, the high albedo response to a remote laser probe, together with glints of specular reflection, suggested extensive ice cover—perhaps over the whole planet. If that implied worldwide glaciation, high-resolution radar measurements would be needed to probe its depth and learn what land or former oceans lay beneath.

Those measurements could only be done on the surface, and that in turn implied their journey to Iceworld would be delayed by at least two extra days. Before the group left the *Pride of Orion,* Hans had suspected something like this might be necessary. With a warm world you could take high-resolution images from orbit. But if a world froze over and you wanted to know what it had been like before the freeze, you had to make measurements down on the ground. Also, Hans himself needed to visit the surface, no matter what the orbital measurements showed. You could never get a gut feel for a world from orbit.

It was useless to try to explain this to the others. He stared at the frosted ball of the planet, enhanced in the ship's display to gleam faintly with reflected starlight. With luck, maybe Darya and the rest would conclude for themselves the need for a trip all the way down.

The trouble was, the *Savior*'s instruments were almost too good. They represented the best technology available to the Fourth Alliance, and from an orbital altitude of no more than two hundred kilometers the imaging sensors and radar altimeters left little to the imagination.

"Descend to the surface, to learn what?" Ben Blesh was watching on the display a revealing picture. It showed a succession of hills and valleys, all coated with a layer of blinding white. "It's obvious what happened down there. The whole globe shows peaks and rifts and flat ocean surfaces, which the synthetic aperture radar confirms. There was no worldwide glaciation—no time for that. It's clear that when the temperature dropped, all the water vapor and carbon dioxide precipitated out. You'd get one fall of water-snow and solid carbon dioxide. After that nothing would change. The air that remains still has some oxygen as well as nitrogen and argon, so things happened *fast.* There's no doubt about the sequence of events. What can we possibly gain by going down to the surface?"

He was asking a question that had occurred to Hans long ago. Before they achieved parking orbit, he had fired off a question to the *Pride of Orion. Suppose that the internal energy source of a main sequence star were somehow turned off in a short time span (weeks or months). How long would it take to cool down by normal radiative cooling? I'm looking for an order of magnitude result: are we talking years, centuries, millennia, or millions of years?*

The first reply from Julian Graves was disappointing. *I have consulted E.C. Tally, who is making his own calculations supplemented by the ship's astrophysics library. Because the answer to your question depends on several other unknowns, in particular the star's stage of progression along the main sequence, and the amount of gravitational potential energy contributed by the star's own shrinkage during cooling, Tally is reluctant to provide a firm answer. He is, however, willing to provide a range of possibilities.*

Hans could imagine. The embodied computer would hum and mutter and hedge his bets until you were ready to scream. Luckily it was Julian Graves who had to sit and listen, rather than Hans himself. Did that mean E.C. Tally was still aboard the *Pride of Orion*? He should have been on his way days ago.

Graves's second answer was a bit better. *At an absolute minimum, with limiting values of all variables, E.C. Tally indicates that radiative cooling would require twenty thousand years. A more likely value, including the gravitational energy provided by stellar shrinkage, would be between eight and eighteen million years. Any shorter value than twenty thousand years would prove that some external agent was employed to expedite cooling. One observational indicator is the ice fracture patterns, if any, on the planet's surface. They will tell you if the cooling was rapid or slow. Here are the characteristic appearances associated with particular rates of cooling.*

Hans examined the images sent from E.C. Tally, and then those of the surface of the world that they were approaching. Ben Blesh's comment was correct. There were visible cracks and fissures, but all were coated with a surface of white. The fusion process in the central star had not simply ceased, to be followed by a slow decline in stellar temperature. The sun had *gone out*, and its surface had cooled from around seven thousand degrees to a few hundred degrees in a very short period—a few decades, or even a few hours.

What would that mean to any unfortunate creatures living on worlds circling the star? One final, rapid sunset, followed by endless night. The land animals would die off first, as rock and soil and sand lost heat in less than a day to the cold of space. Life would linger longest in the oceans, heat sinks protected by their own thermal inertia and by thickening shields of ice. It was not impossible that some living organisms would survive there even now, drawing chemical energy from hydrothermal vents in the deep ocean floor. But the experience of every known world said that intelligence had no chance of evolving in such locations.

"Well? Did you hear me? What can we possibly gain by going all the way down to the surface?"

Ben Blesh's repeated question brought Hans out of his reverie. He should be asking himself the same thing, when the instruments were able to tell them almost everything.

What was happening to him? A troubleshooter who indulged in the luxury of idle introspection was heading for *real* trouble.

"If I could tell you what we would learn, Ben, we wouldn't need to go down. I'm convinced that this world has something to tell us, but it won't speak to us while we're in orbit."

His answer sounded weak, and he knew it. He meant that the world would not speak to *him* until he set foot on the surface. There was a question to be answered of paramount importance, but it would not form itself clearly within his brain. What he had given Blesh was the instinctive reply of a ground hog, someone who needed to feel a planet's ambience vibrating in his bones.

It might be, of course, that instinct was wrong.

Until the ship touches down on Iceworld, I make the decisions.

Hans clung to that thought as the shuttle plunged into

the outer edges of the atmosphere. He couldn't wait for the high-acceleration phase of descent, when for a few blessed minutes the others would be too weighed down in their seats to complain.

It had been a tough half day, with even Darya turned against him. "Hans, you haven't given us any real idea what you hope to learn. Why bother with this?"

She was saying exactly what Ben Blesh had said. Everyone had asked the same question in a dozen different ways. "Because I'm right," wouldn't do for an answer. The entry from orbit came as a positive relief.

Air was beginning to whistle and scream past the ship, while the gee forces within rose steadily. Hans had at his fingertips ample drive power to make their entry easier. One touch, and the autopilot would take over. They would ride easy and be feathered in to a gentle landing.

He decided to do it the hard way. It was time to see if the "survival team" specialists were as tough and well prepared as they imagined.

Apparently they were.

Hans was rustier than he had realized. There was never a moment of danger since the autopilot would take over in an emergency, but the landing was nothing to boast about. He had picked the final site with great care after inspection of hundreds of images, without discussing it with the others. Now he was within visual range, coming down too fast and overshooting. He corrected, but at a price. During the final two thousand meters the deceleration was enough to weld Hans to his seat.

As the ship whomped down onto the icy surface, he felt his innards drive down into the bowl of his pelvis. Darya, sitting next to him, gasped in surprise or pain. It should have taken a minute or two before anyone was ready to move but while the ship was still skidding forward across the ice, Lara Quistner and Ben Blesh released their harnesses and stood up.

Blesh said, quite casually, "Hull integrity maintained. Check monitors and confirm exit station."

"Check." Lara Quistner was already by the main hatch

and staring outside. "Clean landing and no external obstacles. All clear for exit."

Not a word from either of them about a botched landing, or why a manual landing had been performed. Hans moved his head from side to side—his cervical vertebrae would never be the same again—and struggled out of his harness. Next to him, Darya said feebly, "Check monitors? To see what? Before we left orbit you told us you were sure that the surface of this world was too cold for anything to survive."

"I did, and it is."

Even so, Blesh and Quistner were right. On a new planet you took *nothing* for granted. Darya was sprawled in her chair, breathing harshly. He made the effort and rose to his feet. He felt awkward and lumbering. Higher gravity, or poor physical condition? Maybe three weeks chained to an iron chair produced permanent effects. Whatever the reason, the heavy thermal suit needed to venture out onto the surface of this world would make him feel worse. The two survival specialists were slipping into theirs with an ease and efficiency that Hans would never match.

"No exit for anyone until all the ship's sensors report in." His voice sounded hoarse and strained.

"Of course not." Ben's perky tone, rather than his words, added *what do you think we are?* "There's plenty of other things to do before we're ready to go outside. Lara?"

Fully suited, she moved again to the hatch and stared out. "I'm turning on external lights so we can add visuals to the sensor reports. When we go outside we can confirm the surface composition using chemical and physical tests."

"That's good, but it's not just our immediate surroundings that I'm interested in." Hans was still climbing into his own thermal suit, and making hard work of it. "We'll be heading for a place about four kilometers away, directly ahead of the ship. Does the surface seem as smooth as it did from orbit?"

"Smooth, and firm enough to support our weight." Lara Quistner was manipulating an external probe. "We can walk there if we want to."

"Quite feasible, from the look of it." Ben Blesh was

crouched at a bank of instruments duplicating those at the pilot's console. "It's level for a couple of kilometers, until it rises into some kind of low hills. It's too cold for sleds, so if we don't walk we'll need a vehicle with wheels. The ship is provided with at least two, for all-purpose surface work. Want me to go ahead and give the instructions to prepare one?"

"Not just yet." Hans felt an irrational irritation. Ben Blesh and Lara Quistner were fast, efficient, cautious, cooperative, and doing everything right. Wasn't that just what you hoped for from a survival team?

It was. Unfortunately, their high-quality performance had another implication: Hans and Darya were not going to be particularly useful.

But then, before that thought was complete, Hans understood why he had come to this world. His instincts were right after all. He hadn't seen anything, but he knew what they were going to find.

It was all psychological, of course, but suddenly his bones didn't ache and he felt twenty percent lighter.

"We take a vehicle," he said. "Get one ready, Ben—and make sure that it comes equipped with a power digger."

CHAPTER ELEVEN
On Deadworld.

The *Savior* was an all-purpose vehicle. Although its designers must have anticipated that its primary uses would be in space-based operations, the ship was well equipped to support surface work. Hans Rebka had a choice of two different types of wheeled vehicle. One was an open form, little more than a bare platform with seats, wheels, and a big cargo area. The other was a fully enclosed car complete with its own atmosphere, in which the riders did not need to wear suits and could eat, drink, or sleep in comfort.

Hans Rebka chose the more primitive form. Even wearing a suit, he felt more in touch with the frozen world when its air was only a fraction of a centimeter away from his skin. Had it not been for the digging equipment—a mystery in its own right—he would have preferred to walk.

If the others questioned his decision on choice of car, they did so in silence. No one spoke as they watched the digger, a hump-backed machine with the blue-black carapace of a gigantic spider, extrude multiple jointed legs and climb effortlessly onto the cargo rack at the back of the car. Rather less easily, Hans led the way to the front of the vehicle and they took their places on hard bucket seats. He engaged the engine and the car began to crawl across the frozen plain.

Above, unfamiliar star patterns twinkled slightly. There was still enough heat in the lower atmosphere to permit small-scale turbulence. Hans glanced at the air temperature sensor. It hovered at a balmy hundred and fifty degrees above absolute zero, far warmer than open space. With no heat arriving from the central star, the planet's metallic core must contain a good deal of slowly decaying radioactive materials. Some warmth continued to seep out from the interior. The air sniffers confirmed the temperature reading. All traces of radon, xenon, and chlorine had precipitated out onto the frozen surface. Oxygen and nitrogen remained, along with a greater-than-expected abundance of argon and traces of krypton. Hans assumed that was a characteristic of the Sag Arm, rather than of this particular planet.

The car, its blue-white beams providing a narrow wedge of light on the surface ahead, trundled along at a sedate five kilometers an hour. The ship had landed close to the planetary equator, and the calm heavens wheeled steadily overhead. The pattern would repeat every twenty-nine hours, with no promise ever of returning day. Although the air felt perfectly still, at some time after the cold began there had been strong winds. The carbon dioxide snow had here and there blown into banks and deep drifts. Hans avoided them and kept his eyes fixed on the edge of the zone of visibility provided by the car's lights. He could detect objects only to a distance of perhaps two hundred meters. After the three-kilometer mark he found himself impatiently trying to see beyond the narrow illuminated cone. He was filled with a combination of excitement and uneasiness. It was one thing to believe that you were right, and quite another to have proof to show to others.

At last, he saw far ahead a change in the landscape. The frozen drifts rose higher and beyond them stood a regular, sawtoothed barrier. He had been waiting for this, but the others must have been keeping their own close watch. Before Hans was sure of what he saw, Lara Quistner said "What is that?" At the same moment Darya Lang put a hand on Rebka's arm. "Hans, we should stop until we know what's ahead."

"I know what it is." Rebka kept the vehicle moving

forward at the same slow pace. "I saw hundreds of these on the high-resolution orbital images. They were all partly covered by blown snow, but they are too regular in shape to be natural."

"Regular how?"

"Nature often makes circles, but it seldom makes right angles. What we are seeing is a wall. I'd say it's close to ten meters high, and it forms almost a perfect square."

"A walled town?" Ben Blesh had been perched on an uncomfortable rear seat. He pressed forward between Hans Rebka and Darya Lang, too interested to be either critical or argumentative. "Back in the Orion arm a fortification like this would mean at least a Level Two civilization."

Darya added, "But no higher than a Level Three. Walled cities go away as soon as the means to destroy them are developed. So these people didn't have explosives and artillery."

"Also, they didn't expect attacks from the air." Rebka halted the vehicle thirty meters short of the wall. "We're talking pre-industrial here. No aircraft, so no spacecraft. An intelligent species—we'll want to confirm that by looking inside the wall—but without the technology needed to escape. These people were in the worst possible situation. They knew what was happening to them, and they had plenty of time to worry about it. But without spaceflight, and pretty advanced spaceflight at that, there was no chance at all of their survival."

The others were silent for a while. At last Ben Blesh said, "Captain Rebka, how long do you think it took?"

"I've been trying to answer that question. So far I've been unsuccessful. The *Pride of Orion* sent me a range of times, but without more information they couldn't offer anything definite. When the fusion process was turned off in these people's sun, the cooling began. I'd like to know if that cooling took place all at once, or over a period of thousands of years." Rebka started the car moving again, but this time directed its course tangentially to the wall.

Lara Quistner said softly, "Left to die slowly, in the cold and dark. It's an awful tragedy. If only some spacefaring species in the Sag Arm had known about it, these people could have been helped."

"Some spacefaring species did know. Stars can explode and stars can kill you off with a solar flare big enough to wipe out all planetary life. We've all heard of cases where that happened. But stars do not simply *go out*. Something or somebody killed these people. Whatever it was acted by design, with a total indifference to the fate of other intelligent beings. That's why we needed to come here. Julian Graves has to know about this world, and what happened to it. We don't know how these people lived, and an hour ago we were not sure of their existence. But this is a pure case of genocide, and the Ethical Council needs to know— even though there's not a damn thing they can do about it."

Hans Rebka had been studying the wall on their left as the car drove along parallel to it. He stopped where the drifted snow was less deep and formed a shallow V-shaped cut like a valley leading right up to the wall.

"A fortified town must have a way for people and goods to get in and out. It's time to use our digging equipment. I suspect that we have reached one of the entry gates."

He was starting to climb down, but Darya again put a hand on his suited arm. "Hans, do we really need to go through with this?"

"I'm afraid we do. What we find inside will probably be unpleasant, but Julian Graves will ask for every scrap of detail that we can give him. Come on. This world is one giant cemetery, and maybe we are desecrating graves. But I think whoever is buried in there would agree that what we're doing is in a good cause."

"Good, perhaps, but too late to be useful." Darya Lang did not argue anymore. They watched in silence as Ben Blesh ordered the digger to dismount from the car, and gave it the instructions needed so that it could perform its task.

Hans Rebka had visited a hundred worlds and experienced most things that the Orion Arm had to offer. Even so, the digger was like nothing that he had ever seen. Before it started into action he imagined it tunneling its way forward, perhaps extruding a variety of shovels and picks to hold in its multiple jointed limbs, then carving a way through the hard-packed frozen drift.

The machine was smarter than that—smarter it seemed than Hans, at least when it came to its own specialized skills. The digger crept forward, crouched low, and poked thin antennalike sensors deep into the drift. After what seemed like a moment of meditation, it said in a clear female voice, "The material to be cleared is ninety-nine point seven percent solid carbon dioxide, with a little water-ice and trace elements. Beyond it lies stone, baked clay, and a combination of iron and a softer fibrous material. A large working area will be needed. Organic beings, please retreat until you are no closer than sixty meters."

When Hans hesitated, Ben Blesh said, "We'd better get a move on. The digger knows what it's talking about, and it won't start until we're at a safe distance."

A large working area sounded like a bad idea to Hans. "Is it proposing to use explosives? That could destroy exactly the things we are hoping to find."

"It has orders to operate in a non-destructive mode." For once, Ben apparently didn't have all the answers. The four of them climbed back onto the car and it retreated on a path at right angles to the saw-tooth line of the wall. Then it was watch and wait for a long while. To Hans Rebka's eyes nothing at all was happening. But at last Lara Quistner said, "It's really moving. I didn't realize it could go so fast."

Hans realized that a broad tunnel was appearing in the body of the drift. The digger was creeping forward into the cleared space. Hans saw what was perhaps a slight fog in the air above the digger's broad back, but otherwise there was no sign of cleared materials. After a few more seconds he exclaimed, "It's applying heat to the solid carbon oxide. Of course. Sublimation, straight to gas with no liquid phase. Does the digger have a fusion engine inside it?"

"A substantial one." Ben Blesh was measuring the rate of progress. "Don't worry, the digger will turn the heat off as soon as it is near a wall or a door or anything else that it recognizes. After that it will be up to us. If we want the door to remain intact, we can't rely on the digger. It knows fabricated objects when it sees them, but it doesn't know what to do with them."

The tunnel was deepening, at the same time as the drift above it was vanishing. After twenty more minutes, the digger halted. It extruded its limbs and retreated. The female voice said, "We have reached a boundary. Beyond this we cannot proceed without material damage."

Hans and the others approached the end of the newly created valley. They scraped at the white surface, gently at first and then more vigorously as their lamps revealed a brown facing. Ben scraped a path in several directions, to determine the outline of the flat surface. "It's some type of door all right. But it's *tiny*. They must have been very small. Do you think we will be able to squeeze through?"

"I hope so." Hans came close and directed his light onto the right-hand edge. "No kind of hinges. It would waste a lot of time if we tried to go over the wall. I don't think anyone will object if we do a little breaking-in."

The entry went easier than expected. If this had once indeed been a fortified gate, age and extreme temperature had rendered the construction materials weak and brittle. The facing caved in at one blow from Hans Rebka's gloved fist. Within half a minute, the whole door was gone and the way inside clear. Ben Blesh pushed forward eagerly, and Rebka allowed the other man to go first. He could not imagine finding anything pleasant, and at this point he did not expect danger.

The reality was more pathetic than threatening. The tunnel through the thick wall led not back into the open air, but to a large closed chamber. Within it, huddled in some kind of sacking intended to keep in warmth, they found five small bodies. The aliens resembled no species known to Rebka, and he had seen many on many worlds. But all had been in the Orion Arm. It should be no surprise that Sag Arm inhabitants had developed along different physical patterns.

Darya Lang cut open one of the sleeping bags. She worked carefully, afraid that the tiny frozen body would crumble to dust at her touch. The creature resembled a cross between insectoid and reptilian forms. Large compound eyes, clouded in death, stared up from a narrow muzzled face. Thin lips had shrunk back to show teeth like triangular knives. Four limbs, protected at their ends by a shiny chitinous covering, wrapped across the segmented body as though making a final effort to hold in warmth and life.

"How long do think they had?" Lara Quistner asked. "Many generations, or just one or two?"

"Unless someone returns for a thorough investigation, we don't know and we never will." Hans Rebka turned away. "You have to wish that it could have been quicker. I'll take the flash of a supernova any time over long, drawn-out cold."

Darya Lang stood up. She had been making a visual recording of the corpses and their surroundings. "I think it was fairly quick. I examined the images taken from orbit, too. I didn't notice these walled towns, but everything went too quickly for glaciation to creep down from the poles."

"Quick, but not quick enough. Does anyone want to see more?"

"What about the other sites, Captain Rebka?" Ben Blesh was commanding the digger to return to its position on the cargo rack. Having objected to visiting this world, he now seemed reluctant to leave. "Might we learn something there?"

"I don't think so. I didn't see much variation in the towns. It will be the same sad story, repeated a thousand or ten thousand times. Starvation, cold, death." As Hans Rebka led the way back to the car, he added to Darya Lang, "Even if it lasted only one lifetime, that was much too long. I'm inclined to agree with you, Darya, this isn't the handiwork of the Builders. Something more inhuman, something more indifferent to organic suffering, has been at work in this system. Let's get back to the *Savior*, file our report with Julian Graves—and take a look at Iceworld. It may prove more dangerous, but I can't imagine anything more depressing than what we found here."

CHAPTER TWELVE
To Iceworld.

The *Savior* leaving the dead world was not the ship that had arrived two days before. Within an hour of lift-off Darya could feel the change in every person on board. It was not hard to guess the reasons.

Before their arrival, Hans Rebka had been fidgety and preoccupied. He knew that he had his own agenda in going there, but he was reluctant to tell others until he could offer proof. Ben Blesh and Lara Quistner had felt the nervousness of anyone about to undergo a first practical test. Now, Rebka's dark suspicions had been confirmed, while Ben and Lara had performed well—no, make that brilliantly. Darya could not imagine a more competent performance.

As for Darya herself, her full confidence in Hans Rebka was restored. She was ashamed for doubting him, when he had never in the past acted out of ego or the need to prove that he was in charge.

The result of all this was a great decrease in tension. The cramped quarters of the *Savior* no longer felt like an overcrowded box, too small for its crew. Rebka, Blesh, and Quistner were off by the communications console, and although she could not hear their conversation, an occasional laugh suggested that it was friendly and relaxed. If some of the laughter was a reaction to the sight of ugly death, that was no more than natural. The fact that they were talking together at all suggested a major adjustment. And it was no huge surprise when Lara Quistner wandered over to Darya and sat down by her side.

"Professor Lang, I've been thinking." She sounded tentative. "I want to bounce an idea off you. We've all heard a lot about the Builders, ever since we were kids, but it was always secondhand information. Everybody says that you are the ultimate authority on the Builders."

"If there is any such thing. And it's Darya, please, not Professor Lang. When you get right down to it there is no such thing as an authority on the Builders. What we *know* is simple. Something built and left behind a set of structures that we label as artifacts. All of them were very old— at least three million years—and most of them employed technology that we still do not understand. A few years ago, one new artifact appeared. Soon after that every one of them vanished. That's it. There you have our complete knowledge of the Builders. Everything else is speculation."

"But Professor Lang—Darya—surely there must be theories?"

"You've got it exactly right. *Theories*, not theory. You name it, someone had it. Maybe the Builders were entities whose consciousness extended over a finite dimension in time, so that they could literally *see* through time the way we can see through space. They could examine possible futures and direct the course of the spiral arm. That idea was mine, but I don't believe it anymore. Or the Builders are still alive, lying idle on the deep gravity slope that surrounds the giant black hole at the center of our galaxy, where time slows so that an hour there is a century or a millennium for us. That was Professor Carmina Gold's, at the Research Institute on Sentinel Gate, and she keeps looking for a way to travel to the center of the galaxy and back in a human lifetime. Maybe this expedition will help—we came to the Sag Arm in just a few days; there could be a chain of Bose nodes leading all the way to the galactic center. Or another theory: the Builders are actually human beings from our own future, coming back to direct the course of spiral arm development, including their own. That was Quintus Bloom's idea, and it made the embodied computer E.C. Tally go into a logical loop so bad we had to cold-start him."

"Quintus Bloom?"

"He was a big name at the Institute a few years ago. He stayed on Labyrinth when it disappeared, and no one to this day knows what happened to him. Then there was the theory that nothing cataclysmic happened to the Builders. They were just like any other species, they grew old, and since they didn't change they slowly died out. That idea was a kind of orphan, no one knows who had it first. Most people attribute it to Captain Alonzo Sloane, an old space wanderer who went off looking for the Lost Worlds, Jesteen and Skyfall and Petra and Primrose and Paladin and Midas and Rainbow Reef. He never came back, though we did find his ship near Labyrinth."

"People with ideas about the Builders seem to disappear rather often."

"Oh, most of them don't—we just remember the ones who did. I've had a dozen ideas of my own to explain who the Builders were and what happened to them, and I'm still here. And I must have read a hundred or a thousand papers by other people. Only one of them could be right, and chances are, all of them are wrong. If you have thoughts of your own, don't be ashamed of them. Maybe they are new, and maybe they are better than anyone else's."

"If you don't mind listening?"

"As I said, I've listened a thousand times, but I'm ready to listen ten thousand more. Hans Rebka tells me that the Builders are an obsession with me. I won't go quite that far, but I will admit they have been my life's consuming interest. Go ahead."

"Well." Lara glanced across at the two men, making sure that they were still deep in conversation. "I knew that the Builders were around for a very long time, and a few million years ago they disappeared. That never seemed to make much sense to me. If they died out, wouldn't you expect to see evidence of where and how they died? When I heard about this expedition, and found out where we were going, it occurred to me that perhaps the Builders didn't die out at all. Perhaps they just moved. Perhaps they decided to make a home in the Sag Arm, instead of in the Orion Arm. I know that they have some way of moving across great distances, because one of the artifacts is supposed to be far out of the galactic plane."

"Thirty thousand lightyears out of it. Lara, I was there. We called it—or the beings that inhabited it, who claimed to be servants of the Builders, called it—*Serenity*. Our party included Julian Graves. We were not sure what carried us out there, or what carried us back. We called them trans-portation vortices, but that was just a name. How a vor-tex worked was a total mystery. They seemed to appear anywhere, and carry you hundreds or thousands of lightyears instantly without involving Bose nodes at all."

"Then if they wanted to, they could easily have moved here."

"Without a doubt. The Builders have—or had—enormous powers, able to do things that still look like magic to us. We're millennia behind them in our most advanced tech-nology, if not millions of years. But I'm convinced of one thing, Lara. I can't prove this, but I feel it in my bones: whoever and whatever killed this star system and all the life within it was not the Builders. For that to be true, they would have had to change much more than their location. They would have had to change their whole attitude toward other living creatures. It's not generally accepted, but I believe that the Builders guided the development of our own local arm. It's thanks to them that we have a stable civilization involving many species and three major clades. If Captain Rebka were listening, I would say four major clades in deference to his feelings. Even though everyone outside the Phemus Circle regards it as a backward place of no great importance."

"I've heard something about that." Lara Quistner glanced across to Hans Rebka and lowered her voice. "They say that all the planets of the Phemus Circle are poor and primi-tive, and all the men are totally sex-mad. Is it true?"

If you're asking about my recent experience, forget it. Hans and I haven't looked each other in the eye for weeks. And if you have ideas about him, get in line. "The worlds I've seen in the Phemus Circle were certainly poverty-stricken compared with some rich planet like Miranda." It was a good, neutral answer. Darya wondered what rumors Lara Quistner might have heard. "As for the men, you'd have to find out for yourself. Someday, maybe you will. In my experience, they are sex-mad—and so are the women of the Phemus Circle. On some of the planets they have to reproduce whenever and however they can, in order to maintain a population at all. But at the same time the men can be prudish. Sometimes the slightest detail will turn off their interest in sex."

Which was quite as far as Darya intended to go on that particular subject, regardless of her personal data base. She had been keeping an eye on the two men, and saw that they had wrapped up their conversation and were over by the autochef. They were poking at the controls. Darya winced. Maybe Ben Blesh knew what he was doing, but Hans Rebka's attempts at food programming were disastrous. Being raised on Teufel a man couldn't afford to be picky. She went on, "I think that the big planet, Iceworld, proves that the Builders were once here in the Sag Arm. It has all the earmarks of a Builder artifact—too light for its size, far too cold to be natural. What you are proposing, that the Builders might still be here and still be active, is another matter. This star system suggests to me that some other group—the ones I called the Voiders—came along after the Builders and did their own dirty work."

"But that doesn't mean the Builders must be gone completely. Maybe they are still around in other parts of this arm."

"They might be. I'm quite willing to admit the possibility of two races of super-beings. But you know how Julian Graves reacted. He talked about the 'undesirability of concatenating implausibilities.' As if we were not sure of the existence of the Builders themselves, when we have seen evidence of their existence all over our own spiral arm. I'm hoping that what we find on Iceworld will persuade Julian Graves to change his mind."

"My idea wasn't new, was it? You had the same thought yourself, long ago."

"Possibly something very like it. But keep thinking. It could be that the Builders became extinct when they *stopped* thinking."

"You don't really believe that, do you?"

"No, I don't. On the other hand, I've been wrong about the Builders so many times in the past, you shouldn't accept my views—or anyone else's—as gospel." Darya saw that Rebka and Blesh were examining something in the autochef, and Ben Blesh was laughing. She concluded, "If you have more ideas when we reach Iceworld, I'd like to discuss them."

It was intended to be an easy way to end the talk and hurry over to protect her own stomach, but it produced a surprising response. Lara lowered her voice and said, "There is something else I'd like to talk you about. But not right now. I want to speak privately."

It didn't sound as though Lara wanted another conversation about the Builders. That was a pity. Darya herself would be more than ready for that, especially after they'd had a chance to examine Iceworld.

Maybe Hans was right after all. Maybe "obsession" was the best word for it.

They had traveled to an alien arm of the galaxy where humans had never been before. They were within an alien star system, and only a day ago they had left a dead and alien world. But *alien* was relative. There were degrees of alienation. The planet they had come from, with its air and oceans and mountains and what had once been a thriving civilization of intelligent beings, felt like home compared with Iceworld.

Darya sat by Hans Rebka's side and alternated her attention between the displays of the ship's sensors and the planet around which the *Savior* now orbited. She had to think of it as alternating attention, because they could not *see* the world in any conventional sense. To human eyes, Iceworld was no more than darkness visible, a black disk revealed by the absence of the stars that it occulted.

Every other imaging sensor, at every frequency from hard X-rays to long-wavelength radio, told the same story. They detected no emitted signal. The planet was simply not there.

Only one seldom-used instrument, a low-resolution imaging device normally used to measure cosmic background radiation, admitted a presence. It reported a unique world where the maximum temperature was little more than one kelvin, and that only in isolated places. In many places the temperature was too small to register—which meant that it had to be less than one hundredth of a degree absolute.

Nothing in the universe was so cold, nothing in the universe *could be* so cold. Radiation falling onto a planet's surface must warm it, raising it at the very least to the 2.7 kelvins of the cosmic microwave background.

"So it doesn't exist," Rebka said. "But there it is."

"Will we be going down?" Ben Blesh was crowding Darya, pushing her aside in his eagerness to see everything.

"Eventually." Rebka was in the command pilot's seat. "Before that happens I'd like to learn as much as we can from orbit. It may take a day or two, but I want to fly over every square kilometer and tickle the ground with something a bit more active."

The *Savior* was moving along a spiraling orbit that would in time cover Iceworld's whole surface like wool being wound evenly onto a great ball. The ship was less than two hundred kilometers above the surface. Such a close orbit would normally decay rapidly because of air drag, but Iceworld lacked the faintest trace of an atmosphere. The planet also seemed perfectly spherical. The gravity field supported the idea of an equally symmetrical interior, and nothing perturbed the *Savior*'s flight. Only Rebka's natural caution prevented them from flying lower yet, fifty kilometers or five kilometers up.

"What do you mean, tickle?" Darya asked. "Don't damage anything down there, Hans. I want to see the place in its unspoiled condition."

"It's a big planet, Darya. Twenty times the surface area of Miranda. And we'll only be using the laser in a pulse mode, one burst every five seconds. Don't worry. We'll get enough burn to give us an emission spectrum for the points of impact, but we'll be touching less than a billionth of the total area."

"We've never experienced anything so cold before. Can you be *sure* you won't ruin anything?"

"Not completely sure. But if it's a choice of risking a little local damage down there, versus risking our skins when we descend, which do you prefer? Hmm." Rebka was peering at a screen that displayed a graph composed of sharp peaks and valleys. "Darya, this is the return spectrum—it looks the same for every laser pulse. But it seems your name for the planet wasn't the greatest choice."

"Iceworld?"

"Right. This is a spectrum of the raw return signal, and over there we have the results after the spectrum analyzer has done its work. It's reporting not a trace of ice—any kind of ice. No water, no carbon dioxide, no methane, no oxygen, no nitrogen, no chlorine, no fluorine."

"No condensed gases of any kind?"

"Worse than that. The spectrum doesn't match any material in our spectral signature library, solid, liquid, or gas. You were right, Darya, this place wasn't formed naturally. It's not made of any known material."

"Are you sure that our laser isn't disturbing things below the surface?" Lara Quistner was watching another display, this one showing a larger area than the immediate vicinity of the illuminated spot.

"As I said, not so we should notice." Hans Rebka checked a dial. "We're at low power and long wavelength. The top tenth of a millimeter of the ground should account for all the return."

"Maybe it does—or maybe low power means something different down there. Do you want to see what I think I'm seeing? Zoom in on a line that trails behind the laser beam, and wait."

It took a while, because as long as the moving light of the laser was in the field of view it dominated what the eye could detect. Even when the image moved far enough to put the pulse out of sight, Darya was at first convinced that Lara was imagining things. At last she saw it, so faint that it was at the very limit of visibility. A blue glimmer like a dust devil spurted up at the place where the laser beam had hit. It seemed to boil out of the surface for a moment, then was gone.

Lara whispered, "They come about twenty seconds *after* the laser has moved on. What are they?"

"No idea." Rebka was changing control settings. "Let's try some signal enhancement, see if we can get a spectrum we recognize."

Before he could finish, a flash of orange startled their eyes. It was bright enough to obliterate all signs of the blue dust devils, then at once it too had vanished. Darya was left with a zigzag afterimage like a bolt of lightning. She blinked, waiting for her retinas to adjust after the overload.

Rebka said suddenly, "Hey. We got one."

"One what?"

"A spectrum from that flash, one that the analyzer can recognize. We'll finally understand what part of the surface is made of. Uh-oh. Take that back. We won't understand."

Ben Blesh protested, "But you just said—"

"I know what I said." Rebka leaned back in his chair. "I can't imagine how you knew, Darya, but you were right. What's down there isn't just something made by a random alien technology of the Sag Arm. It's an *artifact*—made by the Builders."

"How can you be so sure, from only one reading?"

"Because the signal analyzer is telling us. I said it *recognized* the return spectrum it just received, and it did. It can recognize the material, because there's a match to a spectrum already in its library. But it can't *identify* it. The part of the surface of Iceworld that produced the signal is of the same construction material used to make Phages. What is that material, Darya?"

"Hans Rebka, you know the answer to that question as well as I do." Darya turned to face Ben Blesh and Lara Quistner. "We've been trying for thousands of years, and still we have no idea what the Phages—and now parts of Iceworld—are made of."

Ben and Lara had heard about Phages—who in the local spiral arm had not?—but Darya Lang and Hans Rebka had actually seem them in action.

While the *Savior* flew its automated survey path over the surface of Iceworld and the ship's computer recorded, sorted, and tried to organize all the sensor readings, Hans and Darya explained.

"As much as we know," Darya said. "You have to remember, Phages have such a terrible reputation that you try not to go near one. The reason you will never encounter them during training is because every exploration vessel employs a Phage avoidance system. They are universal eaters. They don't look dangerous, just a gray regular dodecahedron. Most of them are forty-eight meters on a side, but we have run across much smaller ones. The big ones can ingest something thirty meters across, and as long as you care to mention."

"But where does it all go?" Lara's wide-eyed gaze suggested that she and her companion were ignorant in certain important survival areas.

"No one knows. It sure doesn't come out again, and mass detectors measure no change in the mass of the Phage. They seem able to digest anything."

Hans added, "Or nearly everything. They can't eat each other, or the structural hulls left behind by the Builders. We used to think that they were completely indestructible, until we saw smashed remains of some on an artificial moon called Glister in the Dobelle system. Now we know that they and some of the other Builder constructs are stabilized by powerful electromagnetic fields. If that field dies away, or you can impose a suitable counter-field, the material becomes weak. You can push your fist right through a wall of it. I know, because I did it on Labyrinth."

Ben Blesh had been listening with the same total absorption as Lara Quistner. He looked away, to where the displays showed the laser beam from *Savior* steadily stitching its way across the surface of Iceworld. Every few minutes, a sensor observing the wake of the laser reported another flare of orange light. A new one had just occurred. Blesh pointed. "Do you think that if we were down there, we could penetrate below the surface by generating the right field?"

"The right field, in the right place." Rebka had followed Blesh's gesture. "Maybe at a place like that one. But remember, most of the surface isn't Builder material—or if it is, it's a type we never met before. But you are correct. Judging from our experience, if we land where we see one of the orange flashes, and generate a suitable field, we will drop through into the interior. We know how to set up such a cancellation field. I wonder if we can define one for an individual suit."

"Of course we can."

Ben's answer was no surprise any more to Hans. The suits provided on the *Pride of Orion* were like everything else associated with that ship: miraculous, compared with anything that Hans had ever seen before. They would feed you, dispose of waste products, deal with wounds (though not the most severe kinds), and even permit a planetary return from orbit unassisted. They did everything but have sex with you, and Hans would not guarantee that.

Ben went on, "So we might as well set up cancellation fields, for our individual suits and for the whole ship. According to the sensors, they are seeing the same thing over and over again. We get either nothing at all, unless you count that weak blur of blue light, or we see a flash from a section of Builder material. If we're going to learn anything new, we have to head down to the surface."

It was tempting to agree at once with Ben. End the boring survey of an unchanging world from a cramped ship, and move on to where they might discover something that mattered. Hans had felt uneasy before their previous planetfall, because even prior to arrival he had feared the sight of a dead world and murdered inhabitants. Iceworld produced no such qualms. Any danger from Builder artifacts always stemmed from too much human curiosity or a total lack of common sense. He and half a dozen others, including Darya, had almost died on Quake during Summertide Maximum; but no rational creature should have been anywhere near Quake at such a time, after numerous indicators had warned of coming planet-wide violence.

Only years of experience made Hans shake his head. "We finish the survey, then if it still looks safe we go down." He glanced at a display showing current progress, and knew his next words would not be popular. "That means two more days in orbit."

"But—" "Two days!" "Why do—"

The response came at once from the other three. Hans cut them off. "I'm sorry. This isn't negotiable. Ben and Lara, I know you're impatient to have your turn and show what you can do; and Darya, I know you can't wait for a chance to explore the interior of Iceworld. I feel the same way myself. But as long as I'm in charge, it's going to be safety first."

His face wore a mixture of uncertainty and bewilderment. Darya could guess the reason for that changing expression. Safety first, when there was no reason to expect any form of danger? Safety first, when Hans was as relaxed about descending to Iceworld as he ever was about anything? Why was he doing this?

But Hans was not ready to hear questions. He ducked his head, and repeated, "Two more days to complete the survey of Iceworld. Then we'll see what else we've learned. And then we make a decision."

CHAPTER THIRTEEN
Orbiting Iceworld.

As the hours wore on Hans felt the cabin walls of the *Savior* crowding in on him. He had established an electromagnetic cancellation field for the whole ship, and also one for each of the suits. Now there was nothing more to do and no way to escape the others. The ship moved constantly over new areas of Iceworld, but the image on the displays did not change. The other three stared gloomily at the monitors, then turned to stare accusingly at Hans. Their faces said it all: *Why are we wasting time up here? Why don't we go down and get on with it?*

They didn't seem to realize that Hans was as keen for action as they were. He was constantly checking the progress of the surface survey, without any idea what he might be looking for. Whatever it was, he didn't see it. Before the first sleep period arrived he lost patience—not with them, but with himself.

"All right. I know that none of you likes this. Let's try something different." He did not need to invite them to where he was sitting at the control console. They were out of their chairs and crowding in on him in seconds. He went on, "Ben, you are better with the display equipment than

I am. Give me a hand to produce displays of what we have, then I'd like everyone's opinions."

The *Savior* was flying a polar orbit. As the planet rotated, on each pass the ship covered a different swath of the surface, with every strip overlapping the others at the poles. Hans and Ben, working together, converted the results they had to a 3-D graphic.

Hans said at last, "That's good enough. Thanks, Ben. As you can all see, we've covered only about one-fourth of the surface, so no one could say this is close to a complete survey. On the other hand, we've covered the polar region many times, and what we see so far there and elsewhere shows an absolutely regular and unchanging pattern. First, the obvious: Iceworld is a perfect sphere made from unknown materials, held at a temperature lower than anything has any right to be. Most places give no return signal, but dotted on the sphere in places about fifty kilometers apart from each other we have a grid of points of something else, places where the laser's return spectrum suggests the surface has a different composition. These areas look like they're made of Builder materials. Each one is a circular patch only a few hundred meters across, but they are all connected by narrower lines of the same material. The grid patches form a network of perfect equilateral triangles."

Hans gave the others a minute or two to digest the display, then went on, "There's an obvious question here. As I said, we haven't had a close look at almost three-quarters of the surface. If we did, would we simply find more of the same, or is there a chance that if we stop the survey now we'll miss something new and important?"

He didn't need or want their reply, and went on at once, "The honest answer is, we simply don't know. So here's what I propose. It's close to the time when we usually go to sleep. Let's do that. By the time we are up again and have had something to eat, the ship will have surveyed another fifteen percent of the surface. We'll look at the whole result, and if the pattern continues as we have seen it so far, we'll make the bet that the rest would show nothing new. We'll go down, to one of the spots that shows Builder material, and tackle the next problem: How do we penetrate below the surface to take a look at the interior?"

It was a compromise, between the two full days needed to complete the whole survey and everybody else's urge to descend at once. Hans knew it, and so did the others, but they didn't realize how strongly he wanted to agree with them.

It was a relief when Darya nodded, and after a few seconds Ben Blesh and Lara Quistner did the same.

They dispersed, to their separate and cramped bunks. Would they sleep? Or would they, from the expression on Lara Quistner's face, lie awake in excited expectation?

Hans couldn't speak for them. He only knew his own plans. *When you have something to do, do it. When you have nothing to do, sleep.* That was just as true if the next morning would bring an arrival at the safe and wealthy world of Miranda, or a descent to the surface of an unknown world colder than anything in the rest of the universe.

Hans removed his shoes and lay down in his bunk. He turned off the light. Within thirty seconds he was at the edge of sleep.

The edge was as close as he got. Hans was skin and bones, so a bunk wide enough for any normal person was ample for him. But that didn't apply when someone was squeezing in next to you, pushing you up against a cold and unyielding wall.

The Phemus Circle reaction was to assume you were being attacked and hit back at once. Fortunately, Hans recognized the perfume even before his eyes were open.

"Shh! Don't cry out." A soft body pushed in closer.

"I wasn't about to." He answered Darya's whisper with his own. "What's happening? I hoped that at some point we would get friendly, but I didn't expect it would be tonight."

"It won't. We need to talk. Move in a bit—I'm falling off the edge."

"There's no place to move *to*. Do you want the light turned on?"

"No!"

"Why didn't you speak to me earlier, when we had space to breathe?"

"It had to be done in private, away from the other two." Darya tried to wriggle into a space that did not exist. The warmth of her body against his was pleasant and it aroused more than memories.

He said hurriedly, "Has Ben been pushing you, trying to persuade you that it's time for him to take over?"

"No. But while you and he were finishing your food, Lara asked for a few minutes alone with me. There's no such thing as privacy on the *Savior* except in the bunks and the bathroom, and you and Ben would both have noticed if Lara and I went there together. The only time we had was when Ben helped you to generate the display of results. But that was enough. Her message came through loud and clear."

"Let me guess. She's nervous about going down to Iceworld."

"Hans, you have it about as wrong as you could get. But I would have been wrong, too, if she hadn't told me her feelings. She says that before our trip to the dead planet she was nervous and unsure of herself, so she accepted that Ben was her senior in the survival team and she let him take the lead in everything. But she feels that she performed well when we were down on the surface."

"She's right. Better than well, perfectly. Neither she nor Ben put a foot wrong. Old Arabella would be proud of them."

"And Lara knows it, at least for herself. But she claims to have seen flaws in the speed and accuracy of Ben's actions. When I told her I hadn't noticed any such thing, she said I wouldn't since I didn't have special training. *She* could tell the difference. And because of that she was asking me for my help."

"Why didn't she come to me? I'm the one in charge." Hans asked from curiosity rather than hurt ego.

"My question, too. She said that you are only in charge for the moment. As soon as we are down on the surface of Iceworld, Ben will take over."

"She's right. Graves insisted on it. A jackass decision, but we have to live with it."

"If Lara is right, we're as likely to die with it. She says that we have never seen Ben when he's on top. He won't take no for an answer from me, or from you. She has— seen him on top, I mean."

"I can imagine it." Hans had a sudden memory of Darya on top, which had not happened in more than two years and was a thought that made no sense at all when a man was trying to focus on more serious matters. He added, "Ben's a take-charge sort of individual. That's not a bad thing—provided the person knows what he's doing."

"You think Ben doesn't?"

"I think Ben can't possibly, but that's no reflection on him. Some things you gain by experience and in no other way."

"Hans, you have all the experience we need. I'd rather Ben didn't try to get *his* experience at our expense."

They were face to face to hear more easily the other's whispers. Darya's breath was warm, and on the word "expense" her lips brushed against his face. To stay on the narrow bunk her whole body had to be in contact with his. He was aware of her all the way from his head to his toes. Despite the total darkness she had to be equally aware of his body's ill-timed reaction.

Hans told himself to think pure thoughts. Think depressing, think about the frozen and dead world that they had come from, think about what might face them tomorrow. Think about anything, except Darya pressing close to him. He said, "We have a job to do. We have to teach Ben without his ever knowing that he's being taught. It won't be easy, because we have no experience ourselves of anything like Iceworld. That isn't my biggest worry, though."

"So what is? I didn't get the feeling from listening to you that you were expecting danger on Iceworld."

"Then that's a failing on my part. The leader of a party should *always* expect danger. I hope Ben Blesh's survival training included that detail. Don't worry, I won't be relaxing too far. But Ben's actions are not what most concern me. My big worry is Lara."

"*Lara?* She's not the bossy one. And you just told me that she was doing a perfect job."

"She was, and she is. But from what you told me, as soon as we arrive on Iceworld she will feel that she has to prove she's as good as Ben Blesh—and maybe better. It's when people want to prove themselves that they do silly things and get into trouble. My job will be to spot any show-off action ahead of time. If I don't, the hardest task will be to prevent Lara from starting something."

"I understand." Darya eased away from him. "Hans, my hardest task right now is to prevent *you* from starting something. You mustn't feel rejected, but this isn't the best time and place."

"Will there ever be a better one? It's been more than two years."

"I'm aware of that. Maybe more aware of it than you are."

Darya did not suggest, as he knew she had every right to, that their two-year separation was the result of Hans's own efforts to overturn the repressive government of the Phemus Circle. She had not pointed out that any visit by her to him would have been blocked by that same government. She had never criticized him for pursuing a lost cause. For herself, she had not left Sentinel Gate for as much as a single day, and if at any time he had made the effort to come and see her, she would have been ready and waiting.

Any time but now. The bunk creaked as she rolled sideways off it. Hans felt a hand exploring his face in the darkness, tasted a soft kiss on the lips, and heard a whispered, "There will be a better time. Goodnight."

Hans was alone again. He drew in a deep breath and told his body to relax. He repeated his own mantra: *When you have something to do, do it. When you have nothing to do, sleep. When you have something to do, do it. When you have nothing to do, sleep.*

Sometimes, repeated mantras are not enough. Sometimes, self-discipline fails. Hans remained awake. He stared into the darkness and imagined possible dangers on the surface of Iceworld. Half an hour later, his mind remained blank and he was still as far from sleep as ever.

CHAPTER FOURTEEN
Iceworld.

After a thousand planetfalls one more should have little to offer, even if it happened to be in a different arm of the galaxy.

Hans puzzled over his own reactions. He had landed on objects ranging in size from minor planetoids to monster worlds twice the diameter of Iceworld. So why the feeling that this was a new experience?

He looked ahead to the broad curve of the planet, felt the pulse of the *Savior*'s drive, listened for the whistle of air on the ship's hull, and knew the answer. Anything the size of Iceworld ought to be a massive object, well able to hold on to an atmosphere. This place wasn't massive, and the surface was utterly airless. The ship was descending through hard vacuum, riding a drive operating at only a fraction of full power.

The more Hans thought about Darya's plan, the less he was persuaded that it could work as easily as she suggested. Accept that the world a few kilometers below the ship was hollow. Assume that somehow they would be able to penetrate the featureless exterior and reach the interior. But now consider that interior. A world with a diameter of seventy-eight thousand kilometers had a volume of two hundred and fifty *trillion* cubic kilometers. The old "needle in a haystack" image didn't begin to describe it. You could wander a space that size for the rest of your life, and never come close to what you were looking for—even if you knew what you were looking for.

Which, as even Darya readily admitted to him in private if not in public, she did not. She was hoping to find sentient Builder artifacts similar to those they had met inside worlds of the Orion Arm. They had been able to communicate with them, even if the information provided was usually cryptic enough to be more baffling than useful.

Last night's whispered session might have ended in sexual frustration, but it had also produced a positive result. Darya and Hans were more at ease with each other now than at any time since his arrival at Upside Miranda Port. Both of them were keeping a close eye on Lara and Ben.

Not that Ben would be easy to miss. As the *Savior* descended, he hovered at Hans's shoulder. Was he going to shout, "Right. Now it's my turn," the moment that the ship touched down?

Not quite that bad. As soon as the *Savior* made contact, feather-light on the frigid surface (courtesy of the autopilot—Hans had learned his lesson), Ben said, "Exit stations, but hold it there. This is a totally alien world. We look, and then we look again before we leap."

The landing site had been selected with as much care as possible, given an almost total lack of information. The most promising areas were the nodes, regularly spaced in a triangular grid on the surface and connected by narrow lines of what seemed to be the same material. It made sense to land on top of a grid patch, since they were composed of familiar Builder materials. If Darya were correct, the *Savior* could then generate an electromagnetic field inhibitor which would allow an individual, or even the whole ship itself, to sink into the unknown interior of Iceworld. On the other hand, those grid areas were also the places where the probing laser had produced a flash like orange fire. Maybe it made more sense to land on the cold and inert spaces between the grid points.

Hans had made the decision—perhaps the last decision

he would be allowed to make until they left Iceworld. They would bring the *Savior* down on the frozen plain, just a couple of kilometers from the edge of a grid patch. They would keep the drive in full stand-by mode. In a few seconds it could propel the ship forward onto the nearby grid point area, or loft it at high acceleration back into space.

Until touchdown, everyone had been in full suits and in Emergency Mode position. At Ben's order to take up exit stations, Lara moved to stand by the airlock. She did not walk so much as float. Hans estimated from the response of his own body that weight on Iceworld was just a few hundredths of the inter-clade standard. Walking would be easy, running impossible. Let's hope they wouldn't need the latter.

The view on all sides did nothing to suggest danger. Iceworld appeared as a black, featureless plain with a horizon so far away that it showed as a ruled straight line below which no stars were visible. The temperature sensors in contact with the surface failed to report any value whatsoever. The surface conductivity was so high that the ship's instruments could not offer a measurement. The whole exterior of Iceworld formed one giant superconductor. That solved one possible problem that had occurred to Hans while they were still in orbit. No matter how slippery the surface might be, a walking person could gain a firm footing through an electromagnetic field in the extremities of the suit.

They watched and waited, expecting nothing and seeing nothing. It was Lara who at last said, "Well?"

There was more than a suggestion of "What are we waiting for?" in her tone. Hans would have ignored her while he watched all the instruments through a second and confirming set of negative readings, but Ben glanced at Hans, shrugged, and said, "We're in no hurry. However, I authorize you to cycle the lock and step outside. *One* step. Then we wait and see how your suit readings run."

Lara was cycling the inner door before Ben finished speaking. The hard vacuum on Iceworld made it in effect an exit into open space. The *Savior*'s cameras in the airlock and outside recorded Lara's passage through the inner door, then there was a brief wait while that door closed and the outer one opened with a puff of air condensing to ice crystals. As Lara appeared, Hans at once referred to the monitors that provided all-around surveillance of the surface. He still sat in the pilot's chair, his hands instinctively hovering over the controls, but there was no reason to take action. Everything remained calm and dark.

"One step, and all's well." Lara was equally calm. "Are you receiving the readings from my suit?"

Ben nodded, then apparently realized that Lara had no video feed from inside the ship. "Yes, we're receiving. Everything is nominal."

"I'm testing the surface traction, and it's adequate. Walking should be easy. Should I test my suit's cancellation field?"

"No. Definitely not. For one thing, you are not above a grid point area, so we would expect nothing to happen. On the other hand, if it did, the last thing we want is for you to sink down alone through the surface. When we penetrate the interior, we all do it together."

"Then I request authorization to take trial steps on the surface."

"Very well. You should move directly toward the grid point, which is at thirty degrees to the right of your present suit vector. But wait for word from me before you begin." This time Ben had not looked at Hans before giving his answer. Now he said, "Captain Rebka, I am going onto the surface also." Before Hans could object, Ben added, "This is not a matter for discussion. I will follow Specialist Quistner, but well behind her. You will move the *Savior* to keep up with us, and the ship will at no time be more than ten steps away from me."

Which if you get in trouble might as well be ten lightyears for all the good I can probably do you. Hans said, "Very well. Ten steps away from you until you give other instructions."

As Ben Blesh vanished through the inner door, Darya motioned to Hans to turn off his radio transmitter and moved to place her suit helmet into contact with his.

"Hans, what does he think he's doing?"

"He's afraid that Lara is handling everything, and he won't

get his share of the action. Don't worry. Give him a few more years, and he'll be willing to offer his share to anyone who'll take it."

"He could be putting two people in danger instead of one."

"That sounds more like my line than yours. But so far, Iceworld doesn't seem to offer enough danger for even one. I hope you are right about the interior, because I've never seen anything deader than the outside. Here he comes. I have to turn my transmitter back on."

Ben was emerging from the outer lock to stand by Lara Quistner. He waved, knowing that Rebka would be watching on the monitors, and closed the lock door. As Ben turned away, Hans instinctively operated the lock door again and set it to its widest opening. Ben did not seem to notice. He said, "All right, Lara. Go ahead."

Her suited figure, illuminated by one of the *Savior*'s outside searchlights, headed away from Ben Blesh and the ship. The plain on which she moved reflected no light, so that she appeared to walk on nothing. Ben waited until she had taken at least fifty steps, then followed. Hans in turn allowed ten paces, then eased the bulk of the *Savior* after Blesh's suited figure. The delicate balance of gravity and thrust would have been difficult for a human, but the autopilot made it child's play. Hans was free to attempt the difficult task of keeping his attention on three things at once: Lara Quistner, moving in a straight line toward the invisible grid patch; Ben Blesh, following; and the view all around the *Savior* provided by the ship's monitors.

Hans wondered if Ben realized that Lara was steadily increasing the distance between them. Probably not. The view from within a suit was never all that good. Hans could tell what was happening, because his vantage point at the *Savior*'s controls placed him much higher. If what Darya had told him last night was true, Lara wanted the feeling that she was exploring a new world alone, without Ben's authority to follow and annoy her.

Whatever the reason, it was still a damn fool thing for her to do and Ben needed to know about it. Hans was about to send word on what was happening when a flicker of light caught his peripheral vision.

It was the faintest gleam of blue, a dust devil far off to the right that ran across the plain and was gone before you could be sure you saw it at all. Staring in that direction, nothing was visible but the black-hole light-absorbing surface of Iceworld. Hans had no idea how far away the flicker had been. He looked across at the readings from the ship's scanners. They had not reported any signal at all.

Imagination?

People did not accuse Hans of an excess of imagination— quite the opposite. Was he letting the spooky silence and dark of Iceworld get to him?

"Ben, and Lara. Do you realize that Lara is getting farther ahead?"

"I don't think that's true." Lara sounded confident and a little too cocky. "I think I'm holding a steady distance. This is interesting. When you get close enough and can look at things from close to a grazing angle, you actually *see* the edge of the grid point area. It glows a pale green."

Ben said at once, "Lara, I am in charge of this exploration party. I don't want you to go any closer, no matter how interesting you think something is. Stay right there until I catch up. *That is an order.*"

An order from Ben, which Lara surely didn't wish to hear. She said, "Very well," but the signal from her suit gave Hans an accurate range-rate reading. She was moving as fast as ever. The edge of the circular grid patch was no more than a hundred meters in front of her.

Hans didn't want to get into the middle of a two-person power struggle, but he had no choice. If Ben was to serve as chief of the party, he must know what was going on.

"Ben, I'm holding the *Savior* a steady ten paces behind you. But Lara hasn't stopped. The distance between you is still increasing."

Another flash of blue distracted him during his final words. This time it came from the left, brighter than the last one. He could follow its trace, beginning well behind the *Savior* and rippling along a straight line that led toward the grid point boundary. Or to Lara? It was impossible to say.

Hans turned off his radio and leaned across to Darya. "Did you see it?"

"Yes." Darya was in the co-pilot's seat. "What is it?"

"I hoped you could tell me." Hans turned his radio back on and kept his voice calm and dispassionate. "This is Captain Rebka. Professor Lang and I are detecting some kind of unknown activity on the surface. Senior Specialists Blesh and Quistner, I strongly urge both of you to return at once to the *Savior*. I then propose that we lift off and hold a safe altitude until we know what we are dealing with."

"Captain Rebka, what is the nature of the activity?"

Wrong response. When you think there might be danger, you run first and ask questions later.

Hans said, "It resembles a blue will-o'-the-wisp or dust devil, similar to what we noticed from orbit in the track of our laser."

"I saw it!" Lara had finally halted, maybe fifty paces from the grid patch. "Ben, it ran right past me on an angle and merged into the green around the edge of the grid. Where the blue met the green I saw a kind of rainbow burst of light. Could you see it from where you are?"

"I saw nothing. Lara, back up and return to the *Savior*. At once. That's an order!"

But Ben was not following his own instruction. He was still moving toward Lara. Under Hans's control, the *Savior* crept after him.

Lara laughed. "Ben, you are overreacting. You must be receiving the readings from my suit. You can see for yourself, everything is nominal and there's nothing to worry about."

"That's not your decision to make. Lara, if you don't go back to the ship at once you'll be in big trouble."

"All right, Ben, I'm on my way." Lara's suit faceplate reflected light from the *Savior* as she turned. "But you are making a big deal out of nothing. We are here to explore, not to ignore anything interesting that we see."

She was moving toward the ship, but the range-rate reading told Hans that she was in no hurry. At her speed it would take minutes to reach the *Savior*. Hans's fingers itched to hit the sequence that would boost them to orbit at maximum acceleration.

He resisted the temptation, leaned back, and concentrated

on the banks of readings from both Lara's suit and the ship's all-around sensors. As she said, everything in her immediate vicinity registered no change. However, that wasn't true of the edge of the grid point area a hundred meters beyond her. Instead of its previous absurdly low temperature of 1.2 kelvins, one spot now failed to report any temperature reading at all. That was impossible. When energy was delivered to a place—and even the blue dust devils must contain *some* energy—the temperature at that point *had* to rise. It could not possibly go down.

Hans felt his skin crawl. "Ben, Lara. I'm seeing surface changes near the edge of the grid patch. Get back to the ship—*now.*"

Even as he spoke he realized his mistake. If anything could keep Ben Blesh outside, it would be a direct order to return from Hans Rebka.

Predictably, Ben said at once, "The responsibility for bringing us in is mine, Rebka, not yours. Lara, if you don't get a move on, I'll come and drag you back."

Hans saw another gleam of light. It was the reflection from Lara's faceplate. Instead of answering, she had turned her head to look behind her. She said, "This is crazy. Captain Rebka, you're seeing things. I'm a lot closer to the grid than anyone else, and I notice no change there at all."

While she was still speaking, one of the displays of the *Savior* lit so brightly that it cast a flickering blue shadow onto the controls at Hans's fingertips. He looked, in time to see another line of fire, bigger and brighter than the first two, racing like a blue fuse across the surface. It rippled well wide of the *Savior,* cleared Ben Blesh and Lara Quistner, and ran on to the edge of the gridded area. Hans saw a flare of light and a semicircular arc of rainbow colors standing up from the dark plain of Iceworld.

This time the flash was so bright that neither Lara nor Ben could miss it. Lara gasped and stood rooted, at the same time as Ben began to move.

"Not that way!" Hans could hardly believe his eyes. Ben was heading toward Lara—away from the *Savior*—into possible danger. Hans's survival instincts told him to boost

the ship away from the surface at once, but he continued
to follow Ben.

Ben shouted, "Lara! MOVE!"

It had the right effect. She jerked into motion, starting
to run across the smooth plane of the surface. As Hans had
predicted, real running in such a low gravity field was
impossible. Lara strained toward the ship with the agonized
slow-motion action of a woman fleeing in a nightmare.

Behind her, the place where the last dust devil had met
the edge of the grid had come alive. A set of concentric hemispheres of blue light grew, reached a size of a few meters,
and vanished. At the same time, a layer of dense blue mist
emerged from the same center and rolled toward Lara.

The fog did not show on the range-rate sensor, but Hans
did not need any help to compare speeds. Unless Lara could
move faster there was no way that she could reach the *Savior*
before the fog lapped around her feet and calves. Ben was
in a different situation. He could turn around and make the
ship before the layer of mist reached him—if only he had
the sense to act immediately.

He didn't turn. Worse than that, Hans realized that Ben
was still moving *toward* Lara. The man was crazy. What
was he hoping to do, grab hold of the blue fog and wrestle
it away from her?

Ben's hopes and intentions did not matter. He was fifty
paces from Lara when the mist reached her and rippled
around her lower legs.

She at once stopped running. Hans heard a gasp, a startled
scream, and then nothing.

"Lara!" He, Darya, and Ben were shouting in unison.

She did not answer. She stood for a few seconds, motionless. And then Lara was screaming again, and she was
shrinking. She did not move, she did not topple, she did
not sway. She simply sank into the blue surface layer, slowly
and steadily. To Ben, limited to the quality of image provided by his suit, it must seem as though Lara drifted down
to and through the surface of Iceworld.

Hans, employing the superior sensors of the *Savior*, knew
better. As the different sections of Lara's body came to within
a few centimeters of the glowing layer of blue, they fractured

and fragmented and turned to powder. As that happened, the sensors showed her body dropping in temperature. She was ice—she was as cold as liquid air—she was liquid helium, just a few kelvins above absolute zero. Finally, the instruments could not provide values.

Lara's disintegration formed a hypnotic sight, but the warning of a different danger forced Hans into action. The layer of blue mist had paused when it reached Lara. Now it was moving again, sweeping toward the *Savior*. Long before it got there it would meet Ben, who stood as silent and motionless as if the tide of blue had already drained him of life and heat.

"Ben! Into the ship."

Ten quick steps would do it, then they could head up and away to safety. Ben was moving now, but he was like a zombie. Long before he reached the *Savior*, the fog would roll up to and over him. Already it was no more than thirty meters away, and what had at first been a gentle ripple forward now seemed like an irresistible advance.

Certain death for Ben and escape for Hans and Darya? Or possible death by impact for Ben and an uncertain fate for Hans and Darya? There was no time to work out the odds, but Hans refused to lose another crew member.

"Sit tight."

That was for Darya, inexplicably trying to stand up from the seat next to him. Hans hit the controls and boosted the *Savior*—not away to the safety of orbit, but straight forward. The ship accelerated at four gees and scooped Ben Blesh into the maw of the airlock's open outer door. The clang as his body hit the back of the lock sounded through the whole ship.

What Hans would have liked now was an instant switch from forward motion to upward motion, but the ship's inertia and the laws of dynamics did not permit that. Although he could alter the direction of thrust in a fraction of a second, until that change took effect the *Savior* continued to move forward. Forward, toward the edge of the grid point. Forward, toward the deadly blue mist that had crumbled Lara to dust and swallowed her body, and forward toward the pulsing spheres of blue light beyond.

Hans was pinned back in his seat by four gees of acceleration. It took all his strength to keep his hands in place on the controls. The *Savior* was turning and rising. The ship would clear the layer of blue fog. But they were not rising fast enough. The aft end, where the main drive was located, would pass through the spheres of blue at the edge of the grid patch.

Hans waited for an impact. He felt nothing, but he heard a change in the sound of the drive. A moment later the crushing force on his body lessened. The *Savior* was losing power. He called for Emergency Mode thrust, which ought to override any other command. Instead of punishing acceleration, the drive turned off completely. Hans felt himself in free fall, dropping with the ship toward the featureless surface.

He braced for an impact that might kill or maim. It never came. Falling in the light gravity of Iceworld, the *Savior* hit the ground, bounced, then hit again and skidded along the surface.

Hans glanced at the control read-outs. The hull had not been breached. All life-support systems showed normal readings. In principle the inside of the *Savior* was still the safest place on the planet.

Hans did not believe that for a moment. Something had touched the lower part of the ship, and seconds later they had lost the drive. Every other part of the ship might be equally vulnerable. He glanced across at Darya to make sure that her suit was fully closed.

"Come on."

"Where?" But she was already standing up.

"Outside. We lost power, and I don't know why. Until we know what happened I think we'll be safer on the surface."

How safe was that? Hans did not know, but already he was cycling the inner door of the airlock. It did not matter that all the air would be lost from the interior of the ship. When they came back in—if they came back in—air could be replaced.

The inner door was open. Hans had never closed the outer one, and he pushed Darya toward it.

"Go ahead."

"Ben—"

"I'll help him." *I lost one crew member, but I'm damned if I'll lose another.* "You go outside, make sure the outer door is clear."

Hans was exposing Darya to an unknown risk, and she surely knew it. The surface could be even more dangerous than the *Savior*'s interior. She went without another word.

Hans moved to where Ben's suited figure lay sprawled by the wall of the airlock. After the first impact as the *Savior* scooped up his body, Ben had then felt another four-gee force as the ship tried to rise toward orbit. Unlike Darya and Hans, he had not been cushioned in a well-designed seat.

The suit tell-tales showed that its integrity had been maintained. That was good, but had Ben survived the multiple shocks? Hans leaned over and shone the head beam of his own suit into the faceplate. Ben's eyes were open, and the pupils contracted as the light struck them.

Alive.

Hans had no time to ask for anything more. He scooped up the suited body and headed for the outer door of the airlock. It was a three-meter drop from there to the surface, but—thank Heaven for low-gravity planets—he jumped and landed without difficulty.

Darya was waiting. She at once pulled him away from the ship. He did not resist. The flat plain of the grid patch, which had before been dark as the grave, was illuminated now by a faint blue.

Twenty paces from the *Savior*, Darya paused. Hans, still carrying Ben's body, turned. At first sight the ship was just as it should be, standing at an odd angle on the smooth surface. But a line of blue flame licked at the outside of the hull, right down at ground level. The flame was not moving. The *Savior* was. While Hans and Darya watched, the whole hull sank downward slowly and steadily as though being absorbed into the surface of Iceworld.

Ignoring Darya's cry of warning, Hans took a couple of paces back toward the ship. Once you were close enough you could see what was really happening. Just above the pale blue line of flame, the hull of the *Savior* was fracturing, cracking, turning to powder, and vanishing.

Logic said that they ought to turn and run, but to where? Hans could see that the whole grid area had become edged with blue light. He and Darya could move no more than a hundred meters or so in any direction without passing across that blue barrier. He turned to stare again at the *Savior*, and noticed a change. The lower half of the ship was gone, and the dust that it had become was slowly spreading outward. Already the outer edge smudged the surface five meters away from the vanishing hull.

Hans stared upward. Somewhere in the sky, hundreds of millions of kilometers away, the *Pride of Orion* would be monitoring their status. They should receive everything up to Hans's order to Darya to head for the airlock. Since then there had been no time for spoken messages, but the beacon would automatically send out its signal for as long as it existed.

That existence would be for only a few more minutes. The chance of anything from the *Pride of Orion* arriving in time to help Darya, Ben, and Hans was a flat zero.

Hans brought his attention back to their surroundings. Another meter of the *Savior* had vanished, and the dust that the ship had been was oozing closer. It might be harmless, but that was not a risk they could afford to take. The boundary of the grid area was still alight with an ominous blue.

Hans took a deep breath. "Darya?"

He knew what they had to do. He just wanted to hear her voice.

"I'm here, Hans."

"We can't stay where we are. I screwed up, and I'm sorry. I thought the surface would be safe. I was as wrong as I could be."

"We all were."

"The ship is done for. We can't go up. There's only one thing left."

"Hans, I know that. I know very well what we have to do." She produced a sound somewhere between a laugh and a sob. "This is my fault, not yours. I'm the one who wanted to come here, and I'm the one who said I wanted to see the interior of Iceworld. If I'm lucky, I'll get my wish."

It was an odd definition of luck, but Hans understood. The powdery layer had advanced to within a few meters of their feet. He said, "No point in waiting. Let's hope we were right about the destabilizing field. I'm going to turn mine on now."

"Me, too. Hans, I hope I'll meet you on the other side— wherever that is."

"You have to. Remember, you promised me there would be a better time? You can't renege on that."

Hans raised his gaze to the upper edge of his suit's faceplate. He glanced in turn at each element of the control sites that would cause his suit to generate a cancellation field. The suit's sensors, tracking his eye movements, turned the field on.

He had time for one more moment of worry. Would the field's active radius be enough to include Ben, whose body Hans was still holding? If not, what would happen to both of them?

And then there was no time for either worries or actions. The weak gravity of the planet seemed to vanish. Hans was in freefall, still holding his burden, dropping down through the deadly surface of Iceworld and on toward the unknown interior.

CHAPTER FIFTEEN
The perfect embodied computer.

E. Crimson Tally had been reluctant to talk at any length to Julian Graves and the others about the changes and improvements made since his first embodiment. That would sound too much like boasting.

For example, having attosecond circuitry seemed on the face of it like a good thing, something you would want all of the time. Years ago, within days of his initial embodiment and activation, he had learned otherwise. Yes, he could think trillions of times as fast as any organic intelligence, and with an accuracy and repeatability beyond their imagining; but as one consequence of that speed he had been obliged to spend almost all his time *waiting*, as he was now waiting. How would Darya Lang like it, if she asked E.C. a question and then had to hang around ten years before she had an answer?

He had learned to get by, sitting quietly and calculating the first ten billion prime numbers or seeking repeating digit strings in pi while he waited for the first word of response, but you could only stand so much of that. Among the improvements in his second embodiment was one that he had specifically requested: he wanted a stand-by mode. And he didn't mean simply the one he'd had before, which dropped his internal clock rate by a factor of a thousand or a million. No, he wanted a *genuine* stand-by mode, in which he could "sleep" the way that others slept, brought back to consciousness only when his senses were jogged by some external event—such as someone finally getting around to answering his question.

Now he had that ability to sleep, and it was better than anyone else's. Like them, he could wake when provided by an outside stimulus. But he could also set his internal timer to a precise interval and become active when a second, a week, a month, or a century had passed.

E.C. Tally's own logic circuits made him amend that thought. He could not be *certain* that sleep for a long interval would work, since he himself had only tested periods up to one day. On the other hand, the required changes had been put in place by Sue Harbeson Ando and Lee Boro, back on Miranda, and those two ladies were perfectionists. True, they had never managed to fix his smile so it didn't make other humans shudder, but that was nerves and muscle connections, not computer functions. He had complete confidence in Ando and Boro. They had certainly tightened and adjusted him in other desirable ways.

Deliberately, E.C. allowed his thoughts to wander to time travel and to the paradoxes that the idea introduced. Suppose that a man went back in time, and killed his own grandfather? Would he then cease to exist? Maybe he would, and maybe he wouldn't. Tally felt quite comfortable, whereas considerations of time travel in his earlier unimproved form had sent him into a loop from which only a cold start could rescue him.

And quantum theory, with all its now-you-see-it now-you-don't peekaboo elements? He was just as comfortable with that. His brain could now handle everything from Lukasiewicz's three-valued logic, to Reichenbach's infinite-valued logic with its continuous range of truth-values.

Tally permitted himself the luxury of one final test. He turned his mind to Russell's statement of the granddaddy of all true/false problems: "A barber in a certain village shaves all those, and only those, who do not shave themselves. Does the barber shave himself?"

Well, if he doesn't shave himself, then since he shaves everyone who doesn't shave himself, he shaves himself. On the other hand, if he shaves himself . . .

E.C. pursued the endless logical trail, on through the theory of types, meta-set theory, and fuzzy logic. It ate up idle time in a pleasant manner. Only the greater pleasure of a call from Julian Graves could exceed it.

"Tally, I know you are eager to leave, but I have kept you here because I have a task for you."

At last. After a full day of idleness. Tally switched his circuits from background to turbo mode. "I am ready."

"This will involve colossal amounts of computation. It will possibly exceed your resources."

"We shall see."

Tally was merely being polite. Of course, it had come nowhere close to straining his capabilities. The amount of calculation was gigantic, but he had it completed, checked, and re-checked in a few hours. Now, surely, he would be allowed to leave.

But no. Once again he was obliged to sit in stand-by mode, this time for an even longer period. At last the second call came.

"The results that you provided are most satisfactory. Are you still prepared for departure?"

"I am completely ready. My ship is also ready." *In fact, I have been ready for days, while you have brooded over the doings of Professor Lang and Captain Rebka and the results that I gave you.* Tally kept the last sentence to himself—another of the many improvements installed in his new embodiment.

"Then you may proceed with your mission. Good luck, and do not forget to keep me informed as to whatever you may discover."

Do not forget. As though an embodied computer ever would or could forget. "I will keep you informed."

Tally took the final steps to free his own ship, the *Tally-ho*, from its magnetic bonds to the *Pride of Orion*. As he did so, it occurred to him that his current embodiment was perfect, in that it could not be improved.

In a sense he was correct. It could not be improved,

because no one had ever managed to define good judgment, still less create a working algorithm to provide it.

Tally had not wasted time while Julian Graves kept him tied to the *Pride of Orion*'s apron strings. For three full days he had studied the stellar system to which their last Bose transition had brought them, working with unmatched speed and focus, endless patience, and the powers offered by his new ability to handle multi-valued logic systems.

The members of the expedition party from the Orion Arm were all in full agreement: they had not chosen this destination. It had been fed to them as Bose network coordinates, derived from the log of the Chism Polypheme's ship. When they arrived at an obviously dead system, everyone said, Oh, that's so typical of a Polypheme. It lied, they always lie. But suppose that the Polypheme had lied, and at the same time told the truth? Then in that case the stellar system to which they had come was both the wrong place to find the Marglotta home world, and at the same time the right place.

E.C. could live with that notion. When the *Tally-ho* pulled away from its docking he knew exactly where he wanted to go. Of course, he would eventually head for the edge of the dark zone, just as he had said he would, and hope in that way to arrive at the world of the Marglotta. Before taking his leave, however, there were points of interest right here in this system.

One of them was Iceworld, but Professor Lang had already staked her claim to that. Tally had read every report beamed back from the *Savior,* and he questioned Lang's assessment that no matter what had been done to it recently, the big, hollow world had begun as a Builder artifact. Unlike everyone else on the *Pride of Orion*, he did not reject Darya Lang's idea of a second super-race (perhaps a race of computers?). But didn't it then make sense that they, rather than the Builders, had created Iceworld?

If so, the rest of the system was wide open as a possible hiding place for *real* Builder artifacts. Tally, after analysis that would have taken any human a million years of calculation, had a candidate.

His conversation with Julian Graves on the subject had been less than satisfactory.

"This body." E.C. Tally indicated on a whole-system display a medium-sized planetoid moving in an orbit far out from the dark star that formed the center of the gravitating set of worlds.

"What about it?" Julian Graves glared at the insignificant object, his great bald brow furrowed with impatience or suspicion. Sometimes Tally wondered if Graves approved of embodied computers. "I've never seen a more average lump of rock."

"Councilor, it doesn't rotate."

"I can see that. But it's very common for planets and moons not to rotate. They become tidally locked to some other body."

"Tidally locked bodies *do* rotate. They turn so that they always present the same face to the parent, which means their day is the same as their year. But they rotate. *Everything* rotates, everything in the universe: electrons, protons, atoms, molecules, moons, planets, stars, gas clouds, galaxies—everything but that planetoid in the display."

"Let me see the data." Julian Graves stared at the screen filled with numbers provided by E.C. and went silent for half a minute.

Tally computed tenth roots for the first million integers and waited impatiently. He knew what was happening. Julian Graves had once been two separate entities, Julius Graves and an interior mnemonic twin. The twin had originally been intended as no more than a memory augment, housed in an added pair of cerebral hemispheres inside Julius Graves's big-domed head. The emergence of a second personality, Steven Graves, had been a surprise to everyone. The two had slowly merged, to become Julian Graves, but for certain tasks it was still better to maintain separation.

Like now. Steven had the computational talent, and it was of an order that even Tally had learned to respect. At quiet moments in the past they had indulged in calculation face-offs, and sometimes—to Tally's amazement—Steven Graves held his own. They had discussed it, and decided that although E.C. had better circuit speeds than human neurons by a factor of ten to the fifteenth, Steven compensated for that by the specialized pattern recognition hardware built into the human brain, and by computational parallelism which Tally could not match.

Now Steven must be performing his own analysis of the data. That deduction was verified when Julian Graves blinked his blue eyes, nodded, and said, "Indeed, the planetoid does not appear to rotate with respect to the most distant parts of the universe. But the observations you have provided, like all measurements, are accurate only to within certain confidence limits. We feel obliged to point out that rotational speeds of objects follow statistical distributions. Thus there is a finite probability that a given rotation speed, no matter how small, will be encountered. That is what we are seeing here."

"May I speak?"

But speaking had done no good at all. He had been unable to persuade Julian Graves that the non-rotating planetoid was worthy of investigation. Tally had terminated the discussion before it could go on too long. He was learning the ways of humans. Better to stop talking, take the *Tally-ho* on its way, and offer direct proof to Julian Graves that Tally was right and Steven was wrong.

Unfortunately that might be no easy task. The ship was closing fast on the planetoid, and the observation chamber at the front of the *Tally-ho* offered a direct view of what even E.C. had to admit was an unpromising object.

Tally's find was so small that although gravity could hold it together, it could not impose the spherical shape common to large bodies. From a distance it appeared as an uneven chip of dark rock, about seventy kilometers long and perhaps half that along each of the other main axes. Tally used a high-magnification scope and searched for any sign of the Phages that often swarmed near Builder artifacts. He saw nothing. He performed a routine laser scan of the surface, and read the reflected spectrum. Rock, rock, and more rock. Of course, since the body was not turning on any axis he could examine only one side of it, but when

Tally calculated the odds not even he could hold out hope that the other side would be any different.

It was time to give up, accept that Steven Graves was right and E.C. was wrong, and move on to his official mission of seeking the edge of the dark zone and the planet of the Marglotta. Except that while he had been busy examining the reflected spectrum, the *Tally-ho* had continued to close on its target. The navigation equipment would not permit a collision—it was far too smart for that—but when E.C. raised his head and glanced again through the port of the observation chamber, the chip of rock had grown to a great uneven lump that filled the whole sky.

And it had changed. The whole surface, uniform from a distance, was marked by a regular pattern of studs. It looked to Tally as though a meticulous, gigantic, insane, and over-active riveter had been given a free hand on the planetoid. He rejected that hypothesis on the basis of its improbability, and upon giving the surface a closer inspection realized that he had confused bulges with indents. Those were not studs, they were holes. The body was riddled with them. He glanced at the range monitor, estimated the angle subtended by one of the holes, and at once knew its diameter: 2.7 meters. More than wide enough to admit a suited human, but not nearly enough to permit the *Tally-ho* to enter.

So what now?

He had agreed to keep Julian Graves informed as to anything he found, but a message sent to Graves would surely lead to an undesirable result. E.C. would be told to stay where he was until the survival team specialists came to offer assistance. It would do no good to point out that Tally's brain, if not his body, could survive an acceleration of hundreds of gees and temperatures up to four thousand degrees. That was more than could be said for any human, no matter how well trained.

E.C. edged the *Tally-ho* sideways and closer to the planetoid, so that he could shine a beam directly down one of the round holes. The blackness within was absolute, with no sign of reflected light. He wondered how that could be, and what material lined the tunnel. It would surely be all right for him to determine at least that much information. Although Graves had told E.C. to keep the *Pride of Orion* informed, he had not suggested that every independent action was forbidden.

Tally commanded the *Tally-ho* to maintain a precise fifty-meters separation from the planetoid. He put on a suit and went across to the communications console.

I have discovered a planetoid to which some intelligent agent may have made modifications. My signal beacon will direct you here, should you feel it worthwhile to investigate. E. Crimson Tally.

That was enough. He really was beginning to understand how humans thought and operated. Be casual. More was less.

He instructed the console to send his message after a five minute delay. That would give him enough time to leave the *Tally-ho* and make his way to the surface of his find.

As soon as he arrived inside he knew why there had been no reflection from the walls of the tunnel. There *were* no walls. The hole that Tally had entered expanded outward as soon as he was inside. The slab had no interior, it was nothing more than a paper-thin shell surrounding vacuum. He could see tiny circles of starlight, entering through the million other holes scattered all over the surface.

As a possible Builder artifact this was a total failure. It contained no mysteries, and it just sat there and did nothing at all.

Tally was ready to retreat when he noted something slightly unusual. While outside the planetoid, the gravitational force exerted on him had been tiny, hardly enough to notice. That was just as it should be for such a small body. But now that he was inside, his suit had to apply a constant thrust to hold him in position.

He turned off that thrust, and at once began to fall. That made no sense at all; or rather, it made sense only if some invisible object of high density sat at the middle of the lump of rock.

It was still of no more than slight interest, but since he was here he might as well take a look. E.C. allowed himself to drop for a few more kilometers. His suit's inertial system kept a continuous track on how far he had fallen, and just how long it was taking. His conversion of those numbers to a law of force was automatic and almost instantaneous, and it occupied only a tiny fraction of his attention. The results were another matter. They concentrated all his resources. Since he was falling freely he had felt no force on his body, but his acceleration had been increasing exponentially. If he fell for another twenty-six kilometers, the extrapolated value was infinite.

Nothing in nature produces infinite acceleration. Tally knew that very well. It was probable that his computer brain would withstand whatever forces it was exposed to. His body was another matter. It was as weak as any human's. If he damaged another embodiment beyond repair, he would never hear the last of it.

Those thoughts were completed inside a nanosecond. He switched his suit at once to its highest level of upward thrust. His inertial positioning system indicated he was still falling. That was no surprise. It took time to cancel out his downward speed, and start him back up toward the surface. Then he realized that the situation was worse than that. His *acceleration* was still in the wrong direction. The thrust provided by his suit was not sufficient to balance the downward force, and that force increased with every passing second.

It couldn't be any type of high-density natural body at the middle of the hollow planetoid. The attraction was too strong for that. So what was it?

Tally had been falling with his body in a vertical position. He looked down, past the boots of his suit, and saw directly beneath him a rolling whirlpool of black oil, curling and tumbling on itself. As he watched, it grew rapidly in size. In another split-second he would fall into its depths.

E.C. felt the enormous satisfaction of one whose theories had been fully vindicated. This *was* a Builder artifact. The proof of that was right below him, in the form of a Builder transport vortex.

As he dropped into the churning heart of the whirlpool,

his attosecond mental circuits had time for a last twinge of conscience. Despite his promise, it was unlikely that in the immediate future he would be able to report his discovery to Julian Graves.

CHAPTER SIXTEEN
And then there were none.

First the *Have-It-All* flew away. The ship vanished into the nearby Bose node, taking with it—to who-knew-where—Louis Nenda, Atvar H'sial and their slaves, along with survival specialist Sinara Bellstock. Next to leave were Hans Rebka and Darya Lang, flying off to Iceworld with Ben Blesh and Lara Quistner. Finally, E.C. Tally departed.

The *Pride of Orion*—what was left of it, after giving birth to the *Savior* and the *Tally-ho*—felt like a dead ship.

At first Torran Veck and Teri Dahl avoided each other's company. Both felt like failures, the specialists that no one had a use for. Neither wanted the company of still another failure. But finally, with the arrival of Tally's message, they had to talk to each other.

"What does he mean, *I have discovered a planetoid to which some intelligent agent may have made modifications?*" Teri Dahl was lightly built, with long, slim limbs, dark-brown hair, and a coffee complexion. Her constant irritation was being mistaken for a child. She was sitting cross-legged on the bunk in Torran Veck's cabin. "If that embodied computer were a human, he'd be a moron. Tally couldn't have been more vague if he tried."

"It's ridiculous." Torran Veck occupied—and overflowed—

the only chair. "Graves received that message hours ago, and since then there hasn't been another word. Suppose Tally is in trouble? We know the exact location of his ship, and you and I are trained survival specialists. Why aren't we heading out there. Why are we sitting doing nothing?"

"Why are we here at all, when Ben Blesh and Sinara Bellstock and Lara Quistner are away on assignments?" Teri glanced at the cabin eye, confirming that it was turned off. It was, but even so she lowered her voice. "When we were in our final stages of training, did you have an affair with one of the instructors?"

"What if I did?" If Torran Veck was startled by the sudden change of subject, he did not let it show. "It wasn't forbidden, and I wasn't the only one. I certainly didn't get favored treatment on any of the tests—Mandy was probably harder on me than anyone else."

"I believe you. I'm not suggesting you had an easy time. But I'll tell you one thing. If I'd had something going with an instructor, after our training was all done there were certain questions I couldn't have resisted asking Mandy."

"Like?"

"Like how well I had done, compared with others. That wouldn't be giving me an advantage. It would just be pillow talk."

"Mm." Torran Veck had a big, fleshy nose. He tended to pinch the bridge between finger and thumb when he was thinking. He held it now. "What gave us away? We agreed there would be no signs of public affection and no favoritism. Otherwise we'd both have been in trouble."

"You overdid it. Both of you. In the classes, Mandy was hard on you when there was no reason. And you never looked directly at her."

"Mm."

"Well? Did you? Ask questions, I mean, about how you had done?"

"Maybe."

"And perhaps how other people had done?"

"So what if I did? Teri, where are you taking this?"

"I didn't have Mandy's ear, but all during training I couldn't help comparing the members of our group. I watched you perform, and Lara, and everyone else. I bet you did the same."

"Of course I did."

"But you had Mandy to confirm your gut reactions. I didn't. I'll tell you what I think, and I'd like your comment. All right?"

"Maybe."

"There were two stand-out trainees in our group. Their names were Torran Veck and Teri Dahl. You and me. We were easily the best of the bunch, and there was hardly a whisker separating our final scores."

Torran stopped holding the bridge of his nose. "Are you sure you didn't have inside information?"

"Not a scrap. But I use my eyes and ears, same as you do. Comments?"

"Some of these are Mandy's, not mine—though I agree with you and her, we were both top of the class, kick-ass compared with the others. Ben's smart, but he has these feelings of inadequacy. That makes him want to do wild things, just to prove he can. He gets scared, but he'll try to be a hero even if it kills him. If Ben gets into trouble it will be because he thinks that when you are in charge it's a weakness to say you don't understand or don't know. Lara is smart, too—hell, we all are. But her personality has a built-in contradiction. She doesn't really want to run things. So she takes orders—but then she resents being given them. She will get into trouble trying to prove that she makes command decisions as well as anyone, when in fact she doesn't."

He paused, until Teri asked, "That leaves Sinara. What about her?"

"Mandy has a soft spot for Sinara."

"So do you."

"A little. I have a soft spot for you, too, but not enough to distort my judgment of either of you. Sinara ought never to have become a survival specialist. She has mood swings. Sometimes she's all dreamy and romantic, sometimes she's a practicing nymphomaniac."

"You would know, I suppose."

"Don't go by rumors. Anyway, Sinara isn't exactly what

you would call a responsible person. If Ben is looking to be a hero, Sinara is looking to find one. Mandy believes Sinara only went into this business because her family wanted her to—father's dying wish and all that. He was in the same line of work, killed in the Castlemaine disaster. But Sinara shouldn't be looking after other people. She needs somebody to look after *her*."

"Now she's off with Louis Nenda and his crew of alien thugs. Heaven help her. I can't see him taking care of anybody but himself."

"Look on the bright side. Maybe this is what she needs to sort her out. But I don't think you asked if you could come to my cabin so we could sympathize with Sinara or anyone else. Where are you going with all this?"

"I'm going to see Julian Graves. But I wanted to talk to you first." Teri uncrossed her legs and stood up from the bunk in one easy movement. "I think you ought to come with me. You've confirmed what I have been thinking, now let's find out what Graves has in his head. He must have been given a detailed report on each of us before the *Pride of Orion* ever left Upside Miranda Port. I want to ask him: Why has he left his best two survival team members—no time for false modesty, Arabella Lund as good as told us that herself—to sit here staring at our belly buttons, while others who are less qualified are taking the risks?"

Teri had felt and sounded totally confident when she talked to Torran Veck. She could feel that assurance draining away when their knock on the door of Graves's cabin was answered with a quiet, "Enter."

The councilor managed to be a formidable presence without even trying. It wasn't his size—Torran topped him by half a head. And it wasn't his manner, which was unfailingly polite and courteous. Maybe it was the knowledge that the misty blue eyes of Julian Graves had looked on multiple cases of genocide. The brain within the bulging cranium had been forced to make lose-lose decisions that condemned whole species in order to spare others. Every one of those choices was graven in the deep furrows on face and forehead.

There was no sign of that traumatic past in the warm
smile that greeted Teri and Torran, or in the friendly, "What
can I do for you?"

Teri's self-confidence dropped another notch. It was Torran
who finally said, "Can we put it the other way round?
Everyone else is busy, working to find a way to reach the
Marglotta home world. Teri and I have been sitting around
for days, totally useless. What can we do for you, or for
anybody?"

"To begin with, you can sit down." Graves waved them to
seats. His cabin on the *Pride of Orion* was bigger than anyone else's, but so crowded with consoles and displays there
was hardly room for its table and six chairs. Teri slid in easily
enough, but Torran had to squeeze through and fitted the
space between table and wall like a cork in a bottle.

Graves went on, "I have been well aware of your lack
of activity, and I expected your arrival before this. Let me
congratulate you on the patience that you have shown.
However, it was impossible for me to meet usefully with
you until certain other activities were complete. When you
learn what those activities imply, perhaps you will decide
that your enforced idleness was not so bad after all."

He placed himself so that he faced Teri and Torran directly
across the table. "You have borne with me for a long time.
I ask you to bear with me a little longer, for what may
initially seem to be a tedious explanation of the obvious.
My aim will fairly soon become clear; but first, a simple
fact: there are at least thirty sentient species scattered around
our own Orion Arm. In my role as Ethical Councilor, I have
encountered and been obliged to deal with more than half
of those. An equal number of intelligent species probably
exist here in the Sagittarius Arm, although the only one with
which I have direct experience is the Chism Polyphemes.
The species vary widely in their physiology, their reproductive
habits, their life styles, and their notions of morality. What
they do *not* vary in—what is common to every one of
them—is the underlying logic of their thought processes.
When it comes to the way that we think, even the most
alien species follows the same patterns as we do. Are you
with me so far?"

Teri said, "We all think the same. Except—" She paused, unsure of herself.

Graves smiled. "My dear, I see that you are not only with my argument, you are ahead of it. As you say, *except*. Except that we find ourselves in a situation for which the laws of logic do not appear to apply. Before we embarked on this journey we were provided—you might say, spoon-fed—a set of Bose transition coordinates to carry us across the Gulf. Our end point was to be the Marglotta home world. We crossed the Gulf successfully. But rather than finding the Marglotta, instead we find this." He waved an arm. "This, a barren system where the central star suffered some unnatural fate, where there is no sign of life, and where one planet is impossibly cold. The general answer was to blame the perfidious Polypheme. As a habitual liar, it had deliberately directed us to this system in order to keep secret the whereabouts of our real destination. Everyone agreed, we should not be here. Everyone was eager to be on their way immediately, to find and proceed to Marglot.

"You may argue that I could have said no. I could have insisted that we do additional analysis. I am, after all, the official leader of this expedition. But as you will one day discover, a leader is not a leader because of the way that he or she behaves. He is a leader only because of the way that he is *treated by others*. On this expedition there are individuals with far more experience than I of unknown territories and hidden danger. Unlike you, they lack respect for authority. Had I attempted to propose analysis rather than action, I would have faced open rebellion. Uncomfortable as I was with my own decision, I therefore permitted them to go. I would, however, remain here. I did not reject the need for action. I merely postponed it, until I could prove a conjecture. And I would keep with me the most competent members of the survival team."

Torran nodded and smiled. Teri did not smile, and she felt embarrassed. She wondered why the councilor was taking such care to lavish compliments. He wanted something from them, but what could it be?

Graves went on, "Let me tell you my difficulty, and see how you react. I have been puzzled since the moment we arrived here by three observations which are either facts, or at least strong conjectures. First, everyone has emphasized that the Chism Polypheme was dead when it arrived at Miranda. Polyphemes enjoy enormously long life spans. Surely this means that the Polypheme never *expected* to die in transit. It thought that it would bring the Marglotta to Miranda, and return with them—and us—to the Sag Arm. Second, the death of the Marglotta on the Polypheme's ship was also not anticipated. They, too, must have expected to reach us and tell us of their problems. They hoped we would go with them to their home world of Marglot. So the fact that Polyphemes are traditional liars is not relevant, unless the Marglotta are also liars. Not one persistently lying species, but two? As I told Professor Lang on another subject, I do not like to concatenate implausibilities. And now for my third observation: there were many Marglotta on the ship—eighteen of them. There was a single Chism Polypheme, and the Polyphemes are justly famous as navigators. If you agree with all this, what conclusions would you draw?"

Teri and Torran turned to glance at each other. He gave a little wave of his index finger. *You first.*

She grimaced. *Thanks a lot. Let me be wrong.* And to Julian Graves, "It was the Marglotta's idea to come to the Orion Arm. They were in charge, and the Polypheme was just a hired hand."

"Precisely. Which means?"

Teri nudged Torran's leg under the table. *Your turn.*

He grunted, and said, "There would be no point at all in the Polypheme trying to keep the final destination secret. The Marglotta would have been right there to answer our questions."

"And therefore?"

"We didn't blunder into this system by accident. It was intended that our ship would arrive, just where we did— and it must be possible to reach Marglot *through a Bose transition point located right here.*"

"Exactly. Which leaves a single question, but one with huge potential consequences: we can reenter the same node by which we came here. It is sitting a few minutes away. But what transition sequence from here might take us to Marglotta?"

Teri and Torran glanced across at one of the displays, where a faint circle of opalescence indicated the presence of the nearby Bose node.

The theory that explained the Bose network in terms of multi-connected spacetimes was so complex that very few people understood it. The practical use was another matter. It was often said that any fool with a suitably equipped ship could enter a Bose node; but that only an absolute fool would try it, without first being in possession of the eighty-four digits that specified the connection between an entry node and the desired exit point. Used correctly, the Bose network had a zero failure rate. Used incorrectly, by specifying an invalid digit stream, one of two things would happen. If you were lucky and you made an error in the *entry point* digits, the string would be rejected and you would pop back into normal space exactly where you had entered the node. If you were unlucky and you made an error in the *exit point* digits, you might know your fate but no one else would. Ships which were discovered by retrospective analysis to have used an invalid exit digit set were never heard from again.

"An impossible problem." Julian Graves was closely watching the expression on the others' faces. "We know where we are, which gives us the input coordinates for a Bose transition. We could follow the method used by Louis Nenda and the *Have-It-All*, pick some other Bose node, generate the entire digit string, make the jump, and hope we arrive where we want to be. With the screening process they propose, that certainly won't be the Marglot system. But it might be a place where someone can tell them how to reach that system. Fairly simple, probably fairly safe, but at best an indirect approach. However, I don't want just any exit node. I want the digit string of the *correct* exit node—in the Marglot system."

Teri said, "Which means we must know the exact string of forty-two numbers. I don't like those odds."

"Nor do I. I asked—or, to be more specific, Steven, who is better at this kind of thing than I am, asked—how much those odds might be improved using other information. We cannot achieve *certainty*, that would be too much to ask for, but can we reduce the risk to an acceptable level?"

Torran Veck raised his eyebrows, which Teri took to mean, *Are you out of your mind?*

But no one spoke, until Julian Graves continued. "What do we know? Well, we have the exact sequences for a couple of thousand Bose nodes in our own Orion Arm, plus everything for the Bose nodes defined in the Sag Arm and held within the data bank of the Polypheme's ship. If Bose digit strings were random, that would not be any use at all. We would be ruling out only a few thousand numbers, and leaving endless trillions of trillions of possible but incorrect sequences. It does not take the computational powers of Steven or E.C. Tally to recognize that avenue leads nowhere. At the same time, I remained convinced that we were all missing something. The clue as to what that might be came when I was pondering the way that the Chism Polypheme at Miranda Port died. We know that a Polypheme will normally live for many thousands of years—we don't know quite how many—before it succumbs to natural causes. That's why it was so surprising to encounter a dead one. But turn that logic around. A Polypheme will live for ages, but it can be killed, like anything else, by violence or by accident. We often emphasize that Polyphemes don't tell the truth, but maybe we should emphasize even more that *they do not take risks.* Think how averse to danger you would be if your normal life expectancy extended over many thousands of years. That tells us something else. No Polypheme would ever expose itself to the totally avoidable risk of attempting a Bose transition with an invalid digit string. And that has another implication."

Torran said softly, "The Polypheme had all the sequences to bring us here. He must also have possessed the correct sequence to return to the final Marglot destination."

"Exactly so. He would not have risked *remembering* it. Nor would he store the sequence in an open file. The number string must have been stored somewhere in the ship's data banks, in a hidden place from which the Polypheme could recall it when it was needed."

"But the data banks—" Teri paused. "They don't have just

millions or billions of numbers, they have many trillions of them. Everything from artifact catalogs to navigational data to engineering data. I'm sure they also contain all the standard encyclopedias for many worlds and many species."

"Quite true. An impossible job, right, to find the forty-two digit sequence that we need? Impossible to us, that is—but not impossible to E.C. Tally. It's a natural for him. Remember, he already downloaded everything in the Polypheme ship's data banks into his own memory.

"I asked him to do four things. First, to take the known digit sequences of every known Bose node, and derive from them as many characteristic string properties and statistics as he could. Second, to sort out from the data banks of the Polypheme ship every discrete and identifiable forty-two-digit sequence—I knew there would be trillions of them. Third, to test every one of those sequences to see if they possessed the statistical properties derived from known Bose node sequences. And finally, to provide a ranked list of matches in order of their goodness of fit, together with some numerical measure of confidence in the result."

Teri muttered, almost to herself, "An absolutely monstrous job."

"Agreed. It is monstrous, even Steven admitted that it would be quite beyond him. But it's meat and drink to an embodied computer like Tally. He ate it up. I had no idea how long it might take him, days or weeks or months. But he was finished in a few hours. Do you want to see the results?"

The councilor did not wait for an answer. A long table of figures appeared on the wall display behind him. While Torran and Teri studied it, he went on, "As you can see, we have no certainties, no hundred percent fit."

"But isn't that wrong?" Torran Veck was scowling at the screen. "If the number one choice really does represent a Bose node, shouldn't it be on the list?"

"I don't think so. The Chism Polypheme didn't want his private navigation secrets revealed to anybody who tapped his ship's data banks. He deliberately excluded the Bose coordinates of the final destination from his 'official' list of nodes."

"Seventy-two percent probability." Teri had scanned the whole list. "That's the best fit. It's not very good. And the next one is way down, at only eight percent odds."

"Is the glass half full, or is it half empty? Seventy-two percent doesn't sound too great, I agree. But it's so enormously better than eight percent, what are the chances that one match so good would pop up at random?"

Torran said, "You tell us."

"I'll tell you what Steven says. It's only one in a thousand that the digit string you are looking at isn't a genuine Bose sequence. But that doesn't mean most of you will survive if you try it and it's wrong. It's all, or it's nothing. And I'm certainly not going to try to persuade you to take the risk. I'd be quite happy if you would agree to stay here, with the *Pride of Orion*, and serve to coordinate whatever anyone else learns."

Teri asked, "While you do what?"

"While I grow another ship, and make a Bose transition with it."

"Forget that." Torran tried to stand up, but there was not enough space at the table to permit it. "We were trained as survival team members. You just told us that we were the best of the group. Arabella Lund as much as said the same thing. If you go, we go. What are *your* qualifications in survival training?"

"Very limited. I could say that I have survived a large number of dangerous situations, but most of those could have been pure luck. However, that is irrelevant. Do you—both of you—wish to make the Bose transition with me?"

In unison, "We do." Torran added, "Damn right we do. If you like *we'll* go without *you*—we were trained in survival techniques. But no way are you going without us."

"Then there are numerous preparations to be made. A new ship must be grown. Since the *Pride of Orion* will be without a crew, it must be left in a suitable condition to receive and relay all messages arriving from others. I must also send word of our proposed actions to Professor Lang's group, and to E.C. Tally. If you will excuse me . . . "

Graves hurried out. Torran Veck, pushing hard, moved the

table far enough for him to move from behind it and stand up. He said, "A bit eager to leave us, don't you think? You know what that means?"

"I have a good idea."

"Graves had all his information days ago, before E.C. Tally left. He has been sitting on it, waiting."

"Right." Teri, penned in by Torran, was at last free to move from her seat. "Waiting until we went stir crazy and came looking for him. He knew that by now we would be so keen to see action, we would go along with whatever he suggested."

"So we were manipulated." Torran shook his head. "By a master. He's damn good at it. Maybe that's what it takes to be an Ethical Councilor—patience and cunning. I hope there's more to it than that."

"We could always back out." They stared at each other, until Teri laughed. "No way, right? Better death than terminal boredom. But we have only seventy-two percent odds in our favor. That means there's a twenty-eight percent chance that we'll make a Bose jump, and end up God-knows-where, or nowhere at all. What then?"

"*Then?*" Torran draped his massive arm over Teri's shoulder. "Why, then we find out how good as survival specialists we really are. Come on, Teri. If we're going to kill ourselves, I'd rather get it over with sooner than later."

The *No Regrets*, created from the shrinking body of the *Pride of Orion* and newly named by Teri Dahl, stood at the very edge of the Bose node. Torran Veck was checking the final matching of entry velocity.

"As good as it gets," he said. "If the exit sequence is wrong, a few millimeters a second won't make any difference at all. We'll be in limbo. Whenever you are ready."

Julian Graves was at an observation window. He was staring not at the nearby pearly radiance of the Bose node, but far off to where Iceworld, invisible to all sensors, orbited its dark primary.

"I wish we could have had word from Professor Lang before we left," he said. "We have received nothing—not even their signal beacon."

"Whenever you are ready."

"I heard you." Graves sighed. "Go ahead. After three days of silence, another minute is unlikely to make a difference. And the *Pride of Orion* will continue to wait for signals, from us or the others, for as long as needed."

Torran Veck guided the *No Regrets* forward into the Bose node. Behind them, the parent ship began its lonely vigil. The power supply was enough to allow it to monitor events for a million years. Even so, Julian Graves was wrong when he said that the ship would wait for their signals for as long as needed. Neither Graves nor the ship's computer knew it, but all members of the *Pride of Orion*'s crew, human and alien, had departed this stellar system and would never return.

CHAPTER SEVENTEEN
Pleasureworld.

Until he ran into Sinara Bellstock on his way into the *Pride of Orion*, Louis Nenda had never met anyone who called herself a "survival specialist." Didn't everybody do their best to survive? Consider the alternative.

Louis listened, at first with interest and then with horror, as Sinara explained.

"Martial arts, of course. We have experience in every known form of weapon. I received the maximum possible class grade for the use of projectile devices. Our work was done in every environment you can imagine—free-fall, high gravity, low gravity, dense atmosphere, poisonous atmosphere, hard vacuum, and intense radiation fields. I trained on frozen ice caps of water and solid nitrogen, and deep in oceans of water and liquid methane."

"Hold on a minute. Are you saying you were taken to planets with all of these?"

"Not exactly. We operated in simulated setups. I mean, our budget was generous, but there were limits. It was all right, though, the training facility on Persephone can mimic any place you care to mention."

There were places Nenda didn't care to mention or ever

think about again. He asked, "What about aliens? Were you trained to deal with aliens?"

"Naturally. We expected that we would have to work with any clade, in any part of the spiral arm. I mean our own spiral arm, of course—no one ever thought we would be sent to the Sag Arm. But we are ready for anything. Did I mention that I had long sessions in unarmed combat?" Sinara gave Louis an enigmatic smile. "Those were with humans as well as aliens. If you would like to test me out, maybe you and I could try a tussle—sometime when we have more privacy."

Was that what it sounded like? Nenda plowed on. "So, for instance, you could tackle somebody like At there?"

He gestured to Atvar H'sial. The Cecropian was sitting at the other side of the *Have-It-All*'s most comfortable cabin, silent but doing the pheromonal equivalent of glowering.

"Well, tackle is probably the right word." Sinara eyed the hulking alien. "She's huge, isn't she? I never met one before, but I know from the simulations that a Cecropian is very strong. I'd do well to hold my own with her."

"Right. Hold your own. And how about that lot?" Nenda's jerk of the thumb included J'merlia, Kallik, and Archimedes, huddled together in a strange heap at the end of the cabin that led to the ship's main galley.

"As I understand it, a Lo'tfian won't fight, no matter what you do to him. We didn't have training experience with a simulated Zardalu, because we were told that they had been extinct for thousands of years. I certainly never expected to meet one." Sinara frowned, as though a suspicion that her training might have been less than complete had crossed her mind. "I was supposed to fight a Hymenopt, though. It seemed unfair, they're so little and cuddly. I heard that the poor things used to be hunted for their fur. Is that true?"

"The Hymantel, you mean? It's tough and water-resistant, and it insulates against heat and cold. Yes, people wanted to make clothes out of them, so they used to hunt Hymenopts. At least, they tried to. I never saw anybody wearing a Hymantel. But did you fight one?"

"Yes. I had to, it was part of the course."

"And how did it go?"

"Oh, I beat it. Rather easily, as a matter of fact. They are not nearly as formidable as some people will tell you."

Lightning reactions, acute vision, impenetrable hide, poison sting.

"A *real* Hymenopt, like Kallik there? Or a simulation?"

"A simulation. We were told that all living Hymenopts are out in the Zardalu Communion. I was surprised to see that you have one as a crew member."

"A slave, you mean." Nenda grunted. "Maybe sometime you'd like to try a tussle with Kallik."

"I might. But I don't think that would be nearly as much fun as one with you."

The terrible thing was, Louis suspected that she was right. He looked at the way she was sitting, sprawled back provocatively with one knee raised high and her bare foot on the seat of the chair. Her calf and thigh had the plump smooth firmness of youth. The big blue eyes and curls of golden hair suggested an innocence quite alien to Louis. He had the feeling that it was equally alien to Sinara.

He stood up abruptly. "We're through the node, and that's our destination neutron star showin' on the screen. I better go to the navigation deck an' check the planetary patterns."

His departure was only partially a pretext. Somebody on the ship ought to be taking practical survival steps, even if they had no formal training. The *Have-It-All* had the best computer that you could buy in the Orion Arm, but past a certain point an organic intelligence had to take over. The ship's detection system had already performed the first checks needed on entering a new stellar system. It had asked and answered the question, were there warning beacons or other evidence that a planetary approach would be regarded as hostile?

Of course there was always the danger that such signals might be unrecognizably different between Orion Arm and Sag Arm civilizations, but thousands of years of trade by the Chism Polyphemes encouraged the idea that the *Have-It-All*'s signal beacon and message of friendly intent would be familiar to at least one of the planetary receivers.

Louis seated himself at the navigation console. Without

a word being spoken, Kallik had trotted along behind and now crouched in the smaller seat at his side. She could react ten times as fast as he could, and in an emergency it was understood that she would take action on her own initiative.

Without looking at her, Nenda said, "So far, so good."

"I concur." Kallik's double ring of bright black eyes had scanned every display around the cabin walls. "The transition went as planned."

"Six planets. That's a hell of a lot for a neutron star."

"It is. But with respect, there is only one of interest. Five lack atmospheres, and they do not emanate structured radiation patterns consistent with the presence of intelligence."

Nenda stared at the fierce point of violet-blue that formed the system's primary. Most of the emitted energy was X-rays and hard ultraviolet, invisible to human eyes. And deadly.

"Think we'll be able to live on the sixth one? There's enough hot stuff coming out of that star to fry us."

"The atmosphere of the planet is breathable. The ionization at its outer edges will provide some protection, but special clothing and masking will be needed if we hope to operate down on the surface."

"Before we get to that, let's find out if there's anybody down there we'll be able to talk to."

"With respect, do you now wish me to seek to establish communication?"

"Better you than me. I don't know a word of Polypheme gargle."

"I will be honored. My feeling is that the unguarded nature of the signals coming from the planet implies pacific intent on their part."

"Go to it, then, see if you can raise anybody. I'll be back in a few minutes."

Nenda left as Kallik opened a communications channel. He headed not back to the main cabin, but farther forward toward the *Have-It-All*'s weapons control center.

Pacific intent was all very well. In Nenda's experience, once you learned to fake that you had it made.

❖❖   ❖❖   ❖❖

The *Have-It-All*'s space-to-surface pinnace held two humans comfortably and four at a pinch. Nenda had given the matter a good deal of thought before he made his decision.

"Look." He was explaining to Atvar H'sial. "She's the most dangerous sort of incompetent you can get. Completely wet behind the ears, but doesn't know it. If she's ever to learn what life is really like, better for her to do it here and now, where all the signs are that it will be pretty safe, rather than trying to learn when we are already in a bad fix. And it makes sense to use humans because that's who the Polypheme we'll be meeting is used to. You and Archimedes would put him right off. Not only that, you'd both have trouble fitting into the pinnace."

The Cecropian did not seem enthusiastic, but at least she didn't give Nenda a hard time. To lie using pheromones needed more skill than he possessed, and in this case he was speaking the exact truth and Atvar H'sial knew it.

The planet that the pinnace was drifting down to had an atmospheric haze that concealed detail. Only when they were below two thousand meters could Louis Nenda and Sinara Bellstock make out the rough terrain of jagged rocks and, lower still, mounds of purple and gray plant life. The spaceport was little more than a long cleared area, next to four low buildings with beyond them a great body of dark water.

"It doesn't look much like *Pleasureworld* to me." Sinara was staring out of the forward port with the enormous curiosity of one who had never visited worlds beyond her native regions of the Fourth Alliance. "Are you sure your Hymenopt understood what they were saying and translated it right?"

"Quite sure." Nenda brought the pinnace in close to the line of buildings at the end of the landing area. "Kallik heard it in Polypheme talk. I heard it myself in a language of the Zardalu Communion, once they found somebody down here who'd traded in the Orion Arm."

"Pleasureworld. That name is ridiculous." Sinara was wearing a heavy leaded oversuit and hat, opaque to both ultraviolet and X-rays. She wore dark goggles, and all exposed skin was coated with a thick yellow cream. She looked grotesquely unattractive. Nenda regarded it as protective garb in more than one sense of the word.

"The name isn't ridiculous at all—if you happen to be a Chism Polypheme or cater to them. There's a huge colony of Polyphemes here, according to Kallik, even though they are not native to Pleasureworld."

"Where *are* they native to?"

"A Polypheme never tells. But they're great travellers, and one of them here says he's totally fluent in human universal. In a few minutes we'll find out if he's telling the truth."

"If they're not born here, why do they come to such an awful place?"

"For the radiation. That's why At and I picked a neutron star as target. The UV intensity on the surface of this planet is a hundred times what our eyes and skin can stand, but the Polyphemes love it. If you went for a walk by the water's edge—which I don't recommend—you'd find hundreds of them out there, sunning themselves. Of course, it makes them drunk."

"Doesn't the radiation hurt them?"

"That's a matter of opinion. Does alcohol harm a human?" Nenda opened the hatch of the pinnace. Reflected radiation poured in and the air took on a smell of ozone, as though a continuing electrical discharge was going on. "We have to go outside, but we won't be there for long. Kallik has arranged for our contact to meet us in a shielded setting. Come on, let's get this over as quick as we can. Even with protection, enough radiation gets through to give you a burn in a few minutes."

Sinara took a quick look around as she moved between pinnace and building. Close up, the plants between the buildings wore lethal-looking spines. The flowers at their tips were gray to human eyes, but in the hard ultraviolet region where the native pollinators of Pleasureworld lived, those flowers must glow and dazzle in a whole spectrum of colors.

She followed Nenda through a stone doorway and tunnel, and found herself after a few more paces in a chamber so dark that she was forced to remove her goggles to see anything at all. As her eyes adjusted, she found herself facing a green thing—alien? plant? animal?—perched on a slab of stone and balancing itself on a long curled tail.

The creature weaved slightly. It said in a croaking growl, "Here at last. What kept you? You brought me in out of a good hot sun-wallow, so this had better be good."

"We'll make it worth your while." If Nenda found the alien at all peculiar, he didn't show it. "I am Louis Nenda, and this is Sinara Bellstock. We are both from the Orion Arm."

"I can see that." The blubbery lips of a broad green mouth turned down in a scowl. "Humans, eh? My name in your talk is Claudius. I'm a Master Pilot, and I've travelled all the Orion Arm. Make it worth my while, you say? How? Backward, primitive place. Nothing there worth having."

"I think I can change your mind about that. I've worked with a Chism Polypheme before. Do you know Dulcimer? He's a Master Pilot, too, and he can vouch for us."

"I know Dulcimer. Master Pilot, he calls himself? Pah! Dulcimer is a hopeless amateur. Do you both know Dulcimer?"

Sinara shook her head, then, not sure that the gesture would be understood, said, "I don't know him."

"Lucky you." Claudius sniffed and bobbed up and down on his thick tail. The alien was a three-meter helical cylinder, an upright corkscrew of smooth muscle covered with rubbery green skin and with a head as wide as his body. One huge eye, bulging and shifty, peered out from under the wrinkled brow. The slate-gray organ was almost half as wide as Claudius's head. The mouth beneath it was wide and seemed to be fixed in a permanent sneer. Between the mouth and the big eye, a tiny gold-rimmed scanning eye, no bigger than a pea, continuously moved across the scene.

The midsection of Claudius was hidden by an orange garment, tight-fitting, from which protruded five three-fingered limbs, all on the same side of the flexible body.

Claudius tightened the angle of his spiral, so that his head moved down to be level with Louis Nenda's. "Tell me why you're here. Better make it quick, and make it good. Or I'll be gone. It's close to noon, and I'm missing the best part of the day."

"This won't take more than a minute. I know of a world,

a world in desperate need of help. It's dead, or it's dying. Whoever goes there will make a tremendous fortune. Either you take what you want because there is nobody to stop you, or the survivors will give you anything if you can save them."

"Ah. Interesting." The secondary eye continued its scanning, but the main optic fixed its attention on Nenda. "Back in the Orion Arm, is it?"

"Until we have a deal, I'm not saying where this world is."

"You can trust me, human."

"I wouldn't question that for a moment."

"Ah. But it's not clear *why* you need me. Unless this world of yours is hard to get to, and you're looking for the best pilot in the galaxy to take you there? If so, maybe we can do a deal."

"I don't think it's hard to get to." Nenda consulted a list, derived from the ship's data bank of the dead Marglotta. "Do you know of planets called Vintner, Blossom, Riser's Folly, Marglot, Meridian Wall, Desire, and Temblor?"

"Of course I do. I told you, I'm the best, and I've been piloting for ten thousand of your years. I know them all, and the best way to get to them. Near one of those, is it?"

"It might be."

"You're a long way from most. And I'll tell you now, I won't go near some of those places. Ships travel to them, never come back. Which one are you interested in?"

"We need to reach an agreement before I'll tell you more."

"Aye. I can understand that." Claudius stretched upward, uncoiling his tail a fraction. His main eye blinked and rolled toward Sinara, then back to Louis. "I think maybe you and I ought to have a bit of a chat, private-like. Man to man, as you would say."

He nodded toward Sinara and winked.

"Now wait a minute." If the first sight of Claudius had overwhelmed Sinara, she was over that. "I'm our ship's survival specialist."

"No danger here on Pleasureworld. What I have to say is personal."

"I don't care." Sinara put her hands on her hips. "I'm

not leaving. Anything you have to say, you say it while I am here."

"Then there will be nothing said. And no deal." Claudius elevated himself to his full height. "That's it for me. I'm off for a wallow-bake."

"Don't be ridiculous!"

Louis said, "Sinara, maybe if you—"

"You want me to take orders from that—that overgrown twisted *cucumber*? I won't."

"If he has something *personal* that he wants to say—maybe about Dulcimer—"

"Exactly." Claudius was nodding. "It's about Dulcimer. Very private, and very personal." He turned to Sinara. "Now, if you had known Dulcimer, like the captain here . . . then I'd have been free to talk to both of you."

"Five minutes. You have five minutes." Sinara snapped her goggles back in place and turned toward the chamber exit. As she was leaving she added, "And Louis, if you are not outside at our ship in five minutes I will be back in here. It's my job to make sure you are safe."

Claudius watched as she left, then bobbed after her on his corkscrew tail to make sure that she was not hiding outside where she could hear what was said.

Nenda said, "What's this about Dulcimer?"

"Forget Dulcimer. Dulcimer's a half-wit, I don't want to talk about him. Or a possible space deal, either. I've got something else in mind. That's a human female, isn't it, under all those coverings and horrible glop?"

"It is."

"Does it always give you so much trouble?"

"None of your business."

"Ah. Because you see, I was thinking." The broad mouth lost its scowl and took on a knowing leer. "Nobody in this part of the Sag Arm has ever seen a human female. Males, yes, now and again, but not a female—though I must say, even the males didn't look much like you. I wonder if they were genuine. Anyway, there's a freak show here on Pleasureworld, the biggest one within twenty lightyears. It's in a main resort, a town called Carnival not more than a few hours away. Now, if you were to take the female to

Carnival, put her in a cage, strip off all those coverings so visitors could get a close look at what's underneath—well, I'm telling you, that would be a star attraction. Let me have her, and we could be partners. We would both do well."

The temptation was enormous. Get rid of Sinara, with all the potential problems she promised, and at the same time cement the deal with Claudius. Atvar H'sial would agree. The others on the *Have-It-All* would not care. You could explain to Julian Graves, if you ever had another meeting with the Ethical Councilor, by saying—

Louis paused. By saying what? That you had sold Sinara?

He shook his head, and Claudius nodded understandingly. "I see. The old, old story. Mating with her, are you?"

"I am not!"

"But hoping to, eh?" The leer on the wide mouth broadened. "In that case, I'll bide my time. Once you've had her a few times, you'll likely be glad to be rid of her. Then we can come to an arrangement."

"It's a possibility. But let's leave that for the future. One deal at a time. What would you require to come with us, and serve as our pilot?"

"Using whose ship? Yours, or mine?"

"Mine. But does it matter?"

"Could matter a great deal. You don't get ships from the Orion Arm in these parts. Different basic principles, different technology. If we went in my ship, then you could leave yours here—"

"Forget it. It took years to get the *Have-It-All* the way I like. I'll not have anybody else's paws on it."

"First the female, now the ship. Bit touchy, aren't you? But if it's to be your vessel I'm piloting, that ups my price—and I'll need to have a good look-see before we talk terms. Some of the clapped-out bits of junk that people bring you, and ask you to fly! You'd not believe it."

"The *Have-It-All* is in perfect shape."

"I'll need to see that for myself. Where's your ship?"

"Synchronous equatorial orbit. We're beaconed, easy to find."

"Then I'll be up to visit. Tomorrow." Claudius nodded, and bobbed on his springy tail toward the exit. "I'm going to catch me a few rays." He sniffed. "Good luck with the female. Whatever good luck might mean in this case, you'd know that better than I would."

As Claudius was leaving he passed Sinara on the way in. She had heard his final remark, and was frowning.

She snapped at Nenda, "Good luck with the female? What did that disgusting object mean by that remark?"

"I have no idea."

But Louis thought of lost opportunities, and wondered how far it was to Carnival.

CHAPTER EIGHTEEN
Claudius.

Louis decided within fifteen minutes of Claudius's arrival aboard the *Have-It-All* that the Polypheme must be a uniquely competent pilot; otherwise, no one in the universe would employ an individual so rude, insulting, and cantankerous.

Claudius had arrived in his own vessel, a stuttering wreck with failing engines and a body so dilapidated and rusted that Nenda would have hesitated to take it in for salvage had he found the hulk in open space.

The fittings of the *Have-It-All* were magnificent, gathered with a true collector's eye that Louis Nenda did not realize he possessed. He just knew what he liked, and he had assembled those through the years from all over the Orion Arm. Claudius had no nose to turn up, but his sneering contempt for all that he saw showed on his other features.

"Vegetables? How can anything that calls itself civilized try to make a ship out of bits of *vegetation*?" Claudius ran the fingers of his five hands over a polished rail of rare Styx blackwood, "borrowed" from a rich vessel of the Fourth Alliance. Nenda, at the Polypheme's request, was giving Claudius a stem-to-stern inspection of the *Have-It-All*— omitting, of course, the concealed weapons ports and their well-hidden controls.

Claudius went on, "Do you lack metal, so that you must resort to such primitive materials?"

"We have metal." Nenda had a sharp and lethal sample tucked away in his boot.

"Then apparently you don't know what to do with it."

Nenda knew exactly what he would *like* to do with it. He put that thought to one side. Claudius was pretending to an equal disdain for the occupants of the ship, but his eye movements betrayed a different level of interest.

"They belong to you, do they?" Claudius's main eye was staring at Kallik, J'merlia, and Atvar H'sial. "You know, these would also be of interest at Carnival. Especially the big and ugliest one. There's nothing like them there. Might they be available?"

"Certainly—but not until our other business is concluded."

Nenda had been providing pheromonal translation for Atvar H'sial's benefit. Now a message came wafting across to him containing overtones of both amusement and warning.

"Louis, I detect in your emanations an element of treachery. I approve—provided that it is directed at the correct individual."

"At, you know me better than that. I wouldn't dream of selling you out to old blubberguts here."

"Very wise. It leaves unanswered the question, to whom would you dream of selling me out?"

But Louis was moving on, beyond the range at which his augment could pick up and read the Cecropian's signals. Atvar H'sial had much more sensitive apparatus. When doors were open she could track and read Louis at fifty meters.

They passed into the next chamber, which normally served as the main cargo hold but which had been modified for special accommodation.

"Nothing here of value," Claudius was saying. "Why, I doubt if I could get more than a pittance for everything—"

He paused. He had caught sight of Archimedes, hanging by three great suckered tentacles from the ceiling. The Zardalu, head down, uttered a dreadful growl. Claudius was not to know that it was Archimedes's sincere attempt at a greeting in human universal.

"What is that?" Claudius was backing away.

"It's all right." Nenda walked forward, passing within a foot of the wide midnight-blue head with its fearsome maw. "This is only Archimedes. He's a Zardalu."

"Never heard of them before." The Polypheme did not move. "From the Orion Arm, I suppose. Is he dangerous?"

"Not at all. He might be, once he's full-grown."

Claudius edged his way past, keeping as close to the cargo bay wall and as far from Archimedes's dangling body as possible. "What's he do on board this ship?"

"Anythin' I tell him to. He's a sort of personal servant an' bodyguard. Anybody tries to cheat me, Archimedes takes care of it." Nenda passed through into another room. "Now this, I'm sure you'll want to see. This is the aft control cabin, where I expect you'll be working. It's an exact copy of the one forrard."

Claudius carefully closed the door to the cargo bay before he bobbed over to Nenda's side. "Let's get down to business. But I'll tell you now, if you want me to ship with a thumping freak like the one back there, the deal has to be something special."

"Maybe. Though from what I hear from Kallik—she's been monitoring signals coming up from Pleasureworld—times are hard for Chism navigators. Paid missions are way down. If you're not interested, plenty of others probably would be."

"Now then, Captain, did I say as I wasn't interested?" The Polypheme curled his form into the other control cabin chair. "You can't expect me to commit to something when I don't even know where you want to go. Some places are more attractive than others."

"We want to go to Marglot."

"That's it, then." Claudius was out of the chair in a single wriggling motion. "I'll say thank you, and good day. No one in his right mind goes to Marglot."

"Why not?"

"Because it sits right at the edge of the dead zone, that's why. Find someone else."

He was halfway to the door when Nenda said, "Fifty percent."

Claudius held his position, but the upper half of the flexible body turned through a hundred and eighty degrees, so that the great slaty eye faced Louis. "Fifty percent what?"

"Fifty percent of whatever our takings are on Marglot. That's twice what you normally ask, and five times what you normally get."

"And less than I'd need to go *there*." But Claudius remained where he was, coiled a little closer to the floor. "Haven't you heard about Marglot?"

"I've heard lots. What in particular?"

"Why, the fact that four ships from planets within thirty lightyears of here headed for Marglot, and not one came back."

"How were their navigators?"

"Lousy. Nothing near as good as I am."

"Well, then." Nenda swung his chair to face the control console. "I'll give you the right of final decision. If we make a Bose transition and you don't like the look of what you see, you take us out of there. I like to make money, but I'm not such a fool as to put my skin and my ship in danger to do it. What do you say? Half of anything we get, and if you're edgy and want to jump away, we do it with no questions asked."

The big eye lost its focus, and its smaller scanning companion slowed in its travel. Claudius stood as still and silent as a twisted spiral of green marble.

At last he nodded. "We put all this in writing, and post copies at Central Records on Pleasureworld. I've got an idea, you see. There's more than one Bose network approach to Marglot. The other ships, for a bet, took the shortest and easiest route. We'll wriggle around a bit for a back way in. How's your power supply for multiple Bose transitions?"

"Ample. Why?"

"It doesn't take longer in travel time, but my alternate route will burn up a whole lot more energy. Let me head over to my own ship and bring my stuff. Then we'll sign the deal. Oh, and there's one other thing."

"I can't give you terms any better than the ones I offered."

"It's not that. It's your friend out there." Claudius jerked five thumbs in unison toward the cargo bay door. "I know you say he's just a growing lad, but I can't do my best navigating when he's close by. My first suggestion is that you dump him in the freak show at Carnival. They'd take him in a hot minute. But if you won't go for that, at the very least you keep your Zardalu away from me—and the farther away, the better."

While the *Have-It-All*'s communications center transmitted the written agreement to Central Records on Pleasureworld and awaited confirmation of its receipt and filing, Louis Nenda strolled back to join Atvar H'sial.

"Well?" The Cecropian's silent question drifted across to him.

"Nothing to it. All tied up and confirmed. Claudius will be our pilot to Marglot."

"As simple as that? No special agreements were necessary?"

"Not really. Except I had to offer him fifty percent of whatever we get."

"Fifty! That is quite outrageous. It is twice what each of us will receive."

"It is. But here's a question, At. What exactly do you expect to receive on Marglot? Not *hope*, now. *Expect*."

"I follow your logic." The Cecropian folded its proboscis into the pleated region on its chin. As the tube inflated, words in near-human speech emerged. "Anundra 'rsnt fe'wns'st."

"A hundred percent if he wants it? My thoughts exactly. Claudius may collect more than he bargains for. But you're gettin' better, At. I mean, better at speaking human. The sooner we're to Marglot and away again, the sooner you'll be able to have more lessons from Glenna Omar."

"Indeed." The Cecropian returned to her normal pheromonal speech. "Glenna was the best."

"I have to agree. The best." Nenda scratched thoughtfully at his crotch. "Not that I've had any recent chance for comparisons."

"You are considering language lessons?"

"Not really."

"Then what?"

"Nothing." Nenda was hurrying out of the chamber even

before he spoke. He closed the door quickly. No point in getting Atvar H'sial excited over involuntary pheromonal signals.

CHAPTER NINETEEN
A history lesson.

To Hans Rebka, sustained free-fall implied one of only two things. Either you were in orbit around some body in open space, where you might remain with no feeling of a gravity field for an indefinite period; or you were dropping, pulled down steadily toward some center of force. In that case you most definitely could not fall for an indefinite period. The drop would end suddenly, unpleasantly, and probably fatally. And since you had started out on the surface of Iceworld, the chance that you were now orbiting some planet when all around you was nothing but total and stygian darkness seemed too slight to take seriously.

Hans saw nothing and felt no forces on his body. The only tangible thing in his universe was the suited figure of Ben Blesh. He clutched it tighter to him and was reassured by a protesting groan.

"Where are we. What's happening? Oh God, I think my arm and ribs are broken."

"Hang on, Ben. I'll get your suit's painkillers into you as soon as I can." Hans turned on the headlight of his own suit, but still he saw nothing. Either the headlight was not working, or he was in some place where light declined to travel. "You'll have to wait a bit longer until I can see what I'm doing."

"Lara. I thought I saw—or I dreamed I saw—Lara—"

"It was no dream. I'm sorry about Lara, but we can't do anything for her. Concentrate on yourself. How do you feel?"

"We must be in space. I'm in free-fall."

"Yes." *But I don't think this particular free-fall is likely to last much longer.* "I know you're hurting, but try to think objectively. Decide the parts of you that you think we will need to attend to first."

And where was Darya? Dropping invisible at their side, or spun away to some other dimension entirely? Had she already landed somewhere, crushed and shapeless, while he dropped forever?

That worry ended in mid-thought with a bone-jarring thump. His boots had hit a solid surface. Ben's body was wrenched from his arms, and Hans heard a cry of agony as brightness grew around him.

He stood upright within a closed room. The nearest wall, without doors or windows, rose to a ceiling at least fifteen meters above. Hans turned back his head, and saw that a uniform glow came from the ceiling. The light had not been present when he first hit the floor. It was still slowly brightening. He and Ben must have dropped right through the ceiling, but there was no sign of it of their passage.

Ben's body lay face down on the floor a few meters in front of Hans. He had to be at least partly conscious, because as Hans watched he made an attempt to raise himself on his left arm. He groaned with the effort and fell forward again. His helmet clattered against the hard floor.

Hans started forward, but someone was ahead of him.

"Darya!"

She turned, and the face behind the suit's visor glowed with excitement. "We did it, Hans. We're inside Iceworld, just as I said we would be! But we have to look after Ben." She was cradling the body in her arms, gently turning it over. "Can you get at the external controls?"

"I will do it for myself." Ben spoke slowly. His face was white and sweating, but his next words were clear and rational. "Drugs first. The suit will know what to give me. When it hurts less, I will see if I can walk."

"Not until I've had a good look at you." Hans heard a

hiss of gases inside the other's suit and saw the white fog inside the faceplate. In thirty more seconds, Ben should feel no pain. "You may think you feel all right, but you could do bad damage to yourself if you move. We have to get your suit off, examine you, and pad and splint you."

"While I suffocate in hard vacuum? No thanks."

Ben was right, of course. Hans glanced at the monitor in his own suit to confirm the pressure reading. A few moments ago it had been a flat zero. To his surprise the suit readout now showed a small positive value. As he watched, it flickered higher. The suit's sensor, tasting the composition of what lay outside, indicated a mixture of oxygen and nitrogen, plus a couple of percent of inert gases, helium and argon.

"Darya, what is going on here? We're getting an atmosphere."

"We've seen it before, Hans, on Glister and on Serenity." Darya's tone was satisfied, almost smug. "I said it's a Builder artifact, and I'm right. This proves it. Artifacts can tune themselves to the appropriate life form requirements. Wait a minute or two, and I bet we'll have air that we can breathe."

"Where *is* here? I assume we're somewhere inside Iceworld, but you remember how big it is. There could be billions of rooms like this. We could spend our whole lives wandering around."

"We could, but I don't think we will have to. Look about you, Hans. This place has no doors and no windows. Remember the games that the Builders can play with spacetime connectivity? I wouldn't be surprised if every grid patch on the surface of Iceworld leads to the same interior chamber. I don't think we need to go looking at all. It will be enough if we sit tight and wait."

That sounded too optimistic for Hans. In any case, there was a job to be done, and sitting tight wouldn't be enough. He looked in through Ben Blesh's faceplate and saw that the pupils of the other man's eyes had contracted to black points. The drugs were taking effect. Ben should be able to talk and think, but he would soon be free of the worst pain.

"Don't try to move. I'm going to take a look at you." Hans began to ease the suit open.

"I'll help as much as I can." For someone in his desperate condition, Ben seemed at ease. "Can't move my right arm, not one bit. When I try to, something grates around inside. Broken bones, I suppose."

Hans eased the suit away from the right shoulder and upper body. The arm was easy, a simple impact fracture of the humerus with no sign of bone projecting or broken skin. He could not splint it, but the upper arm of the suit itself could be stiffened to form a kind of exoskeleton. The bone would have to be set properly later, but for the moment holding the arm in a fixed position would be enough.

The ribs were another matter. From the feel of them at least four were broken. The good news was that none had been driven inward to puncture a lung. Hans could use the suit's own supplies to pad and strap them. That might do the trick. In olden times before antiseptic methods, when it was dangerous to cut deep into the body, strapping had been the accepted and safest method of treating broken ribs. It could work here.

But where was *here*? As Hans worked on Ben, he glanced around the room. Darya was prowling the featureless perimeter. A successful job on Ben would leave the injured man, like Hans and Darya, free to die of dehydration and starvation. The room had breathable air but no sign of food or drink. The suits would feed them for a week or two, but eventually supplies would be exhausted.

Hans reached down to touch the floor. His gloved hand disturbed a thick coating of dust. This room had been unoccupied—for how long? Thousands of years, maybe millions. Perhaps the last time anyone had been here, this whole stellar system had been alive, with a blazing star at its center.

Hans opened his own suit—no point in using its air supply when the room they were in could provide for them. He did everything he could for Ben, then slipped the other's suit back over his body and right arm.

"Now I want you to try to stand up. Can you manage that?" He watched closely as Ben came to his feet. Hans

had allowed the suit to continue to provide the medication
needed to compensate for shock, but he had set a slightly
lower level of painkillers. He wanted Ben to be aware of
and favor his injured side, while still not suffering excessive pain.

Ben raised himself. He moved slowly, but smoothly.

"That's good. Can you sit down again—close to the wall?"

"I think so." Ben moved all the way to a sitting position.

Hans nodded approval. "That's right. Now stay there. You'll
be better off leaning against the wall and resting."

And so would Hans himself. Suddenly he was bone tired.
How long since they had last eaten? He said to Ben, "Can
you drink something?"

"I don't know. But I don't really want to."

"Make the effort. See if you can manage a fortified drink."

Ben nodded. Hans took his own advice, sipping slowly
and carefully and rolling each sip of tart liquid over his teeth
and tongue before he swallowed.

"Darya, why don't you come and sit down with us?"

She glanced back at him and shook her head. She had
to be running on adrenaline—he had seen her like this
before, too wound up to sit or even to stop moving. She
would pay for it later.

If they had a later.

Hans leaned his head against the wall and closed his eyes.
His position was not comfortable, but comfort was a relative term. If he could manage to sleep shackled naked to
an iron chair, he could certainly relax now. He was passing into a trance not far removed from sleep when he heard
a mumble from next to him.

"Do you know what you are? A screwup, a total hopeless screwup."

Was Ben Blesh talking to Hans? But then he went on,
"You say you're a survival specialist. You told Arabella Lund
that it's what you'd always wanted to be, what you dreamed
of doing. But look at you. You didn't help anyone to survive. You couldn't even save yourself. Other people had to
do that for you. What are you going to do now? Some big
deed of heroism, something that will save everybody? You

think you'd die to achieve that, but I doubt that you'll have the chance. You're a screwup, a burden on others. You'll drag them down, unless you take the decent way out and kill yourself so they don't have to look after you."

Hans could not help listening, but what he heard did not worry him. A combination of shock, injury, and medications was at work on Ben Blesh, allowing deep-seated thoughts of inadequacy and self-doubt to emerge. Ideas like that normally lay in the mind's lowest levels, hidden away from the rest of the world. Hans didn't think any the worse of Ben because of them. He wondered what would emerge from his own mouth in similar circumstances. Nothing to be proud of, you could be sure of that—but nothing to be ashamed of, either, if he did as well as Ben. The other man wanted to be useful, to save others, to die himself if he had to.

As Hans drifted away again toward sleep, he reached a decision. When they emerged—if they emerged—from the interior of Iceworld, he would treat Ben Blesh with a lot more respect. It was the old story. You could train a man or woman as much as you liked in the peace and quiet of a training camp, but character developed and showed itself only in the rough-and-tumble messiness of the real world.

In situations, in fact, just like this one. Ben Blesh was discovering, the hard way but the only way, his own strength of character.

"Hans, Hans—they're here!"

Darya's urgent tone jerked him out of his dream state. He sat upright, stared around, and saw nothing. The room was as empty now as when they arrived.

"What's coming? Who's coming?"

"I don't know. But Hans, look at the floor."

He glanced down. Beyond his outstretched legs the floor of the room was dusted with sparks of orange light. They intensified as he watched. He touched Ben's left arm—the good one. Ben said, "It's all right. I'm all right. I'm awake."

Darya backed up toward the wall. Hans could see the sparks intensifying at the center of the room, forming a brighter disk of orange. Darya moved to his side and they waited, huddling closer together as the orange circle brightened. And then, just as slowly, it began to fade.

Hans took his first deep breath for ages. "False alarm. Darya, you are the Builder expert. Do you have any idea what's going on?"

She silenced him with a wave of her hand. "No false alarm. Something *is* coming. Look."

The center of the sparkling circle was changing. At its middle a dot of silver had appeared. While they watched that dot grew in size, bulging through the floor and slowly rising. The rounded bulge lifted farther to become a hemisphere, paused, then rose again until it was a wobbling sphere of quicksilver supported on a slender silver tail. At the upper end a narrow neck formed, bearing a pentagonal silver tip. The five-sided head turned, questing.

"What is it?" Ben sounded nervous, like the youth that he was. "Is that a Builder?"

"It's not a Builder. But the Builders made it." Darya raised her hand toward the trembling sphere. "Can you understand us? Oh, Hans, of course it can't. We're in the Sag Arm. No Builder construct here will ever have heard human speech, even if all the languages in the galaxy are somewhere in its data base."

Ben said, "So what happens now? Do we sit here until it gets tired and goes away again?"

"No. We *train* it. It will learn our speech, but it needs a sample to analyze. We have to keep talking, to it or to each other. It shouldn't matter which."

The silver sphere was beginning to make sounds of its own. A steady hissing was interrupted now and again by a high-pitched whistle and deep rumbles like a volcano ready to erupt.

"Talk about what?" Ben asked. Hans could relate to that question. His own mind had become a total blank.

"I told you, talk about anything at all. It needs *samples*." Darya took a step forward and recited in a monotone, "In this life stage a Ditron is solitary, energetic, and antisocial. Attempts to export S-2 stage Ditrons to other worlds have all failed, not because the organism dies but because it never ceases to feed voraciously, to attack its captors at every opportunity, and to try to escape. A confined S-2 will solve within minutes a maze that will hold most humans or Cecropians for an hour or more.

"The S-2 life cycle stage lasts for fourteen years, during all of which time the Ditron grows constantly. At the end of this period it masses twelve tons and is fifteen meters long. . . . "

Hans realized that she was quoting the Ditron entry from the *Universal Species Catalog,* which she apparently knew by heart. He had to hope that Darya was right, that it made no difference what you chose as a sample of human speech— because the Ditrons when fully grown to their S-3 stage were brainless bipeds, sometimes kept by Cecropians as pets. It was hard to imagine that anything in the Sag Arm cared to learn about their life cycle.

Darya paused, and the rumblings from the sphere rose in pitch. Meaningless grunts shaped themselves, added sibilants, and interrupted those with what sounded like a series of pure vowel sounds.

"Eeeee—ooooo—aaaaa—"

Darya said urgently, "Hans, come on. Help me out. We need *variety* here. It has to hear other voices and other words."

Variety? Well, Hans could hardly do worse than a lecture on Ditrons.

"The inhabitants of the worlds that comprise the Phemus Circle are by far the poorest of all the clades. Part of the reason for that is natural. The planets tend to be metal-poor and near the edge of habitable life zones for their parent stars. But another part of the reason for their poverty has nothing to do with nature. It is a consequence of a repressive central government, which provides itself with many luxuries while finding it to its own advantage to make sure that most worlds remain marginally habitable. The residents of these oppressed planets endure shortened and impoverished lives—"

"Hans, I didn't ask you for a revolutionary manifesto. You nearly got yourself killed trying to change the Phemus Circle government."

"You told me to speak. You didn't tell me it had to be on a subject that you personally find acceptable."

The sphere muttered, "Septable. Septable. Ax-sept-able."

Ben said, "I can't believe this. It's actually working. That thing is trying to make speaking noises."

"Eaking—eaking—speaking."

"Come on, Ben. It needs to hear as many different voices as possible. Just *talk*, it doesn't matter what about. Whatever is on your mind."

"On my mind? Nothing's on my mind. Or my body's on my mind, and not much else. I've been doing what Captain Rebka told me to do, and trying to assess my own condition. I'm not in great pain, but I'm in rotten shape. I count five ribs gone, and I feel the ends grating against each other whenever I move. Talking is all very well, but if we ever get to *ask questions*, I have a few. Professor Lang, you know more about this than anybody. Can it do something to help us? I don't mean just *talk* to us, I mean get us out of this place."

The sphere said, abruptly and quite clearly, "Get us out of this place. Who are you?"

Rebka muttered, "One hell of a question, that. Answering it could take days."

Darya waved to him to keep quiet. "We are humans, from a place far from here, in the Orion Arm of this galaxy. One of us is badly hurt and needs help. Who are you? Are you a Builder construct?"

The quicksilver surface rippled. "We are—Builder construct. You are—humans. How you come?"

"From the surface of this artificial world. *Through* the surface. You must have noticed when it happened."

"Not notice. We were not—active. We became active because of a presence here. Your presence. No one—no thing—nothing—came for much time."

"How much time?"

"We do not know your measures. Since one galactic revolution, divided by one hundred."

Hans said, "The galactic rotation period at the distance of the Sagittarius Arm from the galactic center is two hundred and fifty million years. Two and a half million years, since anything was here!"

The pentagonal head on its long neck nodded. "For long,

long. Nothing. Since the outside of world changed, nothing came."

Darya asked, "No Builders? Where are the Builders?"

"We do not know. It is possible that they reside by the
great singularity at the galactic center. The Builders designed
us to work with beings where time travels fast—beings like
you."

Darya nodded. The theory that the Builders hovered near
the event horizon of a black hole was not at all new, but
she did not accept it. However, the idea that this construct—
perhaps all constructs—had been developed because humans
and others like them simply lived *too fast* to permit direct
Builder interaction—that was new, and suggestive.

She thought of the midges that made life a misery on
worlds like Moldave. They were a nuisance, and each one
lived only a day. But it was hard for something as "slow"
as a human to get rid of them. They were too quick, in
and away before you could do more than register their
annoying presence. Were humans like that to the Builders?

She said, "Did the Builders change this world?"

"The Builders—change this world? No. Something else.
Something not Builders."

"I told you!" Darya turned to Hans. "You didn't believe
it, but there is another agent in the Sag Arm, as powerful
as the Builders."

"If what we are hearing is true. After a few million years
alone, an intelligent being could contrive its own version
of reality. That happened to a construct on Serenity, and
another one on Genizee." Hans addressed the sphere. "Do
you have a name?"

"A name? We have an—an *essence of being*. This must
be turned into your words. We are—we were—Guardian of
Travel."

"No longer?"

"Not since long. When changes came, travel ended. No
thing came, no thing went."

"Do you have other powers? One of us is hurt." Darya
pointed to Ben Blesh. "He needs help."

"We cannot help. We are Guardian of Travel."

"Do you still have that power?"

"We do not know. Perhaps. No thing came, no thing went for long since."

"You must try to help us. If we stay here, we will all die."

"Die?"

"Cease to exist. Become inorganic. No longer possess sentience. If we stay here, we must die."

"In how long time?"

"Too soon to measure, on your scale of things. We need help *at once.*"

"We cannot help. Perhaps we can send you. Perhaps not. But first we must know other information. Information that is important to us."

Hans murmured, more to himself than to the others, "You see, it's the same all over the galaxy. You never get something for nothing. It wants to trade us, information for help."

"We're not in a great bargaining position." Darya turned again to the sphere. "What do you want to know?"

"We seek to know what happened to this world. To this stellar system. It was not planned this way. This was to be a—a *connect point*. We, Guardian of Travel, were to serve as a center of passage, to and from many, many places. Instead, we have become Guardian of Not-Travel. The ways from here are few. They have gone from many to one. The outside of this world has changed from passage to non-passage. Can you explain?"

"I don't even understand the question. I'll tell you what we know, but it isn't much. Some other great force is at work in this arm of the galaxy. We know little about it, except that it seems separate from the Builders, and it works *against* the Builders. What they form, it destroys. What they build, it makes useless. This world is an example. It is possible to land here, but anything that does so will be, as we were, in danger of destruction. One member of our group already died. The rest of us were lucky to survive for as long as we have. Even if we knew a way to go out again to the surface of this world, we dare not do so. We would surely be killed."

The sphere was silent for so long that Darya said at last, "Do you not understand me? Do you not believe me?"

"Believe you? Not believe you? We cannot say. The right word is . . . we do not *comprehend* you. It is not possible for a force to arise within this galaxy that could match the Builders, or threaten their works."

"Until recently I would have agreed with you completely. Now I can only tell you how it seems to us. Will you help?"

"We can try to send you. That is all."

"To a place of our choice? We would like to return to our ship, which orbits the star of this system."

"That is not possible. We said already, the ways from here are gone from many to one. We can send you, but to only one place. One world."

"Which world?"

"We have no name for it. It is a world."

"Wait one moment." Darya turned to the other two. "Not much of a choice. Either we stay here, or we go to some place we've never heard of and never been."

"That's a no-brainer." Hans gestured at the bare walls surrounding them. "Stay here, and we die. Go somewhere else, anywhere else, maybe we live." He said to Guardian of Travel, "This place you would send us to. What is it like?"

"Like? It is not like here."

"That's wonderful, just what we needed to know. Where will we be if we go? Do we arrive at a ship in orbit, on a world, at the middle of a star, what?"

"You would wish to go to the middle of a star?"

"*No!* Look, what sort of place would you send us to?"

"A world. A planet. A special place, of unique importance to those who made me."

"Will we be able to breathe the air?" Darya turned to the other two. "The Principle of Convergence may not apply in the Sag Arm. We expect habitable planets to develop similar atmospheres, but suppose it isn't true here?"

The sphere trembled and said, "Unless you need different from what was made here, you will be able to breathe the air of the other world. Do you wish us to try to transport you?"

"Not yet. Is this world inhabited?"

"We do not know."

"Does it have life?"

"It did. But our information is old."

"We have to take a chance. It looks like our best option. Our *only* option." Darya looked to Hans and Ben for agreement, then said to the sphere, "Very well. If you can send us to this other world, do it."

"We will attempt. One question: do you wish to be on the surface, or in orbit around that world, or elsewhere?"

Hans said, "Darya, are you *sure* we're communicating with it?" And to the sphere, "The *surface*, of course. Why would we want to be in orbit?"

"We do not know. Your kind is alien to us. For the world where you are going, there are other choices. You could if you wish go to the world center, where a Builder super-vortex waits."

"And does what?"

"It waits. When it is used, it changes the rotation speed of the world. It makes it slower, or faster. It was used, but not for long."

"That's not something we need or want. Thanks, but no thanks. The surface will be fine."

"Then if you will prepare yourselves, we will seek to make necessary arrangement. One more question. Do you expect to return here?"

"We are not sure. Perhaps."

"In case you do, a transfer field will be maintained for your use on the world of your arrival. It will be opened at regular intervals. It will not move. You should mark its exact location in case you wish to enter it."

As the sphere sank slowly back into the floor, Darya said to Hans, "Why on earth did you tell Guardian of Travel we might return here? Do you think we will be coming back?"

"Not if I can help it. I wanted to keep all our options open."

"If we return here, it will be to die."

"I know. Maybe I felt kind of sorry for it. It sits here waiting for umpteen million years while nothing happens. Then we arrive, and after an hour of talk we're off again. And it sits another zillion years by itself."

"Hans, that's ridiculous. It was in stasis all that time. It as good as said so. You don't feel *sorry* for Builder constructs.

If you're going to feel sorry for anybody, feel sorry for us. At least Guardian of Travel knows what's going to happen to it. We have no idea. Look at that."

That was a funnel of blackness, rising at the center of the chamber.

Ben stared uneasily, and tried to back closer to the wall. "What is it? Are we going to die?"

Hans snorted. "Yes. Everybody does. But it won't happen to us *yet*. That's a Builder transport vortex, a fairly small one. We have to move into it if we want to escape from here. Don't worry, it feels strange when you are inside, as though you are being torn in a hundred directions at once. But you're not. You come out at the other end in one piece."

"Come out where?"

"Ah, that's the question of the year. Some world where we'll be able to breathe the air, some special planet with a Builder super-vortex at its center. And that's all we know. A place where we can find something to eat and drink would be nice. At the very least, I hope we find something like trees and sticks so we splint your arm." Hans looked at Darya. "Are we ready?"

"Might as well. Waiting won't do any good. I'll go first."

Darya stepped forward into the black funnel. A cloud like a spray of black oil rose to engulf her body, and she vanished.

"One down, two to go." Hans held out his hand. "Come on, Ben, let's get this over with. Otherwise, Guardian of Travel may decide it's so fond of our company it wants us to stay."

Ben clutched at the outstretched hand. He closed his eyes and took a deep breath. Together, he and Hans walked forward and were swallowed up by the roiling darkness.

CHAPTER TWENTY
Tally on down.

E.C. Tally was not built to feel surprise; the sensation of novelty, yes. Also a certain feeling of satisfaction, coupled with a heightened need for self-preservation, whenever a truly different experience presented itself.

As it was presenting itself now.

Entry to a Builder transport vortex always offered an element of uncertainty. You might feel that you were there for a split second, a minute, or no time at all. And to E.C., even that split second was a long period of subjective consciousness. He had therefore done the logical thing and placed himself in intermediate stand-by mode a microsecond before his embodied form encountered the swirling darkness at the center of the planetoid.

Now he emerged and returned to normal cycle speed. The absence of acceleration on his body already told him that he was again in free-fall, but that was not enough to tell him *where*.

He looked about him. That "where" would surely have justified surprise, had he possessed the capacity for it.

He was in space. More than that, he was in orbit. Below him, filling the sky, floated a substantial planet, all grays and muted greens. And this was more than just any old orbit, it was a *low* orbit. His suited body was racing forward, fast enough that he could see the planetary surface skimming past. His instant mental calculation told him that his orbital period was no more than an hour and a half. The Builder transport vortex had dumped him close to grazing altitude, not far above the limit of the atmosphere. He knew that there must be an atmosphere, because the ground below was hazy in places. Even now he was passing over a clouded region.

E.C. looked in the opposite direction, above his head. Another great world hung there, almost as big in apparent size as the one that he orbited but much farther away. He could see banded patterns of green, white, and orange around its middle. The superb eyes of his embodiment detected a slight broadening at the planet's middle. The other world was in rapid rotation, and from its appearance it was almost certainly a gas-giant.

One hemisphere of that great world was in shadow. E.C. looked to his left, seeking the source of illumination for both that planet and the one he was close to. There it was, a shrunken but fiercely brilliant disk of greenish-yellow. His external sensors and internal geometric algorithms combined to tell him a few things almost instantly. That sun was too distant, with its tiny disk, to provide life-giving warmth to any planet. Yet the one around which he moved was clearly a living world, with the telltale evidence of green photosynthesis. The banded planet, farther off, was not merely warm. It was *hot*. He detected emitted radiation in the thermal infrared, consistent with a temperature close to eight hundred degrees. Therefore, although the sun formed the primary source of light for the whole system, the heat that warmed the world below came from the gas-giant's thermal radiation.

And did the world below possess more than vegetation? Might intelligence reside there?

Tally recalled Sue Harbeson Ando's last words to him as he completed his most recent embodiment. "You ruined two perfectly good and valuable bodies by rushing into things. Be *patient*, E. Crimson Tally. Learn to take things slow and easy."

Slow would be difficult. His orbit took him zipping across the surface of the planet at better than eight kilometers a second. But he could be patient, evaluating everything before he made his next move.

First, he would inspect his general environment in more detail. This system was well worthy of study. It was unlike any that he had ever seen or heard described. From the look of the general geometry, the gas-giant and its satellite world— the one around which he was orbiting—moved roughly in a plane about the parent star. Assuming that was the case, days and nights on the nearby planet would be of roughly equal length. There would be one oddity. Close to noon at the middle of the hemisphere facing the gas-giant, the light of the star would be cut off for a while, occulted by the body of the gas-giant. E.C. was approaching that position now. He stared down. The terrain here was hidden by a dense cloud layer, but it was the part that received continuous maximum heat from the gas-giant. Beneath the cloud you might expect to find a hot, damp world where plant and animal life luxuriated.

His own orbit had a short period. Already he was past the place where the gas-giant stood at zenith, and was rushing on. The day-night terminator lay far ahead, but the land beneath him was changing. The hazy green of vegetation took on a darker hue, interspersed with patches of white. Those grew in number and extent as he moved on, showing brilliantly in the reflected sunlight.

After a moment or two, Tally comprehended what he was seeing. The light from the distant sun provided ample illumination for vision, and it allowed photosynthesis to continue—provided that the temperature on the surface was high enough. But the star was so far away that it offered only a meager supply of heat. Without the warming influence of the hot gas-giant, the world below would be frozen, hundreds of degrees below zero. It was not so cold as that, but lifegiving warmth was provided only to the hemisphere that permanently faced the gas-giant. The other side faced always *away* from the source of heat, so any warmth had to be delivered to it by convective air currents between the two hemispheres.

Tally glanced behind him and confirmed his theories. The warm giant planet was sinking toward the horizon, while the surface beneath him was becoming a near-continuous ice sheet.

And now came something new and strange. As the big planet vanished from view, his suit, with its antennas constantly scanning the surface below, picked up a curious burst of radio sound. It did not seem like something intended as a structured radio transmission. More like the random cross-chat of a group of people all wearing suits and talking to each other at once.

He picked up another source, then another—and then scores and hundreds more of them, as his suit tuned in to the exact range of transmission frequencies.

Thousands and thousands of people down on the surface, all talking to each other in tight little groups while wearing suits? That did not rank high on E.C.'s level of probabilities, but he had no other explanation.

The radio bursts remained frequent as he moved over the cold side of the planet. He waited, until at last his orbit carried him around to a place where the gas-giant appeared again over the horizon. The clusters of radio noise disappeared. He looked down. He was over the night side of the world. He sought the lights of towns and cities, but saw nothing. He also detected no highly structured radiation, consistent with a civilization sending evidence of its existence out into space.

Tally visualized the cycle of events on the world around which he moved. It was tidally locked to the gas-giant; therefore, all parts shared the same sequence of days and nights, with day length dictated by the period of revolution around the gas-giant. He computed that to be 39.36 hours, rather more than one and a half standard days. This was the length of the day/night cycle, with light provided by the distant primary star. E.C. did not yet have enough data to estimate the length of the *other* year, the period of revolution of the gas-giant about the star.

The star formed the source of light for the whole planet. At the same time, only one side of the world enjoyed a supply of heat. The other received nothing but the feeble warmth of radiation from the distant parent star. Presumably it stood locked into a permanent Ice Age. Yet the evidence of life—assuming that those radio bursts were such evidence—came from the frozen hemisphere.

What could it possibly be like down there, on a planet where heat and light derived from two totally different sources? E.C. ran his atmospheric convective models using a variety of different initial conditions and assumed atmospheres, and found his results inconclusive. There was only one way to obtain answers that were undeniably correct. He would have to head down, and see for himself.

But not quite yet. *Slow and easy.*

There was one other peculiarity about the world below. E.C. had visited dozens of planets, and he held stored in his data bases information about thousands more. This was like none of them, and it failed to conform to any theoretical models. The magnetic field that he measured was huge, orders of magnitude higher than seemed possible for such a planet.

Tally could imagine only one explanation. At the center of the planet must be a rapidly spinning metal core, whose dynamo effect generated the magnetic field. But then, that core must somehow be physically decoupled from the planetary mantle and surface, since the inside was turning hundreds of times as fast as the outside. E.C. filed that oddity away, for future analysis.

At the moment he faced a more immediate issue. He would probably not gain more useful information from orbit. It was time to consider a descent.

He analyzed the problem. Simple re-entry was easy. The suits on the *Pride of Orion* were designed to permit a descent with no help from a ship. Once down, however, he would be stuck there—the suits, sophisticated as they were, lacked the power needed for an ascent to orbit.

He would worry about a return when the time came. For the moment, the question was, what insert parameters should he use to land as close as possible to one of the bursts of radio signal?

He was hampered by a lack of knowledge of atmospheric parameters. He could estimate the gaseous mix, but the density profile was much more difficult. E.C. was forced to adopt a fatalistic attitude. He would make his best estimates, and fly in. If he was grossly off, not even this suit could fully protect him. It would burn away with the heat of re-entry. His human embodiment would survive only a few seconds longer. It was conceivable that what would finally reach the ground would be only E.C. Tally's grapefruit-sized brain. It would be in perfect working order, but lack a means of sending information to or receiving information from the outside world.

Well, thank heaven for his stand-by mode. If he had to, he would switch off and wait—wait, either for his awakening in a new embodiment or for the end of the universe, whichever came first.

E.C. made the orbit adjustments needed for a re-entry vector that would bring him in at a scruff of radio signal nearest to the warm hemisphere. It also lay at the planetary equator, so it should be easy to reach. He waited for the exact microsecond, then initiated the suit's built-in drive. He felt a burst of deceleration, powerful but of short duration. Then there was nothing to do but watch and wait.

The planet sped by beneath him. He had changed attitude, so that the feet of his suit now led the way. A new deceleration, slight at first but slowly increasing, told him that he was within the upper limits of the atmosphere. The forces on his body grew and grew. His suit's extremities glowed white-hot with frictional heat. E.C. felt satisfaction. All was nominal, all was normal. If the profile continued he would land within a few kilometers of the estimated center of his target source of radio noise.

Upon landing his body would require food and drink, but after that a walk across the surface—with, or even without his suit—would be no problem.

E.C. watched as the glow of frictional heating faded. His thoughts were already moving on, to who or what he might encounter on the ground. A central part of his reason for existence was the collection of new data. He was without a doubt going to exercise that function before the current day cycle on his new planet was complete.

❖❖   ❖❖   ❖❖

A suit brought you to the surface at an acceptably low speed, but it made no guarantees as to the type of terrain that you might encounter. Tally plopped down feet-first into cold and sticky swamp, coated with a spongy layer of some kind of moss. Even so, he was lucky. A landing fifty meters to his left would have dropped him into standing water of unknown depth.

His legs pulled free with an ugly sucking sound, and he squelched his way toward a higher point of land. He tried to avoid treading on the dozens of small creatures that lay on the ground in front of him, until he realized that none was moving. He bent low and picked one up. It was dead. Presumably they were all dead. Tiny mummified bodies crackled and crunched unpleasantly beneath his feet as he walked.

When he was completely clear of the gluey mud he checked his location. He was just seventeen kilometers from his target. Not bad at all, given the uncertainty in his information about the planet. He could be at the source of the radio signals in just a few hours.

But first things first. He must make observations. This was an unknown world, with unknown dangers. Tally stared around. The gas-giant hovered just above the horizon, where it would remain permanently. It would be many hours before the arrival of night, but a cold, gusting wind blew from his right—the direction opposite to the source of warmth. He was in a permanent "temperate zone." The surface received a constant supply of heat, but a supply much diminished by the large slant angle from the heat source. At this location, the contribution from the parent star would make a critical difference. Life survived easily enough but it would never run riot, as it should in regions where heat from the gas-giant had its full impact. At night, the temperature at this location would fall far enough for open patches of water to form a surface layer of ice.

Atmospheric mixing would guarantee the same general composition of the air over the whole planet. Tally's sensors indicated that an unusually large percentage of that air consisted of the inert gases neon and argon. But he, and most other species from the Orion Arm, could breathe it with no ill effects.

He cracked open the faceplate of his suit and sniffed the air. The wind had a chill edge, more bracing than cold. Faint and unfamiliar odors filled his nostrils. It was a pity that the wind came from the cold side of the planet. The scents of life would be stronger and more revealing if they came from the hot side. But idle wishing for circumstances different from what you had was a waste of time. He had chosen this landing spot for other reasons.

Slow and easy.

Was there anything else that he ought to do before he sought the source of those scruffy bursts of radio noise? Tally could think of none. Here he was, and here, until someone came with a ship able to take him back to space, he would stay.

Choosing his path carefully so as to remain on dry land, he started to walk in the direction exactly opposite to the hovering gas-giant; away from warmth, toward the cold side. Toward the unknown source of the radio signals.

When you had little or no information, it was unreasonable to have any expectations. But somehow you did, even if they were often wrong.

Tally had noticed in the final moments before he landed that the local terrain contained plentiful hills and valleys. But the path that he was following, homing in on the intermittent radio chatter, constantly ascended. He was moving higher and higher, and the external temperature constantly dropped. By the eighth kilometer of his march, Tally was forced to close his faceplate so as to ensure the well-being of his flesh-and-blood embodiment.

He formed a working hypothesis. The source of the radio signals needed, or at least preferred, a cold environment. Either they located themselves on the side away from the source of planetary heat, or they found places high enough for the air to be thin and the radiative heat loss to open space to be high.

Well, as Julian Graves had remarked for some reason, after listening to E.C. Tally's description of the unfortunate circumstances that led to the destruction of his second embodiment, "It takes all sorts of oddities to make a universe."

Tally confirmed that the temperature control of his suit was set to a level comfortable for his body, and marched on.

Up, up, up—but that could not continue much longer. He was approaching an isolated peak, from which the land fell away in all directions. The vector of the radio noise pointed directly to the summit.

Tally stared ahead. He was seeking some evidence of intelligent activity. He found none, until he came close enough to the top of the mountain to observe that it formed a clear, flat line. The top had been sheared off.

He paused to give his body a breather. The last two kilometers had been hard going. The upward path had grown steadily steeper, over fresh snow that concealed hard-packed ice. Now was the time to be extra careful. With the line of the summit just ahead, this was no place to slide into a crevasse or fall over an icy precipice.

He scrambled the final thirty meters on hands and knees, digging his gloved hands deep into the snow to make sure that he could not slip backwards or sideways. And then it was suddenly easy. He had topped the final rise and stood on a level plain, clear of all snow and ice. He saw, no more than fifty meters away from him, a hundred moving figures. Sunlight reflected from glittering silver carapaces, scarlet heads, and multiple scarlet limbs.

Oddly enough, they did not seem to notice him. Well, that would change soon enough.

Tally walked forward, until he came to within ten meters of a rounded building that stood roughly in the middle of the cleared area. There he halted and opened the faceplate of his suit. The air was freezing, but this was necessary.

"Good afternoon." As Tally spoke he sent the same words through every transmission channel of his suit. He stared at the sun, to make sure that he had it right. No point in getting off on the wrong foot. Yes, it was certainly afternoon, with sunset of this planet's long day still maybe six hours away.

He said again, "Good afternoon. My name is E.C. Tally. I am an embodied computer, incorporated in a human form. I am eager to establish communication with you, and to exchange information."

The beings all around him stopped moving. They remained silent, but the buzz of radio noise in his suit receiver rose to a crescendo. The task of analyzing that frenzy of signal activity was a difficult one, but Tally was well-suited to tackle it. How fortunate that this work had come to him, with his unparalleled computational and analytic ability, rather than to some organic being poorly equipped for such demanding activities.

The silvery beetle-backed creatures were closing in, forming a ring around him. Tally closed his faceplate. If Sue Harbeson Ando could see him now, she would be proud of him. He was protecting his latest embodiment. Since talk would probably be at radio frequencies, he was avoiding the inevitable wear and tear on his body that would be produced with an open faceplate in such extreme temperatures.

The beetlebacks were larger than a human, but low-built. He squatted down on his haunches, to bring his head level with theirs. It was time to start in on a tricky task for which he was uniquely well qualified: that of cross-species—in this case, cross-galactic arm—communication.

CHAPTER TWENTY-ONE
In Limbo, and out of it.

Teri Dahl sat alone in the forward observation chamber of
the *No Regrets* and wondered about the name she had chosen
for their ship. Outside the port there was nothing—no stars,
no faint galaxies, no dark occluding masses of gas. That
had been their first hope when they emerged from the Bose
node, almost a full day ago. Perhaps they were in the middle
of a dark gas cloud that made the rest of the universe
invisible; but tests using the sensors of the *No Regrets* showed
that outside the ship lay nothing but the hardest of hard
vacuums.

Teri could feel the stirrings within her brain of old legends and myths. All the species of the Orion Arm had
discovered spaceflight long after the beginnings of their
recorded history. When everything was written down or
stored in computer data banks there should be no room for
uncertainty. The mechanism for the creation of myths was
that of oral memory and imperfect traditions. And yet the
stories lived on. Ships had been lost, that was an undeni-
able fact. A group of unfortunate travelers might enter the
Croquemort Timewell and be trapped there until time itself
came to an end. Or perhaps you and your party would enter
a hiatus, a singularity of spacetime from which you would

emerge within half a minute—or this year, next year, some-time, never.

A rational mind rejected all such fancies. If the Croquemort Timewell existed and a ship vanished into it, how would anyone ever learn that fact? It was all imagining, the fancy of uneasy minds. And yet, beyond the *No Regrets* stood nothing.

For the first few hours, Teri, Torran Veck and Julian Graves had stayed together, comforting each other with useless reassurances that this would soon be over and they would pop out into open space. Teri had endured false optimism for as long as she could, then crept away to be alone. She retreated to the observation chamber and stared—stared so hard looking for something, anything, that her eyeballs felt ready to pop out of her head.

She was frightened, and ashamed of being frightened. So why was it reassuring when suddenly the door to the observation chamber slid open and Torran Veck came lum-bering in?

"Oops. Sorry. I didn't know someone was already in here."

"Torran, if you are going to lie, you have to learn to be better at it."

He grinned at her, quite unabashed. "All right. I knew you were here. I've been trying something, and I got a result. But I don't understand it. You're smarter than me, so I thought I'd ask you to help me out."

"That's a lie just as big as your last one." Teri felt oddly comforted. "Where's Julian Graves?"

"I don't know. But I don't want him in on this, in case it's nothing. It's bad enough to make a fool of yourself in front of one person."

Torran had twice Teri's body mass, and when he sat down next to her, he as usual seemed to overflow the seat. "You came out here to find out if you could see anything," he said. "In a way, I did the same thing, except that I went into the control room in case any of our sensors reported finding anything."

He shook his head at her excited look. "Sorry. Not a peep from any recording instrument that we have. They all insist that the ship is nowhere in the universe. But then I did something stupid and irrational."

"You mean more stupid than entering a Bose node when you don't know where or if you'll come out?"

"About that stupid. I sent a call for help."

"You did *what*?"

"I know. It was totally dumb, but I felt desperate enough for anything. I generated a message saying who we were, that we were lost, and if anyone heard this, please would they come and help. I sent it. I didn't expect any reply, but I sent it anyway."

"And you had a reply?"

"No." Torran shrugged. "Hey, let's be reasonable. What are the chances of anyone picking up a call like that? Zero. But something peculiar did happen. A few microseconds after my message was sent out, the ship's radio receivers recorded a signal. I call it a signal, but it would be more accurate to say it was a burst of static. I couldn't make any sense of it, nor could the ship's computer. But it was something, where before we'd had absolutely nothing.

"I sat there for a while, then I said to myself, Teri's brighter than you. Why don't you go and bounce it off her? And here I am."

"Did you apply Lund's First Rule of Oddities?"

Arabella Lund had been full of "rules," and one of her most basic was this: *Anything in the universe can happen once, or at least it can seem to happen. If you want to obtain information, make it happen again.*

Torran nodded. "I did the same thing, three times over. I found identical results: send a signal, and microseconds afterwards we get a funny squiggle of radio sound on our receivers."

"How did you send your message? I mean, was it in some particular direction?"

"No, I used omni-directional. Hell, if there was help to be had anywhere I wanted to hear from them. What is it, Teri? You've got an idea, haven't you?"

"If you can call it that. It may be half-baked, but I want to try something. Let's head back to the control room."

"Do we need Julian Graves?"

Teri gave him a drop-dead-right-now glare. "You didn't want to seem like an idiot in front of Julian Graves, but you don't mind me doing it?"

"Sorry. What are you planning?"

"Wait and see. You didn't tell me in advance." Teri led the way to the control room. Once there, she ignored the radio wavelength equipment and went across the optical section. "Which one of these lasers provides the best collimated beam?"

"The blue-green. It diverges only one percent in fifty kilometers."

"I hope that will be tight enough. How many microseconds after you started to send your call for help did the receivers begin to record radio noise, and how long after you stopped sending did the noise you received end?"

"I'll have to check. It was small enough that only the instruments could pick it up—so far as I was concerned, they seemed simultaneous." Torran moved across to the receiver displays. "Ninety-four microseconds, plus a fraction, for the delay at the beginning. And the signal went on for a hundred and sixty microseconds after my call ended."

"That's close enough." Teri was at the laser station. "I'm going to send a one-second pulse from the blue-green laser. Watch the display. See anything?"

"Yes. A faint green dot showed on the screen—and it lasted about a second."

"We'll find when we measure it that it lasted *exactly* one second. Now I'm going to work my way around the full sphere, using one-second pulses every five degrees of arc. We'll measure the exact time of return, and then we will know where we are—or at least, we'll know the distance to the boundary."

"*What* boundary?"

"Don't you get it, Torran? We're not in limbo, or in the Croquemort Timewell, or a spacetime hiatus. The ship is sitting *inside* some other object, with an interior surface that screens out external radiation and reflects interior radiation. The reason that you got what looked like random returns from your signal is because it went out in all directions, and the distance is not constant to all parts of the boundary wall. So the return was scrambled, with bits of your message jumbled together. It took ninety-four microseconds round-trip time to the nearest point on the boundary, and a hundred and sixty microseconds to the farthest point.

"Now, I'm going to assume that the velocity of propagating radiation is the same here as in open space—that seems pretty reasonable. So at three hundred thousand kilometers a second, we are fourteen kilometers away from the nearest point of the boundary, and twenty-four kilometers from the farthest point. I also find a zero Doppler shift in frequency between the outgoing laser pulses and their returns, so our ship is at rest relative to the boundary. The advantage of using laser pulses in precise directions is that we— or rather, the ship's computer—can calculate and reconstruct the shape of the space we are inside, and also our ship's distance from any point of the boundary. If we find places where the structure of the wall seems different, those are the logical spots where we should look for a way out."

"Teri, you're a marvel. Can we start that work at once?"

"I'd like to. But I think we ought to tell Julian Graves what we have learned. Do you know where he is?"

"Last time I saw him he was in his own cabin. Contemplating his navel, from the look of him. But you are right, he does need to be told. Come on."

Julian Graves was in his own cabin. He was not actually contemplating his navel, but he was engaged in a pursuit that seemed just as unproductive. He sat in a chair, lightly strapped in position so that he would not move around in the ship's free-fall environment. He was staring intently at a fixed point in space. Torran and Teri finally realized that a tiny green marble hung there, about a meter in front of Graves's face.

Teri said, "Councilor, we have important news. We are not in limbo, or in some form of spacetime hiatus."

Graves nodded. "I know. In a few minutes I was proposing to come and tell the two of you the same thing."

Torran said, "But how could you possibly know that? You have been sitting in your cabin, and there are no instruments here."

"Oh, but there are. The human eye and the human brain are both instruments, potentially of a high order. It is true that at no point have I looked beyond the ship itself, but

I did not need to. I noticed an oddity in the control cabin some time ago. The ship's drive appeared to be off, since we felt no accelerations. However, the drive monitors indicated that the drive was—and is—turned on, although at an extremely low level. Since our position sensors insist that we are at rest in inertial space, the only explanation is that the ship itself resides in a field of force, albeit a very weak one—far too weak to be apprehensible to human senses. If that is the case, then although the drive holds the ship itself in a fixed position, objects *within* the ship that are free to move should do so. They experience a small body force."

Graves leaned back in his chair and placed his fingertips together. "You know, sitting here it occurs to me that maybe the worst mistake we have made on this whole expedition has been to assume that processes in the Sag Arm resemble in any way the familiar ones of our own Orion Arm. There are Builder artifacts here, and none is in any way like those with which we have experience. To paraphrase an old philosophical thought, the Sag Arm is not only more strange than we imagine; it is more strange than we *can* imagine."

Torran's glance at Teri sent a clear message: *He's gone gaga. The councilor is off his head.* He said to Graves, "The human eye and brain may be instruments, but there is nothing here for them to look at and work on."

"Oh, but there is." Graves pointed to the green pill-sized ball hanging before him. "We are not in free-fall, you see, even though our bodies feel as though they are. We are not even in the microgravity environment provided by the gravity forces of the ship itself. Steven calculated and compensated for those. An external gravitational force is acting on everything in this ship. A minute one, to be sure, which is why we can't feel it. But if you observe the green sphere, you will find that it is being accelerated very slowly away from me and toward the rear bulkhead. There is a slight asymmetry, a preferred direction to this environment. I can estimate its magnitude by observation of the little marble. However, I have no explanation as to its origin."

Teri said, "Councilor, *we* have an explanation." Her glance at Torran said, *Equal credit for this, all right?* "Here is what we have learned. . . . "

The *No Regrets* stood at a fixed location, five kilometers off center in a spherical region of radius nineteen kilometers. The space was bounded by a wall of unknown composition, impervious to external radiation and reflecting anything directed to it from inside.

"But we shouldn't try to take the ship to either the nearest part of the boundary, or the farthest." Teri was leaning over Torran Veck's shoulder as he sat at the controls of the *No Regrets*. "Our best hope is one of the poles."

It was their shorthand description for the only two points of asymmetry they had discovered in the spherical space. The "poles" were places where the return laser signal was much weaker than elsewhere, and they held out hope for an easier passage to external space.

"I have a vector to the nearer one," Teri went on. "The distance is 12.3 kilometers."

"Marked, and entered into the navigation system." Torran was far more cheerful when he could do something that involved physical activity. "We can be on our way any time. All right to go ahead?"

"Proceed." Julian Graves sat with his eyes closed and seemed half asleep. "I am sure that it is not necessary to remind you to proceed with extreme caution. We cannot afford to progress from a safe situation to a hazardous one."

It seemed to Teri that Julian Graves was playing a little fast and loose with words. *This* was a safe place, where you had no idea how you had arrived and or where you were, and a surprise could pop up to destroy the present calm at any moment?

Teri couldn't speak for the others, but she wanted *out*—out to a place where you could see stars and planets again, even if the one seemed ready to go supernova, and the other might be a world where nothing had ever lived or ever could.

"We're closing in," Torran said. Even crawling along, twelve kilometers for any form of spacegoing vessel was no distance at all. "We are six hundred meters away from the boundary. The drive is working harder to keep us in place,

which means that a stronger attractive force is drawing us
toward the wall. Nothing to worry about—we could stand
a pull a thousand times as hard and still have spare drive
capacity to keep us balanced. But there's no way of knowing
how things will change as we approach closer to the boundary. Our instruments have monitored our progress so far,
and the ship's computer did a fit and came up with an
inverse cubic relationship with distance. That can't go on—
it implies an infinite force at the boundary—but what we
have isn't enough to worry about. Even so, I'm not sure
we ought to approach any closer."

That degree of caution from Torran was unusual. Teri
leaned over him as he sat at the controls. "What's the
problem?"

"The boundary point that we are approaching is nothing
like you found in other places with your laser probes. There,
everything was smooth and reflected light evenly in all
directions. Take a look for yourself at what's happening at
the pole. I have a broad beam laser illuminating the area
straight ahead of us. See how the wall looks? It's all broken and granular. Not only that, there are big changes from
moment to moment in the Doppler return. Unless some
physical effect is going on different from anything that we
know, some parts of the boundary are approaching fast, while
others retreat—and they *alternate*, in a random manner. I
don't know of any type of force field that could produce
those effects."

Torran turned to Julian Graves. "Councilor, I have halted
our forward progress. I think that the ship ought to remain
at its present distance from the pole. However, with your
permission, I would like to go outside in a suit and investigate what lies ahead."

Two days ago Teri would have resented that suggestion.
Torran was seeking a star role and pushing her into the
background. It didn't feel like that anymore. Nothing specific had happened to make it so, but now she and Torran
were a team who would share risks and rewards. Except
that she would not in this case be sharing the risk—that
would all be Torran's.

She didn't intend to argue the point directly. Talk of risk, or of sharing risks, might make safety-conscious Julian Graves veto the whole idea. She waited in silence, until finally the councilor nodded.

"Very well. You may go outside and investigate. But nothing foolhardy. If you find something inexplicable, turn around and come back."

Good advice from Julian Graves, but if Teri understood Torran at all—and she was learning hour by hour what made the man tick—he would not follow it. The job of a survival expert *was* to take risks, rather than exposing the whole party to them. Teri knew what she would do in Torran's circumstances, and the thought was a bit scary.

Teri also needed an answer to a question that might arise in another set of circumstances: What would she do if, while Torran was outside, he *did* get into serious difficulties?

"Nothing unusual at the moment." Torran's voice came on cue, exactly as if he had heard her inner thoughts and was reassuring her. He had not wasted a moment after Julian Graves's go-ahead. Already he was leaving the *No Regrets*. "I'm checking the drive setting I need from my suit to compensate for the body force I'm feeling from the boundary. It is exactly the same as the ship is experiencing. I'm going to take myself a little closer to the wall."

Teri and Julian Graves watched the suited figure slowly diminish in size. Was it Teri's imagination, or did the outline of Torran's suit seem a little blurred, as though it was out of focus? She blinked, but the slight fuzziness remained.

"Torran, we're getting an odd optical effect here. Your image shows indistinct edges."

"I know. I can't feel it, but my suit sensors insist that I am experiencing a small high-frequency oscillating acceleration. The strange thing is, it's not in the direction of the boundary—it's at right angles to that."

"Torran Veck, do not place yourself at any increased risk."

"I won't, Councilor. I'm a survival specialist, and I'm as keen to survive as anyone. I now show a distance from the boundary of two hundred and seventy meters. The total body forces on me suggest that I can go to less than a third of that, and still accelerate safely back to the *No Regrets*. I'll take it slow."

Torran's figure in its protective suit began to shrink in size. Teri found that she could no longer make out details. Arms, legs, trunk, and head had changed from clear black outlines to gray blurs.

"Torran, we can't see you clearly any more."

"I believe it. There are differential accelerations on different parts of my suit, and now I can actually feel them. There's a high-frequency torque, as though parts of me are being twisted in different directions. The overall body force is quite tolerable. I can go a good deal closer with no danger."

Teri thought, how can he know that, when we are in a situation that no human has ever experienced before? Julian Graves said, "That's far enough. Torran, come back. We need to do an evaluation of what you have found so far. You can always go out again when we are finished."

"Sure." But that single word wasn't quite right when it came to Teri's ears. It was distorted, as though sounds, like images, were suffering interference on their way to the *No Regrets*. She heard one more drawn-out and garbled word— "Da-a-amn-a-a-ation!" Then Torran's blurred figure pinwheeled as though spinning fast around a central axis. At the same time it shrank in size.

"Torran! Can you hear me?" But Teri felt with sickening certainty that he could not. For there was no longer any sign at all of Torran Veck. In a final split second he had vanished at monstrous speed into the granular unknown of the boundary wall.

Teri was now obliged to operate one-on-one in her argument with Julian Graves. She wished Torran could be there to offer his support, but in a way it didn't matter. Whether she could persuade Julian Graves or not would make no difference. She knew what she had to do, and she would do it.

She said. "You have more experience with the Bose Network than I do. Have you ever heard of a case where someone made a transition, and was delivered to an end point from which there was no escape?"

"I have not. But ships have disappeared."

"If we sit here and do nothing, in the future the *No Regrets* will be listed as one of them. We have a choice. We can stay and wait for something to happen, with no assurance that anything ever will—other than that we will eventually die. Or we can accept that the boundary itself contains some kind of Bose transition mechanism, but of a type never experienced in the Orion Arm. Remember, Councilor, you were the one who said that the Sag Arm may be stranger than we can imagine. I think that our decision should be an easy one: we follow Torran, and take the *No Regrets* up to and through the boundary."

"That might offer nothing more than a swifter and surer form of our demise."

"It might. But it makes no sense at all for this to be a Bose node if there is no way to leave it. And the obvious method of departure would be through another Bose transition."

"You make a logical argument." The blue eyes of Julian Graves were old and knowing. "Suppose, my dear, I tell you that I do not agree with you. What then?" He waited for a moment, then added, "Do not agonize over how to present your answer. I know it already."

He gestured to the pilot's chair. "It awaits you. All I say is, proceed slowly. Normally I would say, slowly and cautiously, but in our case the second qualifier does not apply. In our situation, caution no longer has meaning."

Perhaps not; but Teri was going to be as careful as she could. The *No Regrets* crept toward the outer wall, meter by slow meter. At last she began to feel directly the body forces that Torran had described. They were not unpleasant, nothing more than vibrations that sent contradictory and exciting tingles through different parts of her. In other circumstances, a woman could get to like that sort of thing.

She halted the forward progress of the ship. "This is almost at the point where Torran lost control. He said '*Damnation!*,' whirled around like a spinning-top, and vanished. I don't notice anything changing. Do you see any differences?"

"Only the big one—why did it happen to Torran, when it isn't happening to us."

"Unless you object, I propose to take us closer."

"I object in many ways. But continue."

Teri glanced at the range sensor. The boundary wall was less than a hundred meters away. Her comment to Julian Graves had not been accurate. Already they were past the point where Torran had encountered trouble. The drive was working harder to hold their position, but still it was nowhere near its limits.

They crept on—and on. Teri felt the force on her body continue to increase, but it was quite tolerable. She had endured two or three times as much in training, with no ill effects. This was, however, inexplicably different from what had happened to Torran.

Closer and closer. At last, Teri said, "Councilor, that's it."

"That is what, my dear?" Julian Graves's face, under a force of two and a half gees, was even more strained and gaunt than usual.

"We have reached the boundary. The bottom part of the ship is in contact."

"Are you sure of that? What happens if you reduce the drive?"

Teri decreased the thrust little by little. She felt no change at all in the forces on her body. The ship was resting on part of the boundary wall, and being supported by it.

She cut the drive all the way, and looked across at Julian Graves. "We are here, and we have gone as far as we can go. The *No Regrets* is at rest on the boundary wall of this enclosure. The very same wall, in the very same spot that Torran went through. Any ideas?"

A field of two and a half gees was much harder on Julian Graves than on the younger and fitter Teri. He sat crumpled in his chair, gloved hands gripping the arm rests.

"Oddly enough, I do. It involves, however, a somewhat dangerous suggestion."

"More dangerous than the fix that we are in?"

"Perhaps not. You have a right to offer an opinion on that point. As you pointed out to me earlier, I have much experience in the use of the Bose Network. A Bose transition is always limited by two different factors. First, and rather obviously, an object cannot enter a Bose node if its size exceeds the physical dimensions of the entry point. In our case, we don't know what that dimension might be, although it appears to be very large. However, the second limiting element is just as important. An object cannot enter a Bose node for a transition if the *exit* node is smaller than the object to be transferred."

"You think that Torran—"

"—was small enough for both the entry and the exit nodes to accommodate him. Yes. But the *No Regrets*, much bigger than a human suited figure in every way, exceeds the exit node capacity. A transition will not be permitted."

Teri glanced across the control board's array of instruments. The drive of the *No Regrets* had easily enough power to lift them away from the boundary wall and accelerate back to the middle of the closed region.

"How confident do you feel that the problem lies in the size of the Bose exit point?"

"Confident? Why, I am confident of nothing. What I am suggesting is a theory, and like any theory it may be wrong."

"People act based on theories."

"Indeed they do. Some of them die as a result." Julian Graves struggled to his feet. "And if I sit here much longer with two and a half gees pressing this old body into the seat, I will feel as though I myself am dying. Come on, my dear. It is time for us to leave the *No Regrets*."

"Right now?"

"If not now, when?"

"But you always say that thought should *precede* action and we should evaluate every alternative."

"Correct. But when there is only one course of action available and no alternative, making a decision becomes easy."

He headed for the airlock. Teri, struggling under the load of a body two and half times its normal weight, followed.

At the outer wall Julian Graves did not hesitate. He stepped forward, and dropped like a stone. He was gone before Teri could look down and follow the line of his fall.

Poised on the edge, she found action difficult. It sounded easy to take one step forward, but what if that single step was the last one you would ever take, and the airlock of the *No Regrets* the last sight that your eyes would ever see?

Teri decided that the time for thinking, especially thinking like that, was over. It was time to act—and maybe to pray.

She stepped out of the airlock.

CHAPTER TWENTY-TWO
Pompadour.

"Quite true, Captain. It's as you say, we *could* leave here today. But there's no one in his right mind as *would* leave here today."

Claudius was sitting at his ease in the aft control cabin. His body was coiled down on a wide chair and he held a small bowl in his upper two arms. From time to time he raised the smoking bowl to his face, and sniffed deep. When he did so his single slate-gray eye rolled in its socket.

"You see," he went on, "you're not dealing with something simple and predictable here, like the Great Galactic Trade Wind. Oh, no. Otherwise we'd have been out of here days ago. But I know the route from Pompadour to Marglot like the tip of my own tail, and I'm telling you, there's real dangers if you try to make the jump at the wrong time."

"Dangers of what?" Louis was feeling mightily frustrated. It didn't take pheromones to guess that the Chism Polypheme was not telling the truth, but Atvar H'sial's silent, *"He's lying, you know,"* was an added irritant.

"Oh, things I doubt that you beings from the Orion Arm have ever seen. Space reefs and sounders, stuff that can swallow a ship up quick as a wink."

"He's lying, Louis." Atvar H'sial was crouched beyond the open door, out of sight.

"Hell, I realize that. You don't need to keep sticking me with it every ten seconds. But what am I supposed to do? Explain that a Cecropian is secretly listening, and she always knows if a Polypheme is telling the truth or not? I'd rather keep that sort of knowledge for use in emergencies." To Claudius he said, "What's your plan, then? Stay here in orbit forever, 'til we run out of supplies an' starve to death?"

"No, no. I'll know when it's the right time to go."

"How?"

"Experience, and what I pick up from other Chism navigators. It's hard to explain to anyone who isn't a Polypheme. But I was thinking maybe I ought to be taking another trip down to the surface."

"You've done that every day for the past four days. What is it this time?"

"Why, as I told you. I collect information. I need to know the latest word on the condition of all the trade routes out of here."

"And I suppose the hot radiation bars have nothing to do with it."

"Why, Captain."

Louis didn't bother to answer. He turned, and left the cabin.

"He has us over a barrel, At," he said, as soon as the door was closed. "If we were anywhere close to home territory, I'd say we chuck him out of the airlock and make the jump ourselves. But we can't take the risk. Reefs are real enough, and so are space sounders. I've never seen 'em myself, but I know people who ran across 'em in the Messina Dust Cloud, and they're not something you want to mess with. What do we do? He goes down to Pompadour every day, and he comes back pale green. You just know he's been cooking himself."

"I have a simple suggestion, Louis. When Claudius goes down to Pompadour next time, make sure that he is accompanied."

"By who? I went down there once, and it's a total dump that looks like it collects all the rabble in the Sag Arm. I'm

not picky, At, but I won't go there again—an' I can't see
you doin' it. As for J'merlia and Kallik, we could make 'em
go, but I don't think we should. They're too good for that."

"I was not proposing any of the parties that you have
mentioned. I was thinking of your female, Sinara Bellstock."

"She's not my female! Anyway, what reason could I give
her for goin' along with old Claudius?"

"Suggest to her that a survival specialist should experience as many different planetary environments and meet as
many alien species as possible. Naturally, you will also ask
her to keep an eye on Claudius, just to make sure that he
does not get himself into trouble. Two ends will be accomplished simultaneously. Claudius knows his way around the
surface of Pompadour, which should assure the safety of
Sinara Bellstock. And her presence will undoubtedly curb
the usual excesses in his behavior."

Louis reached up and patted the Cecropian's chest plates.
"At, if I've never said it before, I'll say it now. You're a raving
genius. I'll go give Sinara the news. You know what? I bet
she'll be delighted. An' so will I. She's been hangin' round
me the past few days tight as a tick on a dog's backside.
I can use a break."

That had been a day and a half ago. Sinara had jumped
at the chance, and Claudius appeared curiously unworried
by the prospect of a companion on his trip. The two had
taken the pinnace of the *Have-It-All* and left almost at once.

Louis Nenda glanced at the clock in his master suite.
He wasn't about to say so to his partner, but maybe Atvar
H'sial wasn't such a genius after all. The day on Pompadour was a long one. Where Claudius and Sinara arrived
on the planetary surface it would have been early morning. Now it would be past midnight. Somewhere, somehow, the odd couple had spent a long day and a long
evening.

What the devil were they doing?

Louis sat restless at the round table, with its finely pat-
terned surface. In the kitchen, Kallik had been unobtrusively
busy. As always, she was sensitive to Nenda's moods.

The Hymenopt entered carrying a covered bowl. "They

will surely return, Master Nenda. There is no need to fear for their safety. I hope that this meets with your approval."

Louis knew that it would. With her refined senses, Kallik was a superb cook. He removed the cover and nodded his appreciation. There was no point in telling Kallik that she had it all wrong. If Claudius did something stupid and got himself snuffed down on Pompadour, Louis wouldn't grieve for a second. But then they would be back to the search for a navigator. Anything you found down on Pompadour was likely to be the dregs.

Louis ate slowly and steadily. No matter where you were, no matter what was happening, it was a rule of life: Eat, or be eaten. He suspected that Kallik had included in the dish before him a hundred delicate flavors of which he was unaware. And one flavor of which he became steadily more aware as he continued to eat. Kallik worried about her master's tense condition. She had added a few drops of one of the many secretions that a Hymenopt's poison sac could produce. They ranged at her will from a lethal neurotoxic poison, to anesthetic, to tranquillizer. What Louis tasted now was close to the last of those, with some new and subtle variation.

Louis could still worry—Where the hell were they?—but he was becoming drowsy and relaxed. He finished the bowl and drank with some suspicion the contents of the tall glass that accompanied the food. He was no connoisseur of fine wines. When you had been raised to regard muddy water as a treat, you tended not to be picky. But the concoction that Kallik had prepared tasted unusually pleasant.

Louis ran his hand over the fine-carved table top. *Carved* was the wrong word. It was actually *chewed* into those distinctive patterns by the worker-termites of Llandiver. He could never go back there, of course, not after what had happened. If he lost this table, he would never find another like it. As Kallik crept in to clear the dishes, Louis wandered through to his bedroom.

When you lived your whole life aboard a ship—or would, if only people would leave you in peace—you indulged your personal preferences. The *Have-It-All* possessed weapons that would make most military captains drool, but there was no sign of any of that here. Louis slept on a bed three meters long and three meters wide. No one would ever call it soft, but most of the time he slept in low gravity or no gravity, where that wasn't an issue.

He sat down on the edge of the bed and removed his boots. He yawned, slowly stripped down to his shorts, and lay back with his head on the pillow. He scratched his hairy belly. Where the hell were they? And if they didn't show, where in this godawful place would he find another navigator? Although you had to hate anything as slimy and supercilious as Claudius, there was no doubt that the Polypheme knew what he was doing. To everyone else on the *Have-It-All*, travel in the Sag Arm was a mystery.

He closed his eyes.

On the water-world of Pluvial, where a day without rain came once in a thousand years, Louis had encountered several of the native Cetomorphs. He rather admired those marine intelligences, and certainly he envied one of their abilities. They slept with half of their brain at a time; the other half remained awake and available for discussion and action. After a while the halves were ready to swap roles and the sleeping side awoke.

Louis had asked them to teach him the trick. It turned out to be impossible. The best that he could manage was a light trance, in which he was neither asleep nor awake, but sensitive to all external stimuli.

He had been in that state for the past several hours, until finally he heard with drowsy satisfaction the far-off but distinctive sound of the pinnace docking with the *Have-It-All*. He had no doubt that Sinara and Claudius were the people aboard, because the ship's security system would not allow anyone lacking correct identification within a thousand kilometers.

He would give Sinara a good chewing-out for failing to call in and tell Louis what they had been up to, but that could wait until morning.

The other noise began five minutes after the docking ended. It was much less familiar. Not at all familiar, in fact. It sounded like two people, singing raucously and off-key.

Louis rolled off the bed and padded toward the door. He felt naked without his boots, but the condition of the ship came first. As he left the master suite and stepped into the dark hallway that led aft, something fell against his chest. It giggled and said, "Oops!"

He called for lights. Sinara Bellstock stood in front of him, although *stood* was hardly the right word. Her arms were around his neck, and her face pushed close against his chest. She made a strange questioning sound and pulled one hand back to run her fingers over the pits and nodules of his pheromonal augment.

"Mmm," she said. "Nice and fuzzy. Never saw one of these before." She leaned close and sniffed his chest. "Interesting smell. I like that."

He pushed her away, trying to avoid contact with bare flesh. That wasn't easy, because she was wearing about half as much clothing as when she left the *Have-It-All*.

"What happened to you?" But he knew the answer. Sinara was drunk, and on something far stronger than alcohol.

"Happened? Happened? Nothing happened. Went down to Pompadour, keep an eye on Claudius. Thaswhat I did, Mr. Fuzzy. He showed me all over—all over the place. Had a real good time. Haven't had a time like that since . . . since . . . I don't know. Never had a good time like that. Real good time. Real, *real* good time."

Her face was against his chest again, and he was supporting half her weight.

"He took you to some dive, didn't he? Got you stoned. Did you know what was going on?"

He wasn't sure she knew what was going on now, until she raised her head, frowned up at him, and said, "Course I knew. Met aliens—lots and lots of aliens. Treated me real nice. Wanted to have sex with me, some of 'em—Claudius too. He said, 'til you have sex with a Chism Polypheme you don't know what sex is."

"I bet. You—er—you didn't, did you?"

"With Mr. Wriggly? Of course not. Be like having sex with a live corkscrew. Didn't have sex with any of 'em. Told 'em the truth." Sinara was weaving patterns with her right index finger around Louis's navel. "Told 'em they didn't have a chance. I was saving myself for my heart's desire, Mr. Fuzzy, back on the *Have-It-All*."

The notion of being anyone's heart's desire was utterly alien to Louis. It took him a few seconds to realize that this was an open invitation, and one that he badly needed. He had been without a woman for an awful long time. The fact that Sinara was smashed out of her mind and might regret this tomorrow was no concern of his. The fact that Atvar H'sial would claim that her worst suspicions had been realized did not matter. What stopped Louis was no concept of morality or post-coital criticisms, but an awful thought. "Claudius got you this way, but what about him? He didn't go to any radiation hot spots, did he?"

"Dunno." Sinara frowned and went cross-eyed with the effort to think. "Lessee. I remember some names of the places we went. The Solar Plexus, Roentgen's Rendezvous, the Gamma Grille, Sunbathers' Bar, the X-rayted . . . I'm missing some of 'em, there were at least five more. What you doing? Don't go without me!"

Louis was trying to move past her and head for the aft part of the ship. She had her arms around him and held on, so she was towed along complaining at waist-level behind him.

"Claudius," he said over his shoulder. "Where did you leave him on the ship?"

"Don't know. Said he had work to do. I wasn't interested in wriggly old Claudius. Did you know, he's totally *hairless*? I like hair. Like yours. Did anyone ever tell you that you have a cute ass? *Oof!*"

Her face had banged hard into Nenda's muscular rear, because he had frozen at the door of the aft control cabin. Claudius sat in the control chair. Every inch of visible skin bore the luminous apple-green that showed the Chism Polypheme to be baked to a turn.

"Claudius!"

"Yes?" The Polypheme turned. His five hands were flying over the controls so fast that Louis could not make out the individual movements. "Ah, it's you, Captain. We're toasty-warm and ready to go. On our way. Shipshape and

Bristol fashion. Up anchor, splice the mainbrace, souse the herring and split the difference. Space reefs and space sounders, I spit on 'em. Marglot, here we come."

"Claudius, don't do it! Not 'til you're off the boil."

But Louis was too late. Inside him he could feel the multidimensional twists and turns that went with a Bose entry. Outside him, Sinara was busy with the personal explorations of his anatomy that normally preceded entry of a different kind.

The combination was certainly a first. Louis resigned himself to whatever came next. The *Have-It-All* was making a Bose transition, while at the same time Sinara continued to satisfy her prurient curiosity. Where either of them would finish up was anyone's guess.

CHAPTER TWENTY-THREE
Marglottas?

Guardian of Travel had promised a transit to another world, but that long-abandoned being had offered no guarantees as to how much time the passage might take, or how it would feel.

Darya was drowning. Her eyes, mouth, nose, and lungs were filled with thick viscous mud. The suffocation had gone on forever, long past the point where she must be dead.

She tried to breathe, tried to cough, tried to scream—and could do none of them. After several lifetimes of misery, a new discomfort was added. Her body was now being *extruded*, forced through a tube far too narrow to admit it. She was changing shape, transformed by remorseless pressure to a long, pale worm. The agony of breathlessness was nothing compared to this.

And then, without warning, the pain ended. Darya felt a final moment of compression and rapid release, as though her body was being expelled like a cork from a bottle. Suddenly she was curled into a fetal position and lying on something soft. Her lungs and eyes were clear. She could breathe and see.

She sat up, but had to wait until a wave of nausea passed. She looked down at her suit, convinced that it must be coated with thick mud. But the outside was spotless, cleaner than ever before, as though the transit had removed every trace of dust and grime.

As she stood up, still unsteady on her feet, the ground a couple of meters from her began to boil and seethe. She backed away. A dark bubble was pushing its way out of the quaking earth. It grew steadily until it reared to twice Darya's height, then suddenly burst and vanished. Left behind where the bubble had emerged from the ground lay two still forms.

As Darya stepped cautiously toward them, one sat up. It said, "Stone me. I wouldn't call that first-class travel. But I guess we weren't promised anything more than a transit. Ben? Are you all right?"

It was Hans Rebka, shuffling on hands and knees across to the other suited figure.

Ben Blesh said, like someone in a dream, "I don't seem to be dead. That's a surprise. But I can't sit up, and I can't move my arms."

"Let me take a look." Hans turned to Darya, as casual as if this sort of thing happened every day. "Give me a hand, would you?"

Darya moved behind Ben as Hans lifted him, and held him in a sitting position. "Where are we, Hans?"

"Lord knows. I wonder if we're even in the same universe as we were. First things first, though. According to my suit's sensors, wherever we are, it has breathable air. That's good. We can remove our suits."

"Wouldn't it be safer to keep them on?"

"For you and me, it might. But Ben's has to come off."

"Why me?" Ben was trying, and failing, to sit up without assistance. "I thought my suit was feeding me pain-killers."

"It was. It is. That's part of the problem. The pain that we felt during the transit was all psychological, but your suit didn't know that. It decided you were being injured worse and worse every minute, so it upped the dosage of analgesics to blot out your discomfort. That's why you can't move. You've been overdosed. Sit still. I have to get you out of there and reset the levels."

As Hans eased Ben out of his suit, Darya knew that she could do little to help. Hans was an expert troubleshooter. She was at best an expert trouble-finder. He had opened their visors. She did the same and took her first breath of alien air. It was hot, humid, and musky.

She stared about her. Guardian of Travel, by accident or design, had dumped them out halfway down a long, smooth incline. At the bottom, a couple of kilometers away, she thought she saw the glint of water. On the other side of the river, if that's what it was, the ground rose away to another hillside. More significant, perhaps, was another feature. Running alongside and beyond the water, straight and flat, a smooth gray ribbon suggested a stone or gravel road.

Darya swiveled her open faceplate to a position where she could read its built-in sensors. No radio signals registered on any frequency. The instruments showed eighty-five percent of a standard gravity and a slightly richer fraction of oxygen. Those accounted for the light and slightly light-headed feeling. Above her head, a greenish-yellow light filtered through continuous cloud cover. It was much stronger far off to one side. Either they had arrived not long after dawn, or soon it would be night.

She said to Hans, "Anything I can do to help?" And, when he shook his head, "Then I think I'll walk a little way down the hill. Seems like there might be a road at the bottom. It would be nice to meet something we can learn to talk to, and find out where we are."

"Don't hold your breath. Not the best way of putting it, considering what we've just been through. But do you notice something odd about this place?"

"Hans, *everything* is odd."

"All right, then, something here is odder than any place has a right to be. You've visited a bunch of different planets. Did you ever hear of one with plant life, and no animals?"

"Never."

"Look around you. Not a beetle, not a bird, not a bat, not a butterfly. No little critters wriggling through the undergrowth, to escape or take a closer look at us. Where are they?"

"Maybe we're in the wrong location for animals."

"Could be. But this sure feels like it ought to be the right location. Warmth, water, soil, plenty of light, lots of plants—what more could an animal ask?" Hans bent again over Ben, who was now unconscious. "Damn these over-eager suits. They're marvels compared with anything I ever saw before, but they do too good a job making sure the person inside doesn't feel uncomfortable. I've got to get him out or he may never wake up. You go ahead. Take a look around. Maybe you can figure out where the animals went."

Until Hans started talking about animals, Darya had been feeling quite good about things. Against all odds the three of them had escaped from the deadly surface and desolate center of Iceworld. They were on a planet comfortably able to support life, and the road by the river was evidence that it also supported intelligence.

Hans must be wrong. A planet didn't need to have animals on the surface. A thriving biosphere could be maintained very well by creatures that lived below ground, feeding on the roots of plants that grew in the warmth and light above.

She was walking over a layer of sturdy greenery that crackled slightly with each step. Every forty or fifty meters a dense clump of a different growth sprang up much taller, some reaching as high as Darya's head. She changed her path toward the water so that she could approach one of them. She closed her faceplate as she came closer. It was unlikely that she would run into anything dangerous, but there was no point in taking risks, Anything that could chew a way in through the ultra-tough material of her suit, with its instant sealing compounds and multi-layered structure, would more than earn a meal.

The growths had the shape of irregular cones with truncated tops. A green layer of overlapping scales, each about as big as Darya's hand, formed the outer layer. She pushed one out of the way to examine the interior. It was too dark to make out details until she used the headlight on her suit. She peered in, flinched, and took a step backward. The green scale fell into its original position to cover the opening.

Darya stood frozen for a second or two, then realized that

she must take another look. Maybe Hans's words had made her imagine things that weren't there. This time she moved the green scale aside and held the light steady. The cone-growth had a yellow axis running up its middle. Five multi-legged objects hung suspended there. Darya thought at first that they were living creatures, and she hesitated to touch one; but they did not move. Finally she found the nerve to reach out her gloved hand and pluck one away from the plant's central bole.

It was dark brown and about the length of her forearm. And it was dead. Not just dead but mummified, so it appeared almost as it must have been in life. She turned it. Two big compound eyes sat on either side of a fanged maw. They seemed to stare accusingly at Darya.

So Hans was wrong. There were animals. She did not find comfort in that fact. She slipped the little creature into an outside pocket of her suit and continued downhill toward the stream.

The water was clear and swift-flowing over a bed of gravel and fist-sized rocks. Darya looked closely, but saw nothing living. The water moved, and that was all. She waded carefully across and kept stepping forward until she came to the gray strip.

It was a road, no doubt about that, and it had been kept in good condition. A pile of stone by the roadside about two hundred meters away was an obvious source of materials for regular maintenance.

Where did the road lead?

Darya stared to her left, then to her right. She saw no sign of buildings, but maybe a kilometer away some dark object stood on the road itself.

She turned on her suit radio. "Hans?"

"I hear you."

"There are animals. I found them. Or at least, I found some dead ones. Now I'm across the stream and standing on a road. No buildings, but I see something else sitting on the road itself. It's within walking distance. I thought I might take a look at it."

"Might as well. There's nothing for you to do back here. I fixed up Ben as best I can, but he's still asleep. One thing, though. We don't know how long the day is here, but it's my impression that the sun is lower in the sky. Don't stay away too long."

Darya stared off to her left. The sun seemed to her to be in about the same position, though it was certainly darker. Rain clouds, maybe? If nothing else, the stream guaranteed a supply of drinking water.

She opened her faceplate. Even if the sun was going down, the air felt as hot as ever. She headed off in the opposite direction, away from the sun. Progress was much faster now that she was on a solid level surface. The dark object on the road grew steadily, transforming from a shapeless blob to a definite oval outline. It was a huge humpbacked body, supported on six thick limbs.

Could that be another dead animal, somehow frozen and mummified in the very act of walking?

As Darya came closer yet, she revised her idea of what she was seeing. Legs, yes, each one solid and thick, but this was no animal. It was a walking vehicle. The great "head" facing Darya contained a transparent window where you might expect eyes to be, allowing her to look through to the interior. Two shapes, pale-yellow and motionless, sat within. The still forms had a disturbing familiarity.

Darya kept walking. The whole front of the vehicle formed a single door. She located the handle, reached out, and swung it open.

A gust of warm air touched her face. It carried the smell of something old and rancid, but that was not what made her shiver. She *recognized* the creatures sitting lifeless on the two broad seats. She had seen them, or their relatives before—although never in life.

She slammed the door closed.

"Hans?" She could hear the tremble in her voice. "Hans?"

"Darya? Are you all right?"

"I'm not right at all. Hans, you won't believe this, but we're on Marglot. I've just seen some of the Marglotta. They are here in front of me. They are dead. I think they are all dead. We arrived here too late."

❖❖   ❖❖   ❖❖

Darya wanted Hans Rebka to see the walking vehicle and confirm her suspicions as to what she was seeing inside it. But there were two problems. Hans should not leave Ben Blesh alone until it was safe to do so; and Darya doubted her ability to navigate the six-legged walking vehicle off the road and up the hillside—even assuming that she overcame her squeamishness at pushing the mummified body out of the driver's seat.

While she tried to decided what to do next, another factor entered. It started to rain. Great spherical drops as big as marbles drifted down from the warm and clouded sky. When one of them burst on the nose of Darya's upturned face, she slammed shut her suit's visor, jerked open the door of the car, and scrambled inside closing it behind her.

Her inspection of the Marglotta, made without touching the bodies, was suggestive but not conclusive. They seemed to have died instantly, and without any warning. The clawed paws of one of them rested on pedals and control bars. The other sat with a rounded dark-brown ball—food, perhaps?—raised halfway to its open mouth.

She said into her radio, "Hans, I don't know what happened here. But whatever it was, it was quick. If it's like this all over the planet, the Marglotta died fast and without any idea what was coming."

"There's no danger now, is there?"

"I don't think so. Why?"

"I'm wondering where we are going to spend the night. The sun is lower, I'm sure of it, and the rain is coming down harder. It would be a major effort, but if I could carry Ben down there we could spend the night in comfort, inside the car and out of the rain."

Darya decided she had to put her feelings about the dead Marglotta behind her. Even if Hans could carry Ben, what would that do to the other man's injured body?

"Let me try something, Hans. Maybe I can work the car's controls and get it walking."

The hardest act was the first one. She had to lift one body out of the driver's seat and place it in the rear of the car. The Marglotta were small, no more than a meter or so in height, so weight was no problem. But as she raised the driver's body, the arms reaching for the controls snapped off. They were as brittle as long-dried twigs. Darya gritted her teeth, hoisted the body over the seat back, and laid it on the flat area behind. She squeezed into the driver's place, trying to ignore the shrivelled corpse by her side.

The controls were simple enough, assuming that Marglotta thought processes in any way resembled those of humans. The condition of the vehicle's power source was another matter. She had no idea how long it might have been sitting on the stony road unused, or even what the source of power might be. The technology level of the road and the vehicle suggested fossil fuel or a stored energy flywheel, rather than solar power, a fusion plant, or superconducting rings.

Had the vehicle been smart enough to switch itself off after it sat for a while without moving? Darya searched for a general power switch and located two candidates. The first operated the six articulated legs, lengthening them until Darya sat uncomfortably high above the road. She reversed that, restoring the car body to its original height. The second switch led to a hum and bone-rattling vibrations. It did not trouble Darya, but flakes of dried skin shook loose from the creature by her side and rustled down to coat the floor of the car.

Darya did not relish the prospect of driving while dead bodies disintegrated around her, but Hans Rebka had to see these things—or what was left of them by the time she got there.

Her hands and feet were on the same pedals and levers that the Marglotta had used. She experimented with them cautiously. They seemed simple enough. One for speed control, two of them for turning right or left, and one for reversing direction. She "walked" the car along the stony road, getting a feel for pace and movement. The rolling up-and-down gait of the vehicle was not unpleasant. Once you were used to it, the feeling was even soothing. Maximum speed was hardly more than a walk, though Darya knew she was ignorant of such things as gears and faster drive modes.

She continued along the stony road until she was level with the suited figures of Hans Rebka and Ben Blesh, then made a right-angle turn toward the hill.

Now came the tricky part. She had to guide the car across the fast-flowing stream, then negotiate the slope ahead of her.

It proved easier than expected. The car contained some kind of stabilizing device, which automatically shortened or lengthened the front and back legs so as to keep the inside always level.

The limited speed of the vehicle made her progress irritatingly slow, but within ten minutes Darya brought the car to a halt ten meters from where Hans and Ben were sitting. The faceplates of their suits were closed to keep out the rain, now pouring down torrentially.

They walked toward her. She was pleased to see that Ben was awake and moving almost normally, though he was holding his right arm close in to favor his broken ribs.

She opened the car's wide front door and the two men scrambled in. Hans Rebka apparently experienced none of Darya's reverence for the dead. He examined the Marglotta sitting in the passenger seat for a few seconds, and nodded. "You're right. Just the way I remember the dead ones, back at Upside Miranda Port. Died the same way, I'd guess, though I don't know how that could be. Well, there's nothing we can do for them now."

He unceremoniously lifted the second body and dumped it over the seat into the back of the car.

"This is a lot better than spending the night outside. Darya, you keep the driver's seat. Ben, the passenger seat is yours. I'll make a place for myself in the back."

"In with the bodies?"

He gave her a puzzled look. "That's what I had in mind. Unless you think I ought to dump them outside? I wasn't going to, because if we decide tomorrow that we'd like to dissect them, by that time the rain could have ruined the bodies completely. They're falling to bits as it is."

He sounded unbelievably cold and casual. Darya had to remind herself that there was another side to the man. In crises, he seemed able to suppress every trace of emotion.

All was calm logic. Maybe that's why he was such a good troubleshooter.

If you wanted empathy and feeling for others, you would take Julian Graves. If encyclopedic knowledge was the requirement, without much judgment to go with it, then E.C. Tally was the person of choice. If you needed someone who through long experience had a sense of Builder constructs and how they might and might not act, maybe you would turn to Darya herself. But if you were in such deep trouble that you thought you would never emerge alive, then you turned to Hans Rebka—and you hoped that sentiment and finer feelings would not interfere with the need for the split-second decisions and hard actions that survival demanded.

Ben was already in the passenger seat, his body turned a little to give him as much comfort as he could find. He needed real medical treatment, but he would not get it here. Hans was in the back. He was moving things around there, and Darya did not choose to turn her head and find out what they were.

She stared straight ahead, out through the car's forward window. The sun was lower yet, dipping toward the horizon with what seemed like infinite slowness. The day on Marglot was very long, and they had to be prepared to endure an equally long night.

The rain fell steadily, soaking into the springy vegetation and the tall conical growths that hid the small mummified animals. The hillside was as bleak a prospect as Darya had ever seen. Tonight they would rest as best they could, but tomorrow they must begin to ask and answer a different question: Was it possible for humans to survive on Marglot, as the food supplies of their suits ran out?

Darya's brain felt turned off. She was not thinking about anything at all as she stared at the hillside ahead. She saw nothing and was expecting to see nothing, when her trance was broken by a change in the light outside. A vertical shaft of illumination was forming, as though a second sun shone through a rift in the clouds to produce a bright column of light. The shaft was about four meters across, and it struck the ground where Darya, Hans, and Ben had been expelled from it.

"Hans!"

"What?" Incredibly, his voice sounded as though she had wakened him from sleep.

"Look outside. In front of the car. Something's happening."

"Huh?" But he was sitting up, leaning over Darya's shoulder. "That wasn't there ten minutes ago."

"No. I saw it forming. What is it, Hans?"

"I don't know. But it's changing."

The column of light no longer ran from heaven to earth. Its upper end was fading, even as the lower part lifted, solidified, and took on a definite shape. It formed a glowing oval whose lower end hung three meters or so above the soaked earth. As they watched it changed further, into a perfect sphere that slowly drifted downward.

It was three meters above the wet vegetation—two meters, one meter, and still descending. As the lowest point made contact with the wet plants, the sphere emitted a flash of light so bright that the photosensitive faceplates of the suits instantly darkened to protect their eyes.

When they could see again the bright sphere had disappeared. But it had not vanished without leaving a trace. Where the sphere had touched down, something remained. Three somethings. Three suited human figures. Three people, back to back, sitting down on the wet hillside with legs outstretched in front of them.

As Darya watched in disbelief, one figure climbed slowly to its feet. It was facing away from the car, so she could not see into the faceplate of the suit. The person within would not at once see her.

A voice said, "Well, I suppose you'd have to say that this is an improvement. When you have been nowhere at all, and sitting under a force of two and a half gees while you were nowhere, almost anywhere else qualifies as better. But as to why we were brought here . . . "

The words tailed off, but Darya did not need to hear more. Only one person in the Sagittarius Arm possessed that deep, hollow voice. The man standing with his back to the car was Julian Graves.

And with him, scrambling to their feet with expressions

on their faces that suggested they were as surprised as Darya, were two others whom Darya recognized. There was no question that they were Torran Veck and Teri Dahl.

Which left only the biggest question of all. It was the one asked by Julian Graves of himself and his companions, but it applied equally well to Darya, Hans, and Ben: Why had they been brought here?

CHAPTER TWENTY-FOUR

Planning a landing.

The interior of the *Have-It-All* had become a place of hushed conversations and secret meetings. Kallik, J'merlia, and Archimedes sat huddled—in so far as anyone could huddle with a creature the size of Archimedes—in the drive room of the ship.

"Master Nenda is very angry." Kallik spoke with the authority of one who knows.

"Does he blame us?" J'merlia asked. Archimedes added, "Do you think he will disembowel me?"

Kallik looked puzzled. "Is there any reason why he should?"

"It is the standard way of registering disapproval among the Zardalu."

"I would advise you not to point this out to Master Nenda. In any case, he is not angry with you, or with any one of us." Kallik's rings of bright eyes glanced in all directions to be sure that no one was approaching. "He blames Claudius, and to a lesser extent Sinara Bellstock."

"But why?" Archimedes's speech was improving fast, although he was still more comfortable with the master-slave language of the Zardalu. "Are we not in orbit around Marglot, as we wished to be? Kallik, it was your assurance that we had achieved our correct destination."

"That is true. At least, we are orbiting a world with four poles. I cannot imagine many such specimens are to be found in the whole galaxy, still less in a small region of the Sag Arm."

"Kallik, I see no poles. Yet you assert that my eyes are superior to those of everyone else on board."

"What do you expect, pointers sticking out of the ground with labels on them? Archimedes, observe. The world below shows a clear demarcation into two hemispheres. There is a daylight side facing the sun, and another side which is in night. The day-night terminator constantly advances, since the world rotates. There is a fixed axis of rotation, and two poles are located at the ends of that axis. Let us call them, for convenience and in accordance with common usage, the *North Pole* and the *South Pole*. However, there is also a second division into hemispheres unrelated to sun position. Note that we have one side of high albedo, a bright half which faces always away from the gas-giant planet around which the planet orbits. Lacking a name, we will for the sake of convenience name that gas-giant world as *M-2*. Then we also have a less bright though sometimes cloud-covered side, always facing toward M-2."

"I see those. But I do not understand their meaning."

"You require training in simple orbital mechanics. Perhaps, on some other occasion, there will be time for such a thing. Meanwhile, observe." Kallik gestured to the screen showing the planet below. "The gas-giant world M-2 is *hot*, with a mean temperature of eight hundred degrees. Marglot—for I am convinced that this world *is* Marglot—revolves around M-2. It is *tidally locked* to it, so that the same face of Marglot is always presented in that direction. That hemisphere, of course, will be warm, and its center will logically be known as the *Hot Pole*. The other face never receives any heat from M-2, and precious little from the parent star. Its brighter appearance, as spectral reflectance measurements confirm, derives from a surface covered with snow and ice. The center of that hemisphere, the coldest place on the planet, is the *Cold Pole*."

"So you believe that we are exactly where we wish to be, at the world of the four poles. Why then is Master Nenda enraged at Claudius and at Sinara Bellstock?"

"Why, because they delayed us. Had we left Pompadour promptly, we would not be the last of the expedition to arrive. Thanks to Claudius and Sinara, we have been deprived of the possible advantages of getting here first."

"Will Master Nenda disembowel Claudius and Sinara?"

"No. Could you perhaps cease this obsession with disemboweling?"

"I will try. But still I do not understand. When we first arrived, Master Nenda seemed pleased. He reported that there were no signal beacons from other ships, and therefore we were ahead of everyone else."

"That was my fault." J'merlia hung his narrow head in a human gesture of remorse. "I was operating the communications console, and I reported to my dominatrix, Atvar H'sial, that no ships' transponders or signal beacons were active in this stellar system."

"Was that a false statement?"

"No. But it was an insufficient one. I failed to search for the much weaker signals from individual suits, which transmit on different frequencies. To my shame, it was Master Nenda himself who thought to look for and discovered such suit signals, emanating from the surface of Marglot. Worse than that, all but one of the other members of the original expedition now appear to have found their way there. The signal from the suit of Lara Quistner alone is missing."

"How can that be?" Archimedes stared out of the observation port, scanning the planet with his great luminous eyes as though an individual suit might be visible to him even from a distance of five hundred kilometers. "If they are on Marglot, they must somehow have been brought there. Yet you found no ships' transponder or signal beacons. Kallik, where are the ships?"

"You ask me the same question that Master Nenda asked. To my shame, I could provide no answer. He is very angry."

"With reason. We have failed him." Archimedes wrapped his great midnight-blue tentacles protectively around his midsection. "He will surely disembowel all of us. Perhaps he will gut Claudius and Sinara Bellstock first, but then it will be our turn. Kallik, you have worked longest for Master Nenda and you know him best. Please speak to him on our behalf. Seek to take the edge off his anger and impose on us a lesser penalty. My bowels are very dear to me."

Louis was indeed angry. Angry at Claudius, who had made a Bose transition when his brains were fried to a crisp. In doing that the Polypheme had endangered Nenda's precious *Have-It-All*, not to mention everyone inside it. Chism Polyphemes were all liars. You could not trust one when he swore that the navigators of his species practiced their art best when they were on a radiation high.

The Polypheme lay on the floor of the middle cargo hold, a limp and wailing mass of cucumber-green misery. He had, he swore, the worst hangover that any living being had ever endured. That generated no sympathy in Louis. He kicked Claudius hard on the back of his blubbery head as he left.

Louis was just as angry with Sinara Bellstock. What she had swallowed, sniffed, injected, or inserted while down on Pompadour was her business. But it was certainly Louis's business when Sinara, after offering a display of physical affection so enthusiastic and vigorous that Louis was willing to keep going while the *Have-It-All* disintegrated around them, had suddenly and completely passed out.

Nothing could wake her. Louis could have continued and she wouldn't even have noticed. But he had tried necrophilia before, and he didn't like it.

He had rolled Sinara to her own cabin and left her there to sleep it off. Then he went to find his clothes, ready to roam the interior of the ship looking for something to kill.

That was when he became really angry. Not with Claudius, and not with Sinara. With Louis Nenda.

How had he so badly misjudged the rest of the crew of the *Pride of Orion*? Darya Lang, quite apart from being a sexy piece, understood the Builders and their works better than anybody. Hans Rebka was a weaselly little runt, but he had been in trouble often and always found a way out of it. Those two might well have hopped and wiggled their way to Marglot. They had headed off to the big dead world in the system where they first arrived, hoping to do just that.

But what about the other witless collection? What about Julian Graves, so stupid that he considered the life of a pea-brained Ditron as important as the life of a human being? What about dinglebrain E. Crimson Tally, who if he had been a human would have died twice already. As for the "survival specialists" . . .

Sinara was a romantic nympho who put pleasure ahead of everything. All right for fun, but for *survival?* And she was the best of them. But they had all, Ressess'tress knew how, beaten Louis, Atvar H'sial, and the *Have-It-All* to Marglot. Sure, one of them was missing, but she might pop up any time. Maybe she was underground. The rest were on the surface, six of them near the Hot Pole and the other—E.C. Tally, from the suit's identification—sitting near the Hot Pole/Cold Pole equator.

How come Tally was so far from all the others? There was no evidence from the radio signals of a ship, pinnace, or aircar anywhere on Marglot. How had Tally traveled such a distance, many thousands of kilometers? Louis could think of only one answer. The Marglotta must have provided transportation. Here was something to make him madder yet. You responded to a call for help across thousands of lightyears, and when you were stupid enough to respond, they were sitting cozy at home and apparently doing fine.

Louis stormed off to find Atvar H'sial. The Cecropian was crouched at her ease before an instrument panel of her own devising.

"Have you been following all this?"

"To the best of my humble abilities."

"At, modesty don't become you."

"I have also received a detailed briefing from Kallik, by way of J'merlia."

"Then you know we've been screwed. We're arrivin' last of the party, and if we can take anything at all with Julian Graves watchin', it will be scrapings."

"You and I agree on the facts, Louis. However, we draw different conclusions."

"At, they're ahead of us and down there—every one of 'em."

"Correct. Six in one location, the seventh in another. But through J'merlia, I commanded Archimedes, whose optical powers are amazing and perhaps even unparalleled, to seek movement on the cloud-free portions of Marglot. He reports numerous small moving objects, all on the frozen hemisphere, but has detected nothing that could be a substantial piece of airborne or ground transport equipment."

"We've got our pinnace, At. We don't need none of the Marglotta's junk."

"True. But Julian Graves and his cohorts need it. Without it, they are confined to a tiny portion of the planetary surface. All the rest—" Atvar H'sial waved an articulated limb toward the window. Marglot hung in the sky beyond it, although with the Cecropian's echolocation vision she could only be inferring the looming presence of the planet from other sensors. "All the rest, Louis, is ours to explore and exploit.

"Consider the options. Are the Marglotta alive? Then we have responded to their call for help, and we are ready for their thanks and willing to begin negotiations—on our terms. Are the Marglotta dead? Then the whole of the planet, except for an insignificant area where the rest of our original party is located, is ours for the taking. We will of course rescue Julian Graves and the others and be prepared to receive their gratitude—eventually."

There was no justice in the universe, and a man had no right to expect any. Louis had known that long before he was a man—before he was weaned, probably, though his memories didn't go back that far.

Even so, it was never pleasant to have your nose rubbed in injustice one more time.

He was sitting in his own quarters, at his desk and working on the difficult question of the landing party, when Sinara walked in.

No, she didn't walk in; she *waltzed* in. The laws of morning-after said that she should be feeling like hell and looking as green as Claudius. Instead she was rose pink and bright-eyed, with a spring in her step. The bottom of her mouth ought to feel as though bats without toilet-training had roosted all night on her upper palate. But when she said, "Good morning—and a great morning it is," she leaned over and gave Louis a kiss on his unshaven cheek. Her breath was as sweet, fresh, and perfumed as the spring violets on Sentinel Gate.

A woman without a trace of conscience, who showed no signs of guilt for anything she had done? That was Sinara. The thought brought back memories of Glenna Omar. What was Glenna doing right this minute, back on the garden world of Sentinel Gate? Louis didn't know, but he had his suspicions.

He gestured to the seat at the other side of his desk. "Sit down."

"Over there? Not over here?" She was standing by him and breathing into his ear.

"Not now. We got work to do. We're heading down to Marglot. Question is, who goes and who stays here?"

"Everyone should go. It maximizes our chances of survival."

"What makes you think so?"

"In our survival training classes on Persephone, we were provided logical proofs, based on long-established game theory results, that the probability of survival in an unknown environment is proportional to the size of that party."

"That's fine, if you happen to regard survival as a game. In our case, I can see three or four things wrong with the idea that everybody should go. First, whoever we send may need backup. If the *Have-It-All* went down to the surface and somehow got smashed up, that would be it. There's no sign of another ship anywhere in the Marglot system. That means we gotta send the pinnace down, and keep the *Have-It-All* up here and out of danger in case it's needed for a rescue mission. It could make it down easy enough on autopilot, but I'd rather have somebody at the controls who can make the right decision if things get hairy."

"So you have to leave Claudius here. He's the best pilot. But I don't think from the look of him this morning he's in any condition to travel."

"That's his problem, not ours. Claudius is a navigator, an' I don't know how good he pilots when he's not juiced up. Anyway, are you willin' to put that much faith in a Chism Polypheme? I'm not. Give him half a chance and Claudius would be out of here an' take the *Have-It-All* with him. He says this ship is no good, but you can see his eye roll when he looks at some of the fixtures. I don't care how bad he's feelin', he has to go down 'cause I don't trust him here.

"Which brings us to the second problem. You flew the pinnace down to Pompadour, so you know it don't have that much space on it. In principle it has a three-person limit, though you can squeeze two in the back if you have to. Archimedes can't go—he'd be bulging out of the hatch with no room for anyone else."

"That gives you one definite stay-at-home on the *Have-It-All*."

"Yeah. Trouble is, Archimedes is stronger than greed but he ain't none too smart. If it came to a rescue mission, it'd be a toss-up whether you'd trust him or the autopilot to take the right action. You need a rescue crew that's smart *and* a good enough pilot to land the ship on top of Julian Graves's bald head and be out of there before he has time to feel the pain. And there's one other thing. You need a rescue crew that won't turn and run, no matter how dangerous it gets. You need a rescue crew that would die rather than leave you behind on the surface of Marglot."

"Kallik and J'merlia?"

"You got it. Put all that together, and it's easy. Atvar H'sial and I go down in the pinnace, and so does Claudius. Archimedes, Kallik and J'merlia stay behind. Kallik is really smart, and J'merlia flies this ship better than I ever could. Both of them are so devoted to At and me they'd come after us if we were marooned in hell. In fact, they're too damned devoted—if we don't stop 'em, they'll be down there every ten minutes to check on us. I'll tell 'em to come if they get my signal, or the pinnace beacon goes dead, an' not before. That leaves only one person still to decide."

"Me? You can't possibly mean me." Sinara stood in her most aggressive hands-on-hips stance. "Let me remind you of something, Louis. I am a *survival team member*. I am trained for trouble."

"You certainly know how to start it. All right, you're the fourth. It will be a squeeze in the pinnace, but we'll manage."

"We'll do more than manage. We'll have *fun*."

"I'm glad to hear you say that. Because I'll be the pilot, and the way space inside the pinnace is arranged, either Atvar H'sial or Claudius will have to sit next to you. I'll give you the choice." Louis looked up at her scowling face. "If you want to hear the rest of it, you might as well sit down again."

"The rest of it? You had this all worked out before I came in. You didn't want me to help, you just wanted me to listen."

"Not true. A second head can help. I *think* I know what I'm doin', but suppose I'm wrong? Here's the other part. We're going down to Marglot, but where do we land?"

"Are you asking me, or are you just going to tell me?" But Sinara sat down again.

"I'm going to explain the situation as I see it. Then I'm goin' to ask your opinion. What we know isn't much and it isn't complicated. We have six people in suits in one place on the surface, near the Hot Pole. Kallik has been monitoring suit signals, and one of the people is banged up pretty good."

"Who?"

"Ben Blesh."

"I bet he got hurt trying to be a hero. That was always his ambition."

"No information on that, an' you're bein' bitchy. The others are all right. But we got one, E.C. Tally, way off in the temperate zone between the hot and cold hemispheres. How he got there, what he's doin' there, your guess is as good as mine.

"Now we come to what we *really* don't know. Who else, or what else, is down there? The Marglotta were advanced enough to commission a Polypheme ship an' fly all the way to the Orion Arm to ask for help. They must have had some spaceflight of their own. You'd expect to see satellites buzzing all over the place around Marglot. We don't. Maybe in the combined gravity field of the sun, M-2, and Marglot, orbital paths are so weird that orbital decay times stop you puttin' up anything unmanned. But that's pure guesswork.

"Then there's the surface. Before you can have spaceflight, you need a pretty advanced civilization. It doesn't have to be out on the surface—Lo'tfian females run everything from their burrows, and only the males wander around above ground. But normally you expect spaceports an' stuff like that. Archimedes plotted out lots of structures that could be cities or industrial plants on the warm hemisphere, but he can't see anythin' moving near any of them. Also, we don't pick up a peep of radio signals from them. The strangest thing is that on the cold side, where Archimedes finds no trace of industrial structures, we pick up scads of radio noise all over the place. An' when I say *noise*, I mean it. The signals are junk, as though hundreds of people in suits were all jabbering at each other at once with nobody listening. One of those babble centers seems right about the place where we pick up the beacon of E.C. Tally's suit."

Louis leaned back in his chair. He would never admit it to anybody, but it was nice to have an audience—especially an audience as attentive, fair-skinned and bright-eyed as Sinara Bellstock. A man could get into lots of trouble with an attractive young woman like that hanging on his words— if he wasn't in twenty-seven kinds of trouble already.

Sinara raised her eyebrows at him. "Do you really want my opinion?"

"I'm waitin' for it."

"Well, I would say the choices are rather clear-cut. There is exactly one place on Marglot where you have a member of our party, and also evidence of surface activity. We should take the pinnace down to E.C. Tally's location and find out what's going on there."

"You got it in one. Can you be ready in two hours?"

"Louis, I'm ready *now*. For anything."

She looked it. Her cheeks were glowing.

"One other thing, Sinara. We have no idea what we may find down on the surface. We all wear suits."

"I know *that*. I'm not a raw trainee, I'm a *survival specialist*. Assume I'm good at *something*."

Louis did, but he wouldn't say what. He watched her

bounce out, happy as if he'd announced they all had the day off and were going for a picnic down on Marglot. She had come to the same decision as him about a choice of destination, but there was one detail of Louis's own thought processes that he had declined to mention: of all the creatures, human or non-human, that you might find down on the surface of the planet, E.C. Tally was the one entity whom Louis Nenda could persuade into believing almost anything.

Unfortunately, others already on Marglot might be able to persuade E.C. just as easily.

CHAPTER TWENTY-FIVE
Fun and games on Marglot.

One more decision had to be made. Louis had not mentioned it to Sinara, because he was still turning it over in his mind. They had not come here to see the sights, so the safest approach would be to fly to your landing point as directly as possible. On the other hand, if there were spoils to be gained on Marglot—something which Louis increasingly doubted—then a survey from a few thousand meters above the ground, and even a landing at multiple locations, would be needed.

He never made a final decision. He didn't have to, because Atvar H'sial made it for him.

"Do you anticipate that we will be obliged to wear closed suits for most of the period while we are on the surface of Marglot?"

"Dunno. Seems like there's a pretty good chance of it, 'specially when we meet Tally an' whatever goes with him."

"Then let me remind you that on similar occasions in the past, you and I have suffered because of our inability to communicate. Sealed suits prevent any form of pheromonal communication, and you have difficulties when I seek to make statements employing human speech modes."

"You're gettin' better, At."

"Do not waste both our times. Your true opinion of my efforts shows clearly as a sub-text. No matter. What is important is that, since you and I will be unable to communicate efficiently once we are on the surface and our suits are closed, we must have an opportunity to decide upon a course of action *before we arrive.* We are able to fly in the pinnace with suits open. I therefore propose that we perform a preliminary reconnaissance of Marglot and formulate our plans, before we land and close our suits to meet with E.C. Tally and whatever surrounds him."

"Got it. I'll define a full low-altitude circuit of the planet before we touch down. Anything shoots at us, naturally we'll be out of there."

Louis thought about his partner again as he took the final steps to separate the pinnace from the *Have-It-All* and begin the swoop toward Marglot. You took one look at a Cecropian and you wished you could wake up; but you were already awake, and when it came to business the pheromonal conversations between Louis and Atvar H'sial agreed point by point. Those conversations were also—Louis was very aware of Sinara, sitting right behind him and breathing down the back of his neck—unclouded by those *other* pheromonal exchanges which prevented clear-headed discussion with members of the opposite sex.

He stared ahead at their nearing destination. From this distance one whole hemisphere of Marglot was visible. It was almost all the cold side. Making a landing down there among the ice ridges of the oceans or the vertical walls of land glaciers would not be easy. With any luck they would never have to try it.

He had his suit open, and he was offering a running commentary on what he saw to the Cecropian at his side. Atvar H'sial was in the observer's seat—a wild misnomer in this case, since her echolocation permitted her to see only what was in the cabin of the pinnace. Louis wondered how she could stand it. She couldn't "see" anything at all unless it gave off or reflected sound waves. For Atvar H'sial there were no stars, no moons, no galaxies—not even the planet below, until they were close to the ground. And, once her suit was sealed, there was also no speech. The urge to open up as soon as they landed would be enormous. But she never complained.

Not like the sniveling wretch in the seat behind her. Claudius had a special suit, one adapted to his strange helical physiology. Insisting that he was dying, he had refused to wind himself into it on the *Have-It-All*, until Nenda brought Archimedes into the picture.

The Zardalu had raised himself to his full height and glared down on Claudius with open maw, while Nenda said to Claudius, "I've told him he can eat whatever of you he can still see one minute from now."

That had taken care of the suit problem, but it hadn't ended the moaning and groaning.

"Such discomfort! Such pain! Such anguish! That a distinguished being of noble lineage should be subjected to treatment like this . . . Never should I have agreed to suffer such degradation. Never should I have left the haven of Pleasureworld!"

With his suit open Nenda was trying to talk pheromonally to Atvar H'sial, but doing it while Claudius made such a racket in the back seat made Louis's head ache. Claudius was loud, and he was shrill.

Finally Nenda set the controls to automatic and turned in his seat to face the Polypheme. He said pleasantly, "We are cruisin' at seventeen thousand meters. The temperature is a hundred and eleven below. There's hardly any air outside, and nothin' but solid ice beneath us. The seat you are in, Claudius, has an ejector mechanism, and it's controlled from the pilot's seat. If you don't stop jabbering, I'm goin' to use it."

Sinara, sitting next to Claudius, said, "Louis, do it! Do it!"

"I may. My finger's on the button. One more squeak and that's it."

Claudius subsided. At last Louis was able to concentrate on the scene below and could again send pheromonal messages about it to Atvar H'sial.

"We might as well go the distance and make a full circuit of the planet, but I'm not optimistic. The cold hemisphere is as bleak and bare as Archimedes said. The sun provides a fair amount of light, but only a dribble of heat."

"High civilizations have thrived on worlds colder than this."

"They have. I suspect they did here. But the Marglotta were right to be scared enough to call out for help. Something came along, and it zapped them. Question is, is it on the surface now, still doin' its thing?"

"I would suggest that whatever malevolent influence was present, it is, for the time being at least, somewhat inactive. I assume that the suit signals from the surface continue to indicate living occupants?"

"They do, though Ben Blesh ain't in good shape. Hold on a minute, At. We're approaching one of the major boundaries. We are still on the daylight side, but we're near the edge of the cold hemisphere. I think I see open water below us—an' greenery. Maybe I ought to take us down as soon as we get where the surface is a bit warmer. If we're going to do that we should act pretty quick, because in another hour of flight we'll be at the day/night divider."

"Take us lower, Louis, but land only if you observe one of the structures noted by Archimedes as possibly indicative of a city or an industrial site."

"I don't need to look for one. We took every location that Archimedes spotted and stuck 'em in the pinnace navigation system. There's a place about two hundred kilometers ahead and almost on our flight path."

"Then we should indeed take a look. And if you are able to descend to the surface so that we may exit this craft, I personally will, in truth, actually be able to *look* with my own sensory apparatus."

"An open suit?"

"Unless you note clear evidence of danger, that is a risk which I am willing to undertake."

The comment confirmed it in Louis's mind. Atvar H'sial was as averse to unnecessary risks as he was, but she was going stir crazy. They had been cooped up in a confined environment for far too long—ever since the arrival of the summons to Miranda when they were working on Xerarchos. That felt like a million years ago.

"Hold it in a bit longer, At. I'll have us on the ground in twenty minutes."

Having said that, Nenda was still not ready to take risks. He reduced their height and speed in the final ten kilometers, and when their target was in sight he flew a slow circle all around it.

What he could see was unimpressive. Seven broad gray strips—roads, or rail lines—converged. Where they met, and for about half a kilometer around that point, a narrower grid of intersecting strips formed a ruled pattern on the surface. All the gray strips were dotted with dark, rectangular objects, scores of them. They looked to Louis to be about the right size to be ground cars, but he didn't want to tilt Atvar H'sial's opinion before she'd had a chance to make her own assessment. Louis could see no sign of buildings or of people. The only thing that moved in the whole silent scene was some kind of flag or banner, fluttering in the breeze at the top of a tall metallic spindle marking the meeting of the seven roads.

"See anything to worry about?" Louis said over his shoulder to Sinara and Claudius; and, at her silence and the Polypheme's disdainful grunt, "Right, then. I'm taking us in."

He dropped the pinnace onto one of the wide gray roads, about fifty meters from the central flagpole. When after a few minutes of silent observation neither the pinnace's instruments nor its occupants saw or heard anything, Louis opened the hatch and stepped outside.

The final descent had been made with all suits closed, but his suit's monitors showed an acceptable atmosphere and no ambient toxins. He waved to Atvar H'sial and said over his suit radio, "All right. Anybody who wants out for a while should do it now."

Sinara was by his side in a moment, the faceplate of her suit already open. Atvar H'sial followed more slowly, setting in motion the complex set of servo-mechanisms that rolled back the head part of her suit. The two-meter fronded antennas slowly unfolded, while the twin yellow trumpet-like horns below them turned to take in the scene ahead. The pheromones that wafted across to Louis were wordless, but they expressed pure bliss.

Louis set out toward the nearest of the blocky objects that

stood on the road. Sinara danced on ahead of him. By the time he reached her she had already opened a door at its front.

"It's a vehicle, Louis." For once her voice was not bubbling over with enthusiasm. "Marglottas inside it—dead. Just like the ones in the ship on Miranda. But it's the same as there, not a sign of what killed them. They look as if they should be perfectly fine."

Atvar H'sial had moved more slowly along the road, making her own careful observations. She said as she came to their side, "The resemblance between these deaths and the deaths on the ship that came to Miranda go beyond the superficial. When first we had an opportunity to examine those bodies, we all remarked on their exceptionally well-preserved condition. They were dead, but in a sense, like these creatures, they were *more than dead*."

"At, I don't know about Cecropians, but with humans being dead is sorta like being pregnant. Either you are or you aren't. There's no in-between."

"I will define my terms more closely. When a creature dies, be it human, Cecropian, or any other form known to me, the life of the organism, considered as a single unit, ends. However, this does not at once imply the death of the multitude of microorganisms that reside within it or upon it. Their activity continues for a period, largely unaffected by the fate of their host. Were you, Louis, to expire at this very moment, the bacteria of your intestinal tract, to name but one example, would persist in their activity. When you die your body will begin to rot, to putrefy, to bloat, and to transform itself into a mass of reeking and putrescent flesh."

"Thanks, At. It's real nice to have somethin' to look forward to."

"The same would be just as true of me, Louis, or of your female here."

Louis had been summarizing Atvar H'sial's thoughts in words for Sinara's benefit. He edited the final phrase—she had enough ideas on that already.

The Cecropian continued, "Yet this process of internal decay had not happened to the Marglotta who arrived at

Miranda, nor to the Chism Polypheme who flew that ship. Nor is it true for these beings." Atvar H'sial waved a paw. "In order for the mummification which we observe here to occur, *all* life processes, external and internal, at the total organism level and at the bacterial level, must cease *together*. All die."

"How could that happen?"

"I do not know. But I am able to confirm that it is true. My ultrasonics permit me to look inside these bodies. No form of life, even at the microbial level, is present within them. But at the same time, plant life here flourishes." The Cecropian pointed to the low greenery that separated the gray roads, and to the ugly gray cactus growths that popped up here and there among it.

"D'you think it's like this all over Marglot?"

"That remains to be confirmed. First, however, we should determine if what we find for the Marglotta in this car is equally true for those in the city."

Louis stared at Atvar H'sial, then turned to survey everything around them. Far off in the direction of the day-night terminator, a line of hills jutted on the skyline. A ragged edge to their outline suggested more ugly cactus growths, encouraged to enormity by the higher altitude. Everywhere else displayed the level gray of roads or a tangled mass of green that clung close to the ground.

"Before we can see how Marglotta do in a city, At, first we gotta find us one."

"But we have found one already. It is here." The trumpet horns on Atvar H'sial's head swiveled around. "The Marglotta, like many beings of good sense, chose to preserve the surface of their world for other purposes. The city is underground, and it is all around us. In certain places, my ultrasonics have detected the presence of large cavities or caverns. Our task is merely to discover some access point. Logically, one or more should be present close to the city center, where the main roads converge."

The Cecropian turned and made her way steadily back toward the flagpole. Louis trailed after her. This was the other side of the story. Now it was At who could see what they needed, while Louis and Sinara were blind. Before you started to feel sorry for a Cecropian, you had to remember that there was more than one way to define "vision."

When they reached the pinnace, Claudius was standing outside it. Either he had recovered from his hangover or his greed was stronger than his discomfort.

"Fifty percent," he said as they approached. "Remember? Fifty percent of everything we find."

"Right." Louis was watching Atvar H'sial, who seemed to have discovered some kind of downward ramp by one of the major roads. "I think we just found a way to explore underground. You can go first and earn your fifty percent."

He knew there was little chance of that. Polyphemes were as cowardly as they were mendacious. He left Claudius behind and followed Atvar H'sial down what began as a steep ramp and rapidly became a dark tunnel.

"Black as a Rumbleside scad merchant's heart. Hope you can see your way in here."

"I can indeed see, most excellently. I judge this to be the entrance to some municipal building rather than to a residence. That would be consistent with its size and central location."

"So unless everybody works in the dark—I've known whole governments seemed to operate like that—there oughta be a way to turn on lights."

They were approaching a wide pair of doors. Atvar H'sial swung them open. Louis, using the light of his suit and of Sinara's who was walking beside him, searched the wall for some kind of switch or bar. He saw nothing, and went on, "Guess we'll have to rely on you, At."

But as he spoke, the darkness ahead was slowly relieved. Light, dim at first, bled in from fixtures in a low ceiling. Atvar H'sial was forced to stoop far over, while even Nenda had to dip his head.

"Motion sensitive." Sinara waved her hand, and the lights brightened. "Smart design. When everyone leaves, the lights fade automatically."

"Or when everything stops movin'. Nobody's left this place for quite a while."

They had entered one end of a huge room. Its low ceiling, although ample in height for the diminutive Marglotta, made the other walls seem even farther away. Big machines of unfamiliar design and purpose stood in long rows, connected to each other in complex ways. One or two Marglotta stood by, apparently responsible for each production line.

"Dead." Sinara spoke in a whisper. "Hundreds of them, and every one dead."

"But that is not the most striking element of this scene." Atvar H'sial, forced to bend far over and walk on all her legs, was almost too wide to fit between the rows of machines. She crept forward along one of the aisles. "Observe the postures. Every one died while engaged in routine operations. They had no warning, no suggestion of what was coming."

Louis examined each Marglotta as he passed down the aisle behind Atvar H'sial. One studied some kind of readout, another was employing a tool with a clawed end. A third stooped at the end of one machine, in the act of picking up or putting down an empty black container. He, Sinara, and Atvar H'sial had entered a busy factory, full of life and action, frozen at a single moment of time.

"You're right, At. All without warning, and all at once." Louis halted. "Unless you think there's more to learn in some other room, I'd say we're about done in here."

"I agree." Atvar H'sial could find no space big enough for her to turn, so she was forced to retreat backwards along the aisle. "What they were producing is unclear, but that knowledge would probably tell us little or nothing. Also, although this machinery appears of sophisticated design and enjoys a high level of automation, I see nothing that we might wish to remove for our own commercial advantage. These machines confirm the notion that Marglot supported a civilization with good technological capability. However, when disaster came, that technology was unable to save the life of even a single Marglotta."

Sinara had been unusually quiet. Now she said, "Louis, are we in danger?"

"Not right this minute. Whatever did for the Marglotta here has been and gone. But we'd better be real careful when we go other places. I'm 'specially thinkin' about those bursts of radio noise we picked up from orbit. They sounded like gibberish, but nothing I've ever seen in nature produces that kind of output."

"One of those sources is close to E.C. Tally's location. He has probably had dealings with them. Won't we need to do the same?"

"Yeah. That's a real comfort. We should get rollin'. Tally's across at the opposite edge of the warm side. We'll take a look as we go, an' see if there's anything interesting at lower altitude that Archimedes didn't spot from orbit."

What they saw was mostly nothing at all. Louis hadn't thought through the tangled geometry of Marglot. Twenty minutes after they were airborne they were still flying over the warm hemisphere, but they were coming to the day/ night dividing line. Louis stared down as twilight faded to night and the landscape below became a pale shadow. It might be warm down there, even hot, but soon it would be lit only by the "moonlight" of the sun's radiation reflected from the giant world of M-2.

He could just about make out the difference between land and water. The image intensifiers on board the pinnace had not been designed for this kind of work, and they did little better than human eyes. Claudius's great single optic would probably see more, but the Polypheme remained at his most uncooperative. Despite Nenda's assurance that nothing valuable had been found in the underground Marglotta factory, it was obvious that Claudius did not believe him.

As the pinnace sped around the curve of the planet toward the Hot Pole, clouds covered everything below. Somehow that lessened the level of frustration. Seeing nothing because you were not trying was better than peering, guessing, and cursing.

"I receive suit signals," Atvar H'sial said suddenly. "Six of them, and all derive from the same location."

"Yeah. I guess they can't go any place. We're pretty close to passing over the Hot Pole. Halfway to Tally."

"Will they be able to detect our presence?"

"I don't think so. They'll be sending like mad, but not able to hear much. But how the blazes did Tally get so far away from all the others?"

"I would like the answer to a different question: What strange skill or luck brought them here ahead of us, when there is no sign of a ship, either on the surface or up in orbit?"

"I'm tellin' you, At, Marglot is one weird place. If I didn't know better, I'd swear the whole place had to be a Builder artifact itself. Four poles, and a bigger magnetic field than any planet has a right to."

"You are making an unwarranted assumption, namely, that Marglot is *not* an artifact. Since we arrived here, I have been of the opinion that Marglot either is itself a Builder artifact, or it is intimately related to one."

"How come you never bothered to tell me that before?"

"To encumber another with an unlikely theory when all substantial evidence for it is lacking is not the Cecropian way."

"You think you got evidence now?"

"I do. We possess an additional fact which tilts the balance in favor of speaking. The Marglotta who went to Miranda feared that they were in danger because of possible Builder action. Now the Marglotta, or at least those on this planet, are all dead."

"But we're not. How do you explain that?"

"Again, I had formed an idea too vague to offer as hypothesis. However, since you ask: it is my suspicion that we have arrived here in a time interval that separates two phases of activity. The first phase led to the rapid or instantaneous extinction of animal life on Marglot."

"Something sure as hell did. What's the second phase?"

"I offer no conjecture as to when it may happen; but the second phase will extinguish the central star, and turn this whole system into one as dead as that which greeted our arrival in the Sagittarius Arm."

Louis glanced up at M-2, as though to confirm that it still stood close to full-moon phase reflecting the light of the sun. "At, you're a real bundle of joy. Next time I ask you what you've been thinkin', remind me that I'd probably rather not know."

He said nothing more, but under his control the engines changed their tone. The pinnace flew faster and faster over the dim-lit terrain beneath.

The darkness deepened. They were still on the night side, away from the sun. As they circled the planet, M-2 hung lower in the sky, providing weaker reflected sunlight to the pinnace.

Louis stared back at the gas-giant planet. "It's gonna be awful dark when we get to the place where Tally is sittin', and daylight will still be hours and hours away."

"Are you suggesting that we should delay our landing, and hover until dawn?"

"No way!"

"I thought not. Since the pinnace can land as well in light or dark, delay offers neither theoretical nor practical advantage."

"Remind me not to tell you what *I'm* thinkin', either. You'll have me as miserable as Claudius if we keep this up."

But in fact, Louis was already feeling his spirits rise. Soon they would be on the ground again, with a chance for action and maybe violence. People like Darya Lang could sit around for years and just think, but there had never been time in Louis's life to get used to that sort of thing. Get in trouble, whack a few heads, get out of trouble—*that* he could understand.

He turned around and winked at Sinara. "Time to close suits, sweetie. We'll be on the ground in a few minutes." To Claudius he added, "You can keep yours open if you like. You'd be a lot more entertaining rollin' around and screamin' in agony."

The low-altitude radar had picked out a place for a landing: a flat hilltop, part of it clear of everything but random patches of old ice. Louis examined the radar image of the ground ahead as the pinnace drifted in. He changed the glide angle a fraction of a degree.

After that he didn't need to work the controls at all. Louis folded his arms and leaned back. The ship touched down gently, and slid to a halt as smoothly and unobtrusively as a Karelian hostess picking your pocket.

CHAPTER TWENTY-SIX

Ben's dream.

Ben Blesh burned.

At the Hot Pole, bathed in the warm outflow from the gas-giant world to which Marglot was tethered by an invisible gravitational string, summer reigned perpetual. With the sun hidden by clouds, day and night temperatures differed by only a few degrees. A human could not ask for a more placid and comfortable setting.

But Ben was burning up. He was not feverish. His suit would not permit such a thing. With its controlled flow of drugs into his body, it could stabilize elements of his physical condition. But it could not determine his state of mind. The source of heat that he felt was a fiery self-hatred and disgust coming from within. He had become a burden to the expedition, rather than a cherished asset. Others might excuse his behavior on the surface of Iceworld; he never could.

They had treated him kindly and gently. Hans Rebka and Torran Veck had cleaned the mummified fragments from the inside of the legged vehicle, then rearranged the interior better to serve human needs. They had carried him to a makeshift bed there, despite his assertion that he was perfectly able to walk and manage the couple of steps up. They had told him to rest and conserve his strength, and to tell them if he needed anything. They had asked him how he was feeling.

He had lied to them.

And then they had left, and forgotten his existence. Except for occasional brief appearances to check on his condition, everyone ignored him. He had his suit open as far as he could without interfering with its medical functions, and he watched the other five through the transparent windows of the vehicle. They gathered in a ring, talking intensely to each other and gesturing in various directions. Clearly, they were making definite plans, and he was no part of them.

He closed his eyes for a moment. When he opened them again, two of the party had vanished.

It was the suit, deciding that he would benefit from a nap. It knew what it was doing from a medical point of view, because unless he moved he felt no trace of pain from his arm or his ribs. Even so, it was infuriating to have so little control over his own body.

He closed his eyes again, and this time when he awoke the whole group had disappeared. Where were they? Exploring—without him? As he watched, the ground twenty meters ahead began to tremble. The air above it seemed to thicken and shiver. A ghostly outline of a sphere formed. It hovered for a few minutes, then gradually faded. The earth once again became silent. Nothing moved, anywhere in the landscape.

Hallucination? That was not recorded as a side effect of any of the suit's medications. What he had just seen had to be real. Guardian of Travel, true to its word, had opened a transfer field leading back to the middle of Iceworld. It would open "at regular intervals." What did that mean to something like Guardian of Travel? Once a day, once a year, once a millennium? Maybe he had seen its only appearance in a million years.

Ben stared and stared, but the shimmering sphere did not return. He closed his eyes again, and when he opened them the brighter glow in the clouds that marked the sun's position had changed. It stood lower in the sky.

Soon afterwards, Darya Lang climbed into the car.

"How are you?" she said. It was what they all said when

they came in to check his condition—that, and little more. But this time Darya went on, "We've been clocking the rate of movement of the sun, and in another two hours it will be dark. We can't possibly all fit into this car, and Teri Dahl has found a much better place for us to spend the night."

"I saw the transfer field again, the one that links this world with the interior of Iceworld."

"Did you? That's interesting." But Darya was not listening, because she at once went on, "Ben, what I'm going to do may hurt you. I have to walk us to the place that Teri Dahl found. I'll keep the car's movements as smooth as possible, but let me know if you feel any discomfort."

Discomfort? Ben felt rage. He wished that he could be anywhere but here. To everyone else in the party he was a useless dead weight. He had missed his chance. He could have walked thirty meters to the transfer field. Given the choice he would rather be back in the middle of Iceworld, talking to Guardian of Travel. They had left before learning everything that the ancient Builder construct might be able to tell them. There was some sort of super-vortex at the heart of this very planet. Suppose that Ben had asked to be sent there, rather than to the surface? That might have thrown him a million or a billion lightyears. It might have killed him—Guardian of Travel had not described it as a transport vortex. So it killed him. In his present mood he didn't care.

"Are you feeling all right?" Darya's voice itself seemed to come from a distance of a million lightyears. The walking car had reached the top of the hill and was making its slow way down the other side.

"If you mean, do I hurt, I don't." Ben saw towering objects ahead, shaped like the truncated cones that dotted the area where they had arrived. But these were ten times the size. "If you mean, do I feel pleased at the idea I'm going to be spending the night inside this crapheap, I still don't."

"You won't be. None of us will."

The car was lumbering toward one of the squat towers. Darya halted it ten meters away.

"Can you walk? If not I'll get some help."

"I can walk." *Or die trying.* Ben eased himself to an

upright position and carefully climbed out of the car. Now
his right side did hurt, no doubt about it. Maybe that was
a good thing. He had heard that when broken bones were
knitting together it was the most painful time. True or not,
he moved like an old man.

"A few more steps." Darya was on one side of him, and
now Hans Rebka walked on the other. He brushed away their
offers of help.

The outside of the cone structure was an overlapping layer
of giant leaves, each one as tall as a human and much wider.
As Ben shambled forward, Teri Dahl pulled one leaf aside
and gestured him through.

"Home, sweet home, Ben. At least for the time being. In
you go. It's safe and dry."

He saw that she and the others were not wearing suits,
and he envied them. He would love to get out of his own,
even though he knew that would be a disaster. It was
working hard on his behalf.

The layers of great leaves ran four deep. Once past them
Ben stood in a wide space, dimly lit by light diffusing in
from high above. The structure was supported by a thick
central trunk at least a meter wide. The floor was dry, proof
that the outer leaf layers were dense enough to keep out
the rain that seemed to fall every few hours. The floor was
bare, but not naturally so. Someone had been busy with
housekeeping of an unusually gruesome kind. A stack of
small mummified bodies stood at the far side of the clearing.

"Don't worry. We'll get them out of here in the morning." Teri Dahl had followed Ben in and seen what he was
looking at. "They're not Marglotta, they're some form of wild
animal. We think they made those, and they probably lived
up there."

Ben turned his head back, feeling the pull on his ribs
as he did so. Ten meters above him, the inside of the hollow
cone bore drooping interlaced layers of thick white fibers,
spreading out from the central trunk and connecting to the
outer leaves. Above them, Ben could see bunches of rounded
globes, glowing golden-orange even in the faded light, each
one as big as his fist.

"They're edible," Teri said, "but climbing up to get them is a pain. We could do it if we had to, but Hans Rebka says there are better things to eat within easy walking distance. Sit down and make yourself comfortable."

Ben didn't have an easy walking distance, and he was not sure he could ever be comfortable again. He moved to the place Teri had indicated and sat down on a pile of springy undergrowth that someone had cut and dragged in from outside.

"Not luxury, but a lot better than getting drenched," Teri said. "Hans Rebka claims that the really heavy rain will come at night, when the temperature drops a few degrees." She came to sit beside him. "We have food, we have shelter, and we certainly have water."

The others of the group had one by one entered, until now all stood or sat inside the cone-house. Julian Graves, coming in just in time to hear Teri's final words, added, "Probably more water than we'd like. We are safe enough here, but we have no idea how we might leave the planet unless some others of the expedition show up. I wish I understood how our two groups came to arrive in the same place, when we took such different paths. Fortunately we need be in no hurry to learn that, or to leave. We can take our time."

Ben saw the others nodding, until Darya Lang said abruptly, "Sorry to be the company killjoy, but that's just not true. Marglot might seem safe enough, and in one sense it is. But we can't stay here very long. If we do we'll be in deep trouble."

"From what?" Hans Rebka was staring all around him. "I'm usually the pessimist of the group, but I don't see anything to frighten us. No floods, no earthquakes, no volcanoes, no ravenous beasts looking to chomp on our rear ends."

"That's the whole point, Hans. No ravenous beasts—no beasts of any kind. While you were exploring, I dug in the wet soil and looked on and in the plants. I found plenty of animal life. It's everywhere. Small and big, everything from half-meter crawlers down to sizes I can only pick up using my suit magnifiers. But it's all like those." She pointed to the heap of shrunken corpses at the other side of the cone-house clearing. "Dead. I don't think there is a living animal anywhere on the surface of Marglot."

Torran Veck shrugged. "So what? I've never been to Fredholm, but I understand that it's the same way. It's a world with vegetable life and fungi, and a bunch of microorganisms that break down dead materials. But it supports a stable biosphere."

"It does. Everything is in balance on Fredholm because it *evolved* that way, over billions of years. The situation here is totally different. This planet had a balanced ecosphere—plants, animals, fungi and microorganisms all doing their bit. Then every animal suddenly died. Marglot is unstable from an ecological point of view. I don't know how long it will take, but the vegetation will start to die, too—plants all rely on some animal forms. Oxygen content will start to go down as photosynthesis stops. I don't know what the end point of the change will be, but long before the planet gets to that stage we'd better be gone. Nothing like humans will be able to live here. Think of it this way, Hans. We seem to be the only living animals on Marglot. It's rarely good to be an anomaly. We need to find a way to escape, and we need to do it fast."

"I don't think you should be so worried, Darya." But Hans Rebka went off to sit by himself with his back against the central trunk.

No one else was eager to continue the discussion. After a few minutes, Ben moved from a sitting position to lie flat on his back. He was actually less comfortable than in the walking car, but he had no desire to go back there. No matter how gloomy the conversation, here he at least was part of it. He was free to offer his opinions.

High up near the top of the tree-cone, the daylight slowly faded. A new sound began, of a gusting wind. The atmospheric circulation patterns on Marglot must follow the moving day-night boundary, even at the Hot Pole. Soon the pummeling of torrential rain began on the sturdy outside leaves.

Night on Marglot. A planet which, according to Darya Lang, was steadily but surely dying. Ben closed his eyes.

In your dreams you encountered situations like this, hopeless corners with no way out. Except that in your dreams, there always was an answer; and you were always the one who found it.

In your dreams. Ben opened his eyes. The interior of the cone-house was dark. He could not hear the others breathing above the sound of the rain.

This was not a dream. This was reality.

CHAPTER TWENTY-SEVEN
Together again.

If there was a heaven for embodied computers, which E.C. Tally most seriously doubted, then he was in it.

He sat at the center of a circle of a hundred and more beetlebacks, just as he had sat for the past three days. The silver beetlebacks neither moved nor slept; instead, they talked continuously. A complex syncopation of chatter of radio signals surrounded E.C.

So much for the Orion Arm theory of organic beings, that some sleep was essential for all forms of animal life! E.C. had delegated the rest functions of his own body to a tiny part of his brain. With all the rest of his intelligence, he listened, analyzed, and spoke.

This was going to be no easy task, as was the case with Builder constructs. All you needed with them was to keep talking for a while, and they would recall or invent the appropriate human speech patterns. The beetlebacks presented a very different problem. Tally was storing away every syllable of radio utterance within his capacious memory, and it was clear that this was not a monologue or dialogue. The beetleback data streams, all one hundred and thirty-seven of them, had to be considered *simultaneously*. They were aware of his presence, and of what he said. He knew this, because after every one of his own speeches or questions, the beetleback radio talk clamored more furiously than ever before returning to a calmer level. They were working as hard as he was, seeking some common ground of communication. He could not vouch for their analytic powers, separately or in combination, but his own search for patterns and correlations in the hundred-plus parallel data streams suggested an effort that might take days or weeks to complete, even with his prodigious computational powers.

This was the kind of task for which he had been designed. This was no trifling exercise, no piffling conversation with a slow-minded human, Cecropian, or Hymenopt.

He crouched on the ground, and while his suit took care of the material needs of his body, including warmth—for the outside temperature had dipped during the night far below freezing—he worked. At the same time as he analyzed data, he studied the physiology of the creatures that surrounded him.

He could not place them—of course not!—within the Orion Arm ensemble of life forms, but their appearance was generally insectoid. Their backs were shiny silver, their undersides jet black. Multi-legged, eyeless, and wingless, they appeared totally insensitive to cold. He could see no sign of suits, and the source of the radio signals was a mystery until it occurred to him that they must have evolved this way *naturally*. They spoke and heard at radio frequencies! The fuzzy antennas sprouting from their wedge-shaped scarlet heads supported that hypothesis. Perhaps they also saw using the same frequencies, although the long wavelengths of radio compared with optical signals would surely provide an image of inferior spatial detail. Maybe Tally himself was to them no more than a fuzzy and indistinct blob.

No matter. Communication could proceed through avenues other than the visual.

Tally talked and listened, and listened and talked, convinced that the growing data set of beetleback signals would eventually lead to a basis for understanding.

It was with a sense of irritation rather than anticipation that he finally received a strictly sonic signal beyond the sighing of the wind. He looked up. A pinnace, its lights bright against the night sky, was drifting in to make a landing on his ice-clad plateau.

Tally moved across to the craft as its hatch opened. It would probably do little good, but the point had to be made.

"May I speak? Just look at them!" He gestured toward the beetlebacks. "They are disconcerted and they are scattering. Your arrival has unfortunately much disturbed our work."

That Louis Nenda—for it was he who first emerged from the pinnace—heard E.C. at all was debatable. He half turned toward Atvar H'sial, who was still inside the vehicle but whose suit was open enough to show the flash of bright yellow trumpet horns.

Nenda said, "Are you sure?" And then, after another few seconds, "I don't know what you think those things are that you're talkin' to, E.C., but Atvar H'sial assures me that they are not organic."

"How does she know?"

"From what she can see inside of them—or sometimes, what she can't see at all. Her ultrasonics are stopped by the carapace. Heavy-duty absorber. But she says the legs are sure as hell mechanical, with oil-driven hydraulic cylinders to move 'em along."

"Aha!" As always, E.C. Tally received new information gladly. "That explains one small mystery. All communication seems to be at radio frequencies, which I had never before encountered in an organic being."

"Never mind the small mystery. What about the big one. How the devil did you finish up here, on Marglot?"

"I am on Marglot? How fortuitous. I entered a transfer vortex, and at once found myself in orbit about this planet. My re-entry, of course, I directed to bring me as close as possible to the group of creatures that you now see around us."

"How did you become separated from the rest of the group?"

"Others? There are others, here on this planet?" E.C. Tally regarded Nenda with the innocent eyes of one in whom duplicity had never been programmed.

Sinara Bellstock had emerged from the pinnace and was

standing next to Nenda. "Lots of them," she said. "Professor Lang and Captain Rebka and Councilor Graves, and all the other survival team members except Lara Quistner. Do you mean you didn't come here with them?"

"I did not. In fact, I wonder how they could have found each other. In my final communication with them, the councilor and two survival team members were still on board the *Pride of Orion*. The others were exploring the large planet in the dead system where we first arrived at the Sag Arm."

Nenda had been glaring at the beetlebacks, which had stopped retreating and were now approaching, little by little. "You say you've been talkin' to them?"

"Not exactly. I have been engaged in data collection, building a base for communication. For the past three days my stock of information has grown to be most extensive. I am confident that, given time for analysis, I will be able to analyze fully and comprehend all that has been said."

"That's good, because I don't like the look of your buggy friends at all. And we have to find out how Graves and the rest of 'em made it to Marglot. Come on, Tally. Into the pinnace, and we're off."

"Without conclusion of our interactions? Also, sufficient accommodation in the pinnace is lacking." Tally had seen the sprawled corkscrew body in the back seat. "It was designed for only two in the rear, and Claudius is already within."

"Sit on top of him." The buzz of radio sound from the beetlebacks was increasing. "Inside now, or I'll grab you and wipe your data banks."

"You would not!" But for E.C. Tally it was the ultimate threat. He scrambled inside as fast as any of the others. As the pinnace lifted he was sitting on Claudius's non-existent knee. The data stream emanating from the Chism Polypheme required no effort at all to analyze and comprehend.

On descent, or even in level flight, the pinnace could manage a four-passenger load with fair ease. Taking off with five on board was another matter. The engines throbbed and labored until they reached a cruising altitude that satisfied Nenda.

Tally visualized their path. If, as Louis Nenda had said, they were flying to a point near what Graves had termed the "Hot Pole," then their course must take them "westward" with respect to Marglot's axis of rotation. This was a direction away from the dawn, so when they arrived at the Hot Pole it would be the middle of the night there.

Another factor, however, might prove to be much more important. Tally listened to the engines. He knew the specifications of the pinnace, and also Marglot's gravity field. The calculation and conclusion were simple. The pinnace could fly with its present load, but it could not return to space any more than he could do so with the aid of his suit alone. Either a larger ship must descend to the surface and provide transportation, or the pinnace would be obliged to make multiple trips to orbit.

As to the question posed by Louis Nenda concerning the means by which other parties from the *Pride of Orion* had reached Marglot and the Hot Pole, Tally gave it not a microsecond's thought—for the simple reason that they would soon enough be in a position to ask the question directly of the people concerned.

To address all these minor issues he deployed only a tiny fraction of his computational resources. The cabin was quiet as it flew through the night sky, and Tally was free to work without distraction on the main problem: understanding what the silvery beetle creatures had said. He was undeterred by Atvar H'sial's revelation that they were inorganic forms. Was he not himself an inorganic form? The chances were excellent that their utterances when finally interpreted would prove to be logical, lucid, and rational, unencumbered by the glandular effusions that so often contaminated the speech of humans and other organic beings.

Although detailed understanding was far away, one point was already clear to E.C. Individual beetlebacks did not possess separate intelligence. They were more like social insects or Decantil Myrmecons, in which each unit was capable of movement and action, but only if those actions supported a decision somehow made by the whole group.

More than that, in the case of the beetlebacks even the group that had met with Tally was not a complete mind. It formed one node of a distributed intelligence, whose parts included every cluster of beetlebacks on Marglot. There were many thousands of those; and, just as each individual beetleback was an expendable unit, the whole complex was itself expendable. It was on Marglot for a reason—the sense of purpose was overwhelming; but once that purpose was fulfilled, the future was undefined.

There was also an *impression*, and Tally could put it no more strongly than that, that the beetleback activity level was increasing rapidly. It seemed to lead to something with no physical meaning: a singularity. Although a singularity could not exist in the real universe, one might exist in the universe as perceived by the beetlebacks. Suppose, for example, that at some point they themselves ceased to function?

Tally looked around the cabin. He felt that he had achieved an important if imperfect breakthrough. But to whom could he express it? Sinara and Claudius were sound asleep. However, the pinnace was not flying on autopilot. Louis Nenda was—let us hope!—still conscious.

"May I speak?"

Nenda turned a fraction in his seat. "You know, normally when I hear you say that, I grit my teeth. But there's so much nothin' goin' on around here, I can use a change. What you got?"

"A partial understanding, perhaps, of beetleback nature and purpose."

Tally summarized his findings, collapsing the results of quadrillions of data sorts, merges, and compressions into a five-minute description. He expected skepticism. His conclusion was admittedly radical. But Nenda merely said, "Give me a second. I want to make sure this gets through loud and clear to Atvar H'sial."

The silence that followed was far more than a second. Tally assumed that some considerable pheromonal discussion was going on between human and Cecropian.

Finally, Nenda said, "At thinks you've nailed it on the button. Your buddies are one small piece of a much bigger operation, and when that's done they'll be history. At believes the Big Chill is on the way. The sun will go out and Marglot will become the ultimate icebox. Does that make sense in terms of what the bugs have been sayin' to each other?"

"I do not know." For the first time since his original embodiment, E.C. felt that the speed of his mental processes was inadequate. First he needed to frame Atvar H'sial's hypothesis in strictly logical terms, then he must evaluate its consistency in terms of the entire mass of beetleback recorded data. "The question is difficult. The necessary analysis may take hours."

"Well, hours is what we've got. About three more of 'em, is my guess, before we touch down near the suit beacons. Go to it, E.C. Oh, an' Atvar H'sial says there's one thing we need to know in particular."

"Ask, and I will seek to determine it."

"It's a simple question: If there's goin' to be a big freeze, how long until the action starts? When is Showtime?"

CHAPTER TWENTY-EIGHT
Help needed from the *Have-It-All*.

Hans Rebka had trained himself to sleep at almost any place and any time. That talent, however, was not an asset in times of danger. Then you normally slept little, if at all.

But when were you in danger? Sometimes common sense said one thing, while a part of your suspicious hindbrain declined to agree. Inside the cone-house everything was quiet. Outside, the rain had ended and the wind died away. With no animal life, large or small, night on Marglot should be both silent and safe.

That certainly seemed to be the opinion of the rest of the party. Hans, with the headlight of his suit reduced to the faintest glimmer, moved quietly from figure to still figure. Torran Veck—Julian Graves—Darya Lang—Teri Dahl—Ben Blesh—all were asleep, though now and again Ben would murmur something unintelligible.

So why was Hans awake? The sound when it came was at first no louder than the rustle of wind across tall grass. It seemed like imagination, until as it strengthened Hans heard a rhythmic undertone. That was the noise of the engine of a ground or air vehicle—and it was approaching.

Hans went to Darya and shook her.

"Best if we're awake, I think." And then, when she stared

at him as though she had never seen him before, "Help me rouse the others. Visitors are on the way."

She blinked up at him. "Can't be. We're the only ones on the planet."

"Not anymore. Trust me." Hans moved on, to shake Julian Graves awake. By the time everyone was sitting up there could no longer be any doubt about the sound outside.

"Best if most of you stay where we are. I'll take a look." Hans expected opposition, but the others were still hardly more than half awake. He slipped out, pushing aside the thick leaf layers.

The night was unexpectedly cold. It was also cloudy. Was the area around the Hot Pole ever anything but cloudy?

He walked around the cone-house in time to see a pinnace making a soft landing about fifty meters away.

Smart thinking. Whoever was flying it had homed in on the suit beacons and knew that they were in the cone-house. But the pilot wouldn't know who else or what else might be inside with them. Rebka walked toward the ship. When the hatch opened and the figure who emerged was Louis Nenda, somehow that was no surprise at all.

The cone-house was big enough, even for eleven. After the excited—and bewildered—greetings, comparisons began.

Comparisons, because you could hardly call them explanations. Each group in turn told what had happened after leaving the *Pride of Orion* and described how they came to be on Marglot. Julian Graves was the last to speak. Long before he was done, Louis Nenda was wriggling and fidgeting where he sat. He raised his eyebrows at Hans Rebka.

Hans waited for Graves's final words, then said to Nenda, "I agree. You're right."

"Right? I'm more than right. I'm damned right, and this is all wrong." And, when the others stared at Nenda, "Don't you see it, any of you except Rebka?"

Hans said, "They don't. We have to explain." He turned to the rest. "There's such a thing as coincidence, but this goes beyond it. Look at the facts. Every group went in different directions and did totally different things. But here we are on Marglot, all of us."

"Not all of us." Ben spoke softly. "Lara isn't here. That was my fault."

"No." Darya turned to him. "It was my fault. I was the one who insisted on going to Iceworld."

Rebka said, "It was Lara's own fault—she deliberately disobeyed Ben's order. Anyway, we've already been over that ten times. We have to focus on today. How did it happen that we all arrived here, like magic?"

"*Just* like magic." Nenda snorted. "Let me tell you somethin'. When I was younger and even dumber than I am now, I wasted lots of time in the Eyecatch Gallery on Scordato. I studied the gamblin' games, an' finally I found one I liked. I watched it played, figured I couldn't lose. Twenty buttons, and twenty different colors that could come up on a screen. The color for any button changed randomly with each play. You paid for ten tries. If on any try you pressed your button and the screen came up yellow, you were sunk—out of the game. Otherwise you kept goin'. Make it all the way, an' you won double your original stake. I worked out the odds. You had nineteen chances out of twenty that you'd make it through any one try, so you had nearly a six out of ten chance—Tally will confirm this—of makin' it through all ten. That was better than evens of winnin'. So I paid my stake, an' I played. I hit green and purple and orange and black, all the way through to my tenth play. Then I pushed a button one last time, an' the screen came up yellow. What I hadn't known was that the game was rigged. If you made it as far as the tenth play, you got yellow no matter what button you pushed."

The others stared at Nenda as though he had switched to some alien language, until Hans Rebka said, "Like the system we found ourselves in when we reached the Sag Arm. It was rigged. No matter what route you took from the *Pride of Orion*, or what method you tried, the screen finally came up yellow—you were shipped here."

Nenda added, "All roads lead to Marglot. I bet there's a thousand more buttons in that system that nobody tried. Me an' At, we did it the hard way. Off through the Bose Network to Pleasureworld, then all the way to Pompadour. But we didn't need to. We could have closed our eyes, pushed any button, and finished up in a transport vortex that would bring us *here*."

"Here," Darya Lang said, "where the animals are already dead. Here, where all other life on the planet is going to die. If Tally and Atvar H'sial are correct, *here* is a place where everything is doomed, even the sun itself. Why bring us here, just so we can die?" She turned to Nenda. "You say you and Atvar H'sial are the stupid ones, but you came here in a ship. And the reason you have that ship is because you *didn't* arrive using a transport vortex. If it weren't for you, we would have no way to escape."

"Minor correction. It's a *pinnace*, not a ship. An' with all you lot"—Nenda counted—"we'd never cram you in. Even if we piled you three deep, we wouldn't get off the ground. Either it's half a dozen trips to orbit, which would really be pushing the pinnace, or else the *Have-It-All* has to come down. Which I hate like hell to do, because that's my last card."

"But if E.C. Tally is right, we will be forced to seek such an escape. And yet—and yet—" Julian Graves sat with his hand hooding his eyes. "Logic is not my strong point, but I am confused. The Builders brought us here. I accept that. I can even accept that they were not aware of our mortal weakness, and expected that we would find a way to survive. But why not bring us here directly? Why have us travel first to a dead system?"

Darya said, "So we could see it. Would you ever have believed that a stellar system could die like that, if you hadn't been there and seen it for yourself? I wouldn't. The Builders wanted us to know that a whole system *could* die, before we were brought to one that is dying."

"But if the Builders destroyed the other system—" Teri Dahl began.

"They didn't. It was the others—the Destroyers—who did it."

"The Destroyers, the Voiders," Torran Veck said. "Sure. If everything doesn't work out with one race of super-beings, invent another. Professor Lang, if you can't make sense—"

"Save the bickering for later." Julian Graves cut him off.

"I make no claims as to my performance, which has so far been pathetic; but I am still the leader of this expedition. It is my conclusion that Professor Lang is right. We were brought to the Sag Arm for a purpose. That purpose is to see what *has* happened, to understand what *can* happen, and to take that knowledge back with us to the Orion Arm. Whatever causes this, we must find a way to stop it—not only for the sake of beings in this arm, for our own home clades." He turned to Nenda. "I am assuming that the *Have-It-All* is still somewhere in orbit?"

"Sure it is. One yell from me and J'merlia can bring it here. But I won't do that 'til we have to, because the *Have-It-All* is my only ticket home."

"That is a policy both wise and practical. Also, we should learn as much as possible before we leave Marglot. However, for my own peace of mind I would like you to do one thing. Please contact your crew on the *Have-It-All* and confirm that they are in a position to land here on Marglot, if necessary at short notice."

"I'll do it—though I'll tell you right now, the idea of this lot clutterin' up the inside of my ship don't exactly thrill me. I'll call from the pinnace. It has better transmission equipment than the suits, an' there are channels that Kallik will be sure to have open. Take me a few minutes."

He moved to the multiple overlapping leaf layers that formed the wall of the cone-house. As he pulled the inner layer aside, Hans Rebka was somehow standing next to him.

Nenda paused with his hand on the side of the leaf. He said, softly enough so that Rebka alone could hear, "I don't remember anybody invitin' you."

"I invited myself." Rebka motioned Nenda to continue beyond the inner layer. When they were standing in the narrow space between the leaves, he went on, "Look, I know what I think of you, and I can guess that you don't think any better of me. But we are both realists. Like it or not, Julian Graves is in charge of this expedition and the others will do what he says."

"Yeah. Old numb-nuts, the Ethical Councilor. He never met an alien he didn't like, even when it was tryin' to kill him."

"I don't think anyone but you and me realizes how much

danger we could be in—maybe Atvar H'sial, because the two of you seem to be on the same wavelength. Anyway, I've got an itch inside that I can't scratch, and it feels like trouble."

"Yeah. But we don't know when an' how." Nenda whistled through his teeth. "All right. I hate to say this, but I'll go along. We work together, 'til we're out of this crappy place an' home in the Orion Arm. Then it's back to business as usual."

"Some business there I can do without. I was twelve hours away from execution when an inter-clade councilor arrived to take me to Miranda. Now I feel like I'm waiting to be executed on Marglot." Rebka pushed his way through the remaining leaves until he was outside the cone-house. There he paused until Louis Nenda joined him. Rebka went on, "Seems like our worries are justified. What do you make of this?"

The two men stared at the ground, then looked up to the clouded sky. Here at the Hot Pole, perpetually warmed by the hot gas-giant around which Marglot orbited, an impossible event was taking place.

All around, large flakes of white drifted down.

It was snowing.

"Want to go back an' tell 'em the news?" Nenda jerked his head toward the cone-house.

"I think you should make your call to the *Have-It-All* first. Let's see what else we can learn."

"Yeah. Graves will start cluckin' an' gibberin' if we go inside, but there's not a damn thing he can do."

They began to walk side by side across the snow-covered ground. Hans guessed that it must have started at least an hour ago. A faint glow of dawn was touching the eastern horizon, and by its light the outline of the pinnace was visible ahead. An outline only, because already it stood covered with a thin layer of snow. Cone-houses, scattered all the way to the horizon, formed steep-sided pyramids of white.

Their suits kept the men warm, but Hans confirmed from his monitor the large and sudden drop in temperature. Snow was sticking to everything, which meant that the air and ground could not be much below freezing.

Make that, much below freezing *yet*. It was not over. The suit record showed a continuing decrease of a few degrees an hour.

They had reached the pinnace, and Nenda slid one door open. He cursed as blown snow and snow from the roof fell on him and on the pilot's seat. "Claudius was right. We should have stayed on Pleasureworld." He waited until Hans Rebka had moved across to the passenger seat, then scrambled in after him. "If we had any sense, we'd take off now, and to hell with it. I know, I know, we can't— but Atvar H'sial would understand if we did."

He went to work at the communications console. "Hope this funny weather don't mess up signals."

"Are you sure they'll be listening?"

"You kiddin'? I've seen better, but this will do."

A grainy image of Kallik had appeared on the pinnace's central display.

"Master Nenda! And Captain Rebka also!" The Hymenopt was hopping up and down in excitement. "We had been wondering and worrying."

"Worryin' why?"

"Marglot is changing. During our first orbits, one hemisphere was warm and one was ice-coated. Now we see clouds everywhere—snow clouds, from their appearance— and there is evidence of tremendous winds blowing between the cold and warm sides."

"No need to worry about us. We're near the Hot Pole— or what used to be the Hot Pole. It's snowin' here, too."

"Just as predicted, from what Archimedes discovered."

"Archimedes? He don't have the brain to predict anythin'. Is there some way he could see what was happenin' down here, even through the cloud layer."

"Not at all. As observations of Marglot became less relevant because of clouds, J'merlia and I assigned to him a different task. We suggested that he use the aft chamber to study the planet M-2, and see what might be learned there."

"Kallik, you two were just tryin' to keep Archie out of

your hair an' out of the control room. You know there's no life on M-2, never was and never will be."

"That is true. But Archimedes came back to us almost at once. He asserted that rapid and inexplicable changes were taking place on M-2. He wondered if we could tell him what was happening."

"Of course, we could not." J'merlia had crowded in next to Kallik. "Where is Atvar H'sial?"

"She's doin' fine. Get on with it."

"Of course. We had no hope of visual data better than those provided by the superior sight of Archimedes." J'merlia rolled his lemon-colored compound eyes on their short eyestalks. "But even we could remark evidence of vast changes. However, it was not until we employed other sensors that the overall situation became clear to us. When we arrived in this system, the average temperature of the gas-giant M-2 was eight hundred degrees. Now, hard to believe, it emits negligible thermal radiation. Our bolometers register a surface as cold as liquid nitrogen."

"Which sure as hell sounds like bad news for Marglot." Nenda turned to Hans Rebka. "Liquid nitrogen?"

"Seventy-seven degrees absolute. It will take a while for the surface here to go that far, because the inside of the planet must have plenty of stored heat. But long before that, you and I and everyone else on Marglot will be—what are you doing?"

Nenda had reached out to the controls and flipped a switch.

"Turnin' off all communications. You were going to say we would be dead, weren't you? If Kallik and J'merlia think that At and me will get killed, they'll go right off their heads. Leave this to me." He switched the channel back on. "J'merlia, is the *Have-It-All* ready to fly re-entry?"

"Of course. It has been perfectly prepared for that, ever since the moment of your departure."

"Good. D'you know where we are, from our suit beacons?"

"Precisely where you are."

"Then I want the *Have-It-All* down here, quick as you can do it—but fly careful."

"Certainly. It will be as you command. We will fly fast, and we will fly carefully, and we will fly with joy."

Kallik added, "Master Nenda, it will be a pleasure and a privilege to come to Marglot and see you again. We have so missed—"

"Yeah, yeah, yeah." Nenda switched off the channel. "You can't afford to get Kallik an' J'merlia get goin' on the grovellin', or there's no stoppin' 'em."

"How long do you think it will be before the *Have-It-All* arrives here?"

"At least a few hours. I told 'em, they've gotta be careful. J'merlia's a hell of a pilot, but he knows that Atvar H'sial will pull off his legs an' use 'em as backscratchers if he damages my ship." Nenda stared out of the window, where the wind was stronger and snow was driving almost horizontally. "Gettin' a bit nasty out there. Anythin' more that needs to be said to the *Have-It-All*?"

"Will there be medical supplies for Ben Blesh?"

"Sure. An' the best robodoc that money can buy."

"Then I think that's it. I'm ready when you are."

"I'm not ready at all. But we might as well go." Nenda swung the door open, and had to shout above the sudden howl of the wind, "Back to the cone-house. Who wants to be the one gives the others the good news?"

CHAPTER TWENTY-NINE
Stranded on Marglot.

Cold, yes. Snow, yes. With no warmth from M-2 and the sun a brilliant but far-distant ball, anyone would expect those. But who could have predicted such a wind? Certainly not Louis Nenda.

On the leeward side of the cone-house the blast shrieked and howled around him. Despite conditions it could never before have experienced, the cone-house was standing up well. The great leaves ripped off one by one, but the central trunk held steady. That was just as well, because if the cone-house collapsed it would fall on Louis.

The snow was now almost waist-deep. He dug and tunneled and carved himself a kind of bunker in it, not much protection but better than nothing; and better by far to be here than sitting listening to the brainless talk within the cone-house. Everyone except Hans Rebka and the silent Atvar H'sial talked and acted as though the game was over and they were all safe from danger. The *Have-It-All* would land, they would board it, and they would fly home to the Orion Arm using the same set of Bose nodes as Nenda had used to arrive here. They were idiots, all of them.

Nenda looked at his suit monitor. Twenty below, and dropping. He had confided the truth to Hans Rebka.

"No point in tellin' everybody yet, but the *Have-It-All* is a *space*ship. Sure, it can fly atmospheric, an' in any reasonable conditions it can take off to anywhere. But I'm not sure we'll see reasonable conditions. With ice loading all over the hull and drive efficiency down to maybe thirty percent, the mass that can be hoisted to orbit will be way down."

"What about the Bose drive?"

"Unaffected. But you can't use the Bose drive unless you're at a Bose node. It'd be a miracle if there was one on the surface of Marglot. Even if there is, we got no idea where it might be."

"So what's your suggestion."

"I don't have one. I'm goin' outside. If conditions are too bad, the *Have-It-All* may not be able to land at all."

And how bad was too bad? Nenda again glanced at his suit monitor. Down to twenty-five below. Where the devil was the *Have-It-All*? Louis wasn't sure which worried him more: the idea that it was too windy to permit a landing, or the idea that J'merlia would attempt it no matter what and smash the ship to pieces.

He knew what would happen, of course. J'merlia, with Kallik's enthusiastic support, would try for the landing no matter how impossible.

He felt a sudden weight on his legs, and thought for a moment that part of the cone-house must have collapsed. He turned. It was Sinara Bellstock, wiping the snow from her faceplate and peering in through Louis's.

"I was worried about you." She snuggled down beside him, half demolishing the shelter that had cost him a great deal of trouble to make. "Captain Rebka said that you had gone outside. You've been carrying a tremendous load ever since we left the *Pride of Orion*. And Torran Veck told a story from pre-space times, about a man who went out into the snow to die so that others of his party might be saved. I thought you might have—I was afraid you might have— but I should have known, you are too brave for that."

It took Louis a moment to catch on. Who in his right mind would wander off outside, to die in the cold? Louis had heard about cases like that, and decided that in the old days there were even more lunatics around than there were today. Sinara, of course, was looking for a hero. Didn't she know that you were a real hero if you helped people to survive—especially yourself?

"I didn't come out here to die." Even with his helmet in contact with hers, he had to shout to be heard above the wind. "I have no intention of dying. I'm looking for the *Have-It-All* and wondering where the hell it's got to. They ought to have been here hours ago."

"What does it look like? I mean, its lights. I know we won't be able to make out its shape in these conditions."

She was right about that. Louis could see maybe forty meters. Everything beyond was obscured by falling snow, changed from its earlier gentle flakes to a torrent of hard-driven ice needles.

"Maybe a searchlight, though that isn't necessary. J'merlia will be landing using instruments only. The ship will be flying in atmospheric mode with wings deployed. There should be navigation lights, one steady red, two flashing red."

"You mean like that?" Sinara immediately pointed off to the left, in the direction of the pelting snow crystals.

Beginner's luck. Louis had stared that way a hundred times, scraping ice from his visor, and seen nothing.

"Exactly like that. Sinara, don't move!" She was starting to stand up. "Wait 'til they land."

He didn't like the look of the way those lights were veering and tilting. The *Have-It-All* had stabilizers, but when you came right down to it the ship was designed for space, not atmosphere. If the wind happened to be too strong, there would be problems.

The navigation lights rolled, pitched upward, straightened, and fell. Louis could not estimate the distance of that final drop.

"Come on. Now we go."

You couldn't run through waist-deep snow. Kallik or Atvar H'sial would have covered the distance in a dozen gigantic leaps. Louis floundered. Even Sinara was better at this than he was, reaching the ship twenty meters in front of him. The hatch was three meters above her head, far too high to reach. She would have to wait until someone lowered a ladder—no easy job in this wind and snow.

The hatch opened barely wide enough to admit a suited human. Louis heard a startled scream. He saw Sinara grasped by a giant tentacle and whisked inside.

Good old Archimedes. Brains weren't everything. He panted his way the final few meters and stood expectantly. He was grasped and whipped up and away like a paper doll.

Kallik and J'merlia were leaping with excitement as Archimedes set him down. But first things first.

"Damage assessment?"

"The structural damage is superficial. But—" J'merlia looked uncertainly at Sinara Bellstock.

"It's okay. You can talk in front of her. She can't learn anything the rest won't know soon enough."

"The engines to permit atmospheric flight present no problems. They are high above ground level. If there is snow and ice to be cleared from them, it will be no more than an hour's work after they have cooled down. There will also, of course, be the need to clear a runway for takeoff. The drive to return us to orbit is another matter. It sits on the underside of the ship. It must be cleared of packed snow and ice, which will be a lengthy task. That, however, is not my main concern. The efficiency of the thrustors is low until they have had a chance to warm up. In space this is no problem. Here, however, heat is constantly carried away by wind, and in such intense cold the *Have-It-All* may be unable to achieve orbit with its projected loading."

"You're talkin' big stuff, right? We may need to lighten a lot, not just dump the odd person out of the hatch and overboard."

"I fear so. Major fittings must be removed from the ship, and even then the attainment of orbit is questionable."

"Lovely." Nenda turned to Sinara. "Did you know, it took me twenty years to put all this together an' get the *Have-It-All* the way I like it?" He did not expect an answer. "Come on. You an' me have to leave."

"But we only just arrived!"

"I know. But it's gettin' colder out there, an' it's still snowin'. Before things freeze solid an' nobody can walk through it, we have to bring everybody over from the cone-house. After that, I give 'em the good news–bad news routine."

"Isn't it all bad news? You may have to strip your ship down to the bare bones, and even then you don't think it will fly out of here. What's the good news?"

"That everyone except Lara Quistner is still alive. If we work real hard an' have a bit of luck, maybe we can keep it that way."

Inside the cone-house Ben had merely been useless. On the way to the *Have-It-All* he became an out-and-out liability.

He had tried. When Nenda, backed by Julian Graves and Hans Rebka, stated that they must move to the comparative safety of the ship, Ben had closed his suit and stood up with the others. He followed Torran Veck. The outer leaves of the cone-house had frozen brittle and snapped off when they were pushed out of the way.

Torran headed straight for the ship, using the path made through the snow by Louis and Sinara. Ben intended to do the same. He had taken only half a dozen steps when the full force of the wind hit him. Without the strength to resist and unable to react quickly, he was blown sideways to lie full-length and helpless. He could not bite back a cry of pain as his rib cage twisted.

Torran turned at once. "Ben? Can you hear me?"

He spoke over the suit radio channel. Ben replied—he hoped it was calmly, "Yes. But I don't think I can move."

"Don't even try. I want you to stiffen your suit all over and make it rigid. Can you do that?"

"I think so."

"Do it now. Tally, Rebka, can you help? We need to turn him over. The back of his suit is smoother than the front."

With his suit stiffened, Ben felt no pressure on his limbs or body. A few moments later he was on his back, staring upward. Tiny flakes of ice, hard as sand grains, pelted his faceplate. He found his body moving, head forward. The others were pushing him like a human sled toward the *Have-It-All*. Except that it must be far harder than pushing a sled. In this temperature, the pressure of his suit on the snow would not cause the melting that made a sled's movement so easy. His progress was a series of unpleasant bumps and jumps.

How much farther?

Ben gritted his teeth and told himself that it was much easier for him than for the ones who were half-pushing, half-carrying his body. He knew he had reached the *Have-It-All* only when one of Archimedes's great tentacles coiled around his body and lifted him slowly and carefully through the hatch.

The Zardalu had to be freezing. He wore no suit. The whole entrance chamber was covered in snow, and it was almost as cold here as it was outside. Archimedes held his position, hoisting humans and aliens one by one from the frozen surface of the planet and into the ship.

When Louis Nenda, the last one, was lifted in, Kallik slammed the hatch closed. Archimedes, shivering all over and with his great body puckered into midnight-blue goosebumps, headed rapidly for the ship's interior.

Nenda said, "Archie has the right idea. Come on, everyone will fit into the main conference room, provided Archie lies down along one of the walls. We can all take our suits off and sit in comfort."

This time Ben was going to walk if it killed him. He didn't know who to thank for getting him this far, but he moved with the others to the *Have-It-All*'s luxurious conference room. And if everyone's suit was coming off, so was his. It took him three times as long as anyone else, but finally he was done and could ease himself into a seat.

He was sitting opposite Darya Lang. She gave him one look and said to Louis Nenda, "Medical treatment." Then, to Ben, "You have as much right as anyone else to know what's going on. But right after this meeting, that arm and those ribs receive expert attention."

Fixing me up so we can all die together? Ben saw Nenda's grim look as the other man sat down at the end of the table.

Nenda began, "Conditions are bad out there, an' I can't see 'em gettin' anythin' but worse. You may think it's no problem, we'll be up an' out of here in ten minutes. That's not true. Here's where we stand."

He described the problems of the ice loading and the reduced efficiency of the engines that had to take them to orbit. He concluded, "So unless somebody has a brilliant idea, there seems to be only one answer: we have to lighten ship in a big way. Anything that can go, must go. Things like this, for example." Nenda tapped the tabletop in front of him. It was a gorgeous expanse of smooth alabaster, into which dust or even crumbs of food were absorbed leaving no trace. "Beautiful, an' valuable. But when things get desperate, in a pinch it's expendable. We'll make an inventory. If you're in doubt, ask me. I know what we need to fly. I also know what we need to survive in space. Reducing us to a minimum is goin' to be a long job—three or four days, I'd say. An' at the end of it we still may not know what our chances are. Also, we'll need a party to go outside again an' clear ice and snow off the engines and the control surfaces, an' make us a runway in case we fly atmospheric. I'll accept volunteers for that in fifteen minutes."

He looked down the table at Ben. "You're not on that list. You come with me now, and we'll fix you up."

Ben forced himself to his feet. His legs felt as though they belonged to someone else as he followed Louis Nenda out of the conference room and along the upper corridor of the *Have-It-All.*

"You don't think we'll make it, do you? Even with everything inessential stripped away, you don't think that in these conditions the ship can reach orbit."

Nenda shrugged. "What I think don't matter. I've been wrong before. Main thing is, we do what we can. Anythin' we can leave on Marglot, we do. Up on the table now, an' slide into the opening."

They were in the ship's medical center, the main part of which was shaped like a horizontal cylinder. Ben went in feet-first and inched forward until he was lying full length and flat on his back.

"That's good. The doc will tell us if you're ready to go dancin' again. Don't worry about the farmyard noises an' all the spaghetti. It's non-invasive. Have fun, an' I'll leave you to it."

Ben looked up. Hundreds of multi-colored tendrils were

descending from a sphere suspended from the ceiling of the cylinder, homing in purposefully on his body. Clucking and chirping came from all around, accompanied by a dazzling array of lights. Ben felt touches in a hundred places at once, delicate pressures in combinations that were never the same twice. This might be a robodoc, but it was like nothing that Ben had ever seen. He wondered for which type of being the unit had originally been intended. It would easily accommodate something far bigger than a human.

He started to turn his head, until an admonishing voice said. *"Lie still. It is beginning."*

The gentle touches of the tendrils went on, accompanied by small chills here and there on his body as though a cool spray was being applied for a second or two. Ben was beginning to wonder how long this would go on—and just what was going on—when the same dispassionate voice said, *"It is finished."*

The array of tubes, fibers and wires retreated into the medusa from which they had emerged. The sounds ended, the lights went off. The voice said, *"Please wait here for at least five minutes before you leave."*

That was it, the whole thing? Ben was mightily unimpressed. There had been no examination, no imaging of his arm or ribs, no adjustment of bones, no careful assessment of torn muscles or ligaments. He said, aloud, "That has to be the most stupid medical procedure I've ever heard of. What did it do?"

He expected no answer, but the voice said, *"All bones were placed into perfect alignment. Instantaneous hardeners were applied to break points. Intercostal muscular inflammation was eased and five hematomas dissipated. There will be no more pain."*

Ben reached across with his left hand to feel his ribs and right upper arm. There was indeed no pain. Also, there was none of the mental numbness and disorientation that normally went with painkillers.

"However," the calm voice continued, *"despite a feeling of well-being, the recovery process is far from over. For the next several weeks, body stresses should be kept to an absolute minimum. New trauma must be avoided at all costs."*

Ben took little heed of that. He felt like a new man. And that new man could, at last, began the action that had formed in Ben's mind as he listened to Louis Nenda in the conference room.

He headed back through the ship to locate his suit. On the way he passed Kallik and Archimedes, but the aliens were busy and gave him scarcely a glance. The conference room had its own terminal and display. Ben decided he wanted something closer to an exit. He found another terminal in a room next to the chamber where he had first entered. Rivulets from melted snow still pooled on the floor.

The message he left had to be fairly short and simple. He didn't want someone to come in and catch him in the middle of writing it.

To all of you—and especially to Sinara. I am going outside again, but it is certainly not my intention to seek death in the cold and snow. Nothing could be more inconsistent with my training as a survival specialist. I am going because I believe that all the measures proposed will prove insufficient to raise the Have-It-All *into orbit from the surface of Marglot.*

I want to help, and I have something in mind. It is a long shot, but it is different in kind from everything else that you are doing. It can certainly do no harm to anyone except possibly me. Do not come looking for me; that would be a waste of time that you should devote to your own plans as stated. Although I do not expect to return, you will know if I succeed. Good luck to all of us, whatever happens. Ben Blesh.

He climbed into his suit and went through to the next room. He opened the hatch and looked down. It was a long drop, but into deep snow. He would suffer no injury. A bigger worry was the hatch. If he left it open when he jumped, freezing air would invade the inside of the ship, which needed all the warmth it could get.

The hatch could be raised upward. If he stood on the edge, grasped the top in both hands, and stepped out backwards, then he could snap the hatch closed as he dropped.

Ben stood for a long time before he moved. If he was

wrong he would die a drawn-out and lonely death as his suit ran out of air, water, and warmth. If he was right he might die even less pleasantly. Not the greatest of options.

But waiting would not improve them. Ben opened the hatch, grasped the top, and stepped out backwards for the blind drop to the surface.

The snow had stopped falling, and for the first time the sky was cloudless. It was full daylight. All around Ben stood a frozen wonderland of pure and dazzling white. He stared up. Light reflected from the surface and scattered so intensely in the atmosphere that M-2 was invisible in the bright sky.

The drifted snow changed the appearance of everything. There was a real danger that he might lose his way. That would be the ultimate failure, a journey that ended not in tragedy but in farce.

Ben studied the faint line that marked earlier movements between the cone-house and the ship. It should be easy to go that far. Beyond the cone-house he saw a lumpy hummock that must be the walking car. It had not moved since its arrival with Ben and Darya aboard, and it ought to provide the bearing that he needed.

He followed the half-covered track to the cone-house. With no wind and with his improved condition, it was hard to believe that he had been unable to cover this short distance just an hour or two ago. He continued into the unmarked wilderness beyond. With snow so deep and a hardened crust of ice, this was much harder going. He told himself that he would only need to do it once.

Snow had drifted against the car. He stepped close and brushed one side clear to provide a line of sight up the hill. He fixed that vector in his suit's locator and began to plow his way up the shallow incline.

The other side of the hill led down to the valley with the stream, now frozen and snow-covered. The road had vanished. Ben could see no landmarks at all. He was forced to operate from memory—unreliable memory, from a time when he had been strongly and continuously medicated. He walked, stopped, hesitated, started again, and finally halted. This was as good as he would get. He cleared a place big enough to sit, then used packed snow to make a steep little bank against which he could lean. He sat down. The scene had an eerie tranquillity and beauty. As far as the eye could see, the valley was an undisturbed white. Above it the cloudless sky shone greenish-blue.

Now there was nothing more that Ben could do. And precisely because he could do nothing, he relaxed for the first time since his injury on the surface of Iceworld. He had been unconscious for much of that time, but those medicated periods had not rested him. He leaned back against the little wall of snow. He adjusted his suit's thermal setting to its most comfortable level. As the long day drifted on, he drowsed.

What woke him was no more than a shadow, a patch of darkness sensed through closed eyelids in a place where no shadows should exist. He came fully awake, opened his eyes, and scrambled to his feet in a panic. Thirty meters away from him a black sphere hovered above the snow. He had no idea how long it had been there, but already it was beginning to sink down into the surface.

Would he be too late?

Ben made the effort of his life, scrambling and sliding toward the sphere. When he came to it he did not hesitate or slow. He hurled himself forward. The dark heart of the sphere swallowed him up, and one minute later it too was gone.

CHAPTER THIRTY
Stripping the ship.

Sometime, someplace, humans and aliens might discover practical telepathy. Until they did, there was always a chance that whatever you said might be misunderstood.

If Louis had not been convinced of this before, the point was emphasized as he was walking along the *Have-It-All*'s lower corridor and happened to glance into the conference room. He had just come from the lowest level, where Torran Veck, Teri Dahl, Atvar H'sial, and J'merlia were beginning to clear packed snow from the drive unit. Now Louis was looking for Kallik and Archimedes to set them to work.

He certainly found them, though what they were up to was another matter. Kallik stood by the conference room table, her round head level with the polished white top. Archimedes was sprawled along the length of it, his blue tentacles wrapped around each end. They flexed as Nenda watched, and the table top warped upward under a mighty force.

"I don't suppose you two would like to tell me what the hell you're doin'?"

"It is the table, Master Nenda." Kallik touched it with a forelimb. "Although we can pass it through the biggest of the cargo hatches, it will first be necessary to remove it from this room. That requires that it be broken into pieces. Indeed, although I had never thought about it before, it is a mystery how it was ever brought in."

"It wasn't. It was secreted on the spot by a bunch of Doradan Colubrids, an' for the moment it stays here. Archie, get down off that table or you'll be lookin' for a new set of guts."

"Master Nenda, you specifically declared the table to be expendable."

"*If*, Kallik. Didn't I say *if*? If things get desperate, an' we're not there yet. What I want is an *inventory*. We need to know the mass of everything that's not nailed down, plus a bunch of things that are. But until that's done, we throw nothin' overboard. Clear enough?"

"Master Nenda, it will be done exactly as you command."

"An' you, Archie, shape up an' get useful. If that table has to go outside in bits, maybe you go with it."

Nenda hurried away double-time through the ship's interior. Kallik was smart, and if she could get it wrong, so could anybody.

Claudius would not be a problem. Louis found the Polypheme coiled down tight in one of the cabins in a trance of terror. Neither useful nor ornamental—now there was a candidate to throw overboard when you needed to reduce mass. Louis hurried on. He was approaching the hatch through which they had all entered, and this part of the ship was colder than everywhere else. That was surprising. The air circulation system should have taken care of that long ago. Even more surprising was the sight of a group of figures in one of the nearby cabins.

Hans Rebka, Darya Lang, Sinara Bellstock, E.C. Tally, and Julian Graves. Almost half the available work force. And doing what? Not one damn thing, so far as Louis could see. They were clustered around a display terminal.

Louis was about to say, "It must be nice to be a guest on board, an' not have to work," when he saw the message on the display.

Sinara came over to him and grasped his arm. "Ben is outside. We must go after him."

"His message tells us just the opposite." Louis was still

reading. "Besides, we have no idea what he thinks he's up to or where he might have gone."

Darya said, "We don't know what Ben is doing, but Hans has his suspicions."

Rebka nodded. "I asked myself a couple of simple questions: What could Ben possibly hope to gain by going outside? And where could he go on the surface, with Marglot in its present condition? The answers are, nothing and nowhere. Most of the time Ben was here he was doped up, so he's seen even less of the planet than we have—and that's only about one square kilometer. But back in the middle of Iceworld, Guardian of Travel told us that a transport system would open now and again, to let us return there if we wanted to. I think Ben went outside to try to find it. He thinks he can use it to get back to the middle of Iceworld."

Louis stared at Darya Lang and Hans Rebka. "An' do what if he gets there? Things don't look great for us, but his chances are better here than they would be on Iceworld. Does he imagine that Guardian of Travel will drop everythin' an' hustle on over to give us a hand? We don't know much about what Builder constructs do, but we've learned a few of the things they don't. They don't leave places they've been sittin' in for millions of years—'specially to help a bunch of recent arrivals like us." He turned to Sinara. "As for us goin' outside to look, that's a bad idea. It's colder than ever an' the wind is startin' up again. Hope I'm wrong, but we may be in for another storm."

"And there are new potential troubles of quite a different kind." Julian Graves had been listening in silence, but now he turned to E.C. Tally. "Tell them what you told me, just before we came in here."

"It is the beetlebacks. Ever since I first encountered them, I have struggled to comprehend their meaning and their mission. This has been a frustrating task, but also a fascinating one. It appears as though there is a complete sharing of information. What one knows, all know. Long ago, I came to the conclusion from their speech that they had been placed on this world for a specific purpose. It is also clear that our arrival came as a total surprise to them. I conjectured that they operated on the assumption that Marglot would lack animal life of every kind. But what were the beetlebacks themselves supposed to do next? From the data available, extensive as that is, I was still unable to determine the nature or timing of that new act. However, it occurred to me that the sudden and surprising cooling of M-2, and hence of Marglot itself, might be a trigger. In the hope of confirming or denying this theory, one hour ago I tuned the equipment of the *Have-It-All* to the frequency employed by the beetlebacks. I hoped for at best a distant signal, provided perhaps by reflection from a high ionized atmospheric layer—although the weakness of incident radiation from the distant solar primary was not encouraging for the formation of such."

Nenda glared at Julian Graves, who said, "I think, E.C., you might dispense with certain explanatory details."

"At the risk of a possible reduced understanding? Very well, if you insist. What I discovered was not a weak signal, but a very strong one. It emanates from forty or fifty kilometers away, and is just one of several similar but weaker signals. Since we saw that the beetlebacks possess no means of ground or air transportation, I am led to another conjecture which I see no way to confirm. Colonies of beetlebacks were placed *all over Marglot*, before our arrival. Those on the warm hemisphere were completely quiescent until the precipitating event of M-2's cooling. The beetlebacks thrive in a world of cold. They find cold essential to their very existence. This world, together with M-2 and the central star, are all headed toward cold extinction. We, as sources of heat, are now an anomaly on Marglot. The beetlebacks, judging from the changes in their radio signals, are heading this way, and I cannot believe that they come for the purpose of assuring our well-being. They are coming here to advance their cause. They are servants of the *Masters of Cold*."

Masters of Cold? Louis wanted to burst out laughing, except that no one else showed that inclination—and he himself could feel the sudden chill in the pit of his belly.

Julian Graves turned to Darya Lang. "Not Voiders, Professor, or Destroyers. Masters of Cold, able through a variety of measures to draw out and banish heat wherever it may be found. To remove the warmth of animals, the latent heat of gases and liquids, even to end the phoenix reaction within the stars themselves."

Darya had a sudden memory, a flashback to the surface of Iceworld. Lara Quistner, standing, screaming, crumbling from the feet up as implacable cold ascended her body . . .

"Humans," she began.

"And not only humans." Graves's skeletal face was somber, and his misty blue eyes stared at some distant vision. "The evidence was there, even before we left Miranda. We remarked on the condition of the bodies of the Marglotta, and of the Chism Polypheme. How had they died? They were apparently unharmed. But at the microscopic level, cells were ruptured everywhere throughout their bodies. As they would burst, were they *instantly and completely frozen*. A small group of Marglotta sought to fly far from danger, and to seek help. But by the time they left Marglot it was already too late. The Masters of Cold, or more likely some non-corporeal servant form, were already on board that ship. When it reached Miranda, those cold forms had vanished without trace. But you were right, Professor Lang, and I was wrong. Another force is present in the galaxy, a force as powerful as the Builders themselves. The Masters of Cold are not builders; they are indeed destroyers."

He added to Nenda, "Now it is more than ever vital that we escape from here, and carry this news back to our own Orion Arm. Meanwhile, I will seek to determine the current location of the beetlebacks. They pose an increasing threat."

Graves swept out, accompanied by Tally, Darya Lang, and Sinara Bellstock. Louis was left staring at just Hans Rebka.

"What's he think we're doing? Sittin' on our butts laughin' an' scratchin'?"

"He's an ethicist, Darya is a theorist, Tally is a calculator, and Sinara is a trainee. This thing is up to you and me, Nenda—or would you rather rely on the rest of them?"

"Don't try to scare me. I'm scared enough already. Got ideas?"

"You say we can fly atmospheric. Suppose we do that,

get as high and as fast as we can, and then turn on the *Have-It-All*'s space drive. Might that do it?"

"Thought of that a long time ago, an' Kallik checked it out. We won't make it to space unless our mass is way down."

"You trust Kallik's answer?"

"Hell, no. Anybody can be wrong, even Kallik. But Atvar H'sial and E.C. Tally came up with the same result. We can get off the ground, but not off the planet. The jury is still out on how well we'd do with the ship stripped to the bare bones."

"Suppose you were to fly atmospheric to the top speed you can reach, then dump those engines and switch to orbital thrustors."

"It's easy to see it's my ship you're tearin' to bits, an' not yours. But I looked at that, too. You can't dismantle and dump the atmospheric engines without a crew outside the ship. If you want to be unscrewin' nuts and bolts an' strippin' off engines while you're hangin' on the outside at Mach Two, be my guest. I put your chances of stayin' there more than twenty seconds at one in a million."

"You thought of it already."

"I did. But keep comin' up with them ideas. I just said anyone can be wrong, an' I'm sure in the group."

"A tight spot."

"Damn right." Nenda studied Hans Rebka's face. "You know the difference between you an' me?"

"You're a crook, and I'm not?"

"Don't be a smartass. The big difference is, we both know we're in deep trouble, an' I hate it. But you get off on it. Come on, admit it."

"I was raised for trouble, Nenda. I was born on Teufel."

"Yeah, yeah. 'What sins must a man commit,' an' all that stuff. I've heard it before, I don't need to hear it again. Question is, what do we do now?"

"We finish the inventory of the *Have-It-All*. We strip out everything we can do without. Then we strip out some things we believe we can't do without. Then we fly. And if we still have too much mass, I know a way to reduce it some more. You and I flip a coin, and the loser jumps overboard."

"Sounds fair to me."

"You have a two-headed coin, right?"

"How'd you guess." Nenda walked over to the port and stared out at Marglot's barren but beautiful landscape. "Fifty-five below. Think that Ben Blesh is somewhere out there?"

"If he is, he'd better be under cover. It's blowing up another storm."

"We better not stay too long on the surface ourselves, or we'll be here forever."

"I'll offer you a better deal than the last one. If we're too heavy when the time comes, I'll go outside and take my chances with Ben Blesh. If we're not too heavy and we do make it out alive, you'll owe me one. We'll go back together to the Phemus Circle and try to overthrow the government."

"You crazy? You've got me confused with a guy who cares about other people. I'll stick with the coin toss. Come on." Nenda led the way from the room. "Let's see what else may have to be chucked out of here, an' break my sorrowin' heart."

CHAPTER THIRTY-ONE
Iceworld again.

One of Ben Blesh's survival trainers had offered a warning: Be extra careful if you are ever forced to operate when sick or injured, because in such circumstances your senses provide a distorted view of reality. A familiar setting may seem to change beyond recognition.

Sound advice, but the converse situation had not been addressed. Suppose that you returned to a place you had only seen before when in shock and in pain?

Ben looked around, and felt certain that this setting was new to him. He had few clear memories of the interior of Iceworld, but surely he had never been in any place remotely like this.

He stared the length of the great chamber in which he stood, then looked side to side and at last overhead. He realized in that moment that he was wrong. He was standing at the base of a gigantic horizontal cylinder, hundreds of meters long and broad in proportion. The sides, studded with "light fixtures" from which no light emerged, curved away and up to meet far above his head. Suspended from that distant ceiling hung a familiar shape: a medusa's head of tubes, wires, and tentacles, all grossly enlarged. He was standing within a robodoc, exactly like the one

on the *Have-It-All*. Either it was expanded hundreds of
times, or Ben had been reduced to the size of a fly. In
his mind, the robodoc stood as a symbol of healing and
security. How could anything else in the universe know
that?

But this confirmed his conviction that he had never been
here before. It also increased his confusion as to what to
do next. When Hans Rebka had been in charge and Ben
was injured, all decisions had been made for him. Now he
had to act for himself.

His suit sensors showed reduced pressure and an unbreath-
able atmosphere, but as he watched it climbed to a density and composition that he could live with. Apparently
something knew he was here—wherever "here" might be—
and it did not intend to kill him.

He opened his faceplate and began to walk along the floor
of the giant cylinder. It was probably wasted effort, since
anything that knew he was here could presumably find him
no matter where he went. The walk was for his benefit alone.
He needed to do *something*, after that interminable wait in
the snow when he had wondered if he would ever move
again.

His first impression of the cylinder had been that it went
on forever, but as he walked he could see that he was
approaching a place where everything—floor, walls, ceiling—
abruptly ended. He walked on, to the point where one more
step would take him into space, and looked down. An
endless sea of gray lay below, without any reference point
to provide a sense of scale. For all he knew, the fog might
be one meter from his feet, or a thousand kilometers. The
cylinder hovered over a void of indeterminate extent.

Ben could take that final step out over the edge and see
what happened. All his survival training—which admittedly
had so far been of no use whatsoever—argued against it.
He turned, intending to walk back the length of the cylinder.

Lara Quistner stood waiting, maybe thirty meters away. She
was wearing her suit, as he had last seen her in life. An equal
distance behind her was an identical Lara, with another behind
that. A whole line of Laras waited on the central axis of the
cylinder, diminishing away into the distance.

Ben would accept the reality of the cylinder. He had little choice, since he was standing on it. Lara, or an infinite line of Laras, was another matter. They must be the products of his imagination.

He walked forward to the nearest waiting figure, reached out, and touched his gloved hand to her faceplate. The shape in front of him rippled and started to change. At the same time, the long line of image figures moved in rapidly to coalesce with the first one. The surface he had touched brightened. In less than a minute Ben stood before a shining spherical body. As the last ripples died away on the silver surface, a slender neck with a pentagonal head emerged from the topmost part.

Ben drew in his first deep breath since leaving the surface of Marglot. If every journey began with a single step, he had just completed a second one. Now to try for a third. Was the object in front of him Guardian of Travel, or would he have to start everything over from the beginning?

"Can you hear and understand what I am saying?"

The initial reaction was not encouraging. The silver globe sank into the surface of the cylinder, until only a small upper part was visible.

"I have returned from the world to which you sent us. You said that we might return."

The long-necked sphere remained silent, but it slowly began to reemerge from the floor. That had to count as progress of sorts.

"I would like to learn more about the planet to which you sent us."

"A special world."

At last, words.

"Did you say that a super-vortex lies at the center of that world?" This would be one hell of a time for Ben to learn that in his shocked and injured condition he had dreamed up the whole previous conversation.

"A super-vortex exists at the center. That is correct."

"Is it a transport vortex?"

"No. There is no way that it can be used as such. It was placed there long, long ago by our creator, to serve a quite different purpose."

"Will it work now, as it did then?"

"We do not know."

Not so good. "If it can still work, is it controlled at the planet I just came from?"

"It is controlled from here, and only from here."

Fifty-fifty on the answers he hoped for. As good as it was likely to get. But the difficult part lay ahead. Guardian of Travel seemed friendly enough to humans, but all its allegiance must lie with the Builders. Also, its sentience was inorganic and presumably completely logical. You had to imagine that you were trying to persuade E.C. Tally—and hope you remembered at least some of the facts correctly from the last time you were here.

"As servant to the Builders you once provided access to many worlds, including the surface of this one. Little by little, the service that you provide was diminished; not because the Builders wished it so, but because another group has been at work, destroying what the Builders made. Now you have access to only one world."

"One world; but a special world to the Builders."

"Special, but not special enough to save it. Unless you take action, that last world will suffer the same fate as all the others." This was the trickiest piece of what Ben had to say. From most points of view Marglot was already a dead world. "That world is not yet in the hands of the Builder adversaries. It can perhaps be saved from possession by them, if you take the right action here."

"If it can be saved by such action on our part, do you wish to return to it?"

That was a question to which Ben had given not one moment's thought. Go back? It was his turn to say, "I do not know. Why do you ask?"

"Because connection to the super-vortex at the heart of the world can be made at any time, while use of a transport vortex to the surface is possible only at precise times, when the configuration of other events permits it."

Die here of eventual starvation and dehydration? Or return to die on Marglot, in whatever strange condition that planet might be at the time of his transfer?

"May I postpone a decision on that?" Ben felt a paradoxical

sense of exhilaration. Sure, he was going to die. But he had taken another step toward his goal, and he would keep stepping as long as he had breath. "Let me tell you what must be done to save the world from possession by the adversaries of the Builders."

"We will listen." The pentagonal disk bobbed up and down on its long silver neck. "Be aware, however, that we too may postpone a decision."

CHAPTER THIRTY-TWO
Escape clause.

"It has happened before, if you are willing to believe some of the ancient stories." Teri Dahl's arms felt ready to fall off and she was taking a brief break. "An old man pushed a rock up a hill all day. Whenever he reached the top it rolled back down and he had to start over."

Torran Veck had been digging furiously, clearing away new snow and old ice from the runway in front of the *Have-It-All*. He paused for a moment. "I don't know what they meant by an old man, but I doubt if he was much older than I'm feeling. We've done this three times so far. How many more?"

"As often as we need, until we can get out of here. I heard Louis Nenda talking with Hans Rebka. No one, not even E.C. Tally, can calculate the weather patterns. At least the temperature seems to be holding steady. Nenda says we just have to keep the thrustors free from snow and ice as often as they become clogged, and hold the runway open."

"That's easy for him to say. He's not down here digging."

"In some ways this is harder on Nenda than anyone else. It's his ship that's being torn to pieces and thrown away. Look at that."

A flash of green showed at one of the upper hatches, and four storage lockers came sailing out to land on the snow.

Torran stared up. "That's Claudius at the hatch. If they have him working, things must really be bad."

"Nenda let him sit inside the shields on the forward reactor for a few hours, and it made all the difference. See how light a green he is? He's drunk. In his condition he's likely to throw himself out along with everything else."

"Who's keeping overall track of things?"

"E.C. Tally. That kind of job was made for him. He knows to the gram the mass of everything being thrown away, and he provides a running total anytime you ask for it—or even if you don't."

"How close are we to a decision, Teri? I've been too busy even to ask."

"Asking won't help. Tally says he doesn't know. Nenda and Rebka do, and maybe Julian Graves. They know all the facts. But not one of them is telling. My guess is that we still have a long way to go, because internal fixtures are bring thrown away faster than ever."

A fat disk, three meters across and half a meter thick, went spinning away through the air from an upper level of the ship. It flew thirty or forty meters before it plowed sideways into deep snow.

Teri said, "I think that's Louis Nenda's special luxury bed. The only one aboard who could throw it like that is Archimedes. I wonder where Nenda will sleep now?"

"Somehow I don't think that's his top priority. Nobody should plan much sleep anywhere for the next day or two." Torran glanced up at the sun. "Uh-oh. I had no idea it was so late. It will be sunset in another hour. We have to get back to work."

"I can't believe it's so close to sundown." Teri looked to the readout in her suit's faceplate. "And my suit agrees with the way I feel. It says we have four hours and more before dark."

"That's strange." Torran paused again in his work. "My suit is saying the same thing as yours. But our eyes aren't lying, either."

They stared at the sun, barely above the horizon, then turned to look at each other.

At last Teri said, "I have no idea what is going on."

"Nor do I. But this is strange enough, whatever it is, we have to report it this minute."

Teri Dahl was right. They did indeed have a long way to go. But she was wrong in thinking that Louis Nenda and Hans Rebka knew how far.

"We're not down to the wire yet, nowhere near it. There's loads more stuff can go." Nenda was in the conference room with Hans Rebka, along with E.C. Tally, Julian Graves, Darya Lang, and Atvar H'sial. Nenda's beloved conference table had long since vanished, torn apart by Archimedes and thrown outside. The chairs had suffered the same fate. The members of the group sat around on the floor.

Nenda went on, "One thing's for sure, if we have a chance at all, it's a slim one. I pulled us together because we need to make a couple of decisions. Tally, what we got up to now?"

"In our present situation, we have no chance whatsoever of achieving orbit."

"That's just lovely. What I had in mind was a bit more detail. Like, maybe, a few numbers, a few facts, some probabilities."

"Those I will gladly provide."

"But not too many of 'em."

"Can there be too many facts? However, let us begin with fundamentals. In order to reach a Bose entry node in this system, the *Have-It-All* must achieve escape velocity from Marglot. We must somehow attain with our drive a final velocity of better than 9.43 kilometers a second. Based on the *Have-It-All*'s present mass, and assuming a drive efficiency of thirty-eight percent, which appears to be the best that we can hope for, our top final velocity would be 7.61 kilometers a second."

"So we're not even close. Not even close to close. You're tellin' us we somehow have to get rid of twenty percent of the ship's original mass."

"Nineteen point three percent, to be more precise. However,

considerable mass reduction is still possible. We have scarcely begun to remove the second class of inessentials." Tally glanced around the conference room. "For example, wall paneling such as that. It is not needed for flight. It must go."

"That paneling is special hardwoods from Kleindienst. I'll never be able to replace it. Go on."

"All non-structural interior bulkheads are expendable. All food refrigeration systems, together with all food that would spoil. All but an absolute minimum of other foods. All water recycling equipment may be dispensed with, since present water supplies will suffice for a trip back to the Orion Arm. All drinks but water. All storage lockers, all furniture except for control chairs, all sleeping accommodations, all soft furnishings, all carpets and drapes. All clothing beyond what people are wearing at the time we leave. All spare suits. Most lighting fixtures. All exercise and recreational equipment. All toilet and bathroom fixtures, unless you feel it necessary to keep one working toilet."

Nenda said, "That would be nice." Hans Rebka added, "Keep going, E.C. This is beginning to sound familiar—just like it was where I grew up."

"All air quality monitoring and air purification equipment. This introduces a slight risk, which the councilor believes to be tolerable."

Julian Graves nodded. "Compared to the risk if we stay on Marglot, it's negligible."

"Most communication and navigation equipment, beyond a bare minimum. All cosmetics. All personal computing equipment. I volunteer to upload their contents into my own internal storage, and will download them again into new equipment if and when the opportunity arises. All interior temperature control and air circulation systems. Individuals must seek their own comfort zones. There are also many smaller potential savings. For example, Kallik assures me that a Hymenopt can go months without food or water, and she is quite willing to do so. My own body can be left behind, and only my brain retained. Should we survive, a new embodiment will present no problem. Though I cringe at the prospect of Sue Harbeson Ando's indignation if I return to her yet again for a replacement."

"I cringe at the prospect of somethin' a lot worse than that. Suppose we do the list, every one?"

"We will achieve a further mass reduction of 7.44 percent. Making the same assumptions as before as to engine efficiency, that provides us a final velocity of 8.27 kilometers a second."

"And we need 9.43 or better. It won't do. We're still more than twelve percent short."

"I don't understand something." Darya Lang had been sitting silent. "Seems to me we're missing out on something huge. What about all the equipment associated with atmospheric flight? There are the air-breathing engines, the extensible wings, the stabilizers, and the landing gear."

E.C. Tally was nodding. "Most of the landing gear is also needed for an air-breathing power takeoff. However, if we were to dispense with the rest, we would achieve a further mass reduction of two percent of our original. This would bring us to a final velocity of 8.44 kilometers a second. However, the consensus seems to be that we should not readily abandon a capability for atmospheric travel. Captain Rebka is worried that we may need to fly atmospheric for other reasons."

"I am. Keep going, E.C. You still haven't mentioned the beetlebacks."

"They are on my list of relevant facts. They move slowly, perhaps because the snow is hindering their progress. But they do move, and groups of them are still converging on our location. Given their possible role in the destruction of Marglot, it is difficult to believe that they come to do us anything but harm."

"So we may have to take a short hop. After that, maybe we burn our bridges and get rid of the *Have-It-All*'s engines for air travel. There's one more thing we need to sort out, an' maybe it's the main reason I wanted us to meet." Nenda looked around at the others. "This isn't a deal where we all get to pick, an' everyone has their personal preference. We're in one ship. Somebody has to make the call: if we fly, when we fly, how we fly. Some of you have been in trouble as often as I have—maybe more. You know you don't run emergencies by committee."

Darya said at once, "Take me out of the decision-making loop. I like to sit and think for a year before I make up my mind."

"You made your mind up about *that* quick enough. But all right."

Hans Rebka said, "I'm not like Darya, I can make up my mind fast. But I don't know this ship the way you do, Nenda. I don't know what it will and won't do, when you can change your mind, how you can cut corners. This one has to be yours. The rest of us can listen, and maybe make suggestions. But calling the shots must be your job."

"I was afraid you would say that. I don't like it much, but I know I'd like anythin' else a whole lot less." Nenda stood up. "All right. I'll say when. Meanwhile, we hold on to the equipment to fly atmospheric. Everythin' else goes."

He paused. The door of the conference room was history, ripped off its hinges and thrown overboard by Archimedes. Now Torran Veck and Teri Dahl stood in the opening, the lower part of their suits still caked with frozen snow.

"You got problems? We're busy here."

"No problems with the runway and the engines." Torran Veck took a step forward. "They're not perfect, but we'll have a hard time doing better. There's something else going on that we don't understand."

"Join the club."

"When we arrived at Marglot, we thought it was tidally locked to the gas-giant M-2."

"It was. It still is. This just isn't a Hot Pole anymore, because everywhere is cold."

"You don't need to tell us that. It's seventy below outside. And Marglot isn't tidally locked to M-2. Its rotation rate is changing."

Nenda didn't believe it. Hans Rebka didn't believe it, Darya didn't believe it. Nobody believed it, until they saw the evidence.

That came from above, and it was not obvious at once

to human senses. Outside the ship it was night, the sky was clear, and stars were visible. The sensors of the *Have-It-All*—those few that remained—made a series of observations and fed them to the ship's computer. Within microseconds, a precise calculation was completed. The computer reported:

The rotational period of Marglot when the Have-It-All *arrived at this system was measured to be 39.36142 standard hours, with a variation of one unit in the final digit probably caused by planetary internal activity. The rotational period as measured in the sequence of observations that was just completed is 14.388 standard hours.*

"Marglot ain't tidally locked any more?"

That is correct.

"It's in free rotation relative to M-2. How the hell can that happen?"

Nenda was talking to the group around him, but the computer answered: *There is no mechanism described in our data banks which can account for such a thing.*

E.C. Tally added, "Nor in mine."

The computer had not finished. *The same sequence of observations that provides a new value for the rotation period also shows that the rotation rate is still increasing, by 0.0644 radians per hour per hour.*

Tally shook his head in a human gesture of bewilderment. "I do not understand that, either."

"I don't understand it, an' I sure as hell don't like it. But I'm forced to believe it. Tally, we need to dump out all the items on your list, fast as we can do it. Everybody helps. If you're in doubt, don't come back an' ask. Chuck it." He waved his arm. "Go on, go on. Get outa here."

It was Nenda's ship, and his control cabin. Everyone moved out—reluctantly—except Hans Rebka and Atvar H'sial. The two men stared at each other.

"You realize it won't be enough, no matter what you tell people to throw out. We still can't reach orbit."

" 'Course I do. I'm not a dummy. I just didn't see any point advertisin' disaster. Suppose you were me, and had to act. What would you do?"

"Clean off the engines, reduce mass as far as I could—exactly the same as you are doing. Then I'd cross my fingers and fly. Don't worry, I'm not trying to second-guess you. I just want to be sure we're on the same wavelength."

"I think we are. Let's go and dump somethin' expendable—or maybe not so expendable. When in doubt, throw it out."

Hans Rebka left, leaving only Louis and Atvar H'sial in the room.

"How about you, At? What's the problem, too proud to work?"

"When my personal existence is at stake? Not at all. I wish to draw to your attention a factor which seems to have been overlooked. But first, a question. In terms of the rotational axis of Marglot, what is the *Have-It-All*'s current location?"

"We're almost at what used to be the Hot Pole, which puts us just about smack on the rotational equator. What's your point, At? It's a bit late for a geography lesson."

"But not, perhaps, for one in elementary mechanics. The acceleration due to gravity on the rotational equator of Marglot is 8.411 meters per second per second. With a rotational period of 39.36 hours, as it was when we first arrived here, and a radius of 5,286 kilometers, the centripetal acceleration on the equator was 0.01 meters per second per second. That is negligible when compared with the acceleration of gravity, little more than a thousandth of it. With a shorter period of rotation, equal to its present value of about 14.4 hours, the centripetal acceleration has increased to 0.08 meters per second squared. This is still a small value, an outward force equal to only about one percent of the gravitational force. It is insignificant when compared to the large reduction of mass needed by the *Have-It-All* in order to achieve orbit. However, the rotation rate is *still increasing*. Let us suppose, as a theoretical exercise, that it continues to increase at its current rate. This will have three effects, two of them undesirable and one desirable. The first undesirable effect will result from atmospheric inertia. The air of Marglot will resist being dragged around with the body of the planet. We must anticipate huge winds from the east, which I note are already arising. Second, the balance of forces on the planet will force it to assume a different shape.

Marglot will become increasingly oblate, bulging more at the equator. That will undoubtedly induce major structural changes. We must expect great earthquakes, of unknown magnitude."

"Wonderful. Just one more reason to get the hell out of here—if only we could."

"We already had reasons enough to leave. But the undesirable consequences are perhaps outweighed by the desirable effect of more rapid rotation. As the planet continues to spin faster and faster, the centripetal acceleration at the equator will increase. Furthermore, that acceleration increases *quadratically*, proportional to the square of the angular rate. Eighteen hours from now, the outward centripetal force at the equator will equal 12.3 percent of the inward gravitational force. The total downward force on an object on the surface at that time will equal the *difference* of those gravitational and centripetal forces. If the *Have-It-All* still exists then, and if there is a surface that permits a take-off, and if the thrustors perform at their estimated levels when we are in the air, we should be able to leave the surface and ascend to orbit."

"That's a whole lot of *ifs* you got there."

"True. But which would you prefer, Louis Nenda?" Atvar H'sial rose from her crouched position. "A substantial set of contingent possibilities, or a single unpleasant certainty?"

CHAPTER THIRTY-THREE
The end of Marglot.

Darya Lang normally worked alone. She did not like to be in charge of others, even when her own safety was involved. Today she was particularly happy to let someone else make the decisions.

On the other hand, those decisions had so far practically made themselves. In order to take maximum advantage of Marglot's rotation, the *Have-It-All* had to be launched to the east, and from as close to the equator as possible. It also had to be launched *soon*. The speeded-up planetary rotation was producing ground tremors that shook the ship, and bigger earthquakes were clearly on the way.

Darya was standing up, although that was never the way you prepared for a lift-off. It was not a matter of choice. Every chair in the cabin had been removed except the one at the controls where Louis Nenda was sitting. Lacking the service of his usual automatic sensor systems, Nenda had assigned Darya and everyone else on board to monitor some aspect of navigation or signals. The only exception was Claudius, off his radiation high and once again a stone-cold corkscrew of green misery.

Nenda might have the only seat, but he was not a happy man. Darya saw him take a last look around at his ship.

The *Have-It-All* had been stripped to the bones. With all interior bulkheads gone the entire interior length was visible. Darya could see them all—Julian Graves, Teri Dahl, Sinara Bellstock, Kallik, Atvar H'sial, everyone, in what had once been luxurious cabins and were now ragged metal frames. The aliens were as inscrutable as ever. The humans looked pale as ghosts. No one had slept for more than thirty-six hours.

The ship's intercom had been stripped out. Nenda had to shout to be heard above the howl of wind on the hull. His voice echoed along the bare walls. "We're all inside, and the hatches are closed. Hold on to somethin'. It's gonna be bumpy as hell 'til we're high enough to be above the worst of these winds."

Tally had been assigned to the display that looked aft from the ship. He said, "Beetlebacks. I see silvery reflections from a group of them. They are heading for the ship, but the winds severely inhibit their movements. Some are being swept off their feet and carried backwards."

"My heart bleeds. I wish we had a few in front, then I could run over 'em."

"But if we could capture one—any one. They share data, and our information gain could be enormous. A delay of a few minutes, until the nearest one reaches the *Have-It-All*—"

"—would be a lousy idea. Sorry, E.C. Say bye-bye to beetlebacks, and hello to a bump or two."

Nenda initiated the sequence for atmospheric take-off. *Bump* wasn't the word for it. Hans Rebka clung to a metal stanchion, while Darya hung on to him. First there was the bone-rattling run over hard ice. That ended at the moment of lift-off, but a few meters up the winds hit the ship with full force. The retractable wings fluttered and shook and seemed ready to break off. The ship tilted, and Darya thought one of the wingtips was going to hit the snowy surface. For a horrible moment there was no space at all between the wingtip and its own shadow on the ground.

The *Have-It-All* shivered and righted itself. As it gained altitude, Darya had a view of a bigger area of the changing planet. Patterns of dark lines crisscrossed the snow. The ground was already fracturing, breaking open into fissures that widened as she watched. Subterranean stresses were growing faster than anyone had expected.

A little higher, and they reached a region where the winds were less affected by local ground contours. The *Have-It-All* steadied. Nenda said, "I'm takin' us to three thousand meters, an' I'm goin' to hold it there for a while. We're not shakin' to bits anymore, but we want to gain all the speed we can as the planet spins faster. The air gets dragged around with everythin' else, so it will boost us." He was inspecting read-outs. "I hate to say this too soon, but you know what? We may make it. If I turned on the orbital thrustors right now, we have enough speed to take us to space. No hurry, though. Let's build up a good margin before we move."

Hans Rebka left Darya behind at the stanchion and dived forward to stand behind Louis Nenda. He said, "I'm not sure there's no hurry. Suppose that the rotation speed of Marglot goes on increasing?"

"It will. That's good. It helps us."

"To a point it does. But suppose it goes too far?" Rebka turned toward E.C. Tally, who was still staring at the aft display—probably longing for his lost beetlebacks. "E.C., would you do me a calculation? Suppose that the spin rate of Marglot goes on increasing. How long before the centripetal acceleration at the equator is equal to the surface gravity?"

"The calculation is rendered more complicated than you might expect, because the change of spin rate of Marglot continues to accelerate. The reason for that, I presume, is the planet's rapidly spinning inner core—which, as I noted at the time of my first arrival in orbit around Marglot, is the source of the planet's anomalously high magnetic field. That core is coupling now to the planetary mantle, and that in turn to the outer crust. To estimate the coupling constants—"

"Could we have a number, E.C., rather than a dissertation?"

"Certainly. The purpose of my comments is to explain that there must be uncertainty in my answer, since the future spin rate is itself uncertain. However, my best estimate is that centripetal and gravitational forces at the equator will be equal fifteen hours from now."

"So in fifteen hours, and probably a lot less because of the internal deformations, Marglot will come apart. Lumps of the planet will be thrown out into space. That will start in the plane of the equator. And Nenda, you are flying this ship—"

"—smack on the equator. Wrong place to be if there's fireworks."

Darya had been watching her own assigned display, one that looked out and down from the ship. She said, "There will be fireworks, and in a lot less than fifteen hours. It has started. Look ahead." They were approaching the night side of the planet. Beyond and beneath the ship the darkness was illuminated by a orange glare. "Volcanoes, and lava flows."

Nenda said calmly, "Maybe I should take us outta here right now." As he spoke, a long tongue of flame leaped skyward in front of the ship. A smoking juggernaut of rock ten times the size of the *Have-It-All* shot past, still glowing bright red.

"Maybe you should." Hans Rebka was equally casual. They spoke so softly that probably no one but Darya could hear either man. "There's already large-scale planetary deformation. It can only become worse, and the equatorial region is absolutely the wrong place to be."

"So we wanna be outta here. I hear you." Nenda turned and shouted, "Grab a hold of somethin' firm again. Orbital thrustors comin' on—now."

He did something that Darya could not see, but she felt the upward surge. The ship shook with its worst spasm yet. Vibrations seemed ready to tear it apart. Her knees buckled, and she clung for her life to the metal post.

"Snow and ice residue in the firing chambers." Hans Rebka had fallen to his knees behind Nenda's chair. "They don't like that at all."

"Nor do I. Let's hope it'll boil outa there in a minute or two."

Darya, struggling to remain on her feet and watch her assigned display, saw the image of Marglot visibly shrinking.

The upward thrust continued and the ride gradually became smoother. The possibility of continued life no longer seemed unthinkable.

Nenda went on cheerfully, "Well, unless something else happens we have it made. We're on our way to orbit. That was a lot easier than I expected. Once I'm sure we have orbital velocity I'll take us out beyond one of the poles. Safer to watch the show from there, all the junk will be flyin' out round the equator."

A show it was certainly going to be. The ship was ascending faster and Darya could see a substantial fraction of the entire planet. The swath of violent volcanic activity was spreading, growing wider while she watched. Far away from the equator, rocks like ruddy sparks emerged in shotgun volleys from the riven surface. Each one had to be at least as big as a house. If any were to hit the *Have-It-All*, Nenda's optimism wouldn't mean a thing.

Julian Graves came wandering on unsteady legs from the aft part of the ship. "What is our status? During that last convulsion I felt sure that we were doomed."

"Nah. Rattled us up a bit, that was all. We're in fine shape. The hard part was gettin' enough speed to take us to orbit. We have that, so everythin' else is easy."

"If we have reached orbital velocity and we are free to maneuver, why are we not heading at once for the Bose node entry point?"

"Too dangerous. The Bose node is close to Marglot's equatorial plane. We got to wait 'til the planet's spin-up is over before we can head for the node."

"I see. Very well. I rely on your judgment as captain. I will pass the word to the others. Everyone has held the station you assigned, but all are wondering as to our fate."

"Tell 'em the worst is over. They can sit back and enjoy."

Graves glared but said nothing. He went staggering away along the corridor, supporting himself against the metal walls and grabbing at the stems of missing light fixtures.

"That was a lie." Hans Rebka was back on his feet and once more standing behind Louis Nenda.

"Not all of it. We are at orbital speed, and I am takin' us toward the pole."

"You know what I mean. It's not dangerous to head for the Bose node. That's half a million kilometers away and it's nowhere near the equatorial plane. Chances of our being hit are negligible."

"Could be. You proposin' to go to Graves back there an' tell on me?"

"No."

"Thought not. You're as nosy as I am. How often do you get to see a whole planet fly apart? But what's causing it, that's what I'd like to know."

"Maybe we can answer that." Hans Rebka turned to Darya. "Do you remember what we were told by Guardian of Travel about the middle of Marglot?—though of course, we didn't know at the time that it *was* Marglot."

It was a struggle for Darya to think back. Their hours on Iceworld seemed years ago. "Isn't there some sort of vortex in the middle of Marglot? A big one, once used to change the rotation rate."

"Used once, and used again. That's what's happening now. The question is, where will all this end? What will be left of Marglot if the spin rate keeps going up?"

"I don't give a toss what happens to Marglot, though I admit I want to watch it go blooey." Nenda swiveled his chair to face the other two. "I'll give you another question. I don't trust the universe when it starts arrangin' things for my convenience. But just when we need it, Marglot speeds up its spin rate—in time to give us the added outward push we need to ascend to orbit. How come?"

Darya didn't think that Nenda expected an answer, but Hans Rebka was nodding. "We're not looking at the case of a benevolent universe, and this isn't coincidence. We owe our good luck to Ben Blesh."

"He froze to death on Marglot."

"I don't think so. He found his way back to Iceworld. Remember, Darya, we had the option of returning there? He did it. And now, from Iceworld, he is controlling events within Marglot."

"So he saved our asses? Pity we'll never get a chance to thank him. You believe that something Blesh did is responsible for *all that*? Sooo-eee."

All that. Nenda's gesture included everything outside the *Have-It-All*, but one feature dominated everything else. The ship had spiraled out and out and up and up, until Darya found herself looking down at Marglot from above. She could span the whole sphere with one hand. Except that it was not a sphere.

Marglot had become a fat ellipsoid. While parts of the world still showed the pristine white of undisturbed snowfall, a broad central belt glowed red and was shot through with sulfurous yellow flames. Marglot was developing its own planetary ring, a disk of hot ejecta expelled by violent vulcanism.

The others on the ship were drifting back into the control cabin, where the only remaining large display screen was located. They were silent as the central girdle brightened and Marglot continued to change in shape. The polar flattening and central bulge were too obvious to miss.

Hans Rebka was talking to no one in particular when he said, "Less and less at the poles, and wider and wider at the equator. Does it go on until the whole planet flattens into a pancake?"

Of course, it was E.C. Tally who answered. "It does not. An ellipsoid of revolution is a possible shape for a solid gravitating body only up to a limiting spin rate. Beyond that rate, instabilities grow exponentially and dissociation is certain. A threshold for the disintegration of Marglot must be reached in the near future."

"Not true, E.C." Nenda turned up the gain on the display. "Take a peek. It's already here."

The planet was changing. The spheroid had widened to become a fat disk of matter. Now that disk was dividing into three distinct lobes. The inner regions glowed white-hot, proof of enormous energies generated and released.

Nenda went on, "See what you got down there? It's Builders, one, Masters of Cold, zero. The whole damned place is doing a meltdown."

It was far from over. Darya could see more rifts developing within the three lobes of the shattered disk. Waves of compression and rarefaction built new nodes of compacted matter and left dark striations between them. They formed and dissolved chaotically as she watched.

Julian Graves had moved to stand next to Darya. He had his hand on her shoulder for support, although he was probably unaware of it. He said quietly, "The death of a world. But we are not witnessing genocide. That occurred before our arrival."

Marglot no longer existed. It had become streams of molten matter, flowing down from what had once been the poles to the equator, then spun off into space. The central region was no longer red-hot or white-hot. It flared blue. The middle of Marglot had turned from a liquid core to a plasma, ionized gas at a temperature of tens of thousands of degrees.

And still it was not over. Within the center of the blue-white maelstrom another shape was coming into view. A spinning darkness obscured the stars beyond. As the whirl-pool of matter outside it was expelled, the vortex grew in size.

Finally it stood alone as a column of absolute black. And then, while Darya's eyes were still trying to recognize its reality, it vanished.

The vortex was gone. Marglot was gone. In their place stood three great lobes of super-heated matter within a broad expanding ring.

Even Louis Nenda seemed overwhelmed—until he leaned back in his chair and said, "Well, there's a first so far as I'm concerned. I guess we'd all rather be here than there. Nothing could live in the middle of that lot."

"Maybe not." Sinara Bellstock had moved to watch the big display along with all the others, clustering into the remains of what had once been a control cabin as fine as any in the Orion Arm. But she had hauled along the small piece of communications gear that Nenda had assigned to her. She still wore the earpiece, and she seemed to be listening to something.

She went on, "Maybe no one can live there for very long. But I'm picking up a distress signal, and it's from one of our suits. It shows weak but definite vital signs. And unless the range and direction are wrong on my readout, it's coming from the middle of that." She pointed to the display of the glowing disk. "Ben Blesh is alive in there, in the place where nothing should be able to survive."

CHAPTER THIRTY-FOUR
Revolution.

It was still the ship's "conference room," even though in its gutted condition it could have passed as a bare cargo hold. And the room was still being used for a "conference," if that word could include a bitter argument plus insubordination by junior staff that verged on mutiny.

"I was not placed in charge of this expedition for the purpose of making popular decisions." Julian Graves had his back to the wall in both senses, leaning against a metal partition that had once held conference displays. "It was my responsibility to bring us safely to the Sag Arm; it is no less my responsibility to take us home again."

The mutineers were Torran Veck, Sinara Bellstock, and Teri Dahl. They stood shoulder to shoulder against the opposite wall.

"We were told that Louis Nenda was in charge of this ship." Torran Veck was for the moment the spokesman for the three, if for no better reason than that he was the only one tall enough to look Julian Graves straight in the eye. "Nenda should still be in charge. The *Have-It-All* is his ship and not yours."

"Louis Nenda was permitted to bring his ship only with the explicit understanding that it would be part of the

expedition's available resources. I relinquished command to
him while we attempted one difficult and specific act;
namely, he had to get this ship off the surface of Marglot.
He did that—brilliantly. But as soon as that was done,
command decisions reverted to me."

"Nenda didn't," Torran said, and the other two nodded
agreement. "Didn't get us off Marglot, I mean. We spoke
to Louis Nenda. He says that if it hadn't been for the
centrifugal force assist, the ship would still be down there—
or more likely, he thinks, it would be a white-hot blob
floating somewhere in the middle of a mess of planetary
debris. Ben Blesh got us away from Marglot."

"I am not seeking to diminish his contribution. But if we
fail to return to the Orion Arm, Blesh's sacrifice will have
been in vain."

"His sacrifice? You talk as though he's already dead. He's
not. Ben's out there. Unconscious, and maybe close to death,
but he's alive."

"I know. But we cannot risk this ship, and with it our
only hope of returning to the Orion Arm, for *any* member
of this expedition. You, or me, or Ben Blesh."

"He saved all of us. You won't even try to save him."

"Not at the cost of rendering pointless our whole journey to the Sag Arm, including the loss of Lara Quistner and
our own close escape from death. Don't you see that what
we have learned exceeds any of us in importance?"

"What *have* we learned? You can't even tell us."

"Not yet. We have a group attempting such an analysis
at this very moment. However, our success or failure to
understand is not the issue. There are other minds in the
Orion Arm, great minds who will take what we give them
and go beyond any deductions we are able to make. I am
truly sorry. I realize that Ben Blesh was your fellow group
member."

"He was more than that. He was our close friend."

Julian Graves knew that to be an exaggeration—he had
watched the survival specialists and sensed the strong rival-
ries within the group; but he was wise enough not to
challenge the statement. He merely said, "I was not his close
friend, but I am a member of the Ethical Council. The

prospect of Ben Blesh's death, while we are forced to stand by and watch, pains me no less than it does you. However, I must not—dare not—endanger this ship and all that we have done in a rash attempt to secure his survival."

Torran glanced at Sinara. They had orchestrated this in advance, and carefully. He had made the accusations, now she would move it to the next stage.

Sinara took two steps toward Julian Graves. "Suppose we could find a way to save Ben that did not endanger this ship at all? Suppose that it merely meant a delay of a day or two in entering the Bose node?"

"I think I know what you have in mind. Professor Lang, Captain Rebka and I already explored that possibility. A day or two's delay would be tolerable. Ben Blesh's suit, like all the suits, has built-in thrustors. They can be used for in-space maneuvering. We thought, perhaps we can simply wait for him to fly out of the region where the planetary debris is located. Then he can rendezvous with the *Have-It-All* in a safe location. The problem is that Ben Blesh is unconscious, and the equipment needed to control his suit remotely, from this ship, was stripped out and left behind on Marglot. No one ever dreamed that we might need it."

"We also spoke with Professor Lang and Captain Rebka, and they told us about your discussion. They thought that a delay in entering the Bose node would not be an issue."

"It never was. No one likes living in a ship in the derelict condition of this one, but everyone would endure it gladly for a few extra days if it meant we could save Ben Blesh."

Sinara said promptly, "Then we ask for a two-day delay in entering the Bose node. We also seek your permission to attempt a rescue mission for Ben."

"Didn't you hear me? Any danger to this ship—"

"There will no danger to the ship. At worst, you will lose three space suits and three members of the survival team group. We feel that it is our right to try to save our colleague and friend, provided that it endangers no one but ourselves."

"I am sorry, but you have ceased to make sense." Julian

Graves's furrowed brow betrayed his bewilderment. "Three suits, and the three of you?"

"It is simple enough. This ship is sitting high above the plane of debris, far from the danger zone."

"It must remain beyond that zone."

"We know. We also know, from the suit signals, exactly where Ben is located. He is deep within the zone of danger, surrounded by all kinds of fragments big enough to destroy this ship. We asked Louis Nenda if it would be possible to fly the *Have-It-All* on a vector that would exactly intersect Ben Blesh's projected suit position."

"Absolutely not!"

"We didn't ask him to do it, Councilor—we only asked if it would be *possible*. He said it would be easy. He also said he could establish that velocity vector when the ship was far away from danger. We ask you to agree to that, and only that."

"With what useful result?"

"Once the *Have-It-All* is moving at the right speed and in the right direction, the three of us, in our suits, leave the ship. We fly on, to rendezvous with Ben Blesh. However, as soon as we leave the ship, the *Have-It-All* uses its engines to change direction. It stays well out of the plane of danger, and heads toward M-2, a million kilometers away. When this ship gets there, it loops around *behind* M-2. That planet is huge, it will serve as a shield to protect you from free-flying debris. This ship then returns on the *other side* of what was once Marglot's equatorial plane. You will again be far enough out of that plane to be at no risk. And there you wait for us. We will fly through the danger zone in our suits, collect Ben Blesh, and bring him with us to safety."

"That sounds completely impossible."

"Some of it may be. It's possible that we will die trying to reach Ben, or die trying to get back to the *Have-It-All*. But the trajectories are quite feasible if you believe E.C. Tally and Kallik and Atvar H'sial. All three performed the calculations separately at our request, and all assured us that everything we are suggesting is well within the *Have-It-All*'s capabilities. The engines are now operating at full efficiency, and given the ship's reduced mass the maneuvers that we have described are easier than ever. Louis Nenda confirms this."

Julian Graves examined one by one the faces of the three people in front of him. He saw something that had not been there on the voyage out: absolute determination.

He leaned his head back on the cold metal wall. "You know, sometimes I think that all young people are mad. And sometimes I am persuaded that the only real progress in the world comes from those who are mad."

He was slowly nodding. Sinara said, "I'm sorry, Councilor, but is that a yes or a no?"

"It is neither." Graves stepped toward the waiting trio. "You know, in my distant youth I believe that I was quite mad myself. I would like to think so. But before we discuss your suggestions further, let me ask one question. You mentioned Darya Lang, Hans Rebka, Louis Nenda, E.C. Tally, Atvar H'sial, and Kallik. Is there *anyone* on this ship, other than myself, whom you have not already consulted regarding your proposed rescue mission?"

The final five minutes seemed to stretch for ever. Sinara stood in the *Have-It-All*'s one remaining useable airlock, next to Teri Dahl and Torran Veck. They were suited, waiting, ready to go—and, inevitably, there was one more briefing.

"Ideally, you would dive in perpendicular to the plane of debris." Hans Rebka was the speaker. "That would minimize your time there, and also your risk of collision with lumps of rock and solidifying magma. Unfortunately, Ben Blesh is heading out on a radial path, directly away from where Marglot used to be. That would make your trajectory at right angles to his, and if you were lucky—or unlucky—enough to run into each other, the impact would kill all of you. So Louis Nenda will fly—"

"Not me," Nenda interrupted. "J'merlia will pilot this one. He can slice things finer."

He went on, ignoring Hans Rebka's irritated look. "J'merlia will take the *Have-It-All* in on a path that's close to radial, same as Blesh's. So you'll be enterin' the debris belt at almost a grazin' angle, an' not much faster than Blesh is goin'. You'll approach him at only a few hundred meters a second. Your suits can handle that speed change easy enough. So you'll slow down, take him in tow, an' get the hell out of there. While all that goes on, the *Have-It-All* zips out an' away an' off toward M-2. 'Course, there's a disadvantage to doin' it this way. If you—"

"Got to make this quick." Hans Rebka cut him off. It occurred to Sinara that the two men were *competing* in the briefing. "Thirty seconds more and the two of us have to be out of this airlock so you can cycle it. Remember, the shallow entry angle will expose you to much more debris on the way in. On the way out, just pick the best path—"

"—an' don't worry about bein' met. J'merlia will make sure that the *Have-It-All* is there waitin' to pick you up."

"That's it, you two." Lacking an intercom, Julian Graves had to stand at the inner door of the airlock and shout. "Out of there, so we can cycle the lock. And the three of you—good luck."

Rebka and Nenda left reluctantly, nowhere near as fast as Graves would have liked. He was waving them on as the inner door closed.

As the outer door began to open with a hiss of escaping air, Teri Dahl said to Sinara, "Did you notice the way that Captain Rebka was staring at us? I didn't like it at all."

"I know what you mean. I've seen men with that look before. He had an expression on his face as though he wanted to screw us."

"That's it *exactly*! But what a time and what a place for it! In an airlock, in our suits, twenty seconds before we're ready to leave the ship. I'd heard that men from the Phemus Circle are sex-mad, but this is crazy."

"Hey, you two should worry." Torran Veck was laughing. "He was looking at *me* in exactly the same way. There was a touch of it in Louis Nenda, too, if you watched him closely. You are reading it wrong. It was lust, all right—only they didn't want to jump your bones, they want to *be* us. They want to go after Ben Blesh, too, so bad you could see it hurting. I think it's the reason for Hans Rebka's existence.

If there's trouble, he wants to be in the middle of it. But we're the lucky ones. We get to go." He reached out to take Sinara's arm in his left hand and Teri's in his right. "Come on. Ten seconds to their ignition. Let's make sure we're out of here before that."

CHAPTER THIRTY-FIVE

The price of rescue.

They did not wish to change their precisely calculated velocity vector, so the push to take them outside the *Have-It-All*'s airlock was a gentle one. Sinara, Torran, and Teri drifted slowly away from the hull, keeping pace with it. The tiniest thrust from their suit jets could take them back into the air lock.

And then that was no longer true. The *Have-It-All* was gliding ahead, increasing speed as though it intended to plunge into the broad disk of debris. Within half a minute, Sinara could see another change. The ship was turning, thrusting itself away from the dangerous whirlpool and beginning the long drive out to and around the far-off bulk of the gas-giant M-2. She watched the pale-blue exhaust of relativistic particles until the wake of the *Have-It-All*'s drive faded to nothing against the background of stars.

She, Teri, and Torran hovered in space with only each other for company. Except that they were not hovering. They were heading for the danger zone of Marglot's remains, a kilometer closer every few seconds.

Inside a ship you could feel a sense of security, no matter how threatening the situation. You were surrounded by older people, experienced people who had seen a thousand dangers and found a way to live through them. That sense of security, false as it may have been, vanished when you had no protection but your suit and were exposed to the enormous openness that made up even the smallest planetary system.

As they approached the whirlpool of matter that had once been Marglot, Sinara's feeling of discomfort increased. She steered her suit close to Torran and Teri, and noticed they were edging toward her.

"Still a long way to go." Teri's voice came over the suit radio. "Two and a half thousand kilometers to the nearest piece with a long-range radar reflectance. Seventeen thousand to Ben, according to his beacon."

That was half a day's journey, given the slow speed at which they were closing in on him. Their suits could pick up his distress beacon, but not his vital indicators. The *Have-It-All*, despite its distance, could monitor those, and Sinara had access to that information if she wanted it. She did not ask. Nor, she noticed, did Teri or Torran.

Half a day's journey, but not a second of it in which they could afford to relax. Sinara had proof of that when her suit's collision avoidance radar gave a loud beep and a great boulder rushed silently past. It appeared and disappeared so fast that her eyes scarcely had time to register its presence.

"I guess I was an optimist." If Teri felt nervous, she hid it well. "The belt of debris is wider than I thought, and our long-distance radar registers only big fragments. Some of the really huge lumps in the belt must still be colliding and fragmenting and ejecting parts of themselves. Look out! Here's another!"

This one was smaller, but Sinara saw it coming. She had time for a sudden spurt to the right, placing herself well out of harm's way.

"Seems as though Julian Graves was right." Teri had made the same sideways jump. "If we were as big and massive as the *Have-It-All*, that lump of rock wouldn't have missed."

"It wouldn't have hit you," Torran said. "It would have cleared you by at least ten meters. We don't want to go hopping around if we can avoid it. We could lose our original velocity vector."

"It wouldn't matter. We can pick up the signal from Ben's suit, and home in on that."

"Not if it cuts off, we can't."

That had unpleasant implications which Torran did not need to spell out. Ben's suit had ample power for the distress beacon. The signal would be lost only if the suit itself was damaged by impact. Ben's chances of surviving in that case were slight.

Torran said suddenly, "Something's wrong. My inertial guidance system shows me shifting away to the right."

Sinara checked her own monitor. "Not just you. All of us. It's a change of direction, but we're not heading off course. E.C. Tally predicted this, and he allowed for it in his calculations of our original vector. The most massive chunks of Marglot still have a hefty gravitational pull, and we are responding to one. Unless there are chaotic effects which Tally couldn't anticipate—"

A rattle on her suit like hard hail cut her off in mid-sentence. It took a few moments to realize that she was being bombarded with small particles. They must be low-speed, because her suit remained intact.

"Lucky this time." Teri Dahl had been hit by the same volley of space-gravel. "If that lot had been travelling twenty or thirty times as fast, we would be riddled."

"That's bound to happen as we get farther in," Torran added. "I don't know about you, but I'm recording Doppler velocity readings that are all over the place. We have material approaching us at ten kilometers a second, other stuff receding at the same speed. If we keep on as we are, we won't stay lucky. Something fast will hit us. Help me out, the two of you. Look for an object ahead that holds its distance from us—the bigger the better, but the main thing is a good match to our velocity vector."

It was a frightening ten minutes, with two more storms of low-speed gravel and pebbles, until at last Teri said, "Got one, I think. Azimuth eighteen, declination minus twelve."

Torran added, "And just about zero relative velocity. Seems perfect. Let's go take a close-up."

The fragment was several hundred meters across, a rough ellipsoid rotating slowly about its shortest axis. They could tuck in close behind it and be shielded from everything in the forward direction. There was still the danger of a hit from behind, but those fragments should be arriving at a lower relative speed.

"Not too close," Teri warned. "I'm reading a temperature of five hundred degrees. This is one hot rock."

"A piece of Marglot's deep interior, by the look of it." Torran was using his suit's light to study the surface. "See the bubbles from out-gassing into vacuum? But I think that phase is over."

"This is only a temporary hiding place," Sinara said. "Once we are close to Ben we'll have to risk open space again."

"If you can call it open space, when it's this big a mess." Teri had turned to keep watch behind them, relying on the other two to warn her if she came too close to the rock. "What I'm seeing is more violent and more random than it was. Everything from sand grains to molten planetoids, all with higher speeds. But for the moment, we take what we can get."

Sinara said to herself, *And after the moment, when we are close to Ben?* But she saw no point in starting a discussion with so few facts.

The three of them huddled as close to the shielding rock and to each other as they could get. After a silence that seemed to last forever, Torran said, "It's no good. We've been holding off, all of us, but I have to know. I'm going to call the *Have-It-All* and make sure that Ben is still alive. If he's not, we'll have to make a tough call. Do we risk dying, trying to pick up Ben's body? Or do we leave him where he is, hang in behind this lump of rock, and hope to ride it all the way out through the debris belt to safety?"

Teri said, "You know what Ben would say. The same as we were taught in survival school. Unless you propose to eat it, a dead body is worth only the cost of its chemicals. But my bet is that Ben is alive. Call the *Have-It-All* and find out—if you can. They may be out of range, or they may be screened from us."

Sinara heard the query signal in her suit. It was loud to her, but would it be strong enough to be picked up by the

Have-It-All? The ship should be a million kilometers away, perhaps already shielded by the great bulk of M-2.

For another three minutes it seemed her worries were justified. Sinara's suit, tuned to the ship's frequency, offered nothing but static. At last she heard, faint and scratchy and barely intelligible, Hans Rebka's voice: "Ben Blesh is alive, but unconscious. He's weaker, but not much. Blood pressure sixty-five over forty, pulse forty-two. Why didn't you report in before? We've been picking up your beacons and vital signs, and that was all."

"Nothing to say. We're fine, all three. We found a rock to hide behind. It shields us."

Sinara recognized in Torran's laconic reply an echo of Hans Rebka. It was probably happening to all of the survival specialists. They were picking their heroes and imitating them. So who did Sinara herself sound like now?

Torran went on, "Don't expect to hear from us again until after our rendezvous with Ben. We'll have our hands full."

"Don't expect to hear from us for a while, either. We're ready to loop around M-2. Tell us when you know your outbound trajectory."

When, not if. Boundless confidence in their survival, which Sinara did not share. But at least the suspense would not go on much longer. The signal from Ben's suit indicated that he was less than a hundred kilometers away. In four more minutes they had to leave the shelter of the rock and make an exact velocity match with Ben.

Teri was already drifting away to Sinara's right, with Torran following her. They wanted to take a peek around the edge of their shield before venturing out into the open. Sinara turned to look back the way they had come. They were now so deep in the belt of debris that the stars beyond were hidden. All she saw was a sea of moving fragments, some white-hot, some glowing a dull brick-red. Without the aid of her collision avoidance radar she would have no idea of their distances—they could be moving mountains, kilometers away, or fist-sized fireballs close enough to reach out and touch. There would be many others, too dark to see and most dangerous of all.

Sinara turned again and saw Torran gesturing to her to join them.

"We've had a good free ride," he said, "but it won't work much longer. Closest approach of this rock to Ben will be more than ten kilometers. We'll have to fly free."

"Can you see him?"

"Not his actual suit. His signal shows he's floating along in the middle of a big mass of rubble and boulders. It must all have been thrown off the surface of Marglot together. He's had partial shielding from all the other junk out here. It explains why he's still alive at all—I couldn't understand how anybody could float free for so long and not get zapped a hundred times."

Teri added, "We should be so lucky."

"We may not be. We'll stay sheltered here as long as we can, and once we reach Ben we can hide in among the same cluster of rocks. But first we have to get there. That gives us an open space run of more than ten kilometers."

"Together, or separately?" Sinara had moved close to the other two. It was a trade-off. Travel alone, and you tripled the odds that one of you would get through to help Ben. You also tripled the odds that one of you would be hurt on the way.

"Together." Teri and Torran spoke at once. Torran added, "If I get whacked, I like the idea that you two might be close enough to do something about it. And if we all get whacked—well, we tried. I'd say our present position is close to optimum for a move. I'm biggest, so I should go first. You two follow behind me in line, and stay as close as you can."

Sinara realized very well what Torran was leaving unsaid. By taking the lead position, he was partly shielding her and Teri—and increasing the probability that he would be hit himself.

She noticed that he was not heading straight for Ben's suit beacon. Instead, Torran was following a clump of materials with zero radar Doppler shift. Since it was moving ahead of them, it provided some protection. Even so, the rattle of lower-speed gravel and pebbles on her suit was non-stop. One lump of rock, fist-sized or bigger, cannoned

off the back of her hardened suit helmet with enough force
to make her ears ring.

She heard a grunt from Torran, then, "All right back there?"

"Doing fine."

"We're about ready for another course change. Hold your
breath. This will be the last one, and I don't see any way
to shield us."

He veered away, and in the moments before Sinara followed she could at last see their target. The rocks and rubble
formed an untidy splotch of black against the ruddy background of Marglot's remains. Somewhere inside that mess
floated Ben Blesh.

Torran had increased his speed, diving in on an all-or-
nothing approach. Sinara did the same until he said, "All
right. Time to turn and decelerate—hard!"

She saw the front of his suit, briefly, until her own suit's
rotation sent her feet-first toward the floating pile of rock.
The backpack on her suit whined in protest as it was called
upon to exert maximum thrust. Her proximity radar added
its warning, as four hands grabbed her.

"Picture perfect," Teri said. "One for the record books."
Then, "Torran! You've been hit!"

The left shoulder of his suit showed a fist-sized bulge of
black sealant.

"You mean, you weren't?" He held up his right arm, to
show two more dark patches. "I was pinged three times,
but only the one on my shoulder got all the way through
past my skin. I compressed that area of my suit to stop the
bleeding, but one of you will have to dig out the pebble
once we're back aboard the *Have-It-All*."

Was he understating his injury? Out here, Sinara had no
way to tell. But he certainly wasn't letting it stop him. She
and the others pawed their way through the untidy pile of
space rocks, using their suit headlights. They followed Ben
Blesh's signal and paid little attention to the heat of the rocks.

When they finally came to Ben he seemed like just another
misshapen lump of gray space debris. His knees were lifted
up toward his chest, his head bent forward, and his arms
were folded. Sinara, with Teri's help, eased Ben's head back
far enough for her to peer in through the faceplate.

"Hemorrhaging around his eyes. He went through high acceleration somewhere along the way."

"Think that's why he's unconscious now?"

"It's only part of the reason. There were impacts, too. Look at the lower half of his suit, and at his right side. The transport vortex must have returned him to the surface of Marglot just when the whole planet was coming apart."

Teri said, "He should never have left the *Have-It-All*, so soon after his treatment."

"If he hadn't, not one of us would be alive." Torran ran his gloved hand over Ben's rib cage. "Any response? That should hurt like hell."

"Nothing. He's under deep."

"That answers one question. He won't be able to help by flying his own suit. We'll have to tow him."

"Why go anywhere?" Teri said. "This is just a horrible jumble of rocks, but it did well for Ben."

Sinara was still examining the unconscious figure. "Depends how long it would take us to reach a place where we might be picked up. Ben's condition is stable, but how long are we talking about if we hang in here? Torran, do you have our vector?"

"Close to it. We're talking forty hours, give or take five. That would bring us to a point far enough out of the main plane of debris for Julian Graves to agree to pick us up. Can Ben stand that?"

Sinara said, "I don't think that's the issue. If we leave here, we're sure to need some fancy jumping and dodging to avoid being hit by debris. I said Ben seems stable, but I think those kinds of acceleration would kill him."

"That settles it. Teri, do you agree? We stay?"

"We stay. Sinara?"

"We stay."

For forty more hours. That was going to feel like eternity. Arabella Lund had made the point during survival training: "If you want to learn what a person is really like, arrange to be with her in two special situations. The first is when you have to make rapid decisions based on pure instinct. The second is when you are forced to spend a day or two together, with nothing to do but wait."

Sinara had seen Torran and Teri in the first setting. Now she would have a chance to observe them in the second. Within the first couple of hours both of them became restless. First they calculated and re-calculated their velocity vector, estimating the earliest time that they might hope to be picked up. After that they went wandering around, wasting—in Sinara's opinion—suit fuel. They explored the jumble of rocks and fragments surrounding them, moving large pieces to provide better protection from incoming debris.

Sinara did not join them; nor, after the first hour or two, did she watch them closely. She had her own preoccupation. Her suit, like every decent suit designed for use by humans, contained information on the species' physiology and medical treatments based on ten thousand years of theory and practice. Of course, only a tiny fraction of that volume of data applied to Ben, but Sinara studied that fraction as intensively as she could. Sometimes sheer fatigue made her close her eyes for a few minutes, but each time that she awoke she at once checked Ben's condition and ran a new prognosis.

Her task was made more complicated by Ben's suit. It was not sitting idle. It monitored his condition second by second, and provided appropriate medications. Sinara could override it at any time, but she did so only once. She drastically reduced the narcotic dose, in the hope that it would return him to consciousness. When after twenty minutes it did not, she fed that information into her own suit and received confirmation that Ben had suffered a severe concussion. There was also edema, a brain swelling that was being controlled by anti-inflammatories. The cause was probably that same concussion.

Sinara's actions absorbed her completely. She was more irritated than interested when Teri came floating over to halt on the other side of Ben.

"We need your opinion."

"I'm looking after Ben."

"He doesn't seem any different now than he was when

we first found him. He'll be fine for five minutes. That's all we need."

"What's the problem?"

"A little disagreement. Come and look at something."

As a result of Teri and Torran's continued labors, the barrier of protective rock fragments had steadily become more complete. Teri led Sinara to six great overlapping basalt wedges that offered between them only an irregular narrow slit through which to see beyond.

Torran was waiting a few meters away from it. "Take a look," he said, "but don't get too close. Sometimes little bits and pieces fly in—though we've not had anything with much speed."

Teri added, "Tell us what you think. Torran and I don't agree."

"No hints, Teri."

"I wasn't going to."

Sinara approached within arm's length of the ragged barrier of rocks. There was no such thing as a safe distance. Any second, a high-speed fragment could fly in through the slit and hit her. She peered cautiously out past one of the slabs.

The same kaleidoscopic litter of debris, large and small, near and far, filled the sky. It was a little less densely packed than before, thinning out as their distance from the sometime planet increased.

Nothing out there seemed worthy of a second look. Had Sinara not in effect been told to *expect* something, she would have returned at once to her vigil at Ben Blesh's side. Instead, she scanned the scene before her a second time, focusing on each area of the sky in turn before moving on. Her attention finally returned to one small region. Something was different there, some oddity that was difficult to pin down.

She used her suit's image intensifiers and narrowed the field of view. She made out a small disk, an oval shape brighter than its surroundings. As she stared, it thinned and dwindled. It lost width until it was no more than a bright line, then vanished completely.

She stared and stared, but now she could find nothing unusual. "That's strange," she began. "I thought there was—"

She paused. Here it came again, a thin bright line that slowly expanded to a fat silvery oval. Just as steadily, it then thinned and disappeared.

This time Sinara had some idea what to expect. She waited patiently for another half minute. Right on cue, the silver line appeared and swelled.

"I see it," she said. "Or at least, I see *something*, over in the upper right quadrant."

"That's the place," Teri said eagerly. "What do you think it is?"

"Well, it could be just a flat rock, a lot brighter on one side than the other. It's rotating, so sometimes we see it edgeways and sometimes we don't see it at all."

"Exactly what I told her. See, Teri, Sinara agrees with me."

"Except that it's nothing like any of the other rocks," Sinara went on slowly. "One side is *really* bright, like silver. We could be looking at one of the beetlebacks. They would have been thrown out into space with everything else when Marglot disintegrated."

"Told you!"

"So what if it is?" Torran was defensive. "I hate to quote Julian Graves to you, but getting back alive to the Orion Arm is our main concern. Saving Ben was one thing, we were right to insist on that. But worrying about some dumb beetleback is another matter entirely."

"Returning to the Orion Arm alive, *with information*. Didn't you hear E.C. Tally complaining during our take-off from Marglot? One beetleback, with all the data it contains, could make a huge difference to what we know." Teri moved away from the other two. "Torran, I don't care what you think. I'm going out there to try to snag it."

"Suppose it snags you?"

"That will be my problem. I don't expect you to come after me if I get in trouble—I don't *want* you to come after me. Your priority is the same now as when we started: getting yourselves and Ben back to the *Have-It-All*."

Teri didn't hang around for more debate. Already she was moving toward a gap in their primitive protective barrier.

"No, Torran." Sinara had seen his reaction. She grabbed

hold of his arm. "Teri is right, and this isn't like Ben. She's taking a risk, but she wants it to be *her* risk."

"She's crazy." Torran shook his arm free.

"If you believe Julian Graves, we're all crazy. And if you believe E.C. Tally, one beetleback could be worth the price of this whole expedition."

Torran hardly seemed to be listening. His attention, like Sinara's, was focused on the diminishing figure of Teri. He muttered again, "She's crazy." But his comment was drowned out by Teri's exultant cry. "It *is* a beetleback. Badly damaged, with most of its legs gone. But since Atvar H'sial says it's inorganic, that should make no difference at all to its information content. I have it, and I'm towing it. Five minutes and we'll be back there with the rest of you."

Five minutes, after all the hours that had passed since they left the *Have-It-All.* That seemed like nothing. It was a total shock when Teri suddenly cried out, "Oh God. I'm hit!"

Torran said, "Where?" and Sinara, "How bad?"

"Not good. Something hit me hard, in my lower back." Teri did not sound the same at all. "My suit sealed itself, but I have no feeling in my legs. Don't do anything silly. I'll still try to return with the beetleback."

"Anything silly." Torran was already accelerating. "Didn't I tell you she's crazy? You stay here."

Sinara, all ready to race off after Torran, hesitated. The trade-offs were difficult to compute. Help Torran, and so improve the chances of recovering Teri and the beetleback? Or stay with Ben Blesh, to make sure that he remained alive long enough to reach the *Have-It-All?*

Torran's voice steadied her. "Sinara, Teri and I did too good a job moving rocks. I'll be hauling Teri and the beetleback but I don't see a gap big enough for us all to fly through. Teri is losing consciousness. Can you work from the inside? Once we're in, I'll help you close the hole."

Dragging rocks out of the way was the easy part. Much harder was looking at Teri's chalk-white face and half-closed eyes as Torran pulled her through after him. Sinara took charge at once, moving the second body into place beside

Ben Blesh. She gave the beetleback one quick glance. It was legless, one side of the scarlet head was mashed in, and the silver back was crumpled along the central line. More to the point, the creature was crippled and immobilized. That was good enough for her.

Was it worth the effort, to capture a beetleback? Well, to Teri it had been, and Torran had gone to the trouble of finishing the job.

He was at Sinara's side. "I didn't have time to check all the suit readings. How is she?"

"Her suit reports a problem between the third and fourth lumbar vertebrae. Her spinal column there is either cut or severely damaged. The regrowth of nerve tissue would be an easy job back on Miranda, but the robodoc on the *Have-It-All* was stripped out and dumped, nothing left but the bare essentials."

"Will she live?"

"She will, if any of us do." Sinara glanced at the time read-out in her own suit. "Survival training, Torran." She gestured at the two bodies in front of them. "We all had it. But tell me the truth, did you ever imagine the real thing might be anything like this?"

"I didn't, but Arabella Lund pegged it exactly. Remember what she told us? 'Survival is ninety-eight percent boredom, and two percent panic.' How many hours to rendezvous?"

"Eighteen, if the *Have-It-All* is on time."

"Will Ben and Teri be in danger of dying during that period?"

"Not according to all the signs."

Torran blew out a long, gusty breath. "Then I say, bring on the ninety-eight percent boredom. I'm more than ready for it."

"You don't want to look at the beetleback?"

"To hell with the beetleback. That's Tally's area, not mine." Torran moved so that he was stretched out next to Teri. "I'm done. Wake me if a rock flies in and kills me. Otherwise, I'm gone."

Sinara could hardly believe her ears. With eighteen hours to go, and with the primitive defense of rocks around them needing constant attention, Torran Veck was proposing to go to sleep?

Her feeling of outrage lasted less than one minute. She went across to peer in through his visor, and saw that his face was as pale and drawn as Teri's or Ben's. She examined the suit's report of his vital signs. He wasn't sleeping, he was out cold. The shoulder wound that he had dismissed so casually was far worse than she had realized. The effort to bring Teri back, and the beetleback with her, had pushed Torran past the point of exhaustion.

Sinara examined, in turn and in as much detail as she could, each of her three companions. She was beginning to understand something else about survival training—something that Arabella Lund had not mentioned. You trusted your teammates to do whatever was necessary to keep you alive. And you in turn did the same for them. *Whatever.*

Seventeen and a half hours to go.

Sinara moved the others so that each of them would always be in her sight. Then she floated away to examine the condition of their protective shield of rocks, and began the tedious and endless task of filling in gaps as they appeared.

CHAPTER THIRTY-SIX

Starting over.

The *Have-It-All* had started its journey as a luxury ship. In its equipment and its fittings—even in its weapons—it served as a symbol of the best that the Orion Arm could provide. Louis Nenda had worked for many years to make it that way.

Now the ship was a stripped-down hulk, a fleshless skeleton of a vessel barely able to support the life that travelled within it. Nonetheless, Louis Nenda whistled cheerfully as he sat in the ruined control cabin of the derelict and made final adjustments before Bose node entry.

"Louis, I sense a contradiction." Atvar H'sial was crouched a couple of meters away on the bare metal floor. "To one who sees as I do, your vocal utterances are extremely ugly. Yet your pheromones display an uncommon happiness."

"Sure I'm happy. Who wouldn't be? We're goin' home."

"This ship is a wreck."

"It is. But we're not dead. As long as you're not dead, you can start over. Also, Julian Graves says that the inter-clade council will pay to restore the ship to the way it was."

"Do you believe that?"

" 'Course not. They're a bunch of idiot bureaucrats. We'll be lucky if we can squeeze two cents out of 'em. But the other side of that is, while they're jawing about what fine people we are, only they don't have any money to reward us, we'll have things easy. They won't be tryin' to kill us off or stick us in jail. Graves says we'll get some kind of award. Even Archimedes, for hangin' outside the ship without a suit an' draggin' in Sinara and the other survival team members. Graves says he's amazed that Archie didn't die doin' it."

"You appear less confounded."

"Hell, it takes more than that to kill a Zardalu. Archie keeps goin' on about how he's afraid I'll disembowel him, but if I did it wouldn't do him in. He'd just go ahead an' grow another set of guts. Graves doesn't know any of that, though, so Archie's up for an award along with the rest of us."

"Do not trust Ethical Councilors bearing gifts."

"At, you're gettin' cynical. It don't become you." They had passed through the node, and Nenda stared with satisfaction at the view on his one remaining display. It revealed an almost total absence of stars. The ship was floating in the empty spaces of the Gulf. "We have a few hours to spare before the next node entry. Want to go hear what E.C. Tally has to offer? He's been workin' non-stop with the damaged beetleback, an' Hans Rebka says there'll be somethin' worth hearin'."

"It was always my impression that you disliked and distrusted Captain Rebka."

"I do. But I never said he was an idiot. If what Tally has found out is good enough to interest Rebka, it's probably worth a listen."

"Do I detect admiration for Hans Rebka?"

"No."

"Respect, then, which is separated from admiration by a thin olfactory boundary?"

"At, stop playin' pheromonal word games. Let's go."

Nenda led the way along the ravaged upper corridor of the ship. Without circulation or temperature control equipment, the air was stale, hot, and humid. At the doorless entrance of the conference room, Louis paused and sniffed. Everyone on board was packed into the chamber. This was the way that hard-worked crew members should be. Sweaty, and smelly, and with clothes that could not be changed or washed for another couple of weeks.

Even the four survival team members looked right. The *Have-It-All*'s stripped-down robodoc hadn't been able to do much more than hold the status quo. Teri Dahl wore a body cast and was clearly paralyzed below the waist, Ben Blesh had a neck brace and his face was a swollen mass of purple-yellow blotches surrounding sunken bloodshot eyes, Torran Veck's upper body was a mass of bandages, and Sinara Bellstock was relatively intact but had the expression of someone in need of about a year's sleep. Instead of being neat and clean and fresh-faced and enthusiastic, each one was bedraggled and filthy. Louis could for the first time believe that the group might actually be earning its keep.

Archimedes was sprawled along one whole wall of the room. Nenda went to sit on the Zardalu's meter-thick mid-section, and Kallik at once hurried over to crouch at his feet.

E.C. Tally was standing at the far end of the room, next to the captured beetleback. It had been in poor shape when it reached the *Have-It-All*, and recent treatment had done nothing to improve that. The dark ventral body plates had been ripped open along their center line and folded back. The interior was exposed, and parts of it had been removed. It was now obvious to everyone what Atvar H'sial's ultrasonic vision had seen at once. The recent evisceration had not killed the beetleback, because it had never been alive. Its innards were a tangle of wires, tubes, junction boxes, and hydraulics. When Nenda entered the room, E.C. Tally had just pulled out a valve. He was apparently in the middle of a lecture describing how the mechanism was constructed, and how it functioned. From the restless look of his audience, he had been at it for some time.

After three more minutes, Julian Graves said, "This is all very interesting, E.C. But some of us would rather hear *what* the beetlebacks did, rather than how they did it."

"But these data are of great potential value."

"I'm sure they are. So why don't you download everything—*later*—into the *Have-It-All*'s computer. Describe

all that you have discovered about the way a beetleback
is built and functions. But tell us, now, what you have
learned about *what* the beetlebacks were doing, and *why*."

"I have learned a great deal, and I conjecture even more.
I will rank and present these findings in order of their
estimated interest to this particular audience. First, regarding the beings who are extinguishing suns and removing
all heat from them and their planets in a region of the Sag
Arm: they are not, in their own terms, *destroying* these
systems. They are rather, with the assistance of their own
constructs, the beetlebacks, *modifying star systems for their
own use*. The beetlebacks, much like Builder constructs,
possess notions regarding their own creators that are of
questionable validity. However, it seems clear that those
creators require extremely cold temperatures if they are to
survive and function. The name we have been using, *Masters
of Cold*, appears entirely appropriate. It is my conjecture,
although not that of the beetlebacks, that the Masters of
Cold are some composite and sentient form of Bose-Einstein
Condensates."

Graves objected at once, "E.C., that is nonsense and you
should know it. Bose-Einstein Condensates exist only with
ambient temperatures within a few hundred billionths of a
degree of absolute zero. No place in the natural universe
is so cold."

"Councilor, I of course do realize that."

"So there is no possible way that the Masters of Cold could
ever have developed in the first place."

"They did not develop. Everything in the data bank of
the beetlebacks points to a different origin. The Masters of
Cold are themselves a *creation*—a creation of the Builders.
They are a form of artifact."

Tally's audience had been listening quietly, but this was
too much for Darya Lang. Sitting opposite Louis Nenda,
she jumped to her feet and burst out, "E.C., that's
impossible. You were not on Iceworld with us, so you
wouldn't know this. But a Builder construct there assured
us that the coming of extreme cold destroyed both that
world and a complicated transportation system established
by the Builders. It's not reasonable to suggest that

constructs which are themselves Builder creations would destroy Builder works."

"I offer only the most probable answer, not a final one. The Masters of Cold are artifacts, created by the Builders. But they are constructs *over which the Builders themselves have lost control.*"

That stopped everyone, even Louis, who had divided his attention between watching the reactions of others and listening to E.C. Tally's explanation as closely as he listened to anything that was no more than a theory. For thousands of years everyone had assumed that the Builders were superbeings who could do anything they liked. That something could challenge or defy Builder technology—people just didn't think that way.

But E.C. was not people. He was an embodied computer, following the implications of the given data by strictly logical processes to wherever it might lead.

Tally continued, "Professor Lang, you yourself proposed the presence in the Sag Arm of two different kinds of superior forms, adversarial to each other. Others here objected strongly to your suggestion, on probabilistic grounds. What are the odds, they said, of two such forms arising? However, those objections disappear at once if one superior form is the *creation of the other.*

"This"—Tally pointed to the gutted beetleback at his side—"is a secondary product, the creation of a creation. Marglot was once a special world, a nexus to many worlds established by the Builders. Had we not arrived there, the whole Marglot system would also have become the domain of the Masters of Cold. They had already taken the first steps, with the extinction of life on Marglot and the draining of energy from M-2. Halting the fusion reaction within the parent star would come next. That order of processes appears different from what we observed in the system where we first arrived in the Sag Arm. It is a disturbing thought, but I conjecture that the Masters of Cold are still learning the fastest and most effective ways of accomplishing their changes."

"So who brought us here?" Julian Graves asked. "Here, all the way from the Orion Arm."

"I am forced to assume that it was the Builders, since a variety of paths constructed by them all led to Marglot."

"Wrong question," Hans Rebka said. "Forget who. *Why?* Why were we brought here?"

"Again, I am obliged to conjecture. We were brought here so that we could be warned of danger, far in the future, to our own spiral arm."

"No, no, no." Claudius was sitting as far away from Archimedes as he could get. The *Have-It-All* had been stripped of spare reactor capacity, along with everything else, but somewhere on the ship the Chism Polypheme had managed to find a source of enough hard radiation to turn his corkscrew body a pleasant pale green. "No, no, no," his croaking voice repeated, while his single slate-gray eye rolled to survey everyone in the room. "That's not the way the real world wags. I don't know about the Orion Arm, but in the Sagittarius Arm you don't bring people a long way to warn *them*. You bring them a long way only if *they* can help *you*."

Louis, about to agree vigorously, decided it was wiser to keep quiet. Let Claudius be blamed for a suggestion that anybody in his right mind would think reasonable.

As the storm of criticism of Claudius's skepticism arose— with Hans Rebka, Louis noticed, abstaining—Julian Graves interrupted.

"We can debate reasons later. Regardless of motive, the fact remains that we *were* brought to the Sag Arm. We *have* been warned of tremendous danger. This expedition is going home with more information—and worse news— than I thought possible. I knew before we left that a second visit might be inevitable, but I did not dream that it would have such urgency. Tally, do you have more warnings to offer?"

"Not yet. May I speak? If I may be allowed to continue with the description of beetleback physiology—"

"You may not. You may listen. Immediately upon our arrival at the Orion Arm, a much larger and better-equipped party must be formed. With what we have seen and learned and now conjecture, inter-clade council approval and funding can be guaranteed. Our prompt return to the

Sag Arm, and to those parts of it in particular affected by—infested by—the Masters of Cold, cannot be delayed for a moment."

This time the wisdom of silence could not compete with the sense of outrage. Louis said, "The hell with that. Councilor, you're forgettin' a bunch of stuff. First, we were damn near killed, every one of us. We escaped because Ben Blesh risked his skin, an' he nearly lost it. Look at him! You could use his face for wallpaper patterns. An we're crawlin' home in a ship—*my* ship, let me remind you—that's been gutted an' bashed an' beaten 'til it's hardly fit to be sold for scrap. An' now you up an' tell us we're goin' right back to the place that did all this."

"My apologies. My terminology was confusing. When I spoke of *our* return to the Sag Arm, I was referring to the combined clades of the Orion Arm. I did not intend to imply that all those here would be included in a second expedition. In fact, I myself will not be going."

Darya said, "But some of us will."

"That is a true statement." Julian Graves coughed. "I must confess that I have been less than totally forthcoming with all of you. But it was not from choice. My actions were forced on me by the instructions by the inter-clade council." He surveyed the grimy and weary group, examining each one in turn. "We jointly possess, without a doubt, more knowledge and experience of the Builders than any similar-sized assembly of humans and aliens drawn from the whole Orion Arm. And yet we also, without a doubt, form a curiously ill-matched team. For instance, my own presence in the Dobelle system, where I first met most of you, was pure coincidence. My task at that time had nothing to do with the Builders. The next expedition to the Sag Arm will be different. It will be designed from the outset to provide complementary skills and experience."

Darya Lang said, "But I will be going, right? I mean, this is the *Builders*. I've spend my whole life studying them."

"You have indeed. Developments in the Sag Arm, however, seem to involve less the Builders than the Builders' own creations."

"But you said *experience*," Darya persisted. "We have experience in the Sag Arm. Nobody else does, in any of the clades."

"That also is a true statement. Professor Lang, perhaps you may have misinterpreted my earlier words. I said that not all this group would return to the Sag Arm. That was a perfectly accurate statement. I did not, however, assert that *no members* of this group would be on the second expedition."

"If not me, then who?" Darya watched in apparent disbelief as Julian Graves nodded his head toward the end of the room, where the four survival specialists sat like a row of zombies. "You can't mean *them*."

"I am sorry, my dear professor, but that is exactly what I mean. The inter-clade council made the decision before ever we set out, that new blood might be needed. That is exactly why the initial expedition included young survival specialists. You, Captain Rebka, Atvar H'sial, Louis Nenda . . . " Julian Graves's wave of the hand took in most of those present in the chamber. "Yes, and me, too. We are, in the council's view, too fixed in our perceptions. New problems, they argue, call for new ways of thought."

It was the best news to come Louis's way for a long time—the best news, in fact, since that long-ago moment when he and Atvar H'sial had arrived on Xerarchos and discovered how easy it was to milk the natives. But apparently Darya did not agree.

"The inter-clade council members are imbeciles."

"Professor Lang, many of the council are friends of mine."

"That doesn't surprise me one bit. You tell them, if they want information about anything that happened on this expedition, they'll have to be ready to *negotiate*." Darya stood up and stared around at the others in the room. "We have to be united about this. No second expedition *for* us, no cooperation *from* us."

She swept out of the room. Hans Rebka followed at once. Louis could not tell from his expression if he was leaving in support of Darya, or intended to try to talk her out of her anger. E.C. Tally said, "Councilor Graves, when the inter-clade council decreed that *new blood* would be needed, how will that affect my own situation? I can if necessary obtain both new blood and a new body."

"E.C., I do not believe that the inter-clade council's words are intended to be interpreted too literally." Julian Graves rubbed his hand wearily over his bald and bulging cranium. "I did not anticipate so extreme a reaction from Professor Lang. Do any of you share her response?"

Graves seemed to be staring right at him. Louis shook his head. "We're law-abidin' people. Whatever the Council says, we gotta live with it."

"Good for you, Louis Nenda. I value your sound judgment and support. Were there to be any exception to the Council's rule, I would argue that it should be you. But now I must try to persuade Professor Lang to adopt your rational point of view."

Graves hurried out, as Nenda picked up a gust of pheromonal laughter from Atvar H'sial. *"Louis, J'merlia translated for me your exchange with Julian Graves. You almost overdid the fine art of hypocrisy."*

"Yeah, yeah. Laugh if you like. But At, now I've got Graves solid on my side. We're goin' home to the Orion Arm, an' we're stayin' there. Let's get out of here. Tally looks about ready to start in again about his beetleback."

Louis, accompanied by Atvar H'sial and the three slaves, started out along the upper corridor that led to the control cabin. He was almost there when Darya Lang popped out of a side chamber and stood smack in front of him, so that he was forced to stop or run into her.

"Darya, Julian Graves is looking for you."

"I know he is. He's a spineless traitor, and I'm avoiding him."

"Where's Hans Rebka?"

"I don't know, and I don't care. Let's not talk about him at all." And then, "Do you know what Rebka told me? He said that the inter-clade council might have a point, and he needed to think about it. I mean, what is there to think about?" Darya grabbed Louis's arm and stared into his eyes. "I can count on you, I feel sure of that without having to ask. You and I have always had this mental bond between us. Physical, too, even though we haven't ever . . . well, you know. But on a long trip, like to the Sag Arm, I feel sure we would. You'll help me, won't you?"

"Of course I will."

"I knew it. Louis, you're an angel." Darya put her arms around him and kissed him on the lips. "We have to make plans as to how we're going to arrange this. It may not be easy to persuade the Council that we need to go, but I'm sure we can do it."

"It won't be easy, an' it will take time. But it can't be this minute. I have to arrange to put us through another Bose node."

"We'll meet later?"

"You bet."

Louis disentangled himself and went through into the control cabin. Its door had been sacrificed on Marglot to the cause of reduced mass, but Atvar H'sial moved to stand at the entrance and prevent anyone else from entering.

"Louis, I feel that I will never understand humans."

"Join the club."

"First, consider the survival specialist, Sinara Bellstock. She could not wait to mate with you on several earlier occasions. But in the conference chamber, her chemical messengers gave off no trace of interest in you. Instead they revealed great interest in Ben Blesh."

"You don't need pheromones to read that. Sinara has found herself a new hero. Now she's hot for Ben." Louis sat down in the control chair and stared at the Bose coordinates. A few more minutes would do it. "An' you know what? I'm relieved. You've no idea how rotten it makes me feel when somebody expects me to be a hero."

"I am not surprised. It is a role for which by both temperament and history you are unsuited. However, the puzzle does not end with Sinara Bellstock. When humans are in an unwashed condition, their pheromonal products are particularly easy to read. Darya Lang was offering you her body in the corridor. True?"

"Some of her body. An' I don't think she was expectin' it to happen right there in the corridor. But more or less."

"And you were giving off conflicting signals. On the one

hand, you sympathize with and desire her. On the other hand, you have absolutely no intention of returning to the Sagittarius Arm under any circumstances whatsoever."

"So? Any trip to the Sag Arm might be six months away. Darya could be tomorrow night. You gonna give me a lecture on morals?"

"I would not dream of doing so. Were you to observe Cecropian mating habits they would, I suspect, render you nauseated."

"Some human ones don't make me feel any too good." Louis had his eyes fixed on the countdown. Another minute and they would enter another Bose node. One more step on the long journey to the Orion Arm, and from this point on it ought to be plain sailing. The *Have-It-All* was doing no more than retracing its outward path. "So maybe Darya an' me decide to play around on the way home. Don't you agree I've earned it?"

"Indeed you have. However, I want to point out one more complication that does not seem to have occurred to you."

"Go on. Screw things up for me when they're goin' great."

"Darya Lang is from Sentinel Gate, and she will doubtless wish to return there. Waiting for you on Sentinel Gate is the faithful Glenna Omar. Do you not see what a difficult choice lies ahead of you?"

Twenty seconds to go to the Bose node. Louis stared around him at the ruined cabin. He could visualize the rest of the ship. Where once had been the most luxurious of beds there were now bare metal floors. The finest robochef in the Orion Arm floated somewhere in the sea of debris that had been Marglot. Showers, once able to provide subtle combinations of perfumed essences, offered at best a trickle of cold water. Whole closets, once filled with Glenna Omar's lingerie and furs and gowns and shoes and jewelry, stood empty.

"Yeah." Louis entered the final transfer sequence. "There's a choice ahead. Only it's not mine to make, an' I doubt it'll be all that difficult once she sees this ship. You don't know Glenna as well as I do."

Space around the *Have-It-All* flickered. The vessel, such as was left of it, entered the Bose node.

EPILOG

From notes dictated by Darya Lang just prior to the arrival of the *Have-It-All* at Upside Miranda Port:

This is a proposed addendum to the volume A SURFEIT OF NOTIONS: Theories of Builder origins, activities, nature, and artifacts. Begin.

It is difficult for an author when she discovers that a major work, over which she has labored for years and which is shortly to be published, contains basic errors. This unfortunately appears to be the case with this volume. The theories presented in the body of the text, concerning the nature of the Builders, are certainly numerous and diverse. Recent events in the Sagittarius Arm reveal that all those theories may also be at best incomplete, and at worst deeply flawed. Every theory offered to date has adopted a central dogma, implicit although never stated. It is as follows: Builder actions, past and possibly present, have had a profound effect on species development within the local spiral arm, and perhaps beyond. The actions of those developing species, however, have had no effect on the Builders and their plans. Influences flow in one direction only.

There is a corollary to the central dogma: The Builders operate at such vast levels of thought and technology that assistance from our clades to the Builders will never be necessary. The contrary hypothesis, namely, that the Builders

371

lack total control over their own works and may require help from clades whom we have previously considered so far beneath them, is close to heretical.

Let us be willing to consider heresy. From recent experience, we can speculate as to the possible nature of such assistance. All Builder activities seem designed to operate over vast lengths of time. Conceivably, Builder actions and reactions are obliged to function in a long-extended mode. Humans, like all species that develop on planetary surfaces, have perforce evolved to respond rapidly to any threat. We are short-lived, but we are fast. *Could our speedy reactions be of value to the Builders? Could our ultimate relationship be not the subservience of one to the other, but some form of symbiosis? Facing great dangers, will we perhaps help and support each other?*

This is such a radical notion that it cannot, of course, be justified by speculation alone. Evidence must be sought, and crucial experiments performed.

That's the point that the dummies on the inter-clade council don't get. Sure, you can send survival specialists to the Sag Arm. Send a hundred, send a thousand, but if you don't send *scientists*, what can you hope to learn? You can't prove general theorems based on a couple of cases—though that's what I've just been doing here, and I certainly hate it. I must find a way to be part of the second expedition, even if I have to sneak on board in disguise.

Disguised as what? Maybe I could bribe somebody. Hans says that in any group of over fifty, you can always find one that can be bribed. I wonder if that applies to inter-clade council members?

What am I saying? *Delete* after "crucial experiments performed," and *Continue.*

Hard evidence will be needed to support such a radically new hypothesis. We note, however, that many of the listed "theories" concerning Builder origins and activities are based upon the analysis of a single event or artifact. In the case of the Sag Arm, forty or more stellar systems offer proof that something on the scale of Builder artifacts and activity is at work there.

At work *there*. Not here, in our local arm. I wonder what Professor Merada and the others at the Artifact Research Institute will say when they hear what we found in the Sag Arm. I can make a guess. They will *say* lots, but they won't do one damn thing. They'll sit around the conference table and talk about it for the next ten years. I don't see much help from them.

But I *have* to be on that next expedition. Who can I rely on? Well, there's E.C. Tally. He certainly wants to go. But if you're reduced to relying on E.C. you are in a bad way. Louis will help me. He and I are becoming very close. There's a price for that, though. Hans would normally help me, too, if I treated him the right way, but I can't handle both of them at once. I don't have the nerve or the experience. Glenna could give me pointers, and she would probably enjoy doing it, but she's back on Sentinel Gate. By the time we get there it will be too late.

Of course, the person who could make all the difference if he wanted to is Julian Graves. He must have influence on picking the members of the next expedition. Maybe if I switched my efforts to him—wait a minute. He's an Ethical Councilor. He'd see through me in half a second. And he'd better never see any of this. *Delete* after "activity is at work there," and *Continue*.

There already exists a plethora of theories about the Builders, and now we are proposing to add another one. It is still in embryonic form, and it, like all its predecessors, may take hundreds or thousands of years to be disproved, or to confirm its credibility. A century is a long time by human standards. However, to the Builders a millennium is no more than the blink of an eye. We must remain open-minded, yes. We must be careful in our work, yes. But most of all, we must be patient.

Patient. Right. Easy to say and hard to do. I'd be a lot less itchy if I could find a way to be assured a place on the next expedition to the Sag Arm. With so much going on there, major new discoveries have to be ripe for the picking. Maybe I could organize an expedition of my own, nothing to do with the inter-clade council. There's always Claudius. He says he can't wait to go home. And there's a

Chism Polypheme ship sitting at Upside Miranda Port, the one that the Marglotta came in.

Maybe I ought to be making advances to Claudius. Hold on. *Claudius!* That goggle-eyed green freak. I'm not that desperate yet. Am I? Oh my God, I think I am.

Delete. . . .